BRIGHT WHITE

Jessica **GERMAINE**

Jessica Germaine
8.4.2018

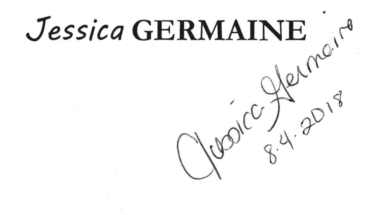

BRIGHT WHITE IS A SPIN-OFF TO MY DEBUT NOVEL. FOR THE FULL EXPERIENCE CHECK OUT *DARK BLACK.*

ISBN: 0985594535
ISBN-13: 978-0985594534

IN LOVING MEMORY OF

FRANCINE "FRANKIE" GARY,

EBONY HALL &

JAMES "BIG FERG" FERGUSON

This book is dedicated to everyone who supported my first novel, ***Dark Black***. Without the readers my work would merely be words on a canvas. Thanks for bringing my visions into reality!

BRIGHT WHITE

CHAPTER ONE: The Intruder

"You must've lost yo' goddamn mind!" was all I heard before a painful sting from my three-hundred-and-fifty-pound mama's hand pierced the right side of my cheekbone. I had planned on having Tre out of her house before sunrise, but the steamy lust we made put us both in a deep sleep that apparently only the sound of her loud voice could wake us from. Mama had a red rage in her eyes that was oh so familiar and a terrible stench of vodka on her breath that stung my nostrils worse than her slap.

"I told yo' fast tail that if anybody's gonna be screwin' in my house, it's gonna be me!" she yelled before heading out of my bedroom into the direction of the kitchen. I knew exactly where she was going.

"We better get out of here before she comes back with t

hat damn bat!" I said to Tre as I watched him confusingly attempt to wipe the crust from his eyes. Mama always grabbed what she called her 'get your mind right' stick when she was ready to tear off in somebody's ass. It had seen the likings of many people's faces. She didn't care if it was a family member, a friend, or one of her lousy boyfriends. If you gave her a reason to pull out that bat, she was going to give you a reason to never mess with her again.

"Damn. This what I get for messin' with young chicks," Tre mumbled to himself, and although I was offended, I was too frightened by Mama's return to jump on him about it. I just stored his comment in the back of my mind so that I could address it later, then continued to fasten my bra.

"Just hurry! I think she's comin' back," I said as I heard her heavy footsteps getting louder and louder.

We had lived in that wooden three-bedroom house on Ordale's east side for the past eight years, so I had become very familiar with the gist of it. A single layer of worn-out, burgundy carpet rested only on the living room floor, and in the hallway where the bedrooms were, laid some dried-up broken tile. Once mama's foot exited that carpet and touched that wood we all knew about it. We had even come up with a formula that calculated exactly where in the house she was going.

Two steps down the hall and a pause meant she was headed to her room. Five steps and a pause meant my little brother's room. And ten meant she wanted me for some petty reason. A whopping twelve steps down the hall was an exit to the back door, and that's how I had planned on making my escape. Of course we would have to hop the gate to get to the front of the house, where I hoped Shannon and Kevin were waiting for us in the car. My best friend and her boo had been getting their groove on in my brother's room across the hall and I could only pray that the sound of Mama's voice had woke them and forced them out the window. If Joanne knew there were more in the house she would have really flipped out.

With only enough time to put on my bra and T-shirt, Tre, who somehow managed to get fully dressed, and I ran towards the backdoor with mama and her bat not far behind us. I hysterically tried to unloosen the three locks that secured the door, only to be interrupted by a firm grip of my hair.

"I told you time and time again, you little grown heffa," Mama said as she yanked me to the ground. "You cannot outrun me."

The forceful tug caused me to hit the wooden floor pretty hard and I landed just a couple inches from the tiny gas heater that magically kept our whole house warm. Mama then held up her bat and pointed it at Tre. He grabbed it with his right hand then used his left to try to unlock the door.

"Chill old lady," he said to her. "You don't have to do this. Don't you see us trying to leave?"

"You should've thought about leaving before you even came! You look old enough to know that this young heffa don't own nothin' around here!"

"I didn't know. I swear," he lied.

"Well you know now and I'mma make sure you never forget!"

Mama was able to snatch away from Tre's grip and began taking swings at him. His experience as a running back must have kicked in because I must say I was very impressed with the way he was dodging her attempts to dismantle his face and body. With her now focused on Tre, I managed to pull myself from off the ground and finish the job he started with the locks. Once the door was open, I grabbed his hand and led us outside. Then we made our way to the front of the house where Kevin's black Toyota Camry was parked. The car was running and the back passenger door was wide open.

"That's my girl!" I yelled, congratulating Shannon for always being on point, although she was the one who convinced me to let the guys come over in the first place.

Mama decided not to follow us out the back door. She figured it would be quicker to use the front instead. When I saw her huge body burst through that screen door, I knew we had better hustle. Mama may have been a big woman, but she was not your average. She could outrun a track star if she had to. Hell, she could drop down and do a split better than me.

"Man y'all hurry up!" Kevin yelled from inside of the car after he saw us approaching. "She's right behind you!"

Before I could turn around to see if he was right, Mama threw the bat perfectly at the back of my calves and the sharp pain that hit my legs immediately knocked me down to the ground. I curled up in a fetal position holding on to my legs, as if my grasp would magically stop the pain. Shortly afterward, the vintage glare from the street light disappeared which let me know that Mama was standing directly over me. I knew there was no way out of this one.

"Mama pleease," I managed to whimper through the pain.

"Mama please my ass," she shot me down. "You wasn't thinking about Mama when you had that nigga up in my house."

Realizing that there was no need for pleading, I used my arms to shield my face as she grabbed me by my hair and began swinging her heavy fists down at my helpless body. I knew my mama was crazy. Hell, I lived with her for seventeen years, but this was the first time she attacked me as if I was a dog on the streets. True enough, I could be a little womanish at times. What teenager wasn't? I figured if she didn't respect her own house, then why should I? It was hard enough having to grow up quickly all because she wanted to neglect us and run the streets. At just ten, I was taking long, hot ass walks down to the market dragging pounds of grocery home all by myself. Shit, I knew how to fry chicken before I knew how to change my pad. I did the ironing, all the chores, and ultimately the parenting because she was either not home or passed the hell out from drinking her life away.

"Didn't I tell yo' lil' fast ass about being hot in the pants," she continued to chant to the rhythm of her swings. "You think 'cause you got that mixed blood you all that and you can do what you wanna do?....YOU THINK YOU CAN LIVE UP IN MY HOUSE....LIE TO ME....SLEEP WITH MY MAN....AND RUIN MY LIFE!"

"Mama what are you talking about? I didn't sleep with your man!" I begged for her mercy. "This is your daughter you're talking to!"

"YOU ARE NOT MY DAUGHTER," she convinced herself. "YOU'RE THAT EVIL, UNGRATEFUL BITCH WHO RUINED MY LIFE!"

"Nooo Mama," I cried as I involuntarily took the pain of her punches. "I'm your daughter! Please snap out of it, Mama. Come back...Please just come back!"

"COME BACK? I WOULD NEVER LET YOU COME BACK IN THIS HERE HOUSE," she pointed. "I should kill you right now just for asking me some dumb shit like that. As a matter of fact..."

Mama stopped in the middle of her sentence and I felt her swings no more. I thought she had enough of tormenting me, but little did I know she had something else in mind.

"You're gonna know what it feels like to be hurt," she said as what half of my conscious mind made out to be her 'get right' stick. A part of me didn't flinch because I just knew she wasn't crazy enough to beat her own daughter down with that bat. But the other part of me wasn't sure. All I knew was that her size twelve Ked sneakers were heading closer to me and I would soon find out.

CHAPTER TWO: Booster Baby

"Aaaaaw...noooo...pleease…stop," I moaned. Pleaseeee."

Shannon, who was peacefully sleeping on the opposite end of her bed, was awaken by my cries and immediately jumped up to comfort me.

"Keisha, wake up!" she demanded. "Are you okay?"

"Yeah, I'm fine." I told her, after realizing I was not stranded in the woods with a bloody infant, but in the comfort of my best friend's home.

"Another one of those dreams again," Shannon asked.

"Yeah," I gasped.

"Was it the one in the alley or the one in the grocery store?"

"Neither," I told her. "The one with the baby."

"Oh that one," she sighed. "Keisha I told you, you need to go see a doctor about dem shits. Everybody has bad dreams, but to have 'em every night like that, I just don't think that's normal."

I quickly rolled my eyes at Shannon then shot her idea straight down. "Hell no! I told you I'm not going to let no freakin' doctor tell me something that I already know."

"And what's that?" Shannon asked.

"That I'm crazy, duh."

Shannon chuckled to herself a little and then became serious. "Keisha, now you and I both know you not crazy. You're just doing the best you can do with the cards you were dealt. My situation is just as fucked up as your's but I don't have those dreams like that. Seriously, go see somebody."

"I'll think about it," I lied. But Shannon knew better.

I rolled over on the flimsy twin-sized bed that Shannon owned and glanced over at the alarm clock for the time.

Only 9:03. I thought.

Since nobody in the house woke up before noon that meant I had a whole four hours to just lay there in bed and try to free my mind of the horrible images I just saw in my head. I never went back to sleep after those nightmares. I would just pick my little brain out wondering what it all could have meant. There were three in particular I would have. It was the one where my mama is beating the hell out of a woman in the grocery store, except every time she hits her I would feel the pain as I helplessly watched. There was another where I am trapped in a car and a male voice is saying, "it will all be over soon beautiful." And then it was one that was the most frightening of them all- the one where a bloody baby is crying hysterically in a wooded area. I had actually witnessed my mama beat a lady down in the grocery store. And the van I was always trapped in belonged to my daddy, but this one about the baby, I didn't have the slightest clue. All I knew for sure was that the dreams got worse once I left mama's house, which happened to be the same night she gave me that terrible beatdown.

Because of the concussion and several bruised bones I suffered, I spent two nights in the hospital and then moved in with Shannon. Mama did me something awful that night and as much as I wanted her to pay for it, I didn't even snitch on the lady. Even when the police swarmed the hospital and drilled me with questions, I just stuck to the story that my longtime rival, Felice Hutchinson, and her homegirls pulled up in a blue Honda and jumped me. Shannon backed me as a witness. I was going to be in even more shit for lying on Felice, but I didn't care. I knew how much their drug dealing family hated the police, so just to have them shook up was enough revenge for me.

“Where you think you going all dressed up this morning?" I stopped myself from pondering and asked Shannon after I noticed how unusually dazzling she looked. She wasn't much of a morning person, so to see her up and dressed that early, I knew there had to have been a good reason.

"Didn't I tell you I was going job hunting this week? You thought I was playing?" she asked.

Shannon did mention it. But I didn't think she would actually go through with it.

"Yeah, I did think you were playing. Hell, what you need to go job hunting for anyway? I'm the one without a place to stay."

"That's why you need to get yo crazy dreamin' ass up and go with me. I tried to wake you but you must have been deep in dem shits," Shannon slightly shoved me. "I'm going up and down the

Tanger Strip. You can start at one end and I'll start at the other. We'll meet in the middle, near Old Navy, then see what we both come up with. How does that sound?"

"It sounds good to me but you know all my clothes are at mom's and ain't no way my small hips can fit in those miracle pants that hold yo' phat booty up," I cracked.

"Oh hush," Shannon gripped her butt cheeks then shamefully blushed. She had a body that made you ashamed to stand around her, but one thing I liked about my girl was that she wasn't boastful about it. She was better than me though. If I had an ass like Shannon's I would have definitely had me a place to stay. Probably wouldn't even need to be job hunting either.

"You right though," Shannon added. "I didn't think about that. And I know Shanetra's pants might be a little too small for you."

"My pride wouldn't even allow me to ask your little fourteen-year-old sister for clothes," I chuckled. "Besides, I'mma just go back to the spot and grab my stuff today. Mama should have done cooled off by now."

"I don't know about JoAnne. You know she's the queen of holding grudges. You be careful going out there by yourself," Shannon warned me. "She might be yo' mama but I don't trust that lady. I'm headed out. Wish me luck."

I rose from the bed and saw Shannon out the room. I knew I wasn't going to get up and go job hunting even if I did have clothes. As much as I was in need of a few dollars, I wasn't into going door to door begging anybody for a damn thing. If I was going to get a job, it was because the job came to me or because I happened to be in the right place at the right time. Besides, the way technology was set up, and if Shannon knew any better, she would have known that any form of job searching could be done in the comfort of her own home.

I chuckled to myself at Shannon's ignorance and immediately grabbed her computer to log into it. I couldn't help but laugh at the picture she had of her and Kevin on her screensaver. Shannon had only known him for a couple weeks but that boy had her mind gone. And I knew that when she gave him the panties that night at Mama's house, she was going to be even more sprung.

Shannon and I didn't talk much about that night because of what happened to me. Normally we would give each other the whole rundown on our partners- strong points, weak points, size, stroke game- we told all. But although we didn't get the chance to catch up this time, I knew by the glow in Shannon's eyes, and the way I heard her screaming from the other room, Kevin had definitely handled his business that night.

I was about two hours into filling out apps before I heard a knock at Shannon's room door. I quickly logged off her computer and hopped back in the bed. I couldn't wait to throw up in her face the fact that I had applied for over seven jobs right in my pajamas.

"Shannon must not be in this muthafucka!" a loud, obnoxious voice surprised me and let me know that it definitely wasn't my best friend coming through the door.

"That sneaky lil' hoe never leaves the door unlock," continued her oldest sister, Shameka, as she entered the room. Following closely behind was her two flunky friends, Bre and Kamilah. They were touting big shopping bags in each of their hands. I quickly shut my eyes and pretended to be asleep.

"Girl, we hit dey asses up good today. That's what you call teamwork bitches." Shameka said as she flopped every bit of her two hundred and fifty pound body on the edge of the bed where I was laying, causing the bottom half of mine to flow down towards her. Kamilah took a seat at the computer desk and Bre continued standing while she began to unload the bags.

"I know right, we got all the orders done in less than two hours. That's thirty minutes better than the last time."

"I know," Kamilah twirled around in the computer chair like a five-year-old. "But at least the last time we didn't have to take a trip to the "flee" market."

"Fa real bitch! I saw that short, stubby ass white heffa walking out the door. I just knew she was on to us. Hollerin' bout 'ma'am, excuse me, ma'am.' My name is *Shameka Juanita Evans*, not ma'am bitch. And if she thought I was stopping, she was just as crazy as her ass looked in those highwater pants she was wearing."

They all laughed before a dead silence struck the room. Shameka was the one who broke it.

"That was a good idea to put that stolen tag on the whip, because she sure was writing it down after we sped off. Little does she know that piece of evidence is gonna lead her to a small town called *Nowhere*."

They laughed again before Bre, who had now laid her slender body across the bed and began playing with her fingernails, became serious. If it wasn't for her hands being up in the air, I probably wouldn't have even saw her. She was thin as a toothpick and nobody even believed she was in her thirties. It wasn't until I saw her take down a chick three times her size that I knew she had to have some experience here on Earth. The girl was small and petite but she was tough as that pot roast Shannon's mom cooked the night before.

"We need to be careful though, next time we might not be so lucky. I don't know if y'all caught it but I did see an officer parked at that Candy's Lucky BBQ joint."

"Oh believe me, I saw him." Shameka replied. "That's why I slowed the hell down. Bre you right tho. It really wasn't a success. We were just lucky enough to have gotten away. We need to be able to get in those stores and walk out without dem folks even the least bit expecting us to be up to something."

"We'll aim for it next time," Kamilah replied. "It's almost 12 o'clock, you know I gotta go take grams to the grocery store at one. Let's go 'head and sort these shits out then start collectin' our chips. Besides, if I don't pay this light bill by tomorrow, me and grams will be spending our weekend in the dark."

"Fa sho," they all said at once.

Over the next hour, I continued to fake sleep as I occasionally peeked at the girls while they pulled clothing after clothing out of the many bags they brought in. Every type of name brand garment you could think of, they had. I listened to them call out name after name as they sorted what went to who. They even used my resting body as a platform to sit some of their stuff down on, and although the plastic hangers would sometimes sting as it hit my lower body, I still managed to play dead.

"And finally, three Old Navy khaki uniform pants and three white tops," Kamilah called out to Shameka then watched her pull them out of a bag. "Good. That goes with Kendra's order."

“And we’re done,” Shameka said as she looked over to the gift bags that she and the girls neatly folded and stuffed with tissue paper. Judging by how beautiful the bags were presented for her clients, I knew Shameka took her job very seriously. Even if it was illegal. Hell, the way she dressed herself in business attire, always carrying a big black briefcase, you'd think she sold insurance somewhere. She took pride in her career as a shoplifter and I knew it was paying off because she had a nice two-bedroom house and a sporty new Tahoe to show for it.

After the bags were sorted, Shameka grabbed her briefcase and immediately pulled out a notepad and one of the biggest calculators I had ever seen in my life. Everybody went in quiet mode as she sat in deep thought and mashed a variety of different numbers on her machine. For some odd reason my own heart began to beat nervously as I waited to see what type of information she would come up with.

“That’s four hundred a piece for the men’s bags, three for the women’s bags, and two for the kid’s. That leaves us with a total of three thousand and six hundred dollars,” she told the girls.

“Holy shit!” I managed to let the words slip from my tongue. Then spent the next three seconds praying that no one heard me.

“Minus five hundred for you and five for you. That leaves me with twenty-six hundred dollars.”

"Oh come on now, Shameka," Bre whimpered. "That's just a fifty-dollar jump from the last time. When are we gonna start splitting this thing three ways. We all take the same risk."

"We can start splitting it three ways when we start using your car, your gas money, and your clientele," Shameka mocked. She knew her homegirls didn't have either of those things. "How many times I gotta tell you? This is *my* business. I make everything possible and I do way more work than you think I do. Hell, I got you making five-hundred dollars in one single day. Do you know it takes some fools two weeks to make that kind of money? You better be thankful I put you on."

"I know that's right," Kamilah agreed from the bed. She wasn't at all rebellious and greedy like Bre. She did secretly feel that Shameka could have given them a little extra cash, but she also knew it beat working at that soup kitchen Shameka saved her from. For that reason, she never complained.

"Speaking of putting on," Bre added. " You ever decided on hiring another chick? I don't think Royce is coming home anytime soon."

"Hell, this is her third time getting caught in two years," Shameka replied. "I know dey gonna make her sit down. I tried to tell her silly ass that the mall ain't no place to go and steal."

Royce was Shameka's right hand girl. But like Bre, she didn't think she was getting a fair pay for her work. One day Royce stole Shameka's contacts straight from her cell phone and tried to underhand her. She reached out to all of Shameka's clients and offered the same service as Shameka did, but at a cheaper price. She was successful at doing it for a while until she got busted by the cops. Shameka didn't want to admit it, but she was secretly happy that Royce got caught, only because of the way she betrayed her. Even still, she went to see her in jail and put money on her books, probably only to rub in her face the fact that she was out and still making money.

"But yeah, I've thought about it," Shameka then began grabbing all the bags so that they could head out. "Every day as a matter of fact. It's just hard to trust someone new right now, especially after what Royce did to me."

The way Shameka put her head down and went into a brief stare told a lot about the way she felt about her best friend's betrayal. Kamilah quickly led the way out the door, probably attempting to snap her friend out of it. I watched them all very closely with the one eye that wasn't hidden under the dusty, brown blanket. Suddenly, a nervous feeling came over my body. Then my heart began to race again as a clever- but risky- idea popped into my head. It was a now or never moment for me to say what was on my mind and I decided to take advantage of it.

"I'll do it!" my slightly confident, but uncertain, voice managed to overthrow the big lump in my throat.

There was another awkward silence but this time Royce had nothing to do with it. I slowly removed the blanket from over my head, as if I was making a grand introduction or something. All the girls carried the same look of surprise on their faces once I was able to see them clearly.

"You'll do what?" Shameka asked, just testing my knowledge of the situation.

"You know...," I said bashfully, "what y'all do…steal shit."

"Girl, you don't know the first thing about going up in no stores," Bre butted in.

"I got this," Shameka said as she threw her arms up in front of Bre's face, seizing her from making any future comments. "But she's right. You don't know anything about it. What makes you so certain you can roll with us?"

"I'm not certain at all," I said honestly. "But I do know that I'm hip to the game and if you give it to me I can catch on quickly."

Shameka and her friends all looked to me, still surprised, but I could tell they were beginning to become a little more open to the idea.

"It might not be so bad," Bre ignored Shameka's request to keep quiet. "Look at her. She's pretty and mixed. I mean, we might know she's a half-black-half-Mexican-trailer-trash-nothing ass chick, but to someone who doesn't know her, they'll think she's the daughter of the mayor or something. All we gotta do is dress her up, fix her hair, and get Ryan to beat her face. I guarantee it, those folks won't think she'll need a reason to steal shit."

Shameka began to scratch the bottom of her chin, clearly thinking about what Bre had suggested. Then she paused for what seemed like forever before finally responding.

"Okay, here's the deal," she said. "We gonna test this thing out because I believe my girl Bre here has a point. Besides, you've always come off very mature to be seventeen, so I think you may can handle it. First thing tomorrow morning take this card here to this address. My girl will know that you're coming."

I looked down at the business card of a woman whose name was Christina Marie. Apparently she owned a fashion boutique on the Southside of Ordale. It was a good ways from Shannon's but I knew the bus route very well.

My thoughts of exactly where this boutique was located and why I needed to go there was quickly interrupted by another card being thrown in my face.

"After you leave there, go here." Shameka said. This card read *Harriet's House of Beauty*. "She will be expecting you too."

"Lastly, I'm gonna give you ah' one hundred dollar *loan* now for you to get miscellaneous shit like a pedicure, a manicure, and breakfast. You should be done with all that by three, so I'll be expecting you to meet us at the Chipotle's on Victory Drive at four. There we can sit down and discuss more. Understood?"

"Yes," I answered, trying very hard to hide my excitement.

"Good," she said. "Four o'clock sharp and not a minute late. Our next big takedown is in five days so I need you trained well."

"I'll be there," I assured her.

“And one more thing," Shameka said, after being the last one to exit the door. "My sister needs to know nothing about this. Got that?"

"I'm two steps ahead of you," I answered. "My lips are sealed."

CHAPTER THREE: BFFs

*"**I** want you out of here right now, you little ungrateful bitch! I let you up in my house and this is how you thank me?"*

Loud thumps, the sound of furniture moving against the already damaged tile floor, and groans of a timid, young voice filled the atmosphere. Hearing them, I used my tiny hands to cover my ears in hopes of shielding out the commotion. It wasn't the first time my mama and her baby sister, Jonell, had a nasty fight but it was the first time it had gotten that violent.

Attempting to escape the rage of my mama, Jonell came stumbling down the shallow hall of our trailer into my room, where she had been sleeping on and off for the past year. Her beautifully innocent pecan face was covered with scratches that were freshly lined with blood and her left cheekbone had a bit of a swell to it. Her nose also seemed to be enlarged, but I saw no sign of trauma to it. In fact, my Aunt Jonell looked much different than the last time she came by.

A few months before, I watched her slender body creep quietly out of my bedroom window. When she returned I noticed a few pounds were added to her hips, thighs, and face. She also had a new shade of dark tint around her eyes that clearly showed signs of heavy stress, yet she still managed to look beautiful.

In a very frantic manner, I watched her carefully as she ran over to the small space in the corner of the room where she kept a raggedy leather suitcase full of her clothes. Even though I had two empty dressers waiting to be used she never even considered placing her belongings there. That strangely puzzled me.

"You got three minutes to get the fuck up out of here!" Mama shouted, after she followed Jonell into the bedroom. "And whatever I paid for stays. As a matter of fact, everything in this muthafucka belongs to me, even the shit you bought in here with you! The only reason I'm being nice enough to let you take anything is because you done gone and got ya lil' fast ass pregnunt!"

Pregnant? My little mind pondered as I slowly began to release the grip from my ears and started to study Jonell very closely. Now that mama mentioned it, I did see a small pudge in her belly. That probably explained the extra weight too.

"You just wait until I tell my husband about the shit you just came up in here and laid on me."

Jonell's eyes immediately expanded as if they were about to pop out of her narrow head. It was like she had seen a ghost or something. Forgetting about her clothes- or the fact that going anywhere near my mama could've have possibly gotten her knocked up again- she immediately ran over to her, dropped to her knees, and folded her hands in a praying position.

"Nooooo please Joanne," she begged. "You promised me!"

Mama snatched away from Jonell and glared down at her with the least bit of sympathy. "Fuck promises. You wanna break up my household, then I sure as hell can break a promise."

Hearing those words and realizing that putting her trust in her hateful older sister was the wrong thing to do, Jonell began to sob.

"Nooooo please don't," she cried. "I'll never come back, I swear. Just don't mention anything to your Jose, please."

"You got three minutes," Mama made herself a little clearer. "Get the fuck out or the ambulance will have to carry you out."

The door slammed behind Mama and Jonell let out a heartbreaking cry. It was painful to witness because I knew she would never in a million years let me see her shed a tear. I would usually catch her weeping silently in the middle of the night while I would lie there pretending to be asleep. If I accidentally sneezed or moved, she'd quickly bury her face under the covers and try to replace her sorrow with fabricated strength.

Finally noticing that I was watching, Jonell quickly began to wipe away her tears and ran over to comfort me.

"Oh God, I'm so sorry Keish," she said sincerely. "Please don't be upset. Auntie's fine okay...Auntie's just fine."

I normally trusted everything that came out of her mouth, but this time I wasn't convinced.

"But you told me to never do that," I said to her.

"Do what?" Auntie Jonell looked puzzled.

"Tell stories," I replied.

A little laughter began to seep through her pain and it was refreshing.

"You're right," she said. "I did say that. And I meant it. But I'm not storying, Keish. I really am fine...or at least I'm gonna be."

"But I don't understand. I saw you crying, Auntie. Are those the tears of joy you once told me about?"

"Not exactly tears of joy," she sighed. "Auntie's just going through a rough time right now, but because I'm a fighter I will get through it. Don't you believe that I'm strong enough to get through it?"

Although I didn't quite understand, I nodded anyway.

"Good."

Aunt Jonell then sat me up on the bed and kneeled on the floor in front of me, placing my hands into hers. She held her head down for a second as if she was trying to get her thoughts together, then she slowly picked herself up and looked me dead into my eyes.

"Keisha, don't be a screw up like me, okay. Promise me you will never let anyone steal your innocence. This thing right here," she pointed at my chest, "is called your heart. Not only does it beat, but it tells you if something isn't, or doesn't, feel right. Bad people come in all shapes and sizes. They can be strangers or people that live right in your house. You better promise me that if something doesn't feel right to you in your heart, no matter who tells you it is right, you don't run away like me. You stand up for yourself and do something about it."

Still clueless, I simply nodded again.

"Okay now, Keisha," she let out a deep sigh, stood up, and stuck out her smallest finger to mine. Pinky swears were our thing.

"I'm gonna hold you to that. I'm also gonna hold you to being the best cousin ever to the baby that I'm going to have soon."

"A real baby?" I asked excitingly. "Yayyyy!"

"I don't think that's a good thing, Keisha," she shhhed me. "I'm only sixteen. I don't know the first thing about having babies."

"But I can help you," I replied.

"No! You can't!" Auntie Jonell blurted out angrily. I jumped at the unpleasant surprise. Seeing how startled I was, she embraced me with a warm hug.

"I'm sorry hun. I didn't mean to yell at you. It's just that it takes more than the help of a little kid to raise a child. A lot of responsibility comes with it. You gots to have money, you gots to have a car, the baby's got to have a dad..."

Aunt Jonell immediately stopped in the middle of her sentence and stared out into space. Her almond-shaped, hazel eyes showed no sign of life in them for about ten whole seconds. It made me feel uncomfortable.

"Gots to have a what?!" I interrupted her thoughts. Hearing me, she shook her head quickly from left to right, pulling herself back into our conversation.

"Nothing," she said quickly before changing the subject. "But listen...I have already given her a name. Do you wanna know what it is?"

"Yes," I smiled brightly. I only hoped it would be the same as mine, or least something close to it.

"I'm gonna name her Charlytte," she said, disappointing me a bit.

"Charlytte?" I asked, as I immediately ran to grab one of my favorite books and placed it on my lap. "You mean like the spider?"

"Yes, just like the spider," Jonell answered. Then she placed her index fingers over one of the letters on the book's front page. "Except instead of spelling it with an 'o', I'm gonna spell it with a 'y.'"

"Why are you going to do that?" I waited impatiently for an explanation.

"Because WHY is a question that I ask myself every morning I wake up and every night before I lay down," she sadly answered as

that lifeless look began to reappear in her eyes. I didn't like it one bit, so I tried to cheer her up.

"Well, I like Charlytte better with a 'y' anyway. The 'o' is ugly, just like my mama."

Aunt Jonell immediately let out a chuckle then nervously peeped over her shoulders in fear that her sister may have heard us. She tried to stop herself from laughing at my remark but she wasn't doing a good job at it. Although she knew how much I hated my mom, she would never allow me to disrespect her. This time, oddly, she didn't seem to mind. Besides, I didn't lie. My mama was ugly-inside and out.

"What did I tell you about saying mean things about your mom, little lady?" she began to tickle my belly. "Huh....What did Auntie say? Huh Keisha...Huh Keisha....Huh Keisha...?"

I kept hearing my name being repeated over and over but the sound of Aunt Jonell's sweet voice was replaced by Shannon's high pitched ghetto tone.

"Keisha!...Keish!" she yelled. "Snap out of it girl, dammit! Didn't you hear me knocking on the door?"

Shannon then put up a wire hanger to my face as proof that she had to use it in order to let herself in the room.

"If I have to work this hard to get in my own shit then maybe your gonna have to go back home. Jeezus!"

I was used to getting this type of attitude from Shannon, especially after I started spending more time with her older sister and less time with her. I didn't pay her any mind though, as I usually didn't.

"I'm sorry, okay" I replied. "Damn. Lighten up a little."

"Lighten up my ass. You must've been having one of those dreams again?"

"No." I replied nonchalantly and hoped that she would change the subject. I normally shared in full details the weird nightmares I had with Shannon, but the daydreams she knew nothing about.

Probably because the nightmares were fictitious things that I needed her to help me make sense of. The daydreams, on the other hand, were real things that actually occurred in my life that I didn't want her to know about.

I usually had them when something I would see or hear triggered me to. Then I would go into a deep trance, lose all sense of the world around me, and enter a zone of my own unpleasant past memories. I realized they were a serious problem my freshman year when I was on the cheerleading squad and I threw Nia Singleton up in the air during a high school football game. The position of the stars reminded me of how the sky looked the last night I saw my Auntie alive. I never caught Nia and the broken ankle she suffered was the reason I was never allowed to cheer again.

"Keisha, we really need to talk." Shannon said as she flopped down on the bed beside me. I was still trying to get my head together from the visuals I just had and I really wasn't in the mood.

"Shannon, can we do this another time." I quickly jumped out of bed and headed for her closet. "Shameka's on the way to get me. There's a pizza spot on Wilmington that she says is hiring. She's gonna take me to fill out an app."

Shannon immediately cracked the phoniest laugh I ever heard. "See now, that's exactly what we need to talk about Keisha. How long are you gonna keep up with this act?"

"Whoa..wait...what act?" I pretended to be confused.

"C'mon Keisha, Shameka's been taking you to get apps for the past seven months. You've been running outta here with that excuse every other day and coming back with everything but a job. I have been knowing my sister much longer than you. You don't think I know what she and anybody who hangs around her does for a living?"

"I'm sure you do know, but what does your sister's life have to do with mine?"

Shannon cracked another laugh, but this one was much simmer. I guess she just couldn't believe the lengths I would go to tell a lie. Hell, I couldn't believe it either. All I know is that Shameka told me not to mention a single word to her baby sister about me working with her and since she was the one cutting me a check, my loyalty went in her favor.

"Look, I'm gettin' real tired of the charade, Keisha. I know you're out boosting clothes with my sister and it's kinda fucked up that we're best friends and you never told me about it."

Tired of having to lie to Shannon and having a little bone to pick with her myself, I forgot all about my vow to Shameka and finally came clean.

"You know what? You're right. I am boosting with your sister and making good money doing so. I don't see you complaining when I'm bringing stuff up in here for you and your baby."

Shannon looked over at the picture on the wall of her, Kevin, and their nine-month old daughter, Precious. I continued.

"Speaking of that, I think it's quite ironic that the day I decided to do business with your sister was the same day you pretended to be going job hunting…but really you were going to your first doctor's appointment for the baby you didn't tell me you were having. Talk about secrets now."

Shannon had a busted look on her face. She knew I had a point, but she still had to argue against it. "I know, but that's different, Keisha. How was I supposed to tell you that I had got pregnant? I was ashamed."

"And I can understand that, but you don't think I was ashamed to tell you that I'm shoplifting. I mean, that's not something to brag about either."

I made my way back to the bed after seeing how down Shannon got when speaking about the baby. I knew it was hard on her, being young and pregnant and having people from the schools, the neighborhoods, even the church, all judging her. I gotta admit though. She handled her business very well as a mother. She was working at Popeye's full time and taking college classes online. Even though I felt like the lucky one because I wasn't tied down with a baby, I was secretly jealous of her bond with her child and the lengths she was going to take care of hers. Not to mention, her and Kevin were a match made in heaven, while I had to fight with his best friend Tre every week about a different chick.

"Look, I'm sorry Shannon. You're right. Regardless of whose keeping what secrets, I haven't been there for you lately like I know I should be. I could have told you that I was boosting, but I didn't want you to look at me as more of a fuck up than you already do. Besides, I gotta do what I gotta do because I'm out here on my own now. Every time I'm out there stealing, I'm thinking about getting another dollar so that I can get up out your mom's crib."

I slid in a little closer to Shannon and grabbed one of her hands to assure her that what I was about to say next was going to be sincere. "Shannon, I know you're a good girl. It's me that's the bad influence on you. It's my gimmicks and my schemes that always have you suffering the consequences. It was my idea to talk to the guys at the corner store. I'm the one who forced you to date Tre's friend. And it was me who suggested we link up with them that night Mama came home and caught us. If it wasn't for that you probably wouldn't be sitting up here with a baby and I know deep down you hate me for it. Just give me some time to get a few more dollars up and I promise I will be out of your way."

Shannon paused and tried to take in everything I said to her before she responded. This was the first time we had a deep conversation about something that always seemed to come natural to us- our friendship. I admit it was a little weird, but we knew it was something that needed to happen sooner or later.

"Look Keisha, you got it all wrong. That's not how I feel about you. True enough, I get in the most shit behind fucking with you," she giggled, "but that's what drives me to wake up every day. Just seeing what the next adventure will bring."

She pulled my hand closer to hers. "I mean look at my family- a house full of bitter people going from city to city because my crackhead mama don't pay her rent long enough to keep a place. All this shit is depressing, but that changed when I met you. Believe it or not, our friendship gives me hope…And you better not ever let me hear you say you think I got pregnant because of you. I made my own decision that night and look what I gained in the process. I have a baby that I pushed out of my pussy so beautiful I had no choice but to name her Precious and a boyfriend who takes good care of the both of us. Now I know what a real mother-daughter bond feels like and I owe some of that to you and your promiscuous ways."

We both shared a quick laugh and I almost got teary-eyed listening to her pour her heart out to me. I was completely wrong about how I thought she looked at me and it was a breath of fresh air knowing that our friendship was still strong even in the distance. I leaned in and gave Shannon the biggest hug ever and she embraced me back wholeheartedly.

"Okay, enough with all this mushy shit bitch," Shannon shoved me away from her. "Christmas 'round the corner and I hear Kid's Playground got some banging winter gear in. My Precious needs to be fly for her birthday."

"I got you sis. You already know I'll do anything for my princess."

"I know, I know." Shannon replied. "Just try to have it by the first because we're overdue for some new pictures. And I'm gonna get Kevin to pay you this time."

"I don't need your money, Shannon. We're friends, remember."

"We are. I just feel that you're risking a lot so you should be paid. And don't think I'm condoning this shit either. Money just real tight since Kevin decided to stop hustlin'. "

"Yeah, I overheard Tre mentioning something about that. You know he don't like me all up in his business so I didn't ask. But what's the deal with that?"

"Nothing really, he just decided to put Precious first. He said he can't be sitting in nobody jail while another man taking care of us. Can you believe that?"

"No I can't," I said. "Seems to me the baby would be more of a reason to go out and get this money."

Shannon shook her head at my comment. "Sometimes everything ain't about money. You'll see that one day."

I heard Shannon clearly but at the same time, I wasn't feeling her.

"Speaking of money," she reminded herself. "I need you to give this to my sister. It's the six hundred dollars Kendra owes her for her order."

"Oh yeah, we almost got busted getting her shit the other night...but it should be four hundred, not six."

"Well I'm pretty sure it's six. She counted it out right in front of me and even had me to run it back by her. I already have it sealed so I wouldn't open it if I were you. You know how Shameka feels bout people going through her shit."

"Yeah I know," I said thinking very hard about why Kendra would be dropping off an envelope with six hundred bucks in it. Shameka had just called and told me that she was coming by with four, so me, Bre, and Kamilah's cut would be eighty-five dollars apiece. "You're probably right. Maybe Kendra spoke with Shameka about us going back to get more stuff. Could be why she gave her the extra two hundred."

I knew that was hardly the case but I had to throw Shannon off. I didn't want her to know I was becoming suspicious of her sister.

"Go ahead and pick up Precious girl," I rushed her out. "I'll make sure she gets it."

"Cool," Shannon said as she grabbed her belongings and her bus ticket then headed out the door.

"Hey Keish," she called out to me before leaving. "Please consider getting yourself a real job. I'm serious about this."

I looked my best friend dead in her eyes and told yet another lie. "I will chick. I promise, I will."

CHAPTER FOUR: The Rat

"You guys can go ahead without me, I feel real awful," I gripped my stomach firmly and groaned in pain. We were in the middle of taking on one of the biggest orders we ever had and having four girls on the job was a must. Shameka, Bre, and Kamilah all scorned at me because of my sudden decision to stand them up.

"Damn Keisha, how much did you drink last night?" Shameka asked as she started to pull the driver side door of the rental car open. Daylight was slowly slipping away and the crowd that raided JCPenny's was beginning to fade, so she knew she didn't have much time to sit and argue against my decision.

"I don't know girl. I think I may have downed the whole bottle, at least that's what Tre said. All I know is that I woke up throwin' up and my head was poundin' like a muthafucka. I wish I could go, I really do, but I don't want to slow y'all down. Besides, just in case y'all need to get out of there quickly at least I'll already be out here in the car ready to roll. "

"Sounds good to me," Bre said from the backseat. "Besides, a three-way split is better than a four anyway."

Bre and Kamilah slapped hands but Shameka didn't partake. She wasn't as excited because she knew that I was the key to getting out of the store safely. After she got my hair fixed in a cute little bob style and stole me some of the finest designer clothes, my high-class looking ass really could have passed for being the daughter of the mayor. I came off as nothing less than a boss chick and nobody ever suspected me of having to steal anything.

"Okay, but next time ease up on the drinking when you know you got a job to do," Shameka said. Then she exited the car, rolled up her sleeve and said the famous line she always said before we went on our missions. "Alright bitches, the robin hoodrats are about to attack!"

I laughed as I watched them head inside the mall, but when they made it out of my sight my chuckles quickly turned into a devilish grin. I had successfully tricked Shameka into thinking I was sick so that I could carry out my real plan of finishing the job that Royce had started. I didn't like the fact that she was playing me and the other girls, getting more money than what she said she was and giving us bullshit ass percentages. That phony count of the four-hundred bucks I had given her in the envelope let me know everything I needed to know about Shameka's two-timing ass.

I immediately grabbed her purse and began to search through it. I knew she'd leave her phone behind because it was a strict rule to never take anything inside the stores that could possibly identify us if we got caught.

"Bingo," I said as I pulled out her shiny touchscreen and started scrolling through her contacts. From spending so much time with Shameka I learned her password and that all her client's numbers had money symbols next to them. One by one, I copied and saved them into my phone. My plan was to steal her customers and give them more clothes for less. I knew it would work because many of them were already asking me personally to get their stuff, especially the guys who were trying to hit on me. My loyalty to Shameka wouldn't allow me to cross her though, but as soon as I learned that she didn't have the same dedication to me, I put it in my mind to start looking out for Keisha and Keisha only.

It only took five minutes to save about thirty numbers in my phone. After I was done I turned on the music and laid back in my seat, before falling asleep then waking up to realize that an hour had passed and the girls hadn't returned. That was unusual because we were always in and out of a store in no less than thirty minutes. I tried not to panic because of the size of the order and the fact that obviously they were down by one person. It was only after yet another hour rolled around that I knew I had better see what was up.

I never went out half stepping for anything or anyone so I spent about five minutes fixing myself up in the car mirror. Then I grabbed my purse, snatched Shameka's keys, and headed toward the mall to hunt for them. The automatic doors made way for my entrance and I immediately soaked in the clean store smell of money that I had gotten familiar with. JCPenny's was clear of most of its customers so I figured it wouldn't be hard for me to spot my crew. We only had women's orders, which prompted me to head straight for the escalators towards that department. On my way I saw a rack of gold-plated pens, grabbed one, looked around and dropped it into my purse.

"Y'all should be thankful this the only thing I'm taking," I said to myself, then preceded to make it to the second floor.

Once I got there, I began to search around but I saw no sign of the girls. I walked swiftly through the entire store checking the men's department, shoes, and jewelry. I even checked the bathrooms. Still nothing.

Disappointed, I decided to make my way back to the car hoping that maybe they had slipped pass me while I was on the inside. A huge smile appeared on my face when I saw people surrounding Shameka's car, but after I got a little closer it faded. That was because I realized those people were not my girls, but police officers with flashlights up to the windows peeping inside.

Shit, I thought to myself as I immediately did a three-sixty turn-around. I didn't know if the officers knew who I was, or if they saw me trying to avoid them, but I didn't look back to find out either. It wasn't until I heard a voice coming from their direction saying "Excuse me Miss, hold it right there!" that I knew they were on to me.

I pretended to act as if I didn't know they were talking to me and what started off as a swift walk turned into a full-fledged run. Both officers took off behind me and at the speedy pace I was going I would have surely lost them if the Loss Prevention store worker didn't take her job so damn serious. Hell, as soon as I made it into the store the chubby, studdish Hispanic lady tackled me down to the floor.

"Get the fuck off me lady!" I cursed at her. "You have no right to put your hands on me!"

We tussled for a minute on the ground but I was no match against the weight of this she-man. She managed to lay me on my stomach, get on top of me and crush me with her body weight. I could barely breathe so to see the officers approaching me had now turned into a bit of a relief.

"Good job. You really should join the team," the officer said to the LP after he hi-fived her. Then he cuffed me while I was on the ground and helped me on my feet. I could now see him better. He was a short, stalky little man with caramel-toned skin. Clearly someone who got his ass beat in his earlier years. The other officer was the complete opposite- tall, white, and linky. He didn't say much nor dare get near me.

"Good job my ass!" I yelled to the both of them. "It's not in your job description to put your filthy hands on me. I'm gonna sue this fuckin place!"

"Good luck with that,'" she clapped back. "Officers you can follow me to the processing room. It's right this way."

Officer Davis, or least that's what his name tag read, instructed his partner to grab one of my arms while he held on to the other. I guess he was afraid that I may try to run again. I began to take the walk of shame as they both escorted me to this room. In order to shield out the embarrassment of being scorned at by shoppers, I immediately closed my eyes and imagined I was a superstar and that the two officers were my bodyguards. Fortunately, my walk down the red carpet was a brief one because the room they placed me in was only a couple feet away.

"Take a seat," Davis said, once we were well inside.

I walked into the small room slowly. It was full of boxes and papers stacked as tall as me. There was one small wooden table with about three flimsy chairs pushed up against it and there were also no windows therefore a small lamp in the corner was its only source of light. One thing for sure, I didn't like to be closed up in stuffy spaces so they had better make this quick.

"Damn. All this for a fucking dollar pen." I cried. "I was gonna pay for it. I was just going back to the car to look for my girls. Here is the pen and a fifty to get me out of these cuffs and on my way."

Officer Davis shook his bald, M&M shaped head from left to right then grabbed a chair and took his place across from me. He didn't know whether to be offended by my sassiness or amused.

"Now young lady, I'm not about to sit here and play games with you. You and I both know that this has nothing to do with a little pen."

"I don't know what you're talking about," I said. "That's the only thing I took."

"Well that's not the only thing your friends took. You know, the ones you drove up here with. We lost them and it would be in your best interest to help me find them."

"Officer, I'm very claustrophobic and I think I'm going to have a panic attack if I don't leave here soon. Can you please just arrest me because I don't know any-"

Officer Davis held his indexed finger up, signaling for me not to say another word. "Ten-four, I'll be right there," he said into a walky-talky, then quickly got up and headed to the door. "Keep an eye on this feisty one. Be right back."

Officer Mobley moved over so that his partner could make his exit. Then we sat silently for what I thought was an hour, but probably was only five minutes, before Davis returned. His demeanor was much different than it was before he left and a long, exaggerated sigh exited his lips before sitting again.

"Well do you see how things work out, Mobley?" Officer Davis turned to his accomplice. "Apparently Mrs. Gonzales caught two of the girls hiding in the bathroom near the food court. I went down and spoke with them separately and guess who they both said was the mastermind behind all this."

Officer Davis looked dead into my eyes, letting me know it was me that the blame was being put on. I just sat silently and processed everything that happened from the time I got caught up until where I was then. Then I busted out into a huge laughter. Both officers looked at each other confused, before Davis spoke up.

"Are you okay, young lady?" he asked, "I said your friends ratted you out. How is that funny?"

I continued to laugh in both of their faces. I admit, I was being a little over-the-top but I was doing it intentionally. "Hold up, so you're trying to say my homegirls gave me up."

Officer Davis nodded.

“I just need to know one thing,” I became serious, “one of the girls has a strong Jamaican accent. That's my very best friend. I expect the other bitches to cross me, but please tell me she wasn't the one who said any of that shit.”

"The girl with the Jamaican accent was the main one who was doing all the talking," Davis informed me.

I sadly dropped my head and pretended to be heartbroken. Just when Davis thought I was about to start talking, I busted out laughing again.

"Gotcha!" I shouted. "None of my friends have Jamaican accents. We all from right here in tha Port. You can't play a player. I may be young but I'm way ahead of my time."

I busted out laughing even harder. Even Officer Mobley tried to hold in his grin. I knew he would have a great time telling the boys in the breakroom how his partner got outsmarted by a kid. A mixed of shame, anger, and embarrassment appeared on Officer Davis’s face while a hue of redness appeared in his eyes.

"I don't have time for this,” he shouted. "Officer Mobley, arrest her for the pen and let's hang this thing up."

Officer Davis emptied out my purse on the table and I watched everything from tampons to jolly ranchers fly out of it. Then he obtained the gold pen and examined it. Suddenly, the normally silent Mr. Mobley, came and whispered something into his ear.

"Good thinking," he said then smirked cleverly into my direction.

"Well apparently you're not as smart as you think you are, little lady. Ya see,” he fumbled through my scattered belongings and pulled out an object. "Me personally, I hate cellphones because I witness so much bullshit that comes with them. I believe that it causes lack of communication amongst people. I've saw where a simple ‘wyd’ cause deadly accidents, but most of all, I just feel like the whole world was better off without them.”

He twirled my phone around with his fingertips in a childish manner. “But on the contrary, I must admit, sometimes these little things come in handy. In fact, over the course of my many years on the force I’ve notice that cell phones have been the key in solving a lot of my cases. Why? Because most people put their lives in them and I’m most certain that when I open yours I will find some indication of who your friends are."

Shit. I thought. *Why the fuck didn't I just leave my shit in the car?* I had slipped big time. Shameka always warned me that one day my bad habit will lead me to my destruction. Unfortunately, she was right. On top that, I had never set a lock on my phone which made his job even more easier. I knew he would immediately see the last text I sent to out Shameka saying, "Bitch what time we hitting up the store today. I'm ready to go make this money."

"Bingo," Officer Davis said as he took a pen and began to copy a few things down in his notepad. He never said another word to me. After he was done, he placed all of my things back into my bag and sat it on the table in front of me.

“Sit tight young lady,” he said as he signaled for Mobley to come speak with him on the outside.

Neither one of them returned for another hour, leaving me to ponder on whether or not Davis found what he was looking for in my phone. The room had gotten cold so I placed my arms inside of my green banana republic blouse. Then I rested my head uncomfortably on the tabletop until I worried myself into a nap.

"Rise and shine, Miss Smarty Pants. Your job here is done."

I woke up to find Officer Davis standing up behind me un-cuffing me from the chair.

"Now I'm not gonna arrest you because I only go after the big fish, but let this be a lesson to you. You should choose your friends and your hobbies more carefully. Besides," he slowly dragged his hands from my wrist up to my shoulders, "those girls in the county would eat your pretty ass alive. And I mean that literally."

I scorned. "Just when I thought you were a good cop."

"I'm a great cop," he stood me up and then began to escort me out of the room, "but I'm a man first. Here is my card. Use it if you decide you wanna give up some more info on your Jamaican friend."

I snatched the card from Officer Davis, whose last remark made me feel like maybe he didn't find anything in my phone. Then I raced back to Shannon's and didn't even try to attempt to call the girls because I knew I had their stuff with me. Just when I thought the night couldn't get any worse, the sight my eyes received when I pulled up on her street revealed otherwise.

"What the fuck!" I screamed as I quickly parked and made my way up to the porch of the shoebox-sized duplex we were all cooped up in. The neighbors flooded their porches to get a good view of what was going on at Shannon's mom's house and she gave them all a show as she cursed and screamed at what seemed like a hundred policemen that filled up her yard. I still wasn't quite sure if they were there for the girls because Mrs. Williams always had something going on at her place. Whether she had gotten her ass beat by one of her boyfriends or was spazzing because she didn't have her daily dose of crack in her system, the police were there more than normal. It wasn't until I walked up a little closer to see Officer Davis talking with Shameka, Bre, and Kamilah, who all sat on the sidewalk wearing handcuffs, that I knew we were busted.

I rushed over to Officer Davis and almost shoved him, but I thought against it.

"What the fuck are you doing!" I asked him. "Why are you here?"

Shameka looked surprised to see me. She was sweating something terribly, her clothes were ripped, and that sew-in Harriet recently hooked up her with was ruined. I knew she must have put up a big fight. Bre also looked roughed up, while Kamilah on the other hand, looked untouched. That was expected though because that scary bitch wouldn't put up a fight to save her life.

"Officer Davis?" Shameka questioned. "Keisha, you know this motherfucker?"

She struggled to stand herself up from off the curb but somehow was successful at it. A few other officers raced over to see what was going on.

"Yes...I mean…No!" I replied. I quickly tried to figure out a way to explain myself without making the situation look worse than it already did. All I managed to do was confuse myself. "Well…I...I...I just met him today."

"Man this bitch ratted us out," Bre informed the girls. "I told you we shouldn't have trusted her ass."

Shameka didn't respond. She just looked to me, hoping that the accusations weren't true.

"No, I didn't rat anyone out." I told them.

"Then how come this pig you *just so happened* to meet today, *just so happens* to be arresting us today?" Kamilah asked.

Bre co-signed. "Yeah, and why are all of us in handcuffs and you ain't?"

Shameka still didn't open her mouth. She just waited for me to explain myself.

"Listen, I can explain all that. But first know that I didn't rat out anyone. I just fucked up when I-"

Before I could get my words out, a fist struck the back of my head and about a dozen officers ran to contain Mrs. Williams. "You lil' heffa, you snitched on my daughter! After all we done for you this is how you do us!"

Mrs. Williams screamed, kicked, and struggled with the officers while trying to get to me. They now had no choice but to cuff her as well. I just stood and watched, the least bit frightened, as she acted like a maniac mostly because she had no drugs in her system. I knew for a fact she was going through some serious withdrawal because before we left to go to the outlet she was rushing us back home. Shameka was the only one of her children who helped support her habit and as long as she was able to count up her merchandise at her mom's spot, she would proudly give her a measly ten or twenty dollars for drugs. That's the only reason Mrs. Williams was so upset, because with Shameka locked up, she knew she had to turn to begging in front of corner stores to get her next hit.

I refused to argue with a crackhead and the love tap she laid across my head probably hurt her fragile ass more than it did me, so I ignored her. When the police were finally able to calm her down, they placed her on the curb next to the rest of the girls.

After I realized I wasn't going to get anything through to them, I looked towards the house for someone I knew would understand me. The horizontal beam of light seeping through the front door let me know that Shannon was peeping and probably listening to the whole thing. She never really cared much for drama, so anytime anything popped off she'd always just look from a distance, only getting involved in something if she absolutely had to.

"Shannon, girl listen to me," I panted, as I ran up the house. "I was at the store and…."

"Don't let that bitch in my house!" Mrs. Williams interrupted once again. "You hear what I said child!"

"Shannon, please don't listen to them. I would never rat on your sister. Come on now, you know me."

"Shannon, you need to put Precious down and whoop that hoe ass!" Shameka now blurted. "Blood is thicker than water. Remember that!"

"Shannon, please." I pleaded. "Don't do this, don't listen to them."

Shannon had a fearful look in her eyes as she stood there with Precious asleep on her shoulders. She said not one word but constantly looked to the curb and back to me. I could sense that the feeling of being stuck between her close family and best friend was becoming overwhelming for her. For that reason, I decided to lessen the pressure by silencing myself, while the girls and Mrs. Williams all continued to make crazy outbursts.

"Chile, if you let that bitch in my house, you might as well start packing your stuff to leave with her. Get that hoe of my property by any means necessary. She's a snitch and a backstabber."

"Shannon, please," I pleaded. "You know I'm more family to you than they are. Who's always been there for you at your worst…them or me? Please don't do this. I have nowhere to go."

Shannon propped Precious's slouching body back up on her shoulders and opened the door a little wider. But, instead of stepping back to let me in, she stepped forward and slapped me dead in my face. Then she cowardly ran back into the house and slammed the door. All I could do was hold one hand across my face and the other across my heart to try to stop it from breaking into tiny little pieces.

CHAPTER FIVE: THE BALL

Boom! Boom! Boom! Went the sound of Tre’s fist as it slammed against the bathroom door of his duplex apartment.

"What the hell are you doing in there?" he fussed. "You said you were gonna be ready thirty hours ago."

I hurried up and brushed the last little bit of smoky-gray eyeshadow up against my eyelid, straightened my fancy red dress, and made my way out the door.

"I know! I know! I'm ready now!" I yelled back to Tre, as he just stood in a daze astonished by my beauty. I had gotten dolled up to go out with him many times before, but never had I put so much effort into looking as gorgeous as I did this night.

We were on the way to the most talked about event in Ordale and half stepping was the last thing anybody wanted to be caught doing. It was his cousin, Hi-C's, all-white party that normally had no more than one hundred attendees but everybody in the muthafucka was somebody. Hell, you could even catch a celebrity or two in that bitch on a real good year.

The party was way too high-class for my jobless ass. You needed to be more than just pretty to be a part of the OMC, Ordale Mafia Circle. Only the real hustlers- dealers, business owners, and big-time moneymakers- made the cut. The only reason I was even allowed to go was because Tre was Hi-C's, the man of the city, first cousin. Tre was also a part of their well-established drug ring. Besides, I was the prettiest of all the girls he fucked with so I was always his top choice when he wanted someone to show off.

The ride to the party was an anxious one for me. I sat quietly in Tre's black BMW and dazed out of the window thinking about what the night would bring.

"You nervous?" he asked, as we cruised down the parkway heading towards Ordale's outer city limits. "Your legs are shaking."

I looked down at my kneecaps, forced myself to stop them from moving, and confidently responded. "Nervous about what?"

"You know, going to The Ball with me. This is the real deal. Nothing like that Uptown teen nightclub shit you go to."

"Oh I don't have to be nervous about shit," I smacked my lips. "The Ball should be nervous about me coming to it."

Tre chuckled at my confidence. He always said it was one of the things that attracted him to me.

"Why do you ask?" I continued. "If you think that I'm not classy enough to go then maybe you should have asked your *registered nurse* friend Paulette when she called you at three o'clock this damn morning."

Tre hissed at my remark but I didn't care. Every other day I would find something that let me know he was fucking around on me and every other day I would question him about it. He was growing tired of it and so was I.

"Keisha, I have told you for the last time to stop going through my shit."

"I didn't go through anything. I couldn't help but wake up to your loud ass ringtone last night and when I went to shut the shit off, that's when I saw it. Tre...," I folded my arms across my chest and shifted my entire body in his direction. Even though we were on the freeway, I only hoped he would take his eyes off the road for a split second and look into mine to see just how much he was deeply hurting me. "I thought you said you were done with her."

"I am done with her,"' he tried effortlessly to convince me. "But I do hustle still and money is money. I don't care who it is or what time they call, if it has something to do with money then I'm available."

"So is that going to be your excuse every time I catch you in a lie? Because if so, then I give up."

"It's not an excuse, it's the truth. And speaking of giving up... what happened to you trying to find a job? It's like you just gave up on that. I told you when you first moved in with me that you could only stay for a month. It's been almost two and you haven't been showing any signs of even thinking about going anywhere."

"Look, I didn't know it was a big deal, okay. Excuse me for thinking that by you coming home to cooked meals and good pussy that you didn't mind me being there. Hell, you're never home anyway. If I'm supposed to be your girl, why is it a problem if I stay with you? Or is it that I'm cockblockin' people like Paulette from coming through?"

Tre shook his head from left to right. "Because we've been over this a million times. I'm in a dangerous business and my home is no place for chicks. It's about caution and safety, not other hoes."

"Yeah, whatever." I sassed him.

"Look, I don't have to explain myself any more than I already have. Bottom line, you need to think about what your next move will be. That shoplifting shit is cool but it needs to be your side hustle. I'm going to give you a deadline to get a legit job and to be out. I mean that shit shawty."

I didn't say another word to Tre after realizing how upset he was becoming. I just continued to ponder out the window and tried to rid my mind of all the evil things I could have done to him in that moment. I didn't understand why he couldn't just let me live with him and I wasn't buying that safety first bullshit he was trying to sell me. What I knew, but didn't want to except, was that Tre just wasn't in love with me. And I never expressed it to him but I was growing very tired of being his sex slave and show-off chick. I was getting bored and my desire for more was slowly beginning to let its way into my mind.

We arrived to the beautiful neighborhood in Connor's Bluff and I immediately shifted my thoughts away from Tre to the nice homes we were approaching. After pulling up to a closed gate, I watched him punch in a few numbers, then get buzzed in by the professional female voice that responded to his call for entrance. As we continued to ride through the neighborhood I was captivated by the subdivision that didn't even look like it was a part of our town. The houses were huge, the grass was exceptionally green, and nobody's property stood less than two stories. We parked at the white one with the black shutters. There were many nice cars surrounding it which let me know we had made it to our destination.

After we finally found a good spot to park, Tre took my hand and led me up to the house like a gentleman, only because there were a few people on the porch that he could put on a show for. A nervous feeling came over me as I did not know what to expect from the inside, but once the door opened and the smooth sound of Maxwell's *Ascension* greeted me I began to feel a little more comfortable.

Wow, I thought to myself as we entered the mini mansion. A beautiful green disco ball hung perfectly in the middle of two identical, curvy stairwells that led up to a balcony on the second floor. The place was laced with beautiful furniture and I'm assuming black was his favorite color because everything in it was jetted. It was just like something I saw in movies and rap videos but better.

Upon entering, mostly everyone continued to go about their conversing, dancing, and mangling as normal. There were a couple girls who started whispering and looking our way. I could only assume they were some chicks who either had Tre before or wanted him, either way I was the one on his arm so anything or anybody else was irrelevant.

"So what do you think about cuz's crib?" Tre asked me after dapping up a few guys who happily greeted him. I couldn't help but silently rolled my eyes at him, yet think about how handsome he indeed looked in his white linen shirt, matching pants, and off-yellow gators. Might I add, his smooth chocolate complexion and perfectly layered waves in his head just made him look even sexier.

"It's okay." I said, trying to act as if I was used to seeing fancy things like that all the time.

"Cool, make yourself comfortable," he replied. "You want a glass of wine or something?"

"Oh so now it's cool for me to drink?" I said sarcastically, reminding him that he never particularly cared for that. It had nothing to do with me being only eighteen. He just felt like it was unladylike. Of course he didn't complain when I would get pissy drunk and fuck him until he cried like a little female.

"A glass of wine should be okay," he said. "Besides, you gon' need to be a lil' tipsy after we leave here tonight."

Tre secretively brushed his manhood up against my backside and gripped one of my ass cheeks firmly. I played along as if it didn't bother me, but I was still upset about the conversation we had in the car and had no plans of giving up anything that night or any night to come.

"Whatever," I replied.

Tre walked off and headed toward the section of the house where the bar was. I immediately grabbed me a spot in a corner and began to scope out my scenery. He was right about the party being like nothing I was used to. Along with the ginger fragrance, you could almost smell the scent of success and money throughout the place. All the men were straight up ballers and the women were beautiful high-class model looking chicks that you could never find in the heart of the city. Even the ones who weren't that cute displayed some of type attribute- whether it had been the jewelry they sported or the expensive dress attire they wore- that let me know they had something major going for themselves. I only hoped to see a celebrity or maybe even the man of the house soon, and even though I didn't know exactly who he was, I was sure his presence would have told it all.

"Here you go," Tre returned to me fairly quickly. “It's an apple martini. You may want to stay here or find another low spot to lay while you sip that. Two years ago the Feds raided this shit and even though they didn't find what they were really looking for, they did lock a couple people up for underage drinking. I'm about to go and chop it up with the fellas for a second. There's a nice balcony if you want to check it out. You can join me after you're done with that."

As Tre suggested, I decided to go over to the patio and check out the balcony. It seemed to be the only place I could be alone without looking like a lame.

"Damn, my baby was right. This is pretty dope," I whispered to myself as I looked from the balcony that gracefully welcomed my presence and blessed me with a gorgeous view of the S-shaped pool in the backyard. Whoever put it all together had a tropical theme in mind because the yard was laced with artificial palm trees and island decors that you knew didn't come from the dollar store. There was also a DJ and bar stand that let me know some dope ass

Summer parties were thrown there. What really caught my attention though, was the lighting. Symmetrically placed around the pool, were different color poles with neon strobe lights that rested on top of them. Each of them scanned the yard in their own unique color creating a beautiful rainbow effect.

It was as perfect as I imagined it would be growing up and I couldn't believe I was getting a chance to experience it. The only thing that was missing was Shannon. Going to functions at this house was what we both dreamed about ever since we had known each other. We'd always talked about what we would wear, how we would rock our hair, and most importantly, who would end up hooking up with Hi-C.

Reminiscing back on those days made me start to miss my best friend. We hadn't spoken since that night she slammed the door in my face, which I felt was the ultimate betrayal. Right or wrong, I would have never left her hanging the way she did me and even though I still had mad love in my heart for her, I wasn’t quite ready to forgive.

"It's called an all-white party for a reason," a deep male voice said to me as he made his way onto the balcony and kidnapped me from my thoughts. "You’re wearing red. Devils are rebellious though."

I glared over at this mysterious guy, rolled my eyes, then focused them down on the pink light as it moved slowly across the yard.

"So you're one of those types," he continued.

I immediately got offended. "And what type is that?"

The guy walked closer to me and I slowly eased back. As I got a better view of him I realized that he wasn't a fearful looking guy, but I still didn't trust him. In fact, I didn't trust any mixed bred dude I saw, and this one with this curly hair, dingy shoes, and poorly coordinated dress attire was surely up to something.

"The type that's too good to have a simple conversation with an old square like me," he replied.

"Oh no," I corrected him. "I have never been that stuck-up type. They don't call me Kool Keisha for nothing."

"Kool Keisha huh," he chuckled to himself. "Well *Kool Keisha*, what do you think about this view? Seems like your loving it."

I rubbed my freshly-painted French manicured nails against the woodgrain board that kept me from falling over and answered him honestly. "I think the guy who lives here makes more money than he should."

The guy snickered. "Yeah, it did cost me a pretty penny for all this."

Hearing those words, my eyes got huge because I realized who I was speaking with. I tried my best to keep a calm composure and only hoped he didn't notice the sweat the quickly started to form across my forehead.

"Herbert Isaac Cooper," he stuck out his arm to formally greet me, "but everyone calls me Hi-C."

"Lakeisha Black," I accepted the handshake then cracked a joke hoping to lessen my sudden rush of anxiety. "But everyone calls me Kool Keisha."

"Never would have guessed it," he cracked back.

We both stood silently looking into each other's eyes for a second. I could tell he was captivated by my beauty and I was surely by his reputation.

"I have never seen you around here before," he said. "What brings you?"

“I'm your cousin Tre’s girl," I told him.

"Ahhhh," he said as if a light bulb went off in his head.

Remembering Tre, I looked into the house and focused my eyes on where he told me he would be. When I spotted him, blood began to boil in my veins as I realized that the chick- the same one who was whispering to her friends when I first walked in- was sitting very close up on him as he played a hand of spades. I wasn't about to have him embarrass me in that way so I immediately knew I had to end my little chit chat with Hi-C.

"Oh hell no," I began to reach for my glittery-gold clutch bag to make my exit. "It was nice meeting you but I have to go now."

Confused by my sudden change of attitude, Hi-C looked in the same direction I was looking and quickly caught on to why I was trying to run off so fast. He then grabbed one of my arms in attempt to stop me.

"Hey, don't sweat that," he calmly said. "She's not worth it, I promise. How bout I take you on a tour of the backyard instead?"

I looked back at Tre, then to Hi-C, who waited with a desperate look in his eyes to see what direction I would go. Fighting off yet another girl over Tre was getting entirely too old and it was the last thing I wanted to spend my night doing. I chose to take the tour instead.

"Okay. But make it quick."

Hi-C cracked a smile that silently said good choice. Then he walked over and hit a button that I saw on the balcony earlier but couldn't figure out what it was used for.

"You might want to hold on to the rail," he informed me before both of our bodies were shaken up as a set of stairs, operated by some sort of custom made motor, slowly rolled out from under us and allowed a pathway to walk down to the backyard. It was a pretty cool thing to witness.

Once the stairs had planted itself on the ground, Hi-C took three steps down first then turned around and reached for my hand. I admit, I felt like Cinderella in that moment but I immediately rid my thoughts of having any connections to this guy. Besides, he didn't seem like the type that fell for just beauty and I was sure that the only reason he was taking me away from the house was to keep his cousin from getting busted. I looked back at Tre one last time, who with the help of this chick wearing the skanky white dress and bright colored panties, seemed to be unbothered by my absence. Then I preceded to make my way down the stairs.

What I thought would be a boring five-minute run through with Hi-C, ended up turning into a half hour of amusement. Every gadget he showed me contained something more within it that kept me interested. For example, the lounge chairs with the massage features, the Karaoke machine that ironically had all my favorite songs up next on the deck, and the turntables that he let me test my skills on as he just laughed at my poor efforts to impress him. I had a blast exploring Hi-C's yard with him and quickly realized that he was a pretty cool guy. Much different than what I expected him to be. That hardcore, gangsta persona that stereotyped most big-time dealers obviously wasn't true in his case.

"I really think it's time for me to go back inside," I said after getting one more massage from the chair. "Tre's probably gonna be looking for me soon."

Hi-C grabbed my arm and helped me up.

"Okay," he said. “There’s just one last thing I want to show you."

Hi-C then led me to a shed in the far back of the yard. It looked a hot mess, tore up on the outside with a horrible paint job.

He can't be so full of himself that he wants to show me the place where he keeps his junk, I said to myself. It wasn't until he opened the door that I received a big surprise.

"Wow!" I uttered, unable to hold in my astonishment. I stepped inside the shed and was welcomed by the clean beige carpet along with the beautiful bedroom set that rested on it. A queen-sized bed with a lovely furry burgundy comfort set sat in the middle of the room and a huge flat-screen TV was mounted up on a wall across from it. Hi-C also took me to the back area of the shed where a nicely decorated bathroom and mini kitchen was. I had never seen anything like it and I was surely impressed.

"Damn. It's like a mini apartment in here," I lusted over the place. "Is this like your man cave or something?"

"Naw, not really," he replied. "Something like a guest room. "

"A guest room?" I questioned, then sat down on the edge of the bed and began to attempt to flick through the cable TV stations. "I've been in regular houses that don't look this good."

"Like I said before," he snickered modestly then took a seat down on the bed beside me and began to show me how to properly use the remote, "it's just a little something for the guests. You like it or do you still think I make way too much money?"

"I still think you make too much money," I laughed but quickly got serious. "But I also think it's pretty thoughtful of you to treat your guest this way. Says a lot about you."

Another quiet moment came upon the two of us and I could only hope that it quickly blew over. Unfortunately, the television commercial that featured Anita Baker's *Sweet Love* played in the background and didn't help the situation. Hi-C stared into my eyes and I bashfully held my head down, trying not to get trapped into his.

Remembering I had a man over in another part of the house, I put the remote down and began to head for the door. "It's really time for me to go back."

"No," he said as he rushed behind me, placed his hand over the door, and turned me around. "Not before you tell me what exactly does it say about me?"

Please don't do this, I thought in my head, while I forced myself not to look directly at him. Hi-C was definitely a charmer and he made sure he kept his eyes locked seductively into mine. They were a strange mixture of hazel and blue that went well with his milky skin complexion. He also had curly brown hair, a neatly trimmed beard, and a goat tee that gave him a pretty-boy look. But it was the small red freckles and obvious signs of a stressful life which showed on his face that added a little streetness to him. Not to mention, he was cut like a body builder.

With one arm still firmly pressed against the door, Hi-C used his free hand to pin my fragile body up against it. We began to stare silently into each other's eyes, causing me to fall for him. Still, I did not consider crossing any lines.

"Really I have to...," I managed to weakly say before I felt his fingers firmly grip around my jawbone and his mouth plant one big wet kiss on my lips. As much as I wanted to draw back, I didn't.

Hi-C and I continued to lock lips until he slowly began to kiss and lick his way down my neck then onto the rest of my body. The dress I had on required me to wear no bra, so it was easy for him to slide it over and kiss each one of my breasts fairly. I softly moaned at the very feeling I received from it, while at the same time tried to mentally fight with my conscious about the bad I was doing.

"Please stop," I moaned. "This is wrong on so many levels."

"Does it feel wrong?" he continued to lead his tongue down my belly button then kissed my black-laced panties. As I tried to grab his head and push him away, he dug his face between my legs even more aggressively. Then he took both my hands and pinned them against the wall with his strong arms.

"Noooo," I moaned as I felt his warm tongue trickle across my goodies, causing me to moist instantly. "It....feels....good."

"Well then shut up and enjoy it," he demanded.

Using only his teeth, Hi-C quickly rolled my panties down my legs. He wasted no time diving into my insides tongue first and licking me like he was competing for something. I scratched the walls passionately and firmly gripped the doorknob to keep myself from falling over in ecstasy.

"Please stop," I continued to resist, even though by now we both knew I didn't want him too.

It was in that moment that I began to think about Tre, but then I also thought about all the women he slepted while we were together. I thought about my morals, my dignity, and my reputation, but none of those things seemed to outweigh the fact that I was getting my pussy ate by the hottest nigga in the city. It was a lifetime opportunity that obviously I couldn't pass up.

“Stop what?” he moaned, then immediately pinned my arms down harder and began to do a drumroll with his tongue on my clique until I let out the ultimate orgasm.

It was a great pleasure to watch my juices pour out onto his face. He smothered himself in it then rose up and kissed me in my mouth once more. Quickly coming to my senses, I immediately pulled my panties up and rushed out the door, leaving him in the dust.

With all sorts of things going on in my mind, I raced back up the stairs only to find Tre pissy drunk with the same chick from earlier now sitting on his lap. Strangely, even though I knew I had just face fucked his first cousin, I was the one who felt disrespected.

“I'm ready to go now." I yelled out to Tre. “Take me home."

Tre tapped the girl on her thigh and signaled for her to rise up off him. She got up slowly and rolled her eyes as she passed me to go back by her girls. I happily returned the gesture.

"What do you mean? We just got here,” he said. "And I know you not tripping about that hoe."

“I’m not tripping over anything or anybody. I'm just ready to go.”

Tre looked at his boys, swallowed a bit more of his Heineken, then laughed to himself. I just knew he was about to do some show-off type shit.

“Since you wanna leave so bad, bitch call a taxi."

He then rose up slowly, pulled out a knot of money, and one by one, threw about five twenty-dollar bills in my face. By now everyone was looking in our direction and I was surely embarrassed.

“You got me fucked up!” I yelled in my own defense, then took his beer bottle and dumped it all over him. Kevin leaped towards me as if he was about to jump on me, but luckily I was saved when somebody stepped in between us.

“Now Tre, you know better than to behave like this in my house,” Hi-C said as he grabbed his cousin’s fist and placed it back on his side. They were so close that I could only wonder if Tre could smell the familiar scent of my privacy on his cousin’s breath.

“Sorry big cuz, but you know how these bitches can get sometimes. Especially hoes that ain't used to nothing.”

“And what did I tell you about disrespecting women?” Hi-C shook his head. “You know Aunt Shirley didn't raise you like that. We’ve been over this a million times. Remember, we understand that they're different types of them in this world, but they all deserve respect.”

Tre sucked his teeth at Hi-C, but obeyed him by sitting back down. By spending so much time with Tre, I learned that his cousin was the only person who could have tamed him. He respected Hi-C a great deal because without the help of him, Tre would just be another black boy from the hood, cute or not.

"Are you okay, Keisha?” Hi-C turned to me. Thankfully people began to look away once they realized there would be no more action.

“Oh I take it you two have already met,” Tre interrupted before I could even get a word out.

"Yeah, I chopped it up with her on the balcony with her just a few minutes ago.”

Tre took a napkin from one of his boys and began to clean himself up with it. “Well she’s actually pretty okay when she isn't trippin’ over stupid shit. What you think about her?”

Hi-C gave me a slick side-eye and while Tre rolled the napkin over his eyes, he licked his lips slowly in my direction. "I think she's pretty *sweet*."

In fear that Tre might catch on to Hi-C’s obvious boasting about our little sexual encounter, I pretended to still be mad.

“I’ll see you at home! And don't bother tapping my shoulder because I ain't rolling over for yo’ ass tonight!"

I yelled as I strutted hard but sexy out the door, then sat alone on the front porch and waited for my taxi to arrive.

CHAPTER SIX: Charlytte's Web

Months had passed since I attended The Ball, and although I was still living with Tre nothing was the same. I knew he was a bit of a show off, but after the way he treated me in front of all those people I knew it was time for me to ditch his ass. Unfortunately, I still didn't have a job, but every day I got up looking and I also began to boost more heavily. It didn't help that I couldn't get the feeling of Hi-C's tongue being between my legs out of my head either. Thoughts of him ruled my mind almost every moment I was awake, and when I was sleeping, there he was in my dreams. I hadn't seen or talked to him since that night, so I could only wonder if he thought about me even half as much as I thought about him. I also knew it would be hard for me to see him again because The Ball wouldn't happen for another year, and judging by the direction Tre and I were headed in, I was almost certain I probably wouldn't be at the next one.

The only thing I could do was just try to keep my ear to the streets for any events that he could have possibly been attending and try to make it my business to be there. One day in particular, I got a call from one of the girls I met through boosting. She was a client of mine and we would occasionally hang out together. She invited me to go with her to a party that was being thrown by some pretty paid Longshoremen and beings that Hi-C had some dealing with them, I figure I would test my luck and see if he'd come out.

I got up with Charmaine around eight o'clock that night. The party didn't start until eleven but I needed a good reason to leave the house. Tre was home ignoring me as usual and intentionally doing the most to piss me off. He was already mad that I wasn't giving him any sex so he'd walked around the house and have phone conversations with his side chicks right in my face. I would have happily checked him about it, but because I didn't have a pot to piss in, nor a window to throw it out, I felt it was kind of pointless.

I left the house without even telling Tre's petty ass goodbye then Charmaine and I hit the mall. We later got dressed at her house and went to Club Odyssey where we partied until sunrise.

"Alright girl, see ya soon." I thanked her for the good time and forced my tired body out of her vehicle. It was after six a.m. "Always a movie when we link up."

"I know that's right," she cosigned. "We showed our asses tonight. Definitely have to do this again."

"How ‘bout next week," I suggested, then pointed my finger in the direction of Tre’s house. "Anything to get away from that dumb ass nigga in there."

Charmaine giggled at my remark. She knew a little about my distant relationship with Tre, but not too much. I didn't believe in putting bitches in too much of my business, especially when it came down to my man. Tre was an asshole but he was still one of the sexiest, richest young niggas around town and I didn't trust a hoe with him as far as I could see her. Besides, the only person I shared my secrets with was Shannon and we still weren't talking.

"It's whateva, just hit me up." Charmaine replied.

"Okay cool," I said, then waved my keys at her. "You can go head. I can get in."

Charmaine threw the deuces then flew her Chevy Camaro down the street. I shook my head at her reckless driving then thought about how Shannon would have never left until she actually saw me go inside the house. It didn't matter if I gave her the okay or not.

I quickly rid my thoughts of Shannon and made my way up to the porch. Strangely, I noticed that there were several black trash bags scattered around the yard. At first I didn't think too much of it because Tre had been stressing all week that he needed to get the yard situated. It wasn't until I got a little closer and opened one of them that I realized it wasn't leaves- but my clothes- stuffed inside of them.

"Man, what the fuck is going on?!" I asked myself, then raced up the porch steps and began to bang on the door.

"Open this fucking door right now, you motherfucker!" I yelled.

It wasn't long before Tre boldly appeared in the screen and stood before me in nothing but his boxers.

"Why are you knockin' on my door like you're crazy?" he asked. "I told you about bringing that ghetto shit around here. I do have neighbors."

"I don't give a fuck about you or your neighbors right now. What I'm concerned about is this." I pointed down to the bags of clothes.

"What about it?" Tre asked, nonchalantly.

"Why is my shit out here and not in there?"

"Because....," he paused and then continued as if it was no big deal, "you don't live here anymore."

“Really Tre! So you're just gonna put my shit out without a warning. I cannot believe this.”

“Without a warning? Are you still drunk from whatever the hell you were sipping on last night?" he asked. "I have been telling you for the longest that you had to go. It's not my fault you thought it was a game."

“I never thought it was a game, nigga. I know you saw me getting up every morning looking for jobs and shit. They just don't fall out of the sky you know."

“Well that's not my problem anymore. I gave you a deadline and it's here. Try going back to Shannon's, your mom’s, or wherever the hell you were last night. If he can keep you til’ six in the morning then I'm sure he’ll be willing to let you live with 'em.

"Oooooh…. that’s what this is about. You think I was out with anotha nigga?” I stuck my phone out to him. “I was with Charmaine. You can check for yourself."

"I'm not doing all that,” he shoved it back to my chest. “Hell, I listen to you moan out my cousin's name damn near every night in yo’ fuckin' sleep. What makes you think I give a fuck about another random ass nigga?"

My face almost dropped to the ground when Tre said those words to me about Hi-C. Now it all made sense why he was disrespecting me around the house the way he was. What was even more surprising was seeing the same chick from the party walk up behind him wearing my red satin robe that he had brought me on Valentine's Day. She grabbed him by his waist and purposely let the gown open up to show me that she was completely naked underneath.

"Baby, I told you not to even open the door for this little girl."

"Excuse me?" I said to her. "Tre, you better tell your little groupie to keep her fucking mouth closed before it really be some ghetto shit going on around here."

"I don't have to tell her a damn thing," he said as he kissed her near her right temple. She blushed at the gesture. "Now get the fuck off my property."

Knowing firsthand the lengths Tre would go to show off in front of people, especially females, I decided not to argue anymore. Besides, I couldn't give the tramp another second to enjoy the advantage that she seemed to have over me. Not to mention, I remember being that girl who sat on Tre's side as he dissed someone for me, and I knew it wouldn't be long before he did the same to her. Realizing there was no way I could win this battle, I figured it was best that I just left it where it was.

"You got it Tre, I'm gone." I threw up my hands and surrendered, but not before I turned to the chick. "Eat it up now bitch because it won't be long before you're standing in my spot."

"Never," she boasted before they both went in the house and slammed the door.

There was a total of six trash bags I had to drag down to the curb that sat in front of Tre's place. I called a cab then waited patiently for it, while trying to tell myself that me sitting out there like that wasn't as embarrassing as it looked. Most of the bags were filled with stolen clothes. I had planned on selling them to make some extra cash.

While waiting on the curb, I decided to roll up a joint, a habit I had picked up on while dating Tre. Then I sat there just trying to put my life in perspective. I began thinking about the things I seemed to have forgotten when I was too tied up with him- like my family, my best friend, and most importantly, Charlytte.

"I'm gonna get it together soon," I looked towards the morning sky and made yet another promise to my deceased Aunt Jonell. I always believed she was up there watching over me. The last time I saw her alive was the time we named her unborn baby and I promised I would be a good cousin to her. Jonell ran away that same night and I was told just a few days later that she died in an alley giving birth. A few months after that, my ten-year-old eyes witnessed a ton of police arrest my dad, my mom began drinking heavily, and we gained a new family member- her daughter Charlytte.

When this happened, everything in my life seemed to change. It was I who held the responsibility of raising Charlytte because Mama for some reason didn't seem to care to. But even though I loved her like I had pushed her out of my own body, it was a responsibility that could sometimes be too much on a young girl like me. Some days the only thing that got me threw dealing with it all was the fact that I knew there was a piece of my aunt inside of her. Besides, sometimes feeling like I was stuck being the middle child of two brothers- Korey and Keyshawn- I often longed to have a sister around.

My siblings and I all grew up fast because everyone pretty much had to fend for themselves in our house. I was ironing at six, cooking dinner at eight, and reading bedtime stories by nine. My naturally sharp mind and swift ability to pick up on things made it easy for me, no matter what age I was, to handle any challenges life threw in my direction. Raising Charlytte was the only major ordeal though, and even that wasn't so difficult. Honestly, it wasn't until I got older and started getting a lil' taste of boys that I began to feel like I wanted to break free from her. To make things worse, when I would try talking to my mama about it, she would tell me that part of living in her house was taking care of Charlytte. Of course, like any other teenager, I feared not having a roof over my head so I pretty much just shut up and complied.

There was this one night though, that Mama did agree to help me out with Charlytte. It was the night of my High School's Valentine's Day dance. We agreed that she'd at least watch her for a few hours while I attended it. The negotiation was a hard one, but after I put up a huge fit about how much being able to go would mean to me, eventually she came around.

It was a monumental day to see Mama volunteer to put her children's happiness before her own bullshit. Although it would have been even more meaningful if I had actually given a damn about going to the dance. Truth was, Shannon and I were planning on ditching it to meet up with two fine ass guys we had recently met at the corner store- Tre and Kevin. So when the day came and Mama never made it home like she promised, I found myself sneaking them in her house and doing things I knew she would not have approved of. Next thing I know, Mama came home earlier than I expected, almost beat me half to death, and a year later I was sitting on the same nigga's curb who was the main reason I was in all that mess. It was definitely time I realized Tre may not have exactly been the best guy for me.

Using the effects of the blunt to help me take my mind off of my past, I sat there puffing and began to wonder what my next move would be. I had a few people I knew would have let me stay with them- even Charmaine- but giving bitches the opportunity to see me at my worst wasn't an option for me. I had too much pride for that. I did have a stash of money in Tre's house too, but I wasn't going to mention it in front of that bitch. All I had left on me was about sixty dollars that thankfully I had saved from the club. Sixty dollars I knew would turn into nothing after the taxi guy coming down the street got through with me.

There was no need for me to wave him down because he obviously knew by the pitied look on my face and the items that surrounded me, I was the person he was picking up. One by one I took the bags and shoved them into his back seat, then with limited space left available to me, squeezed myself in as well. I could only wonder if Tre was watching from the window. I hoped that he and Ashton Kutcher would have run out of the house and say I was being punked, but after we began to ride off of his street, I knew that was nothing more than wishful thinking.

"Where you headed, young lady?" the taxi guy asked.

I didn't know for sure, but I knew there was one place I needed to go before I made a final decision. I directed him to my old neighborhood and then gave him a ten-dollar bill just so he would wait for me.

"Be right back," I said to him, after we reached our destination.

Mama's house hadn't changed a bit since the last time I saw it, but because she wasn't much of a fixer-upper, I hadn't expected it to. I took a deep breath as I walked up the three layers of concrete steps that led me to the same yard where I was beaten mercilessly. It was hard for me to try not to remember the pain I felt on that night, but it seemed much harder preparing myself for what I would say to little Charlytte when I finally laid my eyes on her.

I slowly stepped onto the porch and tried not to let the evil spirit that always seemed to linger around our house discourage me from knocking. I knew Mama wouldn't be home because every Wednesday and Saturday she got up early and cleaned a wealthy doctor's house. While I waited for an answer, I looked around the screened-in porch to see everything in its exact same place as when I left. Those two wooden chairs I used to watch Mama and her best friend, Evelyn, sit and drink on was still standing on its weak legs holding on for dear life. The dull flowers that never got watered, but also never seemed to die, was still trying its best to give a little life to the place. And that big nail that could have easily poked one of her children's eyes out still stuck out from the screen door.

I hesitated at first, then knocked. No one answered for a minute, but then I saw one layer of the blinds slide up just about where Charlytte's height would now be. Mama had programmed in us to never ever answer the door when she wasn't home, so I knew I would have to make myself known in order to get her to open up .

"It's me," I said to the person on the other side. "It's Keisha."

Before I could repeat myself the door swung open and I had to jump back just so that the nail in the screen wouldn't split my belly wide open. Charlytte charged full speed towards me, gave me the biggest hug ever, and held onto my waistline like her life depended on it. I embraced her back and tried to stop the tears from falling from my eyes.

"Aaaw, look at you girl," I said as I practically had to pry her grip away from me.

I pushed her a step back so that I could get a full view of her. Charlytte wasn't one of those type of little girls you'd see and immediately say "aaaw how cute", not because she wasn't pretty, but because the way Mama took care of her made her look like a pitiful child. Not to mention, the insecure and down spirit that she picked up at a very young age made it hard for me to believe that she'd grow up and be as loveable as I was. Still, there was something about her that always told me she would turn out to be someone worth knowing.

"I missed you so much," she said as she stood before me in a dingy oversized white t-shirt that was falling off of her right shoulder, some holey jogging pants, and a hairstyle I knew she must have tried to do herself.

“I missed you too,” I replied. “And look at your hair, it's grown so much."

"I did it myself," she bragged to me. "You like it?"

It took everything in me not to say ‘no’ but I managed to at least smile at it. Charlytte's hair did grow since the last time I saw her, but there was nothing pretty about it.

"What are you doing up so early, little lady?” I quickly changed the subject, after noticing that her hands were filled with soapy water.

"Auntie Jo told me to get up and wash the dishes. She gone now. Went to clean the Tillinger's."

"And where's Keyshawn?"

"Spent the night down the street," she pointed.

"With who?"

"I don't know," she shrugged.

"Does Mama know," I asked.

"I think so," she replied.

"You're not scared being here by yourself," I asked her.

“A little,” she began to look sad, "but I'm more scared when Aunt Joanne is here."

“I can definitely understand that," I told her. "Is she still very mean to you?"

Charlytte immediately busted out into tears, which gave me my answer. A part of me hoped that during the time I had been gone Mama would have possibly changed her evil ways, but who was I kidding? I grabbed Charlytte and hugged her once more.

"Don't cry baby, I'm here for you okay."

"Then why did you leave me for?” she sobbed. “Why you stop carin' about me?"

"Why would you say that Charlytte? You know I still care about you."

“That's not what Auntie Jo said,” she sobbed. "Auntie said you don't care about nobody but yaself."

"Listen to me, don’t pay attention to anything that woman says. Remember what I told you about actions speaking louder than words. Who was the one who fed you, looked after you, and took the best care of you? Was it me or Mama?"

Charlytte pointed one of her small fingers in my direction.

"That's right. So it’s only *my* word that you need to trust."

I picked Charlytte up and carried her to one of the rocking chairs where I took a seat and placed her on my lap. I could feel the legs on it begin to shiver beneath us, but I didn't panic though. If my mama could sit her fat ass on it, I knew Charlytte and I would be fine.

"I never stopped caring about you, babygirl,” I said as I began to wipe her eyes. “I’ve just been working and trying to make it out here on my own. Sometimes it gets hard and I barely have time to think about what’s going on in the world around me. I'm so sorry."

Charlytte put her hands over my lips, signaling for me to say no more. "I'm sorry too and I know why you left me?"

"Huh?...What do you mean?" I questioned her. "Why do you think I left you?

"Because I didn't help you when Aunt Joanne was hurting you with the bat and I didn't come save you when that guy who was making you cry in the room took you away."

"What guy was hurting me?...In where?" I asked Charlytte before a light bulb went off in my head and I figured out what exactly she was talking about. The night we snuck the guys into the house I was so upset with Mama for not coming, that I took my anger out on poor Charlytte and made her sit at the window to be a look-out for us. Shannon and I had some pretty rough sex with the guys that I'm sure she could hear taking place. The way Tre had me screaming when he put his enormous manhood inside of me for the first time, Charlytte probably couldn't help but think I was being abused in there. I also remember saying some pretty mean things to her, even told her that I wished she was the one that died instead of Auntie Jonell. I didn't mean any of it but how could I explain that to her now? She was only seven at the time.

"Aaaw Charlytte," I sympathized with her, "no baby girl, it's not your fault. There was nothing you could do to help save me from Mama. You were too young to get involved in that… And Tre didn't harm me. We were just in the room playing a fun game that only grown-ups play. He's actually helped me a lot since I left here."

"Well I still don't like 'em," she rolled her eyes and smacked her teeth. She had gotten that sassiness from me. Sometimes I thought it was cute to let her get on the phone and say cuss words to my guy friends.

"Why not?" I asked. "You don't even know him."

"Because he laughed at my scar."

I thought back again. We were drinking that night but I do remember Tre making a funny remark about the scar Charlytte had. It came from an operation she had to undergo the day her mama died. It went diagonal across her face, starting a little under her right eye and ending up on her left cheekbone. I never knew the full story of what happened, but the way Mama's mood would go from bad to worse whenever anybody would mention even the slightest thing about that situation, made me feel that something terrible happened to my Aunt Jonell, and her baby, the night she died.

"Don't worry about that. Guys can be mean sometimes. It's just their way of showing you that they like you," I tried to convince myself. "That's just the way they are. Besides, who cares about what anybody says about your scar anyway. Didn't I always tell you're beautiful even with it."

Charlytte nodded.

"Good," I said, then quickly stood her up after I heard the horn of the taxi cab signaling for me to bust a move.

"I have to go now but I promise I'm gonna come back for you. I'm serious Charlytte, as soon as I get my own apartment you're gonna come live with me. Now it's not gonna be today or tomorrow, but sooner than you think."

A joyous look began to appear across her face. I had given her hope and she seemed to be satisfied simply with that. I just prayed that she understood it wasn't going to be anytime soon. Charlytte was the type to wait by the front door every day. Can't say that I blame her though.

"Now I need you to go back in the house and pretend like you never saw me. I don't want Mama to beat your butt for opening up the door."

I kissed Charlytte on her forehead, gave her one last hug, then painfully watched her drag her tiny body back into her world of misery. Before closing the door, she did something she had never done before that reminded me so much of when I was a little girl looking to her mother for comfort.

"Pinky promise?" she stuck out her index finger to mine. Instead of correcting her, I just smiled and wrapped my same finger around hers.

"Cross my heart." I replied.

Charlytte closed the door and I made my way back to the cab. Before pulling off, I stared out the window and looked towards the house one last time. I couldn't get the image of Charlytte's face- the pain it displayed as we said our goodbyes- out of my head. For her to be only nine, the way she held in her tears and showed her strength, just did something to my spirit. I didn't care about anything- not Tre, not Shannon, not even boosting- in that moment. My main concern was coming up with a master plan that was gonna get my babygirl out of that hellhole she was living in. I was gonna do it and I was gonna do it by any means necessary.

The cab driver turned around and banged on the metal railing that separated us, interrupting me from my thoughts. I didn't know how long he was trying to get my attention but I didn't care.

"Where you headed now, Miss?" the big belly sixties-afro-hair-wearing man asked.

"South," I replied.

"How far deep?"

I closed my eyes and took not only a big breath, but a big chance.

"Connor's Bluff."

CHAPTER SEVEN: The Stylist

A nervous feeling came over my body as I walked up to the familiar two-story white house with the black shutters. With me, were two trash bags filled with stolen clothes that I had to drag about ten blocks to get to Hi-C's spot. I didn't have car access through the security gate, so my only option was to have the cab driver let me out at the fence. I was still wearing my light blue denims and white blouse from the club and I'm sure the sweat that poured from my body gave off an aroma of liquor, weed, and perfume combined. I took a deep breath before pressing on the huge, lion-faced doorbell then waited anxiously for an answer. Not long after, I heard the knob turn and a woman with a foreign accent speak.

"Hello, how ma y I help you?" she fully opened the door, allowing me to get a better look at her.

Wow! I thought to myself after laying my eyes on one of the most gorgeous women that I had ever saw in my life. Her skin held a smooth, dark chocolate tone and did not carry one single blemish. Her eyes were slightly chinked and her full-sized lips were decorated with red gloss. What was most beautiful about her though, was her hair. It was long, silky, and jet black. Some of it effortlessly fell across her shoulders, while the rest hang long down her back. Judging by her curly roots, you could tell that it was all natural too.

"I'm…I'm so sorry to bother you," I stuttered. "But I was in the neighborhood and I wanted to know if you, or anyone inside, was interested in buying some clothes from me."

The woman looked down at the bags I held by my side then back to me. Because of the confused look she displayed on her face, I could tell she wasn't used to receiving visitors under these circumstances.

"So let me get this straight...," she opened the door a little wider and leaned on it for support. I couldn't help but notice how nice her body was also. "You come to a neighborhood where house payments are *at least* two G's or better asking residents to buy some stolen clothes."

It didn't make sense to me either, but I was desperate. All I could do was nod my head at her and shrug innocently.

"Don't take this the wrong way," she continued, "but I believe I speak for myself and this entire community when I say I think that you'd get better business in the hood of which you come from."

My reflexes almost caused me to put a nasty cursing on the woman who stood before me, but then I remembered my whole reason for coming to Hi-C's home and decided against it. I figured I would just come up with another way to speak with him or maybe catch him when she wasn't there. Besides, judging by the business attire she had on, I knew she was a busy woman who was always on the go.

"You're right," it took everything in me to humbly say. "Sorry to bother you. I'll be leaving now."

Just as I was about to turn around, I hear a male voice holler out from the inside of the house.

"Aye Ice, who's that at the door?"

I knew it was Hi-C. That baritone was one I could never forget.

"Some girl trying to sell some shit," she leaned inside and hollered back. "But I believe she's the Feds."

“The Feds?” he questioned. Even my eyebrows went up.

"That's what I think. You wanna come check her out or you want me to send her on her way."

"Naw, let me see what slick bullshit they got going on now. "

Hi-C came to the door, swung it open, and showed no emotion when he saw my face. Unlike me, I quickly turned away because I didn't want Miss Foxy Brown to see the glow that suddenly appeared in my eyes.

"She ain't the Feds," he said to her then began to walk back where he came from. "Let her in."

The woman immediately stretched out her arm to me, and gave me a look that clearly said ‘bitch you better not even think about coming up in here.’ Then she stopped Hi-C as he walked off, pulled the door in slightly, and began to speak to him in another language. I didn't know what she was saying but I could tell by the firm hand gestures, neck rolling, and constant dirty looks she was giving me that it wasn't anything nice.

Without even getting upset or rowdy like she was, Hi-C calmly said about two words in this same strange language and the aggression she displayed quickly went away. Then he planted one passionate kiss on her lips, smacked her on the ass, and watched her walk away to gather her belongings. As she stepped outside to leave, she intentionally bumped into me and said "don't touch anything." She was staring hard at Hi-C when she said it and that let me know she wasn't talking about nothing laying around the house. It didn't bother me though. I was just happy to have him to myself for a minute. Besides, I had already had her man and didn't come there for any other reason than to see if he could help me out with a place to stay.

Hi-C stood in the doorway wearing a long black robe and signaled for me to come inside. I dragged my bags into the house and without saying a word, I followed him down a hallway that seemed longer than the ten blocks I just walked. We literally passed about five bedrooms, a small gym, and a mini kitchen before making a stop to the last room at the end of the hall. I waited quietly as Hi-C tapped a code into a security device that eventually let us both inside.

"Step into my office," he said as he held up both his arms and welcomed me.

I slowly stepped into the room where one beautiful, clearly custom-made cherry wood desk sat. On one side of the desk was a black, leather office chair designed for a king and across from it was a comfortable seat I assumed was for his guests. Sitting on top of the desk, was a gold name plate that read Herbert Cooper. Directly on the side of that was a gold-plated pen holder with a matching pen resting inside of it. Hi-C also had a built in compartment where he kept rolling papers, about twenty packs of Dutch Master Palmas, and cream flavored black-n-milds.

"Take a seat," he told me.

I obeyed, then continued to look around the room that was decorated with photos going all the way around the wall. The way they were strategically placed- from baby pictures to adult pictures- they clearly told the story of his life and his road to success. He even had one where he was shaking hands with our city mayor. It baffled me why Edward Delowich would be in the same photo with a big-time drug dealer, but even I knew how crooked politics could be.

Hi-C gave me some time to gather what little information I could from the photos. Most of them seemed self-explanatory, except for the largest one, which was of what appeared to be him in his younger years and one other mixed boy who favored him. They were standing with an elderly white couple. There was also a black woman sitting so far in the background that I could barely make her out.

"So, what do you think about my wife?" Hi-C finally spoke, interrupting me from my scrutiny.

“Your wife?" I asked, while I tried desperately to think of something nice to say about her. "Well, she's pretty."

"One of the main reasons why I married her," he answered.

“But wait…you never told me you were married.”

“You never asked. By the way, how's Tre?" he quickly reminded me that I was in no position to judge. “He seemed pretty messed up when he left the party."

"He's okay, I guess." I replied.

“That cousin of mine is something else,” he said taking a seat. I watched carefully as he grabbed the beautiful gold pen and began to twirl it between each of his fingers. “Always has been.”

“Believe me I know,” I happily agreed.

“So what brings you here?” he changed the subject. “Didn’t think I would ever see you again.”

“I was just in the neighborhood,” I lied.

“So lemme get the straight, a young lady I had the *pleasure* of meeting at my party comes stumbling on my doorsteps saying she was *just in the neighborhood.* Is there a piece to this puzzle that I’m missing?"

"No, there's nothing else,” I said. “Like I said, I was just passin’ through.”

Hi-C smirked and shook his head slowly from left to right. Then he locked his fingers together with the pen still in his grip, and placed his hands on the desk. Finally, he leaned towards me so that he could look me straight into my eyes.

"Let me explain something to you really quickly," he said in a calm tone. "I am a busy man…and the reason I am a busy man is because I am a successful man... and the reason why I became a successful man is because of the choices I made using the most important element in life, time. I know you see this big house and these nice cars and you're probably thinking that's what I live for, but you're wrong. I live for time, because that's the only thing in life that you can't get back once it's gone. I lose money. I can make it back. I lose time, that's it. What I'm simply trying to say is… please don't waste mine because I value it too much. Now I'm going to ask you one more time, what really brings you here?"

I took a moment of silence to debate on whether I should or should not keep it real with Hi-C. Then I began to think about Charlytte and how much she needed me. I closed my eyes tightly and decided to let it all out.

"Look, it's like this, ever since I left this house I cannot seem to get you out of my head. I know you probably think it's about your money and who you are, but I'm telling you it's more to it than that. I can't explain it, but it is."

I let out a huge sigh and continued. "Truth is, Tre kicked me out this morning and now I have nowhere to go. I wanted to see if you could help me- maybe let me live out in your guest room- just until I get on my feet. If I knew you had a wife I would have never come here. I apologize for any disrespect. I'll be leaving now."

I immediately grabbed my belongings and preceded to let myself out of the house. I just knew I had made a complete fool out of myself for telling him those crazy things. There was no way he could have felt any type of way about a clueless girl like me.

"Sit back down," he demanded. "I didn't dismiss you."

Oh my. I thought myself, slightly turned on by his aggression.

"How much money do you have on you now?" he asked.

"About fifty dollars," I answered.

"And about how much can you profit from a bag of clothes like that?"

"Probably about a thousand dollars per bag."

"A whole thousand...really?"

"Yeah easily," I bragged. "I get top notch shit and I have very loyal clientele."

"Okay. And how much do you usually make per week, at your best?"

"About $1500-2000."

Hi-C shook his head in disbelief. "And you only have fifty dollars to your name now?"

"I have more," I replied. "But Tre won't let me back inside and I refuse to have told him that I had money stashed there, especially with that bitch in the house."

"Hmmm," he scratched his chin. "Looks to me you have a hustler's drive but the sense of a three-year-old."

Hearing those words, I looked down at my feet ashamed of my own stupidity. I admit, I hadn't really ever had anything planned as far as managing the money I was making. I would get it and spend it, spend it and then go back to get it again. That was one thing I didn't pick up from Shameka, who was grimy as hell but did have her shit together as far as her business was concerned. Hi-C calling me out on it made me realize something I had seemed to overlook as long as I knew I could call on Tre when I needed something.

He continued. "No offense but the key to being successful is not how much money you make, but what you do with it. You have to understand that in order to make your hustle worthwhile. Tell me something, what does this shoplifting thing mean to you?"

"Huh?" I questioned him. "I don't understand?"

“I mean, I know it's a hustle for you, but does it drive you? Do you get some sort of adrenaline rush from doing it, or is it just something that earns you a quick dolla?”

"Honestly, I hate shoplifting. It makes me feel low and dirty, so that part of it definitely doesn’t drive me. What does drive me though, is fashion. Seeing all the different clothes, feeling the different types of fabrics, and just being able to put folks in them. I mean, things that people can’t normally afford they can rock because of me. I love hearing ‘girl thank you for hooking me and my kids up' or ‘sis, you got me lookin’ right with this fit’. That’s where my passion lives… in styling and making people feel good.”

Hi-C soaked in everything I said to him and began to scratch his chin as if he was thinking hard about something.

“Hmmmm....so you're good at styling huh?”

“Good?” I boasted. "I'm the best to ever do it. I can tell just by the way a chick wears her ponytail what suits her. Hell, judging by those fuzzy slippers you're wearing now I think you’d probably look great in-"

"Surprise me?" Hi-C cut me off.

“What?”

“Don't tell me what you think I would look good in, just surprise me.”

“I don’t understand.”

"The reason why I'm asking you all this is because I've been looking for somebody who could put me up on my clothing game. I’ve never had a passion for dressing. In fact, the homies crack on me all the time about how out of touch I am with it. I never really cared much about how I looked and still don’t to this day. It’s just that I'm starting to involve myself in more, shall I say, *politica*l things. These guys that I'm going to be sitting at the round table with believe how you present yourself is the most important attribute when it comes to conducting successful business. I think I need somebody like you to be able to hook me up. Do you think you can handle that?"

I blushed at Hi-C's offer and tried to hide my excitement. "I'm sure I can handle it."

"Ok cool. I have a major meeting in less than a week and I need some business attire, suit and tie preferably. I don't want you stealing anything though, too risky. I'm going to give you the cash to pay for my stuff and whatever's left you keep for your services. I'll advise you to use that extra change to help you survive on these streets because my wife would never allow you to stay here. I'm going to walk you back to your car now. It was a pleasure doing business with you Keisha."

After hearing him mention me having a car, my excitement quickly turned into shame that I clearly showed all over my face. That was another thing I knew I could have had if I managed my money correctly.

"What's the matter?" he asked. "Please don't tell me you don't even have a car."

I shook my head slowly.

"A license at least."

I shook my head again.

"You really have a lot to learn, babygirl," he sighed. "Don't worry though, you're in the right hands. Leave your stuff here and hop in with me. I have connections at the DMV and we're going to go get you a license because I most definitely need you driving."

CHAPTER EIGHT: TRAFFICK'HER'

Hi-C was in fact smart when it came to the streets, but when it came to fashion he didn't have the slightest clue what to do with himself. I took care of that problem for him though. Any event he went to I made sure he was killin' shit. He even began to make headlines in our local magazines that didn't just focus on him being a popular street figure. Now he was Hi-C the man of the city and the fashion killer.

Even better, everyone in Ordale knew that it was me who was keeping him dressed. That helped me build my own clientele as a stylist. What was first a petty shoplifting hustle had now grown into a legitimized styling business that I named Kool Keisha'z Klothing. Although it was something I did because I enjoyed it, the main reason was to explain the two-story townhouse and other expensive things I had accumulated from the way I really made my money- drug trafficking. That's right, I had gained Hi-C's trust over the months I had styled him and he eventually allowed me to become a part of the OMC, which he later opened up and told me that was part of his plan all along.

Once a week, I moved large amounts of cocaine for him from city to city and he paid me lots of money to do so. First, I stayed at a cheap motel until I got my money up then within a year I had my own spot. It was located in a neighborhood not too far from Hi-C's and almost as beautiful. The two cars I owned was also something I was proud of earning on my own. One was the latest model, dark-blue Chevy Impala that I showed off when I stepped out and the other was a twenty-year-old Toyota Camry that I used for trafficking.

Eight years had passed since I had gotten close to Hi-C and everything in my life seemed to be going perfect. The only thing that really ate at my conscious was that I never kept my promise of going back to rescue Charlytte like I told her I would. It wasn't that I couldn't do it, it was just that I was so caught up in the fabulous drug life that I couldn't seem to make her a priority. I would just go over from time to time to drop her off a few dollars and show my family that I was doing fine without them. I could tell Mama was jealous and curious about how I was getting my money, but she didn't complain as long as some of it was going towards her rent. Charlytte, on the other hand, was different. The older she got the less hesitant she was to take anything from me. She even became less excited to see me, sometimes to the point where she'd go inside her room when I walked inside the house. She was a teenager and I guess she was getting smart enough to scope out my bullshit. She didn't want money, or gifts, or clothes from me. All she wanted was for my word to be my bond. I had failed her on that, and unfortunately, I was too paid to care.

One weekend I had to make a run to Atlanta and decided to mix business with pleasure by partying there because it was my 26th birthday. When I returned back to Ordale, about five o'clock Sunday afternoon, my body was drained and I wanted to do nothing more than to go straight home. Unfortunately, a package I was carrying needed to be dropped off to Hi-C. Normally his right hand man, Cederick, would meet up with me and take it to him but he had to make an emergency run out of town and told me he wouldn't be back for a few hours. I didn't mind though, because any day I could avoid meeting up with Cederick was a good day for me.

Cederick was a true hustler too, but I just couldn't stand the dude. He was Hi-C's most trusted friend who sold dope ass well, but also got his money from turning innocent young girls into tricks. He'd build those babies up then tear them down like artificial Christmas trees. Some of them were even as young as thirteen. For that, I had no respect for him.

I had informed Hi-C of Cederick's departure and he told me to bring whatever I was carrying to his home, which I didn't visit much ever since I had gotten my own spot. When I made it there, the garage was closed and that let me know I needed to prepare myself for his wife. I didn't see her much but when I did I happily spoke to her. I just always felt the need to remind her that I was the same low-class bitch who sat desperately on her doorstep, and by the help of her man I came up and damn near surpassed her ass.

I rang the doorbell and it wasn't long before Isis opened up. She was wearing night attire and judging by her damp hair I could tell she had recently showered. She was still beautiful as hell and the way the moisture caused her hair to curl up nicely allowed me to see just how versatile it really was.

"Baby, it's for you," she said sarcastically. Then walked away without even acknowledging my presence. I didn't care. I let myself in and still spoke to her.

"Hey Icey, how are you girl?" I faked my excitement. "I'm loving those curls."

Isis smacked her lips, flopped down on the couch, and began flicking through the channel.

"Got my package?" Hi-C startled me by quietly appearing from the hallway.

"Yeah, right here." I said, as I handed him a black tote bag that I assumed was full of money. He never brought drugs into his home.

"Good," he said, then took the bag from me, sat it on the kitchen counter, and went through it. It was money indeed.

"Who did you meet up with this time, Pablo or Albino?"

"Albino's creepy ass came this time. I hate that motherfucker."

"I do too," he said. "But remember what I told you. Say nothing. Just give...receive...nod and be on your way."

"You don't have to tell me twice," I replied.

I watched Hi-C carefully as he walked out of the kitchen towards Isis and handed her the black bag. He was in his bedtime gear as well, but that's how he usually carried himself around the house.

"You mind running this?" he kissed her.

Isis pushed the bag away from her face. "Hi-C don't try that shit with me today. Really, I'm not in the mood. Why don't you get your *stylist bitch* to do it?"

Hi-C immediately jacked Isis up and pressed his body firmly against hers on the couch. I had never seen him get that angry with her, and because she was his wife, I was surprised he was allowing me to.

"What did I tell you about disrespecting women, especially up in my house?" he said to her.

Isis pushed Hi-C from off of her as if his weight meant nothing. He was a strong man but she was a strong woman. Not to mention, she had a glass of Patron that she was drinking on the rocks. That probably added to her strength and also her frustration.

"Hi-C, I'm not afraid of you…and stop this hypocrite shit you do. I'm sick of it!" She yelled. "It's okay for you to fuck her in this house, in our bed, on this couch but then you wanna make me out to be the disrespectful one. Get the fuck outta here!"

"What are you talking about Isis? Be real babe, you knew what type of man I was when you met me but I guess as long as you could live good you were satisfied."

"I was never satisfied. I just dealt with it and prayed that one day you'd change."

"I don't see how in fifteen years you'd think I'd change. That lawyer man you fuckin' got you delusional or something?...What, he didn't give you any when you were out with him all last weekend? Is that why you mad today?"

"Please stop," Isis cried. "That has nothing to do with it. And you have no proof of those accusations."

Regardless of proof or those fancy lawyer terms she was using, Isis never denied fucking this attorney guy and the way her eyes lit up when Hi-C mentioned him let me know that she really wasn't as innocent as she seemed. Besides, if I was married to a man with a disappointingly small penis like Hi-C's, I would have had a side piece too. He was the reason why lines like 'you can't judge a book by its cover' existed because he definitely fooled me when I first slept with him. Come to find out all he's good for is head and hustling, and if I knew it I'm sure Isis did too.

I pretty much run this city," he boasted. "You'd be surprised to know who's all on my payroll. I know more than you think."

"Whatever," Isis tried to change the subject. "I don't care who is on your payroll. I'm just tired okay. I'm tired of getting my car windows busted out. I'm tired of people blogging about us. I'm tired of being followed by the undercovers. And I'm really fucking tired of seeing this bitch!"

Hi-C suddenly slapped fire to Isis's right cheek, so hard that even I felt it. The way she looked stunned, I couldn't tell if she was more surprised that he smacked her or more surprised that he did it in front of me. Hi-C didn't come off as the woman-beater type, so I was kind of surprised too. Although it really didn't bother me much because I felt that she got what she deserved. I just continued to stay in my corner and eat all of it up.

"I TOLD YOU ABOUT DISRESPECTING WOMEN IN MY HOUSE! I WILL NOT TOLERATE THAT SHIT FROM YOU OR NOBODY!" he yelled.

Isis slowly wiped the cheek he hit her on and although tears started pouring down her face she managed to remain calm. "I don't know what it is about her, and I can't understand for the life of me why, but it's becoming more and more clear that there's love somewhere involved. I knew that the first time you got her pregnant and here I've been waiting on a baby for years. Look at me, I'm damn near forty and I'm realizing that I have thrown away some of the most valuable things chasing what I only *thought* were valuable things."

Isis walked up closer to Hi-C, then placed her hands gently across his beard as if she was about to kiss him. "I won't lie and say I have the strength to throw away almost ten years of marriage but I will say that you better start enjoying what you have left of it because one day you gonna wake up and I will be gone. Maybe not today- or tomorrow- but one day. That's not a promise…it's a vow."

Hi-C locked eyes with his wife and it was the first time I had seen a grown man shed a tear. I could tell he knew he had lost Isis and I hoped he didn't blame me for it. He didn't say another word. He just grabbed the bag of money and disappeared down the hall with it.

With Isis and I alone now, I immaturely tried to hold in my laugh from seeing her get her ass popped. She knew it was amusement for me, but she didn't seem to mind that I witnessed it. In fact, as she walked slowly in my direction, she continued to let her tears fall from her face. It was almost if she wanted me to see her pain, like she was secretly trying to tell me something.

I immediately tried to straighten my face when I saw her getting closer. I couldn't help but notice that at her weakest she still carried the strength of a lion. She was wise, she was independent, she was beautiful, and even though she appeared a bit broken she was tough. I wasn't half the woman Isis was and secretly I knew it.

“And you,” she stopped once she got up on me, “from now on the best way to acknowledge me is to *not* acknowledge me. I see you 'round here with your phony smiles and fake compliments, and I will no longer stand for it. You would have x’ed me out at any given time if the opportunity was present and I'm cool with that because I understand the fools we turn into for the men we love.”

Isis moved in closer to me and we were now face to face. “Babygirl wake up, Hi-C don't love nothing but money, power, and respect. That’s all he lives for and as long as you’re helping him gain those three things, he’s on your side. But just watch, the minute you ever try to want out or find your own way, he'll cross you out like a game of tic -tac-toe.”

"Think about it," she touched my belly as I held my head down in shame. "A man that loves you doesn't force you to get abortions.”

Isis shook her head and continued on. “I was once you, poor thing. Driving 'round with keys in my trunk, that’s until I found myself in a small room having to decide between my loyalty and my freedom. I could have been doing life right now but by the grace of God, I was spared. It was then that I secretly made a promise to myself that I was going to live a better life. I've been an assistant for six years, working to become a lawyer, and eventually with this money of his I’m stashing, I’m going to own a firm of my own. Believe me, I’m going to get back my fifteen years from that man one way or another.”

Isis grabbed her keys from off the kitchen counter and headed for the door, but not before she turned back to me and spoke once more. “Oh and don’t let this innocent, pretty girl look, fool ya. I always keep two burners on me, if you ever feeling froggy. One in my purse,” she said, then lifted her vest to show another small revolver tucked on the inside of her jacket. “And other on my side.”

I just looked stunned, heart now pacing a bit, because I was uncertain what this clearly scorned woman was capable of doing to me, especially in her own home.

"Remember," she continued after thankfully tucking away her weapons, "sometimes in life being smart is playing dumb, so don't ever think you have an advantage over me. You can let Hi-C know that I'll be back in a few hours. That should give you plenty of time to stroke his 'little' ego. I got a date with a nine-inch attorney."

Isis laughed to herself and then strutted her voluptuous body out the door.

"That is one bad bitch," was all I could say to myself.

CHAPTER NINE: THE BASH

I brought in my 26th birthday with a blast in the A, but in the months after I found myself getting my only dose of excitement by taking daily walks to the ice cream truck that conveniently sat across the street from my house. I hadn't been quite the same since the talk I had with Isis on the day I dropped that package off. As much as I disliked her, some of the stuff she said really got to me. Especially the part about my abortions.

I had two of them under the orders of Hi-C. I was nineteen the first time and twenty-four the second. Hi-C's reasons for not wanting me to have his kid was because he said he just wasn't ready and breaking Isis's heart was definitely out of the question. I didn't agree with the abortions at all, but in my head being loyal to him sometimes meant taking extreme measures. So, if sacrificing the love he had for his family over the love I had for mine was what I had to do, then so be it. Besides, no matter how depressed I got about the situation it still didn't change the way I felt about the man who upgraded my life. I still wanted nothing more than to see his wife out of the way so I could be the next chick to have the glorious title of being a hustler's wife. I figured the best way to achieve that was to play my position and wait on Isis to deliver her promise of walking out on him.

Eventually I grew tired of moping around the house so I decided to step out and go to Hi-C's Annual Pool Bash for reasons other than it being mandatory. There was an important issue that had come up which needed to be addressed by him, and everyone, even members from other parts of the country had to be there.

Normally when matters like these came about, Hi-C would host a big party and have a small private meeting within it. It was his way of throwing off the Feds from being able to tell who were guests and who were OMC members since any move he made was always under surveillance. Conveniently during this situation, the pool party that was hosted at Hi-C's house every year was coming up, so he decided to have us all just meet there.

I knew about The Bash ever since I could remember being a little girl and it was definitely a big deal. The scene always looked like a rap video with beautiful men and women flooding the atmosphere. In fact, some of the well-known local and mainstream rappers did take advantage of the event by coming through with cameras to get footage for their upcoming videos. I loved that type of attention so it wouldn't be unusual to catch me dancing in one of them. Hi-C wasn't big on outside cameras at his place but since it was a part of his cover-up he'd allow it with only the people he trusted.

A little after the party really started to jump off was when Hi-C called for the OMC to meet him in his dining room. He'd let us know by flashing the pole lights that surrounded his pool one solid green color. One by one we'd all find ways to end our mangling and secretly try to slide off without being noticed. I was already sitting alone so it was nothing for me to make my exit down the hall.

When I got there, most of the other twenty-five members were already taking their seats around a circular, black table that was big enough to fit us all. He'd usually have a glass of some expensive wine poured up for each of us but I saw none this time. That let me know our meeting was going to be a brief one.

I quickly spotted Hi-C at the top of the table wearing a pair of the most tasteless lime green swimming trunks that were covered in Hawaiian palm trees. He even had the nerve to have a matching robe on top of it. I found a seat next to my girl Poncha who flew in from L.A. Other than Shannon, she was the realest friend I had. Poncha was the type of chick who was solid and genuinely sweet. Like myself, she was beautiful, about her money, and never with the bullshit. She took me in after Hi-C linked me up with her when I had to make a couple runs to Houston. She lived there at the time and happily showed me the big city and we had a blast shutting shit down. She never stayed in one state long because her husband was military but even though we were distant, it still felt like we were right next door.

After everyone was settled in and ready to get the 4-1-1, Hi-C gave his opening prayer and we listened to him talk for about twenty minutes. He informed us about how one of our team members, who got busted with a large number of dope, was possibly working as an informant for the Feds. He ran through precautionary rules to consider when out handling our business and told us what and who to watch out for. Afterwards, he closed the meeting by stressing the importance of remaining loyal to the squad.

After Hi-C dismissed us, Poncha and I joined Alicia, another girl I met through Hi-C. She was relaxing between two lounge chairs, just waiting on us to bring her some company. When we sat down Alicia offered to go get us some drinks and I was glad because that gave Poncha and I a chance to talk more about what was just said in the meeting.

"So, what do you think about the shit Hi-C was talking about?" I asked her after we both took our places. "You think Squirrel's really' snitchin?"

"Well I personally haven't met the dude but with a nickname like that I can believe it."

"I've met him at a few of the parties. He seems like a solid dude. I really don't know though."

"Me either, but like Hi-C said, we just gotta be more careful about how we move."

"Yeah, tru dat."

There was a brief moment of silence between us and I used the opportunity to scope out the scenery. I spotted Alicia waiting in line for our drinks then watched Cederick as he came and brushed up behind her. She smiled at him and they began to carry a conversation. Although she claimed she hated him just as much as I did, I always got the feeling there was or had been something going on between them. Either that or he was just displaying his usual hoe-ish ways. I had also spotted him going in and out of the shed before the meeting. I figured he had one of his tricks up in there, but since I hadn't seen any guys coming out pulling their pants up I wasn't exactly sure. Either way, I knew he was up to something.

"You ever thought about what you would do if you ever were cornered?" Poncha snatched me from my speculations.

"You mean questioned by the police?" I asked. "I have been in a situation like that before and I didn't tell. I think that I could hold it down."

"Yeah I feel you, but this ain't no bullshit ass shopliftin' shit. We talkin' 'bout trafficking and felony drug charges. You do know that we move enough shit to easily get us double-digit prison sentences?"

"It's not an easy truth to accept," I sighed, "but nonetheless I am aware."

"It's a risky game," she said, "and what I've noticed about being in it is that you always expect the unexpected. It's always the people you see stressing how loyal they are, that are the ones who fold the quickest. You never really know what you'd do until you're in that situation."

"I feel you," I replied.

Poncha leaned in closer to me and began to look around carefully before whispering, "Wanna know what I really heard about this whole squirrel situation?"

I perked up then moved in closer also. I was so thirsty for the info that drool began to appear from my mouth. "Yeah, what?"

"Well you know how Hi-C's always saying that if we get busted not to say anything to the cops and he'll send one of the lawyers at Isis's firm to take care of us?"

"Yeah, he says it every meeting."

"Well I heard Squirrel did just that when he got busted but Hi-C never sent that lawyer like he promised. That's when the telling rumors started. So you be the judge."

"Oh wow, I didn't hear that," I said, astonished. "But honestly, you think Hi-C's the type to leave dude stranded like that? I don't believe that's in his character."

"Listen, it's a dog eat dog world out here. At the end of the day, it's every man for themselves in the drug game."

I got quiet again and really started to think. I had known Hi-C in more ways than one and I couldn't picture him just doing anyone dirty like that. Hell, I remember riding with him in his Range Rover down the highway, and we spotted a homeless old man walking the strip. Hi-C passed him at first, but then he turned around thirty-minutes down the road just to go back and lay a whole stack on him. If he did that for someone he didn't even know, I could only imagine the lengths he'd go for his own people.

"Keish, even though we live on opposite sides of the country you're still like my best friend. I literally can trust you with my life so it's nothing for me to tell you how I really feel about this whole ordeal."

"I'm all ears," I replied, looking back at Alicia who was still smiling with Cederick. I knew we had a few more minutes to chat privately because she hadn't even ordered the drinks yet.

"I don't know why, but lately I've just been thinking 'bout my future in this shit. I wanna live to be one hundred, so where am I going to get money when I stop this because hustlin' sure as hell don't come with a retirement plan? That's why I have started to save up for when this shit is all over. And honestly, I have made up my mind that if I ever get caught up, I'm sorry but I can't sit in no jail while them niggas run free. We all risk our lives doing this shit, and yeah we get paid good money, but we all know who the real dough goes to. Think about it, how many times has Hi-C ever just said here goes something extra for you guys for your sacrifices? He stresses this family bonding shit, but how many times have we had these parties just off the strength? Anytime he wants the OMC fam together it's always about something that can help or hurt his business. Don't get me wrong, Hi-C's a pretty solid guy and he taught me everything I know, but at the end of the day it's every man for themselves. That's how they see it and that's how I see it too. Besides, I'm working on getting me some property overseas. If I ever need to hideout, you know I can call my folks over there. And if you ever need to getaway, just know that you can always count on me too."

Poncha stuck out her hands to me and we gave each other dap. I didn't fully agree with her views, but her conversation did tell me that she trusted me a whole lot. She was talking about moving across the continent, but if I would have given Hi-C the heads up on what she told me, I don't think she would have even made it back to LA. I wasn't like that though. I was loyal to my friends just as much as I was loyal to my man. What Poncha shared with me would never leave my lips.

"Well since we're sharing secrets," I said. "Can I ask you a question?"

"Anything babe, what's up?"

"Have you and Hi-C ever like….uhmmm....you know…hit it off?"

“You mean like...fucked or something?....Hell no!" she shouted, then looked around after realizing she had gotten a little too excited.

"Girl I love chocolate men for one, and for two, you think I would be working for Hi-C if I did? One thing about that man is that he does NOT mix business with pleasure. If he can fuck you, he won't hire you. Trust me on that one,” she laughed, then shoved my right shoulder. "Girl don’t tell me you got the hots for Mr. Herbert Cooper. You be careful with that shit. Isis got that Jamaican blood in her and she will voodoo yo ass about her man."

We both started laughing, but secretly I couldn't help but wonder why Hi-C made so many exceptions to the rules for me. I was the only one he allowed in his home, I was the only one who ever rode in his car, and he definitely mixed his business with our pleasure. I just couldn't understand, why me?

"Naw, it's nothing like that," l lied. "I only asked cuz I heard she was the one fucking around on him. Hi-C seems to be a faithful guy, so I was just wondering if he had those player tendencies. Hell, if he can resist yo’ fine Paula Patton looking ass then I know he must be a pretty good dude.”

Poncha squeezed her beautifully proportioned breast together and rubbed her hands through her long, silky authentic hair that women paid hundreds for.

"Solid he is," she flattered herself and then we both laughed before greeting Alicia who was walking up with our drinks. Just when I was about to grab mine, Brandon, the star football player from our city’s university ran up and snatched me from my chair. Then he slammed me into the pool. I didn't mind though because I knew it would be sooner or later before someone would toss my ass in there. It happened to me every year. That was a tradition at the pool bash called ‘*wet now, wet later.’* Any girl a guy was choosing on would get dunked in the pool by him and if she was interested just maybe they would hit it off later.

“Brandon, you play too damn much.” I yelled at him and then winked to let him know that we could most definitely hookup afterwards. I was free-spirited when it came to sex. I wouldn't say I was a hoe or anything like that, but whatever I wanted I got. Besides, I didn't believe in that six-month rule bullshit. In my opinion, just ‘cause a girl made a guy wait six months didn't make her wifey type, and just because she gave it up on the first day didn't make her a hoe either.

I wiped the water from my eyes then got yet another surprise when I saw this petite little girl run up and hug me. She didn't even mind that I was soaked. I had to wrestle her from off of me and became slightly worried when I got a glimpse of her face and didn’t recognize her. Alicia just sat there, but judging by the way Poncha put her hands in a fighting position, I knew I had nothing to worry about.

"Oh my God Keisha!” this mystery girl screamed out. “I can't believe it’s really you!”

“Do I know you?” I asked her.

"It's me Keisha,” she said again.

I still was confused, until I got a better look at her face and saw a mark on it that I could never forget.

"Charlytte?" I asked.

The young girl smiled and then it all came back to me.

"Oh my god! Yes Charlytte! It’s been so long!” I said. "Give me some love girl.”

We hugged again but this time we both were able to enjoy it.

“Girl you have gotten soooo big." I said before noticing that her dress attire was up to par. "Fresh to death too…and look at that ass girl. Yep, you’re most definitely my lil’cuz."

Charlytte looked nothing like I expected her to look at fifteen. I always thought she would have grown up to be a loner- the type to walk around in gothic jeans and oversized black t-shirts- but this lil' heffa standing before me was sharp down in a cute denim outfit. Her hair was laid as well. I didn't know how she gained access to a party as exclusive as this one, but I definitely was going to make it my business to find out.

"What are you doing here girl?" I asked.

"I'm just a friend of Cederick's," she replied.

Oh lord, that's not good. I thought to myself.

"Ooooh Ced, that's what's up sis," I managed to say. "Doing big things I see. How bout I take you to grab a drink and you can come kick it wit' us for a little while? We got some catchin' up to do."

Without even waiting to hear a response from her, I quickly grabbed Charlytte's hand and headed to the bar. I knew she was only fifteen but judging by how womanish she appeared, I could tell she was no stranger to taking a shot or two. Besides, my real motive was to get her as loose as possible because I was on a mission to know every detail about why she was hanging with Cederick. I wanted to know how they met? How long did she know him? And most importantly, where was she getting the money to buy that expensive ass hair she was rockin'? I needed to know it all.

I must have said 'excuse me please' over a hundred times as Charlytte and I dashed through the crowds of people that occupied the party. What was more amusing was to see the amount of attention she was getting, even though I was the one wearing the two-piece. I must admit though, she was definitely cute even in her bedroom slippers that scrubbed the concrete as I carried her through the backyard.

We made it to the bar and just when I was about to order her a Long Island, a large hand gripped mine and broke Charlytte away. I looked to see who it was and there was Cederick standing in front of her as if he was protecting her from me.

"She'll pass on the drinking," he said, then glared at me with a devilish look in his already creepy ass eyes.

"But that's my cousin," I heard Charlytte say soon after he began to shamefully drag her in the opposite direction. Her eyes pathetically stayed on me all the way up until they made it to Hi-C's shed.

CHAPTER 10: Choices

My next run had come a week after the pool party and as usual I had to meet up with Cederick so that he could load my trunk up with the dope I would be carrying. It was always in the same low-key wooded area on the outer city limits of Ordale that we'd make the exchange. Little-to-no communication would occur between us as the slam of my Camry's trunk would let me know he was done and it was time for me to be on my way. This time was different though. It was the first ever I had looked forward to meeting up with him and it was for reasons that had nothing to do with me shipping any drugs. I needed answers about his connection to my baby cousin and I wasn't going to let him leave until I got them.

Cederick took only a short second to load my car. Then nodded his head once, threw up the deuces, and headed back to his SS Monte Carlo.

"Hey Ced," I called out, then waved my left arm out of the window to let him know that I wanted his attention. Cederick caught my drift and made his way to the passenger side of my car. He entered cautiously and took a seat. The scent of the marijuana that was clinging to his reddish-orange Polo shirt and dark denim jeans soothingly brushed up against my nostrils, somehow bringing a little ease to the troubling situation.

"Everythang aight?" he asked. "I told you not to let Albino intimidate you."

"It's not about the drop," I informed him. "It's about something else."

"Well what's up? Talk to me."

"The girl you snatched up at the party," I took a deep breath then exhaled, "that's what I'm concerned about."

"You mean your cousin?" he surprised me by knowing that we were kin.

"Yes her," I replied. "So you do know she's fam, right?"

"Yeah, she told me that night you were somebody to her, cousin…sister...I don't know, I can't remember exactly," he replied. "Look, I didn't mean to embarrass shorty like that, but you know how Hi-C feels about babies being at his parties, especially after the time he got busted for that underage drinking shit. You know the Feds wanna lock his ass up for anything and we don't need no heat. She wasn't even supposed to leave the shed, and you, being an OMC member and all, was even more reckless for taking her to get a drink when you knew her age."

"True that," I said shamefully. I knew he had a point, but it still didn't change how I felt about her being around him.

"But it ain't even about none of that," I told him. "I just wanna know what she was doing at the party in the first place?...Like what's the deal with you and her? Let's be real here, you and I both know how you roll and what that shed is used for."

"How *I* roll?" He put one hand up to his chest and looked at me as if I had just insulted him. "And what do you mean by that? Keisha, just get to the point of what you trynna say. I hate that talking in code bullshit. What's really good?"

Losing my patience with Cederick, I finally just came out and told him what was on my mind.

"What are you doing with my fifteen-year-old cousin? And you better not be planning on turning her into a trick because it's not going down like that as long as I can help it!"

A feeling of relief came over my body once I had gotten those words out to him. But not taking too kindly of what I said, he turned his entire body around and faced me. His evil-looking eyes pierced mine and I quickly looked away. They always made me uncomfortable.

"Let's get something straight right now" he said. "I don't take too kindly of people telling me what I better do and not do. And second, I never turned anybody into anything. No pistol of mine has ever been put up to a bitch's head, and even if it was, they still got a thing called a choice. Now depending on what they're willing to sacrifice when they make their choice, now that's on them."

Cederick turned his body back around and began to stare out of the window towards the trees.

"Open your eyes, Keisha. My girls doing the same thing you doing- hustling. Only difference between your hustle and their hustle is that they're putting their bodies on the line, and you, well your freedom. Who are you to judge what I do to get money and who takes advantage of the opportunity that I may present- definitely not force- to them?"

I rolled my eyes and turn my head in the direction of my window as I listened to Cederick explain himself to me. He was trying to do exactly what he tries to do to those girls- manipulate me with his bullshit. Little did he know I was not one of those teenagers he had sucking dick for bus fare. I saw right through his games and I wasn't playing any of them.

"So you really gonna try to compare me doing runs to your lil' bitches selling pussy. You know that makes no sense. Going on runs don't put me at risk of catching some shit that can kill me and it definitely doesn't do to me what you did to Peaches Mosley. That girl was prom queen of our high school class and now I can barely even recognize her. Please come again Cederick. Have a heart. Leave my cousin alone."

Seeing where our conversation was beginning to lead us, Cederick in a calm, but obviously frustrated manner, opened the car door and planted his Rockports on the grass. Then he exited my vehicle, closed the door behind himself, and leaned into my window.

"If she's so much of your family and you're going so hard for her, then why are you living up in a nice ass two-story townhouse while she's homeless and getting raped by an old ass creep just to have a place to lay her head."

A still look appeared on my face. I was speechless.

"Exactly," he said. "Don't come preaching to me about a gotdamn thing. Say what you wanna say about me but that girl ain't stop smiling since I took her under my wing and she damn sure ain't the same dirty ass lil' girl she was when I first scooped her up from that cheap ass motel. So if anything, you're welcome."

"Whatever Cederick," I replied, pretending to be unbothered.

"Whatever nothing. I'm out here giving her confidence and you ain't giving her shit. You gotta meet Albino by four. Don't be late."

CHAPTER 11: BAILey ME OUT

Pure silence was all I could bare to stand while riding to Tampa because my head was clouded with thoughts of the info Cederick had just laid on me about Charlytte being raped and all. If it were true, a part of me could not help but feel like it was my fault she had gone through that. Surely, had I kept my word of going back for her she wouldn't have been homeless in the first place. This fancy lifestyle I was caught up with was definitely getting in the way of me tending to the things that should have been most important to me.

I normally always rode with a blunt and a water bottle that contained some Patron in it that I would consume on my way back from the drop. It always seemed to make the time go by faster, but most importantly it was necessary after many hours of being paranoid on the road carrying illegal shit. It didn't matter how many times I did it, the nervous feeling I received was one that I could never seem to shake.

I usually only drank or smoked after I made my deliveries, but this time, being so stressed, I decided to do it on the way going. Not thinking that the very second I lit my joint, a police officer would pull up behind me and hit the blue lights.

"Fuck!" I screamed, as I was now face to face with my biggest fear.

I quickly stuffed the blunt into my panties, then closed my eyes really tight and began to pray that everything would go smoothly. When the officer made it up to my car, I slowly rolled down my window and hoped that the smell of marijuana didn't greet him before I did.

"Hello, how are you?" a phony smile appeared upon my face as I tried so desperately to look innocent. "Is there a problem, sir?"

The officer began to explain why he was pulling me over, and had I not been distracted by how amazingly charming he was, I would have paid him some attention. Unfortunately, the way the sunlight beamed perfectly on his neatly combed curly hair, the nicely-form set of lips that complimented his pearly white teeth, and his broad, muscular frame put me in a zone that made me lose focus on all that I could have possibly been locked up for.

"...did you not realize you were going that fast?" he continued. "Are you in a hurry or something?"

"Hurry...wait...what?" I stuttered.

"Are you okay young lady? You seemed to be discombobulated," he strangely and rather quickly jumped to conclusion. " Are you under the influence of something?"

I got myself together quickly after hearing those words. "Wait a minute officer...that's definitely not the case. Besides, don't you think it's a little too early for me to be under the influence of anything?"

The policeman whose name plate read OFFICER BAILEY didn't feel the need to answer.

"License and registration please," he simply replied.

I reached into my glove compartment, grabbed the only piece of paper that was inside and then handed it to him. I still wondered if he smelt the weed.

"What again did you say you pulled me over for?"

"As I stated before," he emphasized. "You were doing eighty-five in a seventy and you seemed to be failing to maintain your lane."

"Seemed to be or was I?"

"You were definitely swerving Miss…," he looked down at my driver's license, "Black. Just sit tight. I'll be back in a second."

Officer Bailey walked back to his vehicle that I now realized wasn't a regular cop car. It was a black Chevy Impala with very dark tinted windows and the blue lights that flashed from it seemed to be built inside the headlights.

I waited for about twenty minutes and the officer still hadn't returned to my car. I had to meet up with Albino no later than 4:30 and I knew for sure that I would now be running behind. One thing about that guy is that he didn't respect anyone or anybody, especially people who were late. Albino was a crazy ass cat from Florida with big stupid dreadlocks and skin that was pale as cotton. His hair was an orange color and his eyes were goldish brown. They would have been mesmerizing had one of them not constantly wiggled from left to right. He got the nickname Albino because he had that albino skin disease.

Growing tired of waiting, I flagged the officer down and watched him as he finally made his way back over to me. He held the body frame of a man in his mid-twenties, but the depth of his voice and the way he carried himself let me know that he was nowhere close to my age. Still that didn't stop me from being mesmerized.

"I know you're only doing your job but do you know how long this will take? I'm on my way to see an aunt of mine. She had a stroke this morning and I'm hearing that she may not pull through. I'm sorry if I was speeding, but I have to see her before, God forbids, the worst happens. My aunt practically raised me since my mom couldn't put the needle down. Please officer."

I put on a sad face and hoped that he'd sympathize with my situation. The officer looked down at me with puppy eyes, leaving me to think that my story had gotten to him.

"Well you would have been free to go, but there's just one problem?" he informed me.

"What's that officer?" I sighed.

"Do you have any drugs in here, ma'am?"

My heart suddenly began to pound, nearly out of my chest.

"Drugs?" I asked.

"Yes," he replied. "Marijuana…weed…kush or whatever y'all call it nowadays. The smell of it damn near made me choke when you let down your window."

Although I got nervous knowing that he sensed the weed, a feeling of relief came over me.

"Oh...weed," I sighed. "Honestly officer, yeah I admit I did smoke a blunt a few hours ago. But it's gone and out the window now."

"Well then you shouldn't mind if I search your car?"

"Search…my….my…car," I stuttered. "Sir, I promise there is nothing left of it. Listen, I really would like to see my aunt before it's too late. Please, she means the world to me."

"Miss Black," he stuck his head into the window. "Unfortunately, if something happens to you on your way there I will be held responsible. You were speeding and swerving and it could have possibly been because you were high. Just let me do a quick check inside the vehicle, and if you're clear, I promise I will leave you with nothing more than a warning."

"Just…just a quick search?" I asked.

"No backup, no dogs, just a quick peep inside." He replied.

“Okay fine,” I gave in. "You have my permission."

Officer Bailey led me to the back seat of his car and made his way back to mine. I watched him carefully as he opened every door, sticking his head and body in and out of my car. All I could do was sit there and pray that he didn't ask to go into my trunk. I didn't worry about him getting in without me though, because of the way Hi-C mechanically rigged my car. You couldn’t pop the lock from inside or attempt to use a key because the only way anyone could get in was by using a separate uniquely-designed chip that I always kept in my breast. The car was also perfectly dented in the back to help coincide with the story that it could not open because it was jammed shut. Hi-C went above and beyond to protect his product.

Officer Bailey took a slow stroll back to my car with nothing in his hand.

"Welp, I didn't find anything, but there is still a stench that I am getting. Do you mind opening your trunk for me Miss Black? Just one last peep.”

I almost died in that moment. “My…my…trunk.”

“Yes, that space in the back of your car that’s used for storing things like your spare tire and stuff,” he said sarcastically.

I tried to remain calm, but deep down inside my body was doing things that I couldn’t describe even if a dictionary was staring me in my face.

“I know what a trunk is, silly" I attempted to joke with him and give him a little bit of flirtatious action at the same time. "But unfortunately that little dent you see on the side there won't allow me to do that. It's jammed shut and believe me, nothing is inside.”

“Just let me see your keys, Miss Black.”

“Officer, the key won’t work,” I gladly handed it to him. “I’m telling you, it’s shut tight."

Officer Bailey took my keys and desperately attempted to open the trunk. For about five minutes, I watched him build up a sweat as he fought with it. When he finally returned, he entered the front seat of his car and began searching around for something, then exited and sat on the hood of his car. I continued to watch him as he sparked up a cigarette and just began to stare out at the cars swiftly passing by. I didn't know what to make of his smoke break, and what he may have been thinking so deeply about, but I did know that if he didn't hurry there would definitely be a big problem in Florida for Hi-C.

After the cigarette was burned out, Officer Bailey returned to his car and sat next to me. It was odd seeing a police officer in the backseat of his own vehicle so my mind immediately began to wonder.

"Now hold up Mr. Officer, I don’t know what the fuck you tryin’, but I ain't giving up no pussy just to get out of a hundred-dollar speeding ticket,” I snapped. "You even think about touching me I’ll sue the whole damn department and make sho’ ya ass can't even get a job doing security for a children's block party.”

Officer Bailey slowly shook his head and leaned in towards me. I still couldn’t help but admire this guy. Even though he was the enemy, there was just something about him and those damn eyes that held my interest.

"Don't flatter yourself, Miss Black," he replied. "Or shall I say Keisha the stylist....or how about Keisha, the daughter of Joanne Black.....the Keisha that grew up in Carver Heights and went to elementary at Garrison, middle at Myers, and high school at Beach....the same Keisha that strangely takes the bubble gum off her SpongeBob ice cream and eats it before she even tastes the ice cream….should I go on?”

I began to immediately think about the ice cream truck that sat across the street from my house the entire summer and that’s when it dawned on me.

OH SHIT! THE MUTHAFUCKIN’ FEDS! I thought.

"What's wrong," he smiled. "Cats got yo' tongue or is it still down Hi-C's throat?"

I just stood in a daze and couldn't speak another word even if my life depended on it. I knew for sure Officer Bailey had an idea of what I was hiding in that trunk and I was certain that the big break he'd probably been laying on had finally come. There was just no way I could go to jail, so I had to do something. Immediately, I busted out into my famous phony laughter. Officer Bailey seemed confused.

"Is this a joke to you, Miss black?" he asked.

"No, not at all." I continued to laugh. "It's just that...that..."

"That what?" he started to get impatient with me.

"It's just that you think you've busted me, but really you don't have shit."

"You sure about that?" he asked, confidently. "I can guarantee when my squad arrives and gets this trunk open we're gonna find some kilos back there."

I still continued to laugh in his face.

"Possibly," I shrugged. "But if you bust me now, what really will you achieve? Getting a couple of keys off the streets, when you know like I know it's *waaaay* more where that came from. Yeah, I'll probably get a few years in prison while the people I'm working for just laughs and keeps getting rich. Tell me again, what really will you achieve?"

Officer Bailey looked at me long and hard.

"Where are you going with this, Miss Black?"

"Nowhere, just arrest me now. Besides, the guys on the receiving end probably are already suspicious anyway. I'm thirty minutes behind without even a phone call to them. With those guys perfect timing is the key to everything."

I stuck my arms out in a take-me-now position and tried to stop them from shivering from my nervousness. I didn't want him to know that I was just bluffing.

"You got one more time to answer me honestly," he put his radio up to his lips, "or else I will call for back up. What are you implying?"

I dropped my arms and let them fall to my side. It was a physical relief. "What I'm saying is that if you arrest me now, yeah you get a couple drugs off the streets, but that won't change the world. What's in my trunk is nothing compared to what's out there and you know it. If you let me go, and pretend as if this never happened, I can finish my delivery and then lead you to the real fish. I mean, I can help you get a bust so big they'll be promoting you to chief."

Hearing those words, Officer Bailey's eyes got huge. I could tell he was at least thinking about it.

"Look," I continued, "I'm really starting to want out of this shit. I'm starting to realize the importance of family and everything I seemed to have forgotten about chasing this little thing called money. If you have been following me like you say you have, then you'll know that I'm the only chick besides his wife that Hi-C will even let close to him. I'm the only one who has access to his home, I know where he keeps his financial documents, and I don't know his connect, but with a lil' bit of investigating I'm sure I can find out. You have to just trust me on this. I promise, I won't let you down. Please."

Officer Bailey forced his pupils away from the captivity of mine. Then he glanced back at the road and again watched each car carefully pass as if one of them held a sign that led him to the right decision.

"Meet me here at eleven o'clock sharp in exactly five days," he handed me a card. "Fuck me over, I will make sure that the next time you see freedom you will be too old and senile to even spell it."

CHAPTER 12: Reunited

The fatal car accident involving a tractor trailer and two compact vehicles that happened on I-95 fortunately collaborated with my story to Albino about why I was an hour late to make the drop. I seemed a little jittery when I arrived but that didn't make me look suspicious because I was always that way when meeting up with him. Although this time it wasn't his weird presence, but the fact that I had just made a deal with the devil, that had everything to do with it.

I had so much more to think about on the ride home and the worst part was that the only person I was able to talk to about it was now a stranger to me. It was at that moment when I needed a real friend to help me with my situation that I started to really miss Shannon.

I had heard it through the grapevine that she worked at a convenience store on the east side of Ordale and I would often stop, get gas from the outside, and just stare at her through the glass window. I never had the courage to go inside, even when I saw her between customers putting her head down in obvious stress. I could see that Shannon was struggling in her life, especially with four children, but instead of offering any assistance I would just ride off and carry on with my life.

"Lemme get two packs of Swishers and a hug from an old friend," I said to Shannon who hadn't noticed me approaching because she had her head down as usual. I didn't know how she would take seeing me again but the wide smile and the way she stormed out from behind the counter let me know that true friendships never died.

"Oh my god, Keisha!" she shouted while almost squeezing the life out of me. "How have you been girl? You look beautiful."

"So do you," I replied, as I stepped back and took a good look at my girl. She surely had gained about a hundred pounds but her nice curves and pretty face was still intact.

"I try....I try...," she boasted, then did a three-sixty spin-around so that I could really check her out. "I might be a big bitch now but I'm still fine."

"That you are," I laughed then watched Shannon strut her even more enormous butt back to her post.

"So what brings you to this side of town?" she asked. "I heard you got that nice ass spot way out there where Kevin's aunt stays. Doing well, I see."

"Just passing through the area, " I lied. "And yeah I'm doing okay."

“Seems like you’re doing a little better than okay,” she said. “Those houses ain’t cheap over there.”

"Girl stop it. What are you doing when you get off?" I quickly changed the subject, trying to dodge discussing any major moves in my life because I felt guilty about rubbing them in her face. "Maybe we should go out for drinks or something, just catch up."

"I'll be outta here in ‘bout thirty. I normally stay until the bus comes just to get some more hours on my check. Then I gotta get the kids from my cousin’s."

I looked across the street at the two homeless men posted up at the bus stop and I pitied Shannon even more.

"You can hop in with me, I’ll take you to get the kids. I haven’t seen them in forever anyways.”

A sign of happiness quickly showed up on Shannon’s face. I don’t know if she was more excited that she was riding with me or that she didn’t have to wait at that pissy ass bus stop.

"I would appreciate that," she smiled.

In exactly thirty minutes, Shannon hopped in my car and we rode to get the kids. Luckily their father, which I was amazed to find out that Kevin and her were still together, agreed to keep them while we caught up on old times. He gave her a curfew though, especially since he worked overnight. I wasn't quite happy with it because I knew it would be in the wee hours of the morning before I could finish laying the shit I had on her. Still, I was thankful for the little bit of time we did have to spend together.

“I can't believe how big the kids have gotten,” I told Shannon, as we waited in the McDonald's drive thru for a quick bite to eat. Their McRibs were in again and I had been craving one. Besides, that sandwich used to be Shannon and I's favorite.

"Yes ma'am, those little monsters are a trip,” she replied. “Especially Precious, the teacher says all she does is talk. Seems like now that she’s in the fourth grade she doesn't know how to act. Remember when she used to be so innocent and sweet?”

"Yeah I remember and always sucking that index finger," I chuckled. "That used to be my baby."

“Speaking of somebody who used to be yo’ baby, how's Charlytte?”

I purposely looked away from Shannon towards the board that contained the restaurant’s weekly specials. The cars had begun to move forward but we hadn't quite made it up to the intercom.

“She's doing good,” I replied, then continued to stare out of my window and pretended to be telling the truth.

“Hold up Keisha,” she sat up. “I know when something's not right. You would have rambled on and told me how good she was doing if that were true. Fa real, how is she?"

I sighed deeply and was now able to look at Shannon since I didn’t have to lie to her.

"I gotta be honest,” I replied. "I really don't know. I haven't been going ‘round there like that."

“Oh my god Keisha, why not? You know how much that girl depended on you and you know your mama doesn't give a shit about her.”

“I know,” I said, then tried to rid my body of the guilty feelings I had successfully tried to escape from over the years. I guess reality kicked in hearing the truth come from a real friend. "But you saw the way my mama beat my ass and embarrassed me that night. It's just hard to go back to that house, too many bad memories.”

"That's understandable,” she said. “But I think that should be more of a reason for you to go back. You don’t want the same thing that happened to you to happen to her, right? I told you that's yo' mama and all but that bitch is crazy."

We both laughed, then I had to remind Shannon not to forget where she came from as well.

"Hell, yo mama ain't too far behind. You saw the way she leaped like a damn lizard and sucker punched me. Swear she did something but I think Precious hits harder than that. How is she by the way?"

"Mama?" she asked. "Well she died two years ago. Overdosed on heroin."

"What?! Oh my god Shannon and you didn't bother to call and tell me."

"I didn't know how to reach you and I really didn't know if you even cared. Besides, happened when she moved back to our hometown. She just up and left Ordale without telling anyone and we hadn't heard nothin' from her until we were getting a call from my aunt saying her body had been found in an abandoned house. You know she was dead there for two weeks before anyone even discovered her?"

"Oh my gosh, Shannon," I reached over and hugged her. "I'm so sorry to hear that."

"It's okay. Really it is," she hugged back briefly, but then politely removed me from off of her. "Ma had gotten worse after Shameka went to jail. I used to think my sister was making her habit worse, but I guess keeping her high was the only way to really keep her alive."

"Shannon please believe me," I said sincerely. "I didn't rat your sister out. I was trying to tell you that before you just slammed the door in my face."

"I know you didn't," she replied.

"Then why did you just diss me like that?" I asked her.

"Because Keisha, I know how my family is. We were raised to stick together. If I would have let you in, my crazy mama would have put the both of us out. I had Precious to think about. It wasn't personal and please believe that it hurt me worse than it hurt you."

Hearing Shannon's explanation made me put myself in her shoes. She did have a two-year-old in her arms and if it was my family on the line I probably would have done the same thing too.
There was a brief silence between us but it was interrupted by the sound of my cell phone ringer going off. I checked to see who was calling and saw that it was Cederick's number that was flashing on my screen. He called from time to time to talk about business but there was nothing going on for another week so it was very strange to be hearing from him now. I really didn't want to answer in front of Shannon, but my curiosity of what he might have wanted overruled my decision.

"What it do boo!" I answered, trying to throw Shannon off while at the same time secretly letting Cederick know that I was around someone.

"Hello, may I speak to Keisha?" a female voice asked.

"Speaking," I replied, immediately recognizing who the person on the other end was. "This must be Charlytte?"

"Yeah it's me," she said.

"Bout time bitch! I swear I was just talkin' about you. What's going on, hun?"

Just as Charlytte began to answer me, the woman working the drive thru began to take my order. I didn't play about my food and wanted to make sure everything was correct, so I gave Shannon the phone and let them chop it up. By the time they were done talking, we had all agreed that Charlytte would meet us at the nail salon on Skidaway. I volunteered to treat her and Shannon, who was in very desperate need of a pedicure, to some services and I was excited because it gave us a chance to catch up on old times. It also allowed me the much needed opportunity to vent to Shannon about my most recent dilemma, while at the same time scope out what Charlytte had going on with Cederick.

We spent about an hour in the salon, then Charlytte, Shannon, and I decided to grab some stuff to make daiquiris with and headed to my spot. I had to have Shannon home by eleven so there was no need for us to do anything fancy. Besides, I did secretly want to show off my nice townhouse and elegant furniture. I had paid a local interior designer almost ten grand to give my apartment the ancient look I dreamed of having ever since I was a kid.

When we got to my house I watched Shannon and Charlytte lust over the place. I took them on a mini tour, showing off my bedroom, my kitchen, and even my walk-in closet. Then I convinced Shannon to make the daiquiris and led Charlytte to the den. I knew that I had a small window of time to speak with her in private, so I had better made it quick.

I turned my surround sound stereo on low, took my place on one of my leather loveseats, then watched her as she got deeply drawn into the big portrait of the African beauty I had mounted on my wall.

"Her name was Amina," I explained to her, "and she was the Queen of Zaria hundreds of years ago. She's believed to had built governments, lead armies, conquer territories and powerful shit like that. I fucks with her because she was a strong warrior and didn't even want no nigga because she knew subjecting herself to them muthafuckas would make her less powerful. In fact, they said after she defeated her enemies in battle, she would take one of their men home with her, sleep with him, and kill his ass the next morning. My kinda bitch."

Charlytte giggled a little bit at what I had just told her and it made me realize that my plan to loosen her up was starting to work. But still, I knew it was going to take more than African stories to make her open up to me. I had to turn it up a notch.

"So you really have never smoked weed before?" I asked, confirming what she already told Shannon and I in the car. Her eyes were still glued on the portrait of Amina.

"No, never." She replied, then looked over to me before glancing down at the weed and blunts I had just laid out on the coffee table.

"Hell, why not?" I asked.

"I don't know," she shrugged. "I guess because I've never really been around it."

"What? And Cederick's a good friend of yours?" I purposely tried to pick her. "As much as that nigga smokes."

Charlytte turned back to the picture and didn't say another word. She was obviously too smart to fall into my trap. I had to think of something else and fast. The blender was beginning to sound from the kitchen so I knew it wouldn't be long before Shannon made her way to us.

"Charlytte, why don't you come over here for a sec?" I tapped on my loveseat and signaled for her to take her place next to me. "I wanna teach you a little something about weed."

"Okay," Charlytte nonchalantly shrugged, then slowly made her way over. I couldn't help but notice how beautiful she had grown up to be.

"See," I sniffed a sack of loud and began to twirl it before my eyes, "weed is not bad for you so don't be intimidated by all this 'it's illegal' bullshit going on. The government is fucked up and sour as hell because if they weren't, cigarettes would be banned and it would be grams of Kush that we'd be buying from our local Wal-Marts right now. Weed just relaxes you, opens your mind, but most importantly, makes you think. And the government don't want nobody thinking."

I looked to Charlytte who was looking at me as if she didn't understand a word of what was coming out of my mouth. I didn't understand much either. I was just trying to say to her the same thing Hi-C had said to me once. I didn't think it was getting us anywhere though.

"Well, do you at least know how to roll up?" I switched to a different subject, something I could relate more to.

Charlytte shook her head from left to right.

"Ok well, if you're gonna be smoking," I said, as I grabbed a Swisher off the table, "you most definitely need to know how to roll your own blunts. We're Blacks and we don't depend on nobody to do shit for us."

I began to break down my weed and I watched Charlytte suddenly gain a little more interest in what I was doing.

"It's simple. See, I like to look at how I roll these blunts the same way I look at how I fuck these niggas. First, you bust it open for 'em."

I took a razor blade and slowly slid it down the blunt.

"Then you shake it for 'em." I told her. Then shook all of the guts into a small black bag.

"Next, you let 'em fill you up, but only if they got some good shit. If it looks like this," I pointed at the bag of weed Shannon offered to match with me. "then don't let that nigga bring that weak shit nowhere near you."

Charlytte and I giggled, but quietly. We didn't want Shannon to know we were cracking on her sac.

"Then once he puts that good shit all the way inside of you, your *rooooll* your body for him and then trap his ass until there's no way for him to escape you."

I demonstrated to Charlytte how I rolled the weed inside the blunt, then looked at each end of it to make sure it was packed in tightly. Last, I put it to my mouth and grabbed my lighter.

"Now I know you know what to do next, right?"

Charlytte shrugged again.

"Chile, you put that fire on his bitch ass and smoke him until he has nothing left to offer you. Then you toss that nigga out with the rest of them bum ass roaches. Queen Amina type shit."

Charlytte laughed at my crazy ass then I gave her a blunt, and Shannon's weak ass sac, so that she could practice on her own. I also made a note-to-self to bless Shannon with some of my weed to replace hers. If we were going to be friends again I couldn't have her carrying that bullshit around.

I allowed the smoke to enter my lungs and do its thing. No matter what I was going through it always gave me the feeling that everything would be alright. Then I sat quietly, pretending to be listening to the sound of Prince's song *Adore*, but really I began to study Charlytte as she sat there concentrating hard on the little project I gave her. Her hair was laid so beautifully that I knew it had to have cost a pretty penny to have it done. Even her outfit was banging, but it was something strange about the way she was made up. It just didn't match her personality. Charlytte seemed a little clueless on the inside but looked to have it all figured out on the out, and it didn't add up. Something or someone else was creating this girl sitting before me or at least that's what my instincts led me to believe.

Shannon came in shortly afterwards with our drinks and the girls followed me to my balcony, where we sat in comfty lounge chairs and got a nice view of the beautiful community lake. At first, I admit I had a secret agenda for wanting to meet up with them, as far as dropping some info on Shannon and getting some from Charlytte, but I decided to just sit back and naturally enjoy the time we were spending together. Besides, it turned out better that way. We began to open up to one another about what was going on in each of our lives and I was even able to jokingly throw the idea of me snitching on Hi-C at them just to see what their reactions would be. Charlytte also spilled some tea about her and Cederick's relationship and admitted to having a huge crush on him, but denied that they had ever had any sexual encounters. I wasn't sure if I believed her, but I decided to just take her word, especially after she began to stress how bad she wanted him. Oddly, I even tried to school Charlytte on how to win Cederick over by telling her how much 'pussy power' she had and using my crazy theory about Adam eating Eve's coochie, and not no damn apple, to help her feel more confident about getting the D. The girls and I laughed until the night fell and enjoyed our little reunion. True, there were a lot of things I didn't get to say to Shannon and much more I needed to get out of Charlytte, but I didn't trip because judging by the good chemistry we all seemed to have had, I knew it wouldn't be long before we got together again.

CHAPTER 13: THE PLAN

Marlon's, a low-key restaurant located on a small beach held just a handful of people waiting to indulge in some great seafood eating. Tybris Island was forty-five minutes away from my hometown but seeing the beautiful ocean and catching a drift of the cool summer breeze always made the drive well worth it. I had already ordered and began eating an appetizer, which consisted of fried mushrooms and jalapeno bites, while I impatiently waited for Detective Bailey to meet me there. I had been sitting for twenty minutes and I was going to give him another ten before I'd bounce and try my best to make certain he'd never see me again.

"Is that your party joining?" the young waitress, full of tattoos and piercings, asked me after seeing a man entering the door looking around. We were the only two of our kind in the place so I guess it wasn't hard for her to connect us.

"Yes, that's him," I said, as I began to stand.

The waitress stopped me.

"I got it. Just sit tight and stay pretty for him," she winked.

I shamefully smiled at her comment and then quickly pulled out my mirror to make sure that I was not necessarily pretty, but together. I was in no way trying to physically impress the detective, it was just a natural habit of mine to always make sure I was on point. In fact, I didn't even care to wear make-up, which was something I rarely left the house without. Besides, most of my face was hidden under the large Gucci sunglasses I wore and I didn’t have to worry about my hair since it was covered up by a black hoodie. Sure enough, I was definitely out of fashion but I would have rather been caught looking tacky then be caught hooking up with a detective.

After making sure I had no signs of fried crumbs on my face or boogers in my nose, I placed my mirror back in my purse just in time for Detective Bailey to make it to the table. He apparently wasn't trying to impress me either because he was only wearing a tank top and a pair of loose jogging pants that were covered in beach sand. I figured he had been out by the ocean. That probably explained why he was late.

"That nice breeze must have caused you to lose track of the time," I sarcastically greeted him after watching him take a seat and grab himself a menu.

Without saying a word, Detective Bailey swung his index finger up to get the waitress's attention. She quickly made her way back to the table.

"May I help you to anything to drink, sir?" she asked. “We have some great happy hour specials.”

"No thank you," he said. "I will just have a cup of water with lemon, no ice."

The waitress nodded. "And what about your lady? Are you interested in hearing more about our specials?"

"Oh no, I'm not his lady," I corrected her. "And no thanks, I'm fine."

She nodded again and walked off carrying a look on her face that said 'I know you're not sitting in front of this fine man and not be fucking him.'

"So you won't be taking advantage of any half-priced cocktails?" he asked. "I know Grey Goose is your favorite."

"Actually, Patron is my favorite," I informed him. " I just don't drink it on the regular. Just because you've been following me around doesn't mean that you know me. And why did you make us meet so close to Ordale, then have the nerve to show up late? Are you seriously trying to get me kilt?"

"Believe me, I'm never late," he said. "By the way, how were those mushrooms you ordered? The way you were devouring them they must have been good."

I looked around the table to find any type of clue that would have let the detective know that I had ate mushrooms before he got there, but I found none. The waitress had already taken my plate so it appeared to me that he must have been watching me the whole time.

"You are truly something else," I said, trying to act unimpressed. "I just read something in the paper this morning about a house on Cedar that had three dead bodies in it. All were shot in the head, execution style. And guess what? The suspects are still on the loose. Don't you think you should be over there investigating some real criminals?"

"And don't you think you're coming off real snobbish for someone who should actually be in jail right now?" he reminded me. "For your information, I don't specialize in homicides, only drugs and narcotics. I'm a special agent who came to Ordale from Oklahoma about two weeks ago. As far as anybody in this town is concerned, the two of us are dating. I would never put you in harm’s way. I didn't manage to keep this job over ten years from being messy. I have a sharp, thought-out-mind and I'm very careful about how I move. You understand that?"

I rolled my eyes and acted as if nothing he said impressed me.

"But enough about that," he began to sit up and give me his full attention. "Tell me something about you."

"For what?" I answered. "As much as you have been following me you should already know plenty. Look, I'm not here for any of that psychological shit, so don't start it. I know exactly how this goes. You're gonna make me think you’re interested in knowing me personally, then once I get you the information you need, you’re gonna take my team down and probably throw me in jail along with them…And why do you want to go after the OMC anyway? We're not running no bloody mafia crew. All we do is the same shit the people who sign the front of your checks do- put a lil' bit of drugs on the streets. That in turn makes people happy while also making people money. That's what life’s all about, right?”

"I guess it depends on whose life you’re talking about," he answered.

"What do you mean?" I questioned.

"It's what life is all about to you because you have no idea what it really means to live. You're a slave to man and you worship the designer, not the creator. Those Gucci sunglasses, that Prada handbag, all that expensive shit you’re wearing is the most you want out of life. That's why you do this. Not to make people happy, but to make yourself happy.”

Detective Bailey grabbed his water from the waitress, who had made it back to us, then waited until she walked off before he spoke again.

"You're so smart until you're almost stupid," he insulted me. "Your pride and your ability to think that you’re wiser than everybody around you is going to cause some major problems for you, young lady. I care more about you than you think I do. I took this job to save my people and lost souls like yourself. And may I remind you that I did put my career on the line by letting you go last week, so I'mma need you to be a little less biggity and a lot more respectful towards me. If it wasn't for my mercy, right now you would have been sitting between some lesbian's legs getting your pretty hair cornrowed."

Detective Bailey had a point. It was hard, but I put down my pride and humbly asked, "So what can I do to help?"

"First just start by telling me whatever you feel comfortable telling me. You don't have to spill too much. I understand that you have to learn to trust me just as much as I have to learn to trust you."

I nodded. "Okay cool. The only thing I can tell you now is that I deliver in Jacksonville to some guys named Albino and Chester, sometimes them both. When I go to Louisiana, it's a black man named Big Foot. When I go to DC, it's a mixed guy named Harry. And the two times I went to New York, it's been to a fat Chinese guy they call Sauce. Now I don't know much about these dudes so don't ask. As a matter of fact, I'm not even allowed to speak to them. I hand them a bag. They hand me one. We nod. Then I'm on my way back."

Detective Bailey reached into his shorts pocket for his notepad and began writing something down. He was good if he was able to recall all those names and cities I had just put him up on.

"And what about Hi-C? What can you tell me about him?"

"Well, he's very cautious and moves quietly, if at all. See everybody works for him so his hands are never dirty. To be honest, he covers his trails so well that it would probably take a miracle to bring him down. I never really try to get into the business side of his life, but he trusts me on a personal, so I think I can get him to open up."

"If he's so cautious, then how do you think you can do that?"

"The three P's," I smiled. "Patron, pussy and pillow talk."

Detective Bailey managed to crack some laughter from under that serious face he always held and it was refreshing. Seeing his nice smile was a plus too.

"Work your magic then," he chuckled.

"I'll see what I can do," I replied, then the both of us became serious again.

"So I take it there's really not much else you can offer up on Hi-C?" he asked.

"Well," I thought once more, "there is one other thing that may be helpful to you."

"And what's that?" he leaned in closer to me.

"He has a particular file cabinet in his office that he guards with his life. I believe he has some type of financial documents in it, or least something that may help take him down. There just has to be a good reason why he protects it the way he does."

"Oh really," he scratched his chin. "Since you have access to his house, do you think you may be able to creep in there and see what it is?"

"Hell no!" I accidently blurted out, then caught myself and simmered down. "Hi-C has all types of high-tech security shit in his house. I'm talking HD cameras, fingerprint scanners, and stuff like that. The only way you can get into this thing is by some serious force and some people that have the right equipment."

"What if my guys do it....yeah...my squad," an idea popped into his head. "I just need a reason to be able to go in there. Like a drug bust or something."

"Exactly," I agreed. "But don't you gotta have a warrant for that type of shit."

"Yeah, but that's nothing," he boasted. "I know just the judge to make it happen. He owes me a favor anyway."

CHAPTER 14: THE BUST

"Aaaaw...got damn baby," Hi-C moaned softly as he enjoyed the feeling of me licking and sucking on each of his testicles fairly. I usually kept it basic when I gave him oral, but the guilt I felt from working closely with a Narcotics Agent, and the fact that in less than two hours there would be a staged drug bust in his home, made me want to please him in any and every way possible.

I had been meeting up with Detective Bailey for almost three months, trying to help him get information on Hi-C. But because of my inability to find anything even close to bringing him down, we decided that seeing what was in his highly-secured file cabinet was probably the best route to go. Courtesy of a judge who apparently owed Detective Bailey a favor, he was able to obtain a bogus search warrant and we planned the perfect evening for it all to go down.

It was a cool Spring night in April, and Isis was on an overnight business trip with her firm. Whenever she'd leave for them- usually every third weekend of the month- I would make it my business to be in her house laid up with her man. Hi-C didn't care that he was disrespecting her by having me over, especially since he had a gut feeling that these so-called 'trips' were actually just getaway time that she could spend with her own side piece.

The bust was planned to happen in the wee hours of the night. I was iffy about being present when it all went down but Detective Bailey felt I would appear a lot less suspicious had I been arrested alongside Hi-C.

He definitely had a sharp mind when it came down to catching the people he went after. He had planned the whole thing to a tee and started doing so when the idea first came to him at the table. Before we left each other that evening, he enrolled a fake contact, *Sharon*, into my phone and began sending messages to me. They were just random *'Hey, what's up'* texts of that nature to give off a vibe that Sharon was a real person and that we were real friends. So, when Bailey's signal text '*What's the move for tonight?'* came to my phone on the night of the bust, it would all fall into play. Once the text was sent, I would respond back by saying either 'Yeah, I'm going out' or 'No, I'm staying in.' The word OUT in the text would signify that it was a no-go and to have his team pull *out*. The word IN meant for them to come on and run up *in* the spot. The squat team had Hi-C's house surrounded by twelve, so the whole time I was freaking on him they were already positioned and ready. At 2:12am exact, was the time when he would send me the message and wait for my cue.

After I had finished pleasing Hi-C, I went straight into the bathroom to clean myself up. I left my phone near him on purpose because I wanted him to possibly see some of the texts that this make-believe person and I had been sending each other. I even mentioned to him that 'Sharon' had been pressuring me into going out with her later on, but I wasn't sure if I would go. He questioned me a little about how we'd met and suggested that I should indeed link up with her and enjoy myself.

I spent about fifteen minutes in the bathroom that was conveniently located down the hall from the master bedroom. The baby blue water theme that decorated it slightly put me at ease, but was unable to completely rid me of the nervous feeling I felt inside. On top of that, being alone in his shower allowed me to do something that I really didn't want to do- think about what was getting ready to happen. Regardless of Hi-C's bullshit, he had been a great man to me. If it wasn't for him, I didn't know where I would be. I thought about just running out there and telling him the truth, but then I thought about spending even a simple day in jail for betraying Detective Bailey and decided to just stick to the plan.

After showering, I dressed myself in a long-sleeved fitted black shirt with matching black tights, then covered up with one of Hi-C's favorite robes. My choice of clothes was made only to prepare me for what the night would bring. I wanted to be comfortable in that holding cell I knew I would soon be spending a few hours in.

"Hey babe," I said after I came out of the bathroom and twirled around once to show him how good I looked in his night clothing. "I've been meaning to ask you, what's up with all this water-themed shit in your damn house?"

When I stopped myself from turning I looked to Hi-C, who even though I somewhat wanted him to, surprisingly had my phone in his hand. The room was very dim so the light from the screen shined in his direction, allowing me to see every hurtful emotion he displayed on his face. There was just no way I left any hints in my phone about the bust, but the way Hi-C was looking I just knew he must have saw something.

"So this is what it's come to Keisha?" he asked as he disappointingly glared down at my cell.

"Look, I can explain," I panicked, "I had no other choice. He was gonna lock me-"

"Motherfuckin' Tre?" he interrupted me. "Out of all the niggas you could have fucked with, you go back to fuckin' with Tre?"

A sigh of relief exited my lips. "Tre?...*Ohhh...Tre*....baby please, it's not what you think. I saw him after the club one night. I was drunk, he was drunk...I'm sorry. It meant nothing."

"Nothing?" he mocked me. "These texts don't look like they mean nothing."

I rolled my eyes at his comment and he continued.

"I can't believe this," he said. "I created this big ass beef with my blood relative and the only reason I didn't trip about him not fuckin' with me no more was because I thought you were worth it."

"What's that supposed to mean?" I shouted. Now I was the one beginning to get heated. "Really I mean, what do you expect me to do? Just sit around and wait for you to leave your wife. Well, I'm tired of waiting Hi-C. I have needs too."

"Needs? Let's not talk about needs because the last time I checked every need you ever had, I made it happen for you. That apartment, that car, that trip to the mountains you had been dreaming about. I did that so what other needs are you implying? Huh?...You trynna say I'm not man enough for you in the bed, where you got to be going out with the enemy making me look bad and shit? I can't handle my biz or something?"

I laughed a little in my head and hoped that I wouldn't be forced to answer that. I'm sure a sixteen-year-old virgin could have handled his business better than Hi-C's poodle-stroking ass.

"You're overreacting," I tried to convince him. "What do you want me to say? I'm sorry okay."

"You're sorry now but that don't take back what you did," he sighed. "And the sad part about it is that I know you're still going to be fucking him."

"Well how about this?" I said, then made a suggestion of my own. "I'll stop fucking Tre the same day you leave Isis."

"What? Keisha are you crazy or something. I've told you already, I'm not going to leave my wife. She's going to have to leave me. I take that 'through thick and thin' shit very seriously."

"But you know she's never gonna do that. You expect me to just sit here and meet up with you wheneva she happens to go out of town? Well I'm tired of these side chick regulations. I thought you told me I was more than that."

I walked over to Hi-C, sat next to him on the bed, and gripped one side of his face with one of my hands. "Baby, I want holidays. I want getaways that aren't secret. I want to be able to brag to the world about the man I love. But most importantly, I want a family."

My eyes began to get teary thinking about those abortions. I wished I would have kept at least one baby to have some type of hold on him, and his money. I was stupid to take his advice and go through with that. And I hated myself for it.

"Please don't start that crying shit," he said after he witnessed a flush of water circle around my eyeballs. "You know just like I know that I'm in no position to do that. I'm involved in too much shit and I have way too many enemies. Motherfuckers in my line of work will come after yo' kids if shit don't go 'dey way. I wouldn't subject a child to this type of lifestyle. When I chose to hustle, I chose to sacrifice certain things. A family was one of them."

"Oh please," I disagreed. "They're plenty of big-time dealers who raise good kids. And you got more of an advantage than anybody because you can afford the best for yours. Hell, ain't much your kid would ever want for. It's lil' muthafuckas in the projects that wish they could simply spend the night in a house like this, let alone live here. I don't understand it. There's got to be a reason you're going on forty and don't want kids. Really, what are you so afraid of?"

"I'm not afraid of anything alright!" he suddenly yelled out. I could tell he was getting very frustrated but I continued to push his button anyway.

"There's gotta be something," I said. "Just tell me."

"Keisha, please. Just leave it alone. I don't want to discuss this anymore."

"Is it trust?" I continued to badger him. I could sense that he was growing impatient with me, but I also knew there was something he was hiding. "Is that what it is? You just don't trust people?"

"I don't have trust issues. Reality is, you gotta trust a lot of people in this business. Keisha, I'm warning you…let...it…go."

Hearing Hi-C use trust and business in the same sentence gave me the perfect opportunity to pick him for the information I needed, and I knew just the way to do it.

"Speaking of business," I said, "you don't even trust me with that shit."

"What do you mean I don't trust you with my business? That's crazy. I trust you more than anybody, even my own damn wife."

"Shit, you damn near took my fingers off the time we were in yo' office and I simply pointed at that file cabinet in there. *Your wife* can count your money and I bet *your wife* has access to that file cabinet. But you trust me more than her. Please."

"I've been married to Isis for almost eleven years," he said, "and even she don't have access to that cabinet."

"Well what's in it so much that you can't show anybody!" I purposely yelled. I figured maybe if I put up a tantrum he would give me what I wanted.

"Keisha, I told you…let that shit go."

"No! This is not even about that damn cabinet," I lied. "It's about the trust you claim you have with me. Well, if you trust me like you say you do, then you'd tell me. Now what's in it?"

"I said leave it alone!" he shouted. "I'm warning you!"

"Warning me? Is that a threat!" I began to get up in his face. "Because I'm not Isis. You're not gonna slap the shit outta of me and think that I'm just gonna sit there and take it. You got the wrong bitch for that."

"Keisha watch your mouth," he said. "I'm trying to be cool with you. Leave it alone, or else..."

"Or else what?!" I put my index up to his forehead. "What are you gonna do? Chop my finger off? Huh? Or does it not bother you since your face is not a fuckin' file cabinet?"

"That's it!" he shouted. "You really wanna know what's in that cabinet?!"

"Yes, I really do!" I yelled back.

"Alright, fuck it!"

Hi-C snatched my hand away from his face and began dragging me down the hall. The strength of his grip crushed my fingertips in a painful way. He moved so swiftly that my legs weren't even able to keep up with each other.

"Ouch, you're hurting me," I cried as I passed by every room in the hallway, looking inside each of them like I never saw them before. I hoped that there was someone in one who could have possibly saved me from this man who had clearly gone mad.

Hi-C made it to his office door and broke the code faster than I ever saw him do it before. Then he threw me down into his chair so hard that I rolled back and the only thing that stopped me was the wall I slammed in to.

"Is this what you want?" he shouted, before pushing his fingertips up against another security device that opened the cabinet. "Here, you got it!"

Hi-C then slammed a folder down on the desk and a few articles seeped out. I used my trembling legs to slowly roll the chair back over to the desk and boy was I excited on the inside. I had finally gotten the information I needed to take back to Detective Bailey and I was glad that obtaining it didn't have to involve guns and hundreds of police officers.

"It's all there," he said, as his body began to weaken and he slowly sunk to the floor. He planted himself down on the carpet and folded his legs Indian-style then began to weep. Hi-C would never get caught putting his bare feet on the floor, so to see him sitting down there in nothing but his boxers let me know that something was terribly wrong.

"You happy now," he cried.

I will be in a second, I said to myself as I finally made it to the desk and opened up a manila folder. Inside, on the very top of the stack, a full-sized portrait of a woman who looked similar -or shall I say damn near identical- to me revealed itself. She had the bob-cut hairstyle, the mixed-looking light skin, the narrowly-structured face, and even the full sized lips like me. It was so weird.

"Wow! she's beautiful." I said, as I grabbed my cheekbones and stared at the photo in pure amazement. "And we look just alike."

"Yeah, I know." he replied.

"Who is she?" I asked.

"My mother," he answered.

"Hi-C what the fuck?" I began to get nervous. "Please don't tell me no wild shit like were related or something."

As crazy as that would have been, it would have all made sense. I never believed my mother was really my mother anyway. There was just no way someone as ugly as her could have created someone as beautiful as me.

"Hell no!" he shouted. "You think I'm some kind of creep or something? Believe me, you're no way kin."

"Sorry, I know. But damn…the resemblance."

"Striking isn't it?" he said. "I saw it the very first moment I laid eyes on you at The Ball and I couldn't believe it myself. I mean, just seeing your face was like traveling back in time, to the days when I felt most loved. To this day I feel that every time I look into those pretty ass eyes of yours, and out of all the chicks I've met in my life, you're the only one who has that effect on me. That's why I keep you around."

I heard everything Hi-C had said to me, and yes it meant a lot, but the only thing I could concerned myself with was the woman who looked just like me.

"Where is she now?" I asked.

"She's dead," he began to sob. "They're all dead. And it's all my fault."

"What? Wait, who's all dead? Herbert Isaac, what are you talking about? Please talk to me."

Hi-C began to blankly stare at something on the wall. When I looked up to see what it was, I realized it was the weird big portrait of him, the little boy, the middle-aged white couple, and the strange young lady in the background. I also notice that this strange woman was the same woman he just identified as his mother. I was surely confused.

"Calm down baby," I told him. "Just calm down and talk to me. I'm here for you."

I wanted to run over and just hold him, but I began to get distracted searching at the other documents in the folder. A part of me was still looking for something in it that I could have taken back to Detective Bailey, but the other part was becoming more concerned with his past.

"Please," I said to him, as I looked at newspaper articles, more photos, and handwritten letters that I had removed from the folder. "forget everything else that happened here tonight. Just talk to me. I need to know what happened, obviously it's eating you alive."

Hi-C took a deep breath and finally began to explain. "Look I never told anyone this, but this house here is not just a house I bought when I got rich off drug money like you and everybody else I have been fuckin' lying to thinks. I was born and raised here. It belonged to the Brockington's, a rich ass white couple. My brother and I had the 'privilege' of living here simply because my mama was poor and worked for them….Mama did all the cooking, she cleaned, she took care of us, and I'm sure if the Brockington's had children she would have been taking care of them too….And she was beautiful, I mean very beautiful, and loved by everyone who knew her. The only person that seemed to hate her was that BITCH!"

Hi-C suddenly threw one of his lion-structured floor pieces at the portrait on the wall, hitting the mean-looking white woman directly in the face. Although the thick glass didn't break, what Hi-C did break was his own rule of never disrespecting women. Really, it was the first time I had ever heard him call one out of her name.

"*Ole natsy ass bitch Linda Brockington*," he shocked me again. "I wouldn't even shit on her grave if I had diarrhea and it was the only thing on this Earth that I could sit my ass on. She was a hateful something and the way she treated my mama was a shame. I mean, any name you could think of, from whore to trash to nigger, Linda called her. And it was even worse when Dave wasn't around."

"Who's Dave?" I asked.

"Her husband, the breadwinner," he pointed to the man in the picture who was standing over Linda wearing a clearly artificial smile. "He owned half of a big insurance company here and he had money out the ass. I liked the guy too. I mean, he was rarely home but when he was it brought a sense of peace to the house. And he always took time out of his busy day to spend with me and my brother. He would play baseball with us in the backyard, teach us how to swim in the pool, take us hunting, all sorts of shit. A real goodhearted dude, and unlike Mrs. Brockington, he treated my mom with the upmost respect….Until I found out why."

Hi-C rose from the carpet and began to look around the room as if he was sizing it up. I watched him with two wide eyes as he started to moved his arms like a person would if they were positioning where to put furniture. Then went over to the counter where his mini bar stand was, pulled it out from the wall, got behind it and squatted.

"I was about right here," he told me. "This was an old room used for storing shit and because of all the junk inside none of us were allowed. Me and my brother would sometimes play hide-n-seek and since I always went out of my way to win, I would go places I knew his scary ass wouldn't dare to look. On this particular day, I hid in this room right in this spot, behind an old rusty dresser. I stayed here for about an hour, and well, ended up falling asleep, only to be wakened by someone busting into the closet."

Hi-C dashed deeper behind his bar stand and began to peep out towards the office door. His demonstrations were so vivid that I only wondered if he actually believed he was back in his past for real.

"I thought it was my brother trynna play tough, so I hid deeper," he continued. "but then when I looked up I saw that it wasn't him, but Mama and Mr. Brockington, sneaking in there. They quickly, but quietly, started doing things my eyes should not have seen, but that's what kept my bad ass looking. I swear I watched them make love all the way til' the end and I wouldn't have gotten caught if all that dust from that old dirty dresser didn't make me sneeze."

Hi-C laughed hard to himself. So hard, that I too wanted to know what was funny.

"What?" I asked. "What's so funny?"

"Nothing," he chuckled a bit more. "You just should have seen the look on both of their faces when they saw me. My mama had a handful of titties trynna explain to me that the shit wasn't what it looked like. Then she snatched me up and dragged me out to the shed- that's where we were living- and beat my twelve-year-old ass like I was a grown damn man."

Hi-C's laugh slowly faded. "It's funny now, but it wasn't back then. I was hurt by that shit. Hell, my mama wouldn't kill a damn spider if it was biting her on her ass and she damn sure didn't believe in hitting her kids. So when she whipped me like that I knew it wasn't just because I was somewhere I wasn't supposed to be. No, I was smart enough to know the real reason, it was because of what I saw."

"Later that night," he continued, "she pulled me around the side of the shed and told me it was about time that I knew the truth about our family. She also made me promise I would not repeat a thing to my brother since he was only five years old. He wouldn't understand that my mother was in love with a white man who was married and he sure as hell wouldn't understand that this white man was our real dad."

Shit. Some Maury type stuff, I thought to myself then looked at the picture, where I now noticed that Hi-C did look like a cross between his mom and Mr. Brockington. That also explained his mixed complexion, curly hair, and weird eye color. Hi-C paused for a second, which gave me a quick moment to glance down at the time. It was now two o'clock. He still had my cell phone tightly in his hand and I knew it would only be a matter of time before Detective Bailey would text me. I wanted to go over and take it from him but I was too caught up in wanting to know more that I didn't bother to move.

"She told me that they were in love and had been for many years. She also told me that they had been ready to move away and start a life together, but the only thing stopping them was miserable ass Mrs. Brockington. She couldn't live with the fact that her husband would rather be with a nigger than her and she sholl 'nuff didn't want the people 'round town to find out. So, she paid lots of money to have a shed built in the backyard so that she could hide us in it."

"Like y'all some damn animals," I said. "And Dave just allowed her to do it?"

"No not really, Mrs. Brockington's dad was the Sheriff and her granddad was a judge. They were all deep-rooted racists, and even I knew that. She threatened that if mama were to run away or tell anyone our secret she would pin a crime on her so big she'd never see the light of day. Mr. Dave knew firsthand his wife had the power to do it, so he just decided it was best that they played by her rules.

"Fucked up," I shook my head.

"Yeah I know, but it gets much worse. One day, my mama comes to me- I was thirteen then- and she was the happiest I'd ever seen her probably in my whole life. She sits me down after dinner and told me that her and Mr. Dave had a long talk with Mrs. Brockington and we were finally gonna do it, finally gonna pack up and live a life together. 'No more hiding, no more being afraid' as she put it."

Hi-C finally came from behind the counter and took his place back on the floor, even though a chair was right in front of him. The little bit of chipper attitude he had before slowly started to wither away, taking him back to that blank and empty stare.

"It was winter and the shed was so cold that night. Mrs. Brockington didn't ever allow us to have heat back there so the three of us would stay warm by bundling up together under one flimsy sheet. Mr. Brockington would sometimes creep a space heater to us, but we'd only have a few hours to enjoy it because he would have to sneak it back inside before he left for work in the mornings."

"I remember I couldn't sleep that night, just thinking about how we were gonna leave and where we were gonna go. I used to steal Mr. Brockington's cigarettes then sneak out of the shed after everyone fell asleep and puffed on them. I never got caught either, mainly because the door was so light and fragile that it never even made a sound as it opened and closed. It didn't even lock."

"I would always go a short ways out into the woods, sit on this little wooden stoop and just think sometimes. On this night, I thought about all of us dressed in little back ninja suits, running through the woods until we got to a car that looked like batman's. Then we'd hopped in and bobbed through traffic while Mrs. Brockington's dad, granddad, and the whole damn police department chased us until we lost them. I remembered quietly jumping and leaping around the woods acting like I was really a ninja fighting off police officers and racists."

Hi-C laughed again, but it didn't last long. "That's until I heard something and I had to dash behind a tree. When I felt it was safe to look, I peeped around to see what my imagination thought would have been a big bear or something, only to find out that it was something much worse- it was FIRE!"

"Oh my god baby," I said, placing my hand over my mouth in disbelief. In fact, if it wasn't for the newspaper article I was holding in my hand that read, BROCKINGTON FAMILY NANNY AND CHILD KILLED IN BLAZE, I probably wouldn't have believed it. There was also another article behind it that had a younger picture of Hi-C, and Mrs. Brockington smiling. This one read HUMANATARIAN AWARD DEDICATED TO LINDA BROCKINGTON FOR THE ADOPTION OF HER NANNY'S OLDEST SON.

"That fire took my mother, my brother, and Mr. Dave."

"Mr. Dave? He died in the fire too?"

"No. Killed himself a week later. Left his suicide note in his shirt pocket. It's in there," he pointed at the folder I was looking over.

I found the letter and began to look over it. Just by the first words... *'I can't bear to live in this world without'*...I knew he loved that woman.

"Investigators said the fire started with the space heater. It was already hard for him knowing that the love of his life was gone, but to know that he was the one who brought us the heater made it all worse."

"Damn," I shook my head. "And what happened to you then? You were the child that Mrs. Brockington adopted?"

"Yeah because of her guilt. But mainly because of the fact that she was a 'hero' in the town's eyes. I hated every second of it because I knew secretly how she felt about my existence, although I can't say she mistreated me. In fact, she put me in the finest schools, dressed me in the finest clothes, and I lived the finest life. But none of it made me happy because those things couldn't bring my family back. I mean everyone envied my life, but I couldn't wait until I was eighteen so that I could fake going to college and ditch Mrs. Brockington's ass."

"Well, what happened to her?" I asked. "Mrs. Brockington."

"She had a bad stroke, but that didn't kill her. As a matter of fact, she made a full recovery and would have been going home the next day. For some strange reason, she died the night they were going to release her from the hospital."

"This is so terrible," I sympathized. Still not believing everything he had just told me. "Hi-C, I never knew you went through this. I can't imagine the pain you must go through and now I understand. Your lack of care for material things…the reason you snapped on Isis for disrespecting me…this house…that shed. It all make sense now."

"Yeah pretty much explains a lot of it," he said. "You see, because I was legally their son, the Brockington's left all their money to me and that's how I got rich. I just used some of it to start my own shit in the game. Everybody thinks I'm the man who came from nothing, but really I'm just a pretender who was born with everything. I just get high off the fame, the respect, and all the love because it's something that I rarely had growing up. My mama would kill me if she knew what I was doing and how I was getting money and every night when the darkness comes I think about it. Keisha, it really is eating me alive and beginning to be too much. I want out so bad but so many people depend on me, everybody from the dealers to the users. I just sit here every day and wait on some sort of breakthrough. Hell, someone to take me away from here, rob me, blow my fuckin' brains out or something, shit. At least that way I can be back with my family."

"Baby, don't say that." I told him. "Please don't talk that way."

"Why not?" he asked. "What do I have here? Who do I have here? I made you kill all my seeds and really all I have left are just a bunch of people hanging around simply because of who I am. Hell, I wouldn't have gotten a woman as beautiful as my wife if I was just a regular Joe Blow. You wouldn't have even…."

"Wait a minute now," I cut him off. "Yes I admit, at first it was the idea of you, but after hanging around and getting to really know you I started falling in love for reasons that don't involve your rep or your money. I can tell you a million reasons other than that of why I think you're special. So please, don't put me in that category."

"I know Keisha and for some crazy, strange reason I believe you," he sighed. "Look, my imagination is just as big as it was when I was a little boy and I still dream just the same. Sometimes I picture myself packing up and leaving all this shit behind- the money, the game, just everything. I mean, I always have this vision of me riding in a classic old school Buick with only the clothes on my back and just enough gas to take me across the country, going somewhere where I can start all over…I really see myself riding down this highway, with the least bit of worries, and when I look over to my right the person whose riding shotgun is always ..well…you."

"Me?" I asked. "But why?"

"Because I love you…I'm in love with you and I don't care what anybody thinks about it. Fuck Tre…fuck Isis…fuck the different worlds that we come from…and fuck this damn dope game. Let's do what my mom and dad never got a chance to do. Let's leave all this shit behind and start fresh…just me and you…us against the world….before it's too late…what do you say?"

I just sat there in my chair, staring down at Hi-C while carefully digesting everything he had just dropped on me. Just for him to be able to trust me with his past let me know that he was sincere about having some type of future with me, but for him to say those three letter words, took it to a whole other level. I didn't care about anything at the moment…not the money…not Detective Bailey…not even the team of men outside waiting on my signal. My mind was made up.

"Okay, I'll go." I said, then looked to Hi-C who now had his face in my phone tapping his fingers on the screen. "Wait, what are you doing?"

"Nothing, Sharon just texted you and wanted to know if you were still going out tonight, but you're not going anywhere. You're staying in with me."

I threw the papers out of my hand and rushed over to get the phone from Hi-C.

"WAIT BABY, NO!"

But it was too late….

PART TWO

CHAPTER 15: OPERATION SHUT DOWN

"**I** can't believe I let that muthafucka play me," I yelled to myself after slamming my fist against the hard, white concrete wall of my jail cell. The impact almost shattered my fragile little bones.

I had been behind bars for almost six days- that's six days longer than what Detective Bailey told me I would have to. And the more the days passed, the more I felt like he had betrayed me. It looked as if he used me to get to Hi-C and was probably gonna eventually throw us all under the jail.

I took my place along the cold, hard mat and was just about to let out a gut-wrenching cry until the smell of my cellmates stink juice box slapped my nostrils. With no shame, she pulled down her pants and let out a long piss. The girl didn't seem to be at all bothered by being locked up and I could tell by her rugged, street demeanor that she was no stranger to the place.

"This fuckin' P.O. better not deny my bond," she said as her urine trickled into the rusty toilet that sat at the corner of the cell. I didn't even respond to her because I didn't care about her or her damn P.O. Instead I just laid down across the thin mat and decided to cry silently, only to be interrupted by a couple stomps and a loud voice that let out the long awaited words I could have done anything to hear. "Lakeisha Black! Time to pack it up!"

Without hesitating, I jumped from my mat and followed the male correctional officer as he led me through what I consider the most joyous walk of my life. I was released, took what little items I had brought in with me, and proceeded to meet this mysterious person who had bailed me out.

"Your party is there," the officer said, pointing to a woman in a housekeeping uniform that I had never saw a day in my life. Even though I was glad to be out of there, I didn't trust leaving with anyone I didn't know.

"That's not my-" I said before the lady quickly grabbed my belongings then pointed to her name badge that read 'O. BAILEY.' Those were the detective's initials so I immediately knew to keep quiet and simply go with the flow. I followed this mysterious lady out the door to an all-black Lincoln with very dark-tinted windows. As she guided me, I couldn't help but admire her beautiful body and nonchalant demeanor. Her face was brown and slim and her hair was pulled back in one ponytail that swayed to the rhythm of her steps. She also had a very militant persona which let me know for damn sure that the dusty housekeeping outfit was just a facade.

This strange lady said no words, nor did I dare ask her a single thing, as we rode about an hour to the Lake Meyer park on the southside of Ordale. The park was always full of people who exercised, played basketball, tennis, and even raced remote controlled cars. She carefully drove me to a secluded, wooded area near a marsh and as we got closer I could see Detective Bailey's unmarked car parked downhill. He wasn't too far from it, gazing out at the water. I could only hope he was thinking of a good explanation of why he kept me behind bars so long.

The woman parked the car, looked back at me, and then said 'get out' without opening her mouth. I gladly exited and she rode off without even acknowledging the detective, who continued to stare out at the lake as I drifted towards him. Being the observant man he was though, I was certain he knew that I was headed in his direction.

"What the fuck!" I immediately lashed out once I got within his reach. I shoved him but not too hard.

"I help you and you just leave me in jail for a whole week. Do you know how miserable I was?"

Detective Bailey flinched at my aggression but seemed to be unbothered by it.

"Helped me?" he laughed, then slightly began to get aggressive himself. "You call embarrassing me in front of my whole team helping me? You played me, Keisha. And you know it. I bet you and Hi-C are having a good laugh at this shit. Shoulda never trusted you."

I snatched back from Bailey's grip and followed him as he walked closer to the water. "I didn't play you. Hell, how was I supposed to know that his security box was filled with pictures? We both got played."

"And how am I supposed to know you didn't drop the dime on Hi-C about me bustin' in on him. You're his girl, right. I mean side chick."

"So now you wanna go there," his words cut me deep. "Look, I never told you I knew for sure what was in that safe. I only assumed because of the way he protected it. That information still has to be inside his home. I just have to find out exactly where, just give me-"

"Look, I'm done with the shenanigans," he stopped me. "I will not risk looking like a complete idiot again. I should have just took my chances locking you up in the beginning like my first mind told me to."

"No, please. I can still get you the information you need. Just let me go to his house, talk to him, and see where his head is at. Then we can go from there."

"I'm afraid you can't do that." Detective Bailey walked towards his car.

"Why not?"

"Because he's still locked up."

What? I thought. I was upset to hear that but I did not want Detective Bailey to think I cared too much. He was already starting to believe that I was on Hi-C's side."

"Why is he...?" I began to shout, but then quickly simmered down. "I mean why would he still be locked up. You have nothing on him."

"Obstruction," he replied.

Obstruction? I thought back the week before to Detective Bailey and his team busting into Hi-C's home and rushing right to the office room. Of course, Hi-C drew his weapon, but it was only in self-defense. Unfortunately Bailey's swift instinct and strong physical abilities caused him to take Hi-C down before he even had the opportunity to open fire. Then he began to resist from the ground causing the squad to get physical, some of them striking him with their weapons. I just stood there hollering 'please stop', while acting like I didn't have a clue what was going on. The officers eventually handcuffed me and led me out of the door.

"Obstruction, *ooooh right.* " I said sarcastically. "And you mean to tell me that none of his fellow soldiers bonded him out yet. Not even his wife."

I knew Isis was upset with him, but I never thought she would stoop that low as to leave him in jail.

"Same thing I said," Detective answered. "We monitored the phone calls he made with her. They were talking in this language that none of my best translators could even understand. I mean they were using English words but none of it made sense."

Code of OMG, I thought to myself. One of Hi-C's very intelligent members came up with it. I was supposed to study it but never made the time.

We currently have him under no bond, but I don't know how long that's gonna hold up with a petty obstruction charge. Weird thing is that he hasn't requested to speak with a lawyer, asked for a hearing, or anything."

"Seems as if he doesn't want to get out if you ask me," I thought.

"That's how it seems. I really don't know what to make of any of this shit," he scratched his head.

"Well then what's gonna happen if he's locked up." I looked out to the water and found myself in deep thought worrying about the future of the only life I knew. "How's shit gonna move?"

"I can't answer that," he said. "Who's the next person he would trust to handle his business?"

"I know just the person," I smiled and began walking away from the detective. "I'm gonna hang out here at the park for a little while and enjoy the fresh smell of freedom. I'll find my own way home."

....

"Knew he'd be here," I said to myself as I pulled around the back of Hi-C's house. I parked my car slightly up the street, crept around front, and peeked to make sure Isis's car was nowhere in sight. It was around 11:00am. I figured she would be at the firm but I wasn't taking any chances. Once the coast was clear, I unlocked the latch on the gate, headed towards the shed, and planted three knocks on its door before watching it sling open.

"Hey Cederick," I threw my arms up and waved after I saw him in the doorway. He had this 'what the fuck you want' look on his face and my heart dropped because I just knew he must have known I had set the whole bust up.

"Your cousin is not here, if you finally care enough to come save her," he said.

A feeling of relief came over me as I remembered the last conversation Cederick and I had about his relationship with Charlytte. I had gotten so caught up in all the stuff regarding Detective Bailey and Hi-C that I had totally forgotten about it.

"I'm not here for Charlytte," I informed him.

"And why am I not surprised?" he answered.

"Look, I just spent seven whole days and two hours behind a funky ass jail cell. I still got the scent of musk, shitty breath, and crabby pussy in my nostrils. And don't get me started on the food, Ramon noodles with Doritos chopped inside of it was the closest thing I could get to a gourmet meal. Trust me, the last thing I'm thinking about is that petty ass argument we had. I'm just trying to find out if you heard anything from Hi-C. I was there when they busted in on him, ya know."

"You don't think I know that you were there," he said. His attitude was still the same, like nothing I just said mattered to him."

"Isis knows too," he began to look around as if he was expecting her to pull up at any minute. As a matter of fact, it's probably best you leave now. I don't want no parts in having you around here without her permission. That's Hi-C's job."

Cederick then snickered to himself, as if something funny suddenly came to him.

"You know," he continued, "you have some nerve trying to preach to me about being a bad influence on Charlytte, but you round here fuckin' a married man and shit. You ain't no better of a person than me."

"And why the fuck are you so worried about who I'm fucking?" I asked him.

Cederick looked away shamefully.

"Listen, I don't care if he's married or not, I love him and he loves me. Now I'm not leaving until you tell me what the fuck is going on."

Cederick looked around before snatching me into the shed. I quickly noticed that he had bags packed across the bed and that Charlytte was nowhere in sight. Although I wanted to ask about her whereabouts, I was more concerned with Hi-C."

"Look," he said. "Hi-C got some information from the cop he got on his payroll. They got something going on called the TMSD 'Twelve Month Shut Down.' What it is, is that the folks are gonna keep him locked up for a year and give him the max for that obstruction charge as there alibi. Then they're gonna monitor his phone lines, see who he's contacting and not contacting anymore, and if the drug activity in the streets slows down. Ya know, shit like that. Since they can't catch him while he's out, they wanna see what they can do while he's in."

"Well that explains why he's still in there," I said. Detective Bailey never mentioned that part.

"Sort of, at first he wanted to sit because niggas was talking on the inside. You know those dudes in there know more about what's going on in the streets than we do. Once he got word that they're not letting him out, he just accepted it. I don't know, it's strange to me too. Maybe he's just trying to remain strong, but Hi-C sure as hell didn't seem to care about having to sit down for a year."

I immediately thought back to the words that Hi-C told me about wanting to get out of the game. Maybe he needed this break to clear his head and try to figure out what he wanted to do with his life. I think he was burned out and if jail was the only break he had from the streets, maybe he was fine with just that.

"I don't know, that is strange." I pretended to act clueless. "Hi-C ain't built for jail."

"I know, dude hates the idea of it. Always has. I don't know Keisha. I just got a tingly feeling in my gut. Something ain't right. It's some snake shit going on. I can't put my finger on it, but I know it is."

"I don't know about all that," I tried to discourage him from the truth. "How long you thought we could hustle out here before people started talking and the folks started to run down on us. Look at the history, it happens to every organization at some point. This shit don't last forever. Maybe it's just time."

"Naw fuck that, hustling is all I know. It's all that any of us knows, even you. You probably wouldn't last a month if the shit was shut down."

"I'm a survivor, I'll do what I have to do. Speaking of shutting down, has Hi-C spoken on what he's going to do if they do keep him for a year. Do we have to wait until he comes home or does he trust us to keep shit moving while he's in there."

"That's what we're working on now. He hasn't decided yet. Between you and me, and a few other people in the crew, I know we can handle it. I've tried to convince him to pass me the torch and I believe he's thinking about it. When I find out you'll be the first to know. Now get out of here before Isis comes home. She doesn't even want me back here anymore, I bet she'll go at your throat for sure and daddy ain't here to save ya ass."

I ignored Cederick's comment, we pressed knuckles together, and then I headed back to my car. I had gotten all the information I needed on Hi-C so my trip to his house was surely a successful one. What wasn't successful though, was my bank account. I was depending on an upcoming run to put five G's in my pocket but the possibility of that happening was slim to none. Crazy, I was getting so much money and never took the time to invest in it. I would just get it and spend it because I knew I would get it right back again. Hi-C would always warn me about saving, but even I thought the OMC was untouchable. Now I understood what he was trying to tell me all along. Unfortunately it was too late. I had rent due, two car notes, a fancy Chanel bag that was calling my name, and time that was surely not on my side.

CHAPTER 16: Peaches -N- Cream

“That's what happens when you disrespect your queen," I said in my toughest, most seductive voice.

"Now take that," I swatted. "And that," I swatted again.

I could never understand what an old ass white man got out of getting chained and spanked by a beautiful black woman, but to each his own. If the old dude was paying one grand for me to beat him with a whip for an hour, who was I to question it? I hated that I had to stoop that low to get some funds, but it was an easy way to make a quick dollar so I just went with it. Most importantly, it didn't involve any sex. After all, I wasn't a prostitute and I wasn’t going back to being completely broke for nothing.

After I got done tormenting Mr. Zinc, a former city council member from Ordale, he paid me in cash and I left without even saying goodbye. He loved that disrespectful shit. Then I headed to a low-budget hotel that was located about forty-five minutes out of the city limits. I had been living there for the past few months. Money was slow so I rented my apartment out to two artsy students under the grounds that my furniture remained untouched. I even charged them an extra three hundred a month because the place was fully furnished. Luckily, the two rich white girls had no problem giving me fifteen a month for the place. My plan was to let them live there until we got the okay to start moving work again, but the decision was coming longer than I expected. Between the thousand dollars I made from Mr. Zinc and the rent money I collected, I had enough to make the cheap two-hundred dollar a week hotel payments while still buying enough clothes, shoes, and VIP tickets to keep people in the city thinking I was still on top of the world.

Everyone was affected by the bust. Even Cederick, who had turned back to pimping girls and robbing folks to make his ends meet. I had even heard from my friend Alicia that he was back snorting cocaine. I also got word that my cousin Charlytte was spotted with a chick named Peaches, who was the biggest trick in the city, so that confirmed to me that she had fallen victim to the life of prostitution. If only I could have saved her. But hey, I had my own problems to worry about.

....

It was a hot summer day and I was headed to the mall to find a nice outfit to wear. I had planned on going out with Shannon and Alicia to the club that night. Alicia had become closer to me than Shannon because I didn't have to worry about her trying to get too involved in my personal business. She was only an associate of mine. Not anyone that would be expecting to come by and see the new place that I had lied to everyone and told that I had gotten. I tried to act like I had my shit together, but really I had fallen off bad. Unfortunately, it was my top priority to try to stay on top, which honestly just added to my struggle. I didn't care though. When you lived under the spotlight for so long, the last thing you wanted was for people to know that you had crumbled. Especially since most of them are praying for your downfall anyway.

I grabbed my purse and headed for my car, only to hear a familiar voice stop me in my tracks.

"So that's how you treat your good ole partner," Detective Bailey crept up behind me, almost giving me a heart attack. "You just move away and don't even call."

"I am not your partner," I replied. "And I didn't move anywhere. I'm just here visiting a friend."

"Does this *friend* happen to be related to the other *two friends* that are now living in your apartment?"

Detective Bailey was stalking me again and I didn't like it one bit.

"Look," I got straight to the point, "just tell me what you want from me?"

"Just wanna talk to you. That's it."

"I'm listening," I sassed him.

"No," he pointed up to the second floor of the hotel, directly where my room was located. "Upstairs. In your *new apartment*."

"Like I said, I'm visiting a friend."

Unwillingly, I led Detective Bailey up to my room. We entered and were greeted by all the fancy clothes, shoes, and purses that were neatly placed around the room. Without question, he knew the place belonged to me and confirmed it with his sarcasm.

"Bit of an upgrade from your last spot," he joked.

I wasn't amused.

"Look, I'm busted okay. You got me. This is where I've been staying. Yep, this is what I've been lowered down too. All because of you and your damn investigation. If this is what you wanted, to see me miserable, well you should be happy because you got it."

"Seeing you in this run down hotel is the last thing I wanted. But the way I look at it, if you can blow seven hundred dollars on club VIPs and expensive bottles of champagne for you and your little posse, then I guess there may be a reason why you're living like this."

"Oh brother," I shook my head because I knew exactly what Detective Bailey was talking about.

He was referring to the last event I attended, which was only a week prior. A hot new rapper came down and I spent exactly seven hundred dollars that night. The detective was really doing his homework on me.

"You don't got nothin' better to do than to harrass poor ol' me," I asked him. "You already know ain't no REAL money being made over here, so what would be the point?"

"Everything ain't always about money, Keisha," he said. "The quicker you learn that, the better off you will be."

"I don't know what world your living in, but in mines money is everything. They didn't make the saying, 'money makes the world go round' for nothing."

Detective Bailey laughed, not with me but at me, and decided it would be best to just get to the point of why he had come there in the first place.

"Look," he handed me a piece of paper. "I'm serving you this subpoena. Your boyfriend has court next week and we need you to testify on what happened the night we busted in on you. I just need you to do exactly what you would do if you didn't know me. Take up for him. Let them know he acted in self-defense."

"I'm confused Detective, so you want me to talk against you."

"Exactly."

I stood there with a blank expression on my face, not knowing what to make of all the mess. Detective Bailey sure knew how to complicate my life. Just when things were already bad, he comes and makes it worse.

"Here's the deal, " he explained. "I never stepped foot in that club to know how much money you spent. A reliable source told me that. To be honest, my only objective was getting folks talking. If I start telling people to keep an eye out for you, they'll know that I'm watching you and they'll least expect that we're working together. You go on that stand, you ride for Hi-C and say whatever you need to say to incriminate me. You want him to believe that you're on his side, even if you have to lie. It seems you're good at that."

I began to understand Detective Bailey's theory and I had to admit, it was a clever one. Of course, people are going to be talking about how the Feds are watching, especially with everyone knowing Hi-C was locked up.

Before seeing him out, Detective Bailey made it his business to let me know how important it was that I showed up. He told me if I didn't he would cut all ties with me then throw me under the jail. I already knew I wasn't built for that life so I quickly decided it would be in my best interest to show up.

“Exactly one week from today,” he reminded me. “Be there or be there."

I walked Detective Bailey out the door and waited about five minutes to make sure he was gone before leaving. Then I headed to my vehicle to continue on my journey to the mall. Before exiting the parking lot, I found myself sitting in a daze, just thinking about how I would feel seeing Hi-C for the first time in three months at the trial. I had not had any type of contact with him, because under Detective Bailey's orders, I wasn't allowed to. I didn't think Hi-C felt any type of way about it though, he was a street dude who knew the game. In our business, silence spoke louder than words. One thing was for sure, the detective had now opened a can of beans that I really wasn't expecting to swallow.

Ordale City Mall was packed as usual, but it was even more thick since a party was going on at a local club in the night to come. Everyone was trying to get their last minute fits and make sure they were fly for one of the hottest acts in our area. A night like this Hi-C would have the VIP section lit, but with him being locked down the vibe wouldn't be the same. Yet still, I knew that the OMC crew would all be there reppin' his name and keeping the OMC legacy alive.

I spent about two hours in the mall and ended up with a nice black dress and a pair of knee-high leather boots to match. To top it off, I found some cute silver accessories in a pricy jewelry store. I knew I went well over my budget but I didn't care when it came to putting on for my city. Besides, I just made another easy thousand from Mr. Zinc, so I had a little something extra to flex with.

Once I was done shopping, I realized I had worked up an appetite. I quickly made my way over to the food court and ordered me some Chinese rice and steamed vegetables. Then I took a seat at one of the tables and decided to devour my meal there. That was before I was interrupted by a tap on my shoulder bone.

"Is this who I think it is?" a strange voice called out. "Keisha Black?"

I turned to see a slightly familiar-looking girl staring back at me. She had a lollipop hanging from her plump lips.

"Peaches?" I asked.

"The one and only," she flattered her worn-out self.

I quickly covered my food so that none of her slutty germs would contaminate my meal. For all I knew, she probably had just got done fucking in one of those bathrooms for a cheap pair of leggings.

Peaches and I were never best friends, but we were good associates back in high school. I secretly did not like her because she was one of the few in the school that was just as pretty as I was. It didn't help that she won prom queen over me either, although I still believe I was cheated out of the crown. Peaches mom had died in a car accident shortly before graduation and people pitied her. That was also probably the reason she started doing drugs and turned trick because after that the girl was never really the same.

"Hey girl, it's good to see ya. Still looking good," I lied.

"You don't have to compliment me. I know I'm a hot mess out here," she admitted. "But it is what it is. Dis da life I was dealt."

"Yeah, I feel you on that." I told her.

"You mind if I sit witcha?" Peaches asked and before I could politely shut her down, she flopped her dusty self right beside me. I quickly closed my plate and prayed that no particles from her body landed on my food.

“I’m sorry. I was just about to head out, hun." I lied again.

“Oh, I thought you were eating here. I literally just saw you sit down."

“Yeah, you know how it is when that hunger strikes. I just needed a quick bite to satisfy my crazy stomach. I'm going to enjoy the rest of it at home."

"Oh okay. I heard that," she smacked on the lollipop and then withdrew it from her mouth. "Which way you headed?"

I knew she was going to ask me for a ride and had I known which way she was going, I would have said the opposite direction. I'm sure Peaches knew not to ask me if I was going a particular place though, because she knew nine times out of ten I was going to lie about it. She was a professional game-runner.

Just as I was thinking about a good lie to come up with, I realized that I had Peaches Johnson standing in my face, the sidekick of Cederick and the person who could give me some real insight on what my baby cousin Charlytte was doing hanging around them. Why didn't I think of this before?

"What, you need a lift?" I asked.

"Yeah, just to Cloverdale, if you don't mind." Then she reached in her bra and pulled out a few damped one dollar bills. "I have gas money."

"Don't worry about it," I said, disgusted. "I was going that way anyway. Come with me. I'm parked at the main entrance."

Peaches followed me out to the car and then we headed to the west side of town. It was only about ten minutes from the mall, but I purposely took the long route. There were some things Peaches and I needed to discuss.

"So Peaches," I said as I turned my radio up just a few notches. Jill Scott's *'The Way'* blessed our ears. "How's life been treating you, honestly girl?"

"Girl life is life. I don't expect much out of it no more. On the bright side, it can't get no worse than it already is. I just get my money from these sucka ass dudes to get by, and then I get on."

"Yeah, I know that's right." I boosted her ego. "Get them before they get you. That's my motto."

"Oh-kay," peaches snapped her fingers in agreeance.

"You still fuckin' with Cederick though?" I asked. "He seems to be kinda low-key lately."

"Peaches rolled her eyes at the sound of his name. "Girl, don't even get me started up on that fool. That's my baby tho. He actually just hit me right after Hi-C went down. "

"Oh word."

"Yeah, I knew it was coming though. Only time he calls is when he needs some extra money. Now he's saying he wants me to find more girls and he's gonna start trynna take percentages and shit. See, I like it when he makes his own damn money 'cause he don't bother me as long as I keep the rent paid in that house. Now he gonna be all in my pockets and shit."

"Sounds like Cederick to me," I said. "So, did you find more girls? Cause I think I know someone who may be interested."

"Oh cool," she said. "Send 'em on down Jefferson then. But naw, I haven't recruited any of these hoes yet."

A sigh of relief exited my body.

"Although there is one girl...," she thought abruptly, "but I don't know what the fuck is up with lil' mama."

Suddenly, a lump appeared in my throat and a rush of adrenaline came over my entire body. I tried my best to act normal though.

"What do you mean?"

"Well girl, Ced calls me one day and asks me to meet him at this hotel. When I get there he comes down to the car and tells me that he has this young girl up in there that needed to get 'broke in' 'cause he was about to introduce her to the game."

"What the fuck is *broke in*?" I asked her.

"Just this thing where he gets me to show them there first lesbian experience. Kinda get them used to being with men and women, but at the same time playing with their minds and self-esteem. Girls who do that feel shitty about themselves and them hoes will more likely be the ones who do anything for you at the snap of a finger. I'm actually the one who put him on to the shit."

"Y'all hell," I pretended to laugh with her while clinching my fist tightly together. A part of me wanted to punch her dead in her dried-up face, but I didn't want to blow my cover. Besides, I needed to hear more.

"Yeah, it's a total mind fuck," she bragged. "But anyway, I get to the spot and there's this young ass chick sitting there naked. She was so scared that her lips were shivering. Kinda reminded me of my first time."

"Wait a minute. First off, was she bad? I would hope Cederick didn't hook you up with no ugly bitch."

"Now don't get me wrong, she definitely was cute. Slim-thick, brown-skinned, with a helluva body. She did have this little scar across her face that was a little creepy, but other than that she got an A+ in my book. But anyway, I go in there, lick her down, and she returned the favor. Little more work, but not bad for her first time."

Peaches began to laugh again and this time it really took everything in me not to smash her face wide open. I couldn't believe Charlytte let Peaches dirty mouth ass touch her. That alone told me how gullible she really was and let me know that she had no clue what was really going on in the streets. Everyone knew Peaches was a hoe. And I mean everyone.

"Girl you crazy," I shot her one more artificial chuckle.

"But I don't know how long this chick gon' last in this world," she continued. "She's just too open now."

"What do you mean, *too open*?" I asked. I knew I must have been beginning to sound like the police, but Peaches didn't seem to think anything of it.

"She's not that little naive girl she was a few months ago. She's wild now. Like really, I never seen a bitch come out of her shell so fast. Matta fact, just last week we were headed to G's spot in Jacksonville and she lifted her shirt up and showed some white man her titties at the gas station. His wife was calling the cops and we had so much shit in the car that we had to peel out fast. I mean like really, who does that? Cederick would have slapped the shit out of me if I would have tried some shit like that. But when this little bitch does it, it's okay. "

Peaches stared out of the window for a second. I could tell something was weighing heavy on her mind.

"I don't know what it is about this chick," she sighed, "but he just treats her different from the rest of us."

"Different?" I asked. "Like he could be in love with her or something."

"Love," she laughed. "You think a man that loves you gonna have you out on the streets selling pussy."

"It's definitely not love," she said, "but it's something."

Maybe it was me, but it seemed as if Peaches whole mood suddenly changed and she ceased from talking for the rest of the ride. I was about five minutes away from Cloverdale before she stopped me.

"I'm good right here sis," she said.

I knew it wasn't her destination but Peaches exited my car and tried to give me five sweaty dollar bills. As much as I could have used them, instead I gave her a twenty.

"You take care, Peaches." I told her. "I mean that."

"I'll try," she said, before stuffing the money in her panties and disappearing down an alley.

CHAPTER 17: Credible Witness

It was the morning of court and I was a complete train wreck trying to get dressed. It didn't start until ten but I wanted to give myself at least an hour head start to get there. I had to make sure I was on time and I also needed to look flawless when I saw my boo for the first time in months.

Some black casual slacks and a matching vest is what I decided to throw on for the occasion. I spent about seven hundred dollars on the pants alone, so of course I definitely looked on point. My hair displayed my usual bob, except this time I had a fancy curl over one eye. My girl Harriet hooked me up on short notice and I appreciated her so much that I tipped her a whole extra fifty bucks for doing so.

Once I was finished getting dolled up and ready, I made my exit out of the hotel. There were only a few people out that morning and that was just the way I liked it. When I entered my car, I said a brief prayer then proceeded to back out of the parking lot, only to feel a sudden rejection.

"What the fuck?" I thought to myself before seeing a man and a woman who were conversing with each other point down at the side of my car.

"Your tire," I made out the guy's lips to say.

"Excuse me?" I asked him.

"Your tire is flat," they both now clearly informed me.

"No way," I said before jumping out of my vehicle and heading to the rear passenger side of my Impala to check for myself.

True enough, my tire was as flat as a year-old Coca cola. I looked to see if I had rolled over a piece of glass but there was no sign of it.

"Oh c'mon! This can't be happening to me. At least not right now!" I shouted, while staring down at my tire for another couple seconds, as if my eyes had the power to breathe life into it.

I had only forty-five minutes to make it to the courthouse that was already thirty minutes away from where I was located. On top of that, I had to find parking in the heavy downtown area. Even if I was to get the tire changed, there was still no way possible I could make it on time.

"This just cannot be happening to me," I said after kicking my car. Then I stood up against it as if I just didn't disrespect it the way I did. Thinking of my next move, I quickly decided to call myself a taxi. I didn't really have the money to spend on one but I didn't care. I wasn't gonna end up in jail again.

I had remembered seeing the cab company's number on the front lobby's wall, so instead of wasting time trying to find it on my own, I rushed inside to get it. Luckily, the checkout counter was free.

"Excuse me," I said to the man working the desk. I was nervous and breathing fairly heavily. "My tire is flat. I have to be downtown to the courthouse in less than an hour and I need the number to the nearest cab company."

The guy carefully looked me up and down before answering. He was one of those flamboyant types so he spoke and moved with strong femininity.

"Ah mean, you kin call a cab but they pretty slow about getting to this area. If you trying to get downtown in an hour you prolly not gonna make it. Yo' bess bet is ta' catch the bus. It's right there across the street," he pointed and then looked at his watch. "It's one that comes in about five minutes and lucky for you, it's first stop is downtown. Trust me, it's the only way you'll make it on time."

"No thank you," I quickly shot him down. "I'll take my chances with the cab."

The clerk, whose name badge literally read BrianNA, shrugged his shoulders before pulling out a sticky note and writing a number down on it. Then he handed it to me and frowned as he watched me rush out the door. Deep down I knew he was right about the bus getting me there faster, but I just couldn't lower myself to that type of standard. I mean, I was Lakeisha Black, one of the baddest chicks in the city, I couldn't be caught dead on a bus.

"Good luck!" he yelled, sarcastically.

Once I made it back to my car, I looked at the phone number, back to the bus stop, and then back to the number again. I had realized it was now eleven minutes past the ten o'clock hour. I kicked my car tire one last time before silently yelling every curse word in the book at it. Regretfully, I decided to just take the walk to the bus stop. It was only a minute away, but seemed like forever. I hadn't felt that ashamed walking anywhere since the time I got caught shoplifting at the mall.

Soon enough, I made it there and sat down on the old, rusted bench. It wasn't that long after that I could feel my heart becoming heavy. The weight of going broke, living in a cooped up hotel room, and selling out my team just to keep myself from serving jail time, was all starting to sink in. I had done a pretty good job of trying to keep everything together, but I knew eventually I would reach my breaking point.

I took some tissue out of my purse and dabbed my eyes so that my tears would not interrupt the make-up that I spent a whole hour doing. I also made sure to hold my head away from traffic so no one could possibly spot me. I knew I was a little ways from Ordale, but it was still a very good possibility that I could be recognized.

Fortunately, the streets seemed to be pretty dead though. In fact, the only sign of life was the old, homeless lady that was walking around picking up things off the ground. I watched her carefully as she wobbled across the open, grassy fielded area and grabbed whatever trash she could find. After she was done she walked over and took a seat by me.

"How are you dear?" she said in her noticeably southern accent, although she had this universally beige skin color that wouldn't allow me to guess her nationality. The wrinkles on her face let me know that she was up in age. Yet the pureness of her skin made it easy to tell that through her hard life of street living, she managed to take good care of herself.

I quickly slid over as far opposite of where she sat.

"I don't have no money," I immediately said as I grabbed my Louis Vuitton bag close to me and hugged it tightly with my own body. She didn't ask me for anything but I just knew she was going to.

The woman just stared at me silently with those large round eyes.

"Oh I'm sorry to hear that sugar, here you go," she replied, throwing her arm towards me.

When I looked down at her hand, I saw that she was handing me a single crumbled up dollar bill.

"I found it over there. It's all I have, but you can take it," she told me.

I was confused. Even in the mist of my horrible attitude towards her she still managed to remain pleasant with me. You didn't see that often where I was from. I was rather touched by this strange lady, but I just couldn't show it.

"Don't need yo' last dollar either," was all I managed to say.

She just looked at me with a smile that was bright enough to make the sun jealous. "I'm not giving you my last dollar."

I sat there staring at the measly bill and tried to contemplate on whether or not I was the one that was crazy. It also didn't help that I was hot, frustrated, and had no time to be entertaining a homeless lady. Just when I was about to go straight off and give her a piece of my mind, a car rolled up and stopped directly in front of us.

"Now isn't this a sight to see," Detective Bailey let out a toothless grin and rolled his dark, tinted windows down to greet me. Without asking a single question, I hopped up from the bus stop and jumped straight into the passenger seat of his car. It was the first time I was actually glad to see him.

"Thank Gosh. You just don't know how happy I am to see you," I said, very appreciatively.

Without saying another word, Detective Bailey pulled off slowly, but not before waving at the lady sitting at the stop. She looked the other way, as if not to see him.

"Crazy old lady," I told him.

"Who Mrs. Burrows?" he asked.

“You know her?"

"Yes."

"Can you believe she thought I was homeless? Tried to give me her last dollar."

Detective Bailey smirked, "Trust me when I tell you she wasn't giving you her last dollar."

I had no clue what this Mrs. Burrows woman or Detective Bailey meant by her not giving me her last dollar, but I was right there and I saw her try to hand it to me. On the other hand, I had no desire to dwell on that dollar or that lady. For I had bigger problems to worry about.

"Ya know, you sure know a lot of people for you to not be from around here."

"I said I don't live in Ordale, I never said I haven't been here before."

"Oh," I said. "Gotcha."

"I gotta say Keisha," Detective Bailey changed the subject. "I'm quite impressed by you this morning."

"And why is that?" I pondered.

"You really were willing to catch that bus to make it downtown after you realized your tire was flat."

"Can't say it was the easiest choice I ever made in my life," I said to him. "But wait a minute, I never told you my tire was flat."

"You didn't have to," Detective said before reaching in his side pocket to pull out an antique pocket knife.

"What the fuck Detective!" I gasped. "It was you who slashed my tire today."

"Last night to be exact. I had to make sure you didn't pull a fast one and try to catch flight. You were gonna make it on that stand even if I had to drag you there myself."

"I really can't believe this shit!" I said, "and I hope you planning on fixing it TODAY. That was totally uncalled for. I thought we were working on building our trust."

"Don't worry, your tire will be fixed before you know it," he replied. "And trust me, we are most certainly working on it. You definitely gained a few points today."

"Points?" I said, unamused. "Detective, I'm glad you think this is some sort of game because it's not. I don't know if you realize yet, but you have officially ruined my life."

Detective Bailey smirked cleverly again, "I guess it all depends on how you define life, or better yet, how you look at the glass. Half full or half empty. "

I was in no mood for his riddles nor 'beat-around-the-bush' talk so I turned my entire body towards the window and quietly stared out of it. Unmoved, Detective Bailey turned his radio to an old school station and we didn't say a word to each other the entire ride downtown. Once we made it, he drove me up to a secluded area at the very top floor of a nearby parking garage and demanded that I be standing outside courtroom B in exactly ten minutes. I nodded then watched Detective Bailey ride off slowly back to ground zero.

Except for me and the few cars that occupied the top floor's lot, it was empty and lifeless. I was up about six stories and couldn't help but make my way over to the edge of the balcony. I just had to get a glimpse of my city from a different angle before heading into the building.

"So ugly in the inside," I whispered to myself while soaking in the gorgeous view. "But so beautiful from up here."

Even though the heart of the city was crime infested, nothing was as pretty as what I was seeing. I had to admit, the buildings, the trees, and the lights collectively gave off a stunning sight that kept me captivated. I looked east and west, locating areas I grew up in and the ones I recently habited. Also, seeing all the thriving businesses allowed me to realize just how much legit money the city offered. Maybe hustling wasn't the only way to be successful here. Just maybe I could use my ambition towards something that didn't involve me testifying in court against my affiliates. Or what if it was all just an illusion.

As Detective Bailey requested, I made it to courtroom B in exactly ten minutes. A middle-aged white woman was at the door obviously waiting for my arrival. She instructed me to sit on a bench outside the courtroom until my name was called and I followed her orders. While waiting, I needed something to calm my anxiously growing nerves so I plug my earphones into my ear and began listening to some smooth sounds of Sade.

"This is no ordinary love...no ordinary love," I sang in my head, feeling every word of it in my soul. The woman eventually tapped me on my right shoulder and signaled for me to enter the courtroom.

Knowing the moment of truth had arrived, I took one deep breath and preceded to follow her through the double doors. I was so nervous that upon entering I only saw the narrow path of which I was led. My heartbeat overruled the sound of the courtroom chatter and I didn't even try to locate Hi-C like I thought I would. Once I got to the stand, I was directed to enter a tiny booth where I was told to place my hand over the holy bible to take an oath. With my hand firmly against the book, I swore to tell the truth, the whole truth, and nothing but the truth, even though I knew most of what I was about to say would be a big, fat lie.

After repeating what was asked of me, another lady approached the bench. She was a middle-aged white women whose tall height made its presence before she did. Her hair was long, dark, and pulled back into one of tightest ponytails I had ever saw in my life and she had a very serious look on her face. She also showed no signs of fear or lack of confidence as she stood before the court ready to take me on.

I, nervous and now a bit frighten, took my seat and was now able to get a better grasp of where I was. It was only then that I began to notice everything that was going on around me and one of the first familiar faces I spotted was of course Hi-C. He was wearing an all-white jumpsuit and looked just about the same, except his jawbone was a little more narrow than it was before he went in. His goatee had also grown out into a full beard but he still looked just as attractive as he did before. Sitting directly behind him was Isis, who wore a lavender pants and jacket set. Her hair was pushed back and hanging down her back like she normally wore it and I couldn't help but notice the clever grin on her face as she pierced me with her chinked eyes. I wasn't surprised to see her, but I wasn't prepared for it either. Most of the other people in the courtroom I had never saw a day in my life, while I did notice just a few members of the OMC laying back in disguise.

The woman who approached the bench made her way directly up to me before projecting her voice loud enough for everyone in the room to hear her.

"Hello. I am District Attorney, Mrs. Lowisky, and I represent the prosecution," she formally introduced herself. "You are called here today because you are a key witness in the case against Herbert Cooper, also known as Hi-C on the streets of Ordale. Do you understand this much?"

"I do," I replied.

"Okay good. For the records, may you state your name?"

"My name is Lakeisha Black," I said.

"And you were present in the home of Mr. Herbert Cooper on the night of April 23. Is this also correct?"

"Yes ma'am," I nodded swiftly.

"Can you describe to me in detail what exactly happened that night?"

I nodded and positioned myself more comfortably in my seat before also speaking loud enough that everyone in the courtroom could hear me.

"Yes. I was with Hi-C and we were at his house," I stopped and looked over at Isis before finishing my sentence, "chillin'. That's when we heard a loud bang at the door and then people dressed in black rushed in. Hi-C thought it was a robbery or something' so he told me to stand behind him. That's when he grabbed his gun, but before he could even get a chance to use it, the officers ran down on him and started beating him for no reason at all. I started crying and screaming for them to leave him alone but they just took me outside and arrested me too."

"Hmmm," Mrs. Lowisky paced back and forth, processing everything I had just said to her. "So the gun he grabbed, did he just happened to be walking around with it or did he have it on him the whole time you were, as you quote, 'chillin?'"

"No. It was on the wall of his office room. Along with three other guns he keeps up there."

"Is this the only place he keeps his guns?" she asked.

"No, there are a few more scattered around the house but he has a big home. That's why he protects it so much."

"Oh no, I completely understand that part Ms. Black. He has every right to bare arms. It is a pretty big house so I'm sure he has to protect it."

"Yes, exactly." I nodded.

I quickly glanced over to Hi-C who held a straight and serious face. I could never tell what he was thinking and this time wasn't any different. Detective Bailey, on the other hand, was standing in the back corner of the courtroom watching me very carefully. As the sweat visibly trickled down his face, it was clear that he was nervous about something.

"But is it safe to say that he keeps guns scattered around his home, which was why it was so convenient for him to grab it and aim it at fellow officers?"

"Yes, makes it very easy for him to protect himself from intruders," I clapped back.

"I see," the woman said.

"And talk to me a little more about when the officers and Hi-C came in physical contact."

"You mean how they attacked him?" I asked. "They beat the crap out of him for no reason at all. Simple as that."

"And when you say they beat him, what weapons, if any, did they use?"

"I saw fists. I saw guns. Listen, there was so much going on at one time that it's hard to say, but I know for a fact that they were beating him. I'm one thousand percent sure of that." Then without thinking I rose out of my chair and pointed towards the back of the room. "As a matter of fact, it was that pig right back there who was the ring leader of it all! He was the one calling the shots and letting it all go down! It was unnecessary. Point blank period! Hi-C is not a violent person and he was only acting in self-defense. Now I don't wanna answer any more questions!"

Detective Bailey put his head down while everyone turned to him. Whispers began to cover the courtroom. I didn't know if I had crossed the line or if he was proud of the performance I gave. Either way, I didn't care. I needed people to believe that I had no ties with the police.

"Order in the court!" the judge intervened and ceased the chatter with his gavel. "And please reframe from name-calling in my courtroom. I won't allow it."

"Yes, your honor." I said, unapologetically before giving my attention back to Mrs. Lowisky.

She continued. "So it is your sworn testimony that Mr. Herbert Cooper was simply trying to protect himself against the officers and that he was only acting in self-defense?"

"Yes, that's exactly what I'm saying," I told her.

"No further questions," she said then strutted back to her seat, only to stop halfway in her tracks. "But wait…just one more thing."

I was ready for whatever Mrs. Lowisky brought my way. I had shut her down before and I knew I could do it again.

"I mean, I know you are Lakiesha Black but what exactly is your relationship to Mr. Herbert Cooper?" she asked. "Are you cousins...friends...maybe something more?"

"I'm not understanding your question, Mrs. Lowisky."

"Let me just get to the point of what I'm asking you," she said.

"You were alone at Hi-C's house late in the night. Are the two of you involved, I mean like sexually?"

Collective gasped filled the room and everyone's eyes became glued to my face. Even the judge looked over in my direction to get the scoop. Uncertain of how I should respond, I looked to Hi-C who still did not display any feelings and then to Detective Bailey who with a silent movement, swiftly nodded to let me know it was okay to be truthful.

"Yes," I sighed.

"Yes...you are related or yes you are sexually involved?"

I sighed again. "Yes, we are sexually involved. But what does that have to do with what happened that night?"

"Oh nothing at all, she mocked. "You're a mature, beautiful woman. I don't see why Hi-C, or any man, wouldn't be attracted to you."

"Thank you for that," I sassed her, while still appreciating the compliment. "So am I done now?"

"Soon, Mrs. Black, very soon. I just have one more question. Just bear with me for a second."

Mrs. Lowisky walked to the bleachers, behind where Hi-C was, and stopped right by Isis.

"Mrs. Black, are you familiar with the woman I am standing here next to?"

I knew exactly who she was talking about but I squinted my eyes and pretended to act as if I could not see that far off. The jittery feeling I had when I first walked in the courtroom immediately came back.

"I...I...am not sure. I can barely see her." I stuttered.

Mrs. Lowisky said something to Isis which caused her to stand up from her seat.

"I am sure you can see a little better now. This woman, who happens to be the only person in this room standing besides myself, are you familiar with her?"

Isis just stood with that same clever grin on her face. She had no shame in what was taking place, or at least that's how she made it seem. As for me, it was the first time in my life that I felt embarrassed about messing around with her man.

"Yes, I am familiar," I blew a heavy breath.

"Who do you know her to be?" she asked.

"Her name is Isis," I responded.

"You are correct. Her name is Isis," she replied. "And can you tell the court what her business of being here today would be?"

That infamous sigh returned yet again. "She is his wife."

"Whose wife?" Mrs. Lowisky continued to press me.

I let out a heavy sigh and then sunk my head, "Hi-C's wife."

More gasps surfaced back into the courtroom and I couldn't describe how low I felt in that moment. I wanted to cry but my pride wouldn't allow me to take it that far. Mrs. Lowisky didn't seem to make it any better either.

"His wife," she scratched her chin. "Well Isis, *his wife*, testified earlier this evening that she was out of town on a business trip when the officers entered the house. Do you believe that she knew you were in her home on that evening?"

"Objection," a male voice called from the other side of the room. "There is no possible way the witness can know what someone else is thinking."

"Your honor, I'm only asking what Miss Black felt in her own mind. She can answer in any way she chooses."

"Overruled," the judge said. "But make sure she understands your question very clearly."

"Understood, your honor." Mrs. Lowisky called out to me. "Miss Black, do you feel in your own mind and heart that Isis, *Hi-C's wife,* knew you were in her home on the night of April 23rd? Be very clear, I'm only asking you what you feel."

"No," I replied. "I don't believe that, this time, she knew I was in her home. But she does know-"

“Thank you,” Mrs. Lowisky rudely cut me off. “I have no further questions.”

"Would the defense like to cross examine?" the judge asked the small group of people sitting at Hi-C's corner. His attorney looked away. "No, your honor. Nothing further."

"Okay Miss Black," the judge said. "You may stand down now."

I don't think I had ever walked so fast out of that courtroom and I was so furious that I could have burnt the whole place down. How dare this thin hair, thin lipped broad humiliate me in that manner? And Isis, she just sat there soaking it all up. I guess she was right, sometimes being smart was playing dumb.

There were no words to describe how I felt and I was just glad that it was all over. I raced up to the top of the parking lot forgetting that I had no car to travel back home in. I found myself in the same spot I was in when I was checking out the view earlier. I must have stood there cursing myself for about five whole minutes before I saw Detective Bailey coming towards me.

"What the fuck do you want!" I began walking away from him.

"Calm down, Keisha,” he tried to stop me. “Just talk to me.”

"Talk to you?" I said. "No, fuck that! You knew all along that they were going to do that to me. I have never been so embarrassed in my life!"

Detective Bailey tried to grab me but I was able to break away. "Don't touch me, I'm leaving now."

"And how are you gonna get home, Keisha?" he flagged his keys at me. "I brought you here remember."

"I'll catch the bus back," I told him. "Can't nothing be more embarrassing then what I just went through."

"Keisha you're not catching any damn bus so just quit it," the detective said before looking over his shoulders. "We are out in public remember."

"I don't give a fuck. I don't care about any of this shit anymore. Just arrest me!" I threw my arms to him. "And you can tell Hi-C and everybody else the truth. I'm serious."

"You don't mean that Keisha. You're just upset right now."

"I mean every word I said. I really don't care anymore. Do I have to jump off this fucking balcony to prove it?"

I began to walk towards the edge of the roof, but Detective Bailey grabbed me again, this time not allowing me to get away. Then he hugged my body tightly, but not in a pleasant way. He was now so close to me that I could feel the air in his nostrils smacking against my cheekbone.

"Keisha, just chill the fuck out," he yelled. "I'm getting sick of you, ya know. You try to act like you have all the sense in the world but really you're as blind as a bat. All this happened for a reason. Don't you get it? There was no way the state was going to convict Hi-C for that obstruction bullshit. We stormed into his house unannounced and he had every right to defend himself. Doesn't matter how big of a drug dealer he is. We needed to make you a noncredible witness and proving you were sleeping with him was evidence enough. Everything was planned and everyone was in on it. Hi-C is gonna be convicted and serve twelve months."

Detective Bailey loosened his grip once he realized that I had calmed myself, but he wasn't finished with me just yet.

"Keisha really, when are you gonna own up to your own shit. You've been sleeping with a married man for years and you didn't think you were gonna ever have to face that? Imagine how that woman felt countless nights knowing the love of her life was in bed with you. You need to start owning up to your mistakes and learn how to face your karma. Every action has a reaction and every cause has an effect. Stop playing victim to situations you created. Nobody's against you. We're trying to help you. Now if you don't want to spend the next twenty years in prison I suggest you follow me to my car, take your ass home, and pull yourself together."

Holding on to every word Detective Bailey said, I simmered down completely. Although I was humiliated, he did have a point. And I still hadn't swallowed enough pride to catch the city bus so I decided it was best to take that ride with him. Even better, once I made it back to the hotel, I noticed that not only was my tire fixed, but the car was washed and sparkly too.

"Didn't I tell you I would take care of it," the detective said as he pulled up and noticed me blushing. "In fact, you have four brand new tires and your car has been washed and waxed too. I hope I'm forgiven."

The detective informed me that he had someone on the job while we were at court. He apologized and said it was the least he could do after he vandalized my property. Of course bygones were definitely bygones. Plus, that was four hundred dollars he saved me from spending on new wheels.

"Why don't you take it easy today? Just stay here, relax, and think about your future."

"That's exactly what I'll do," I told him. "Thanks Detective."

"It's all good," he said. "And if ever you need me, I'm just a phone call away. Remember, I'm on your side."

Without responding, I checked my surroundings to make sure no one could have possibly saw us and then exited the detective's vehicle.

CHAPTER 18: The Intruder

After Detective Bailey dropped me off, I entered my hotel room and fell straight across the single queen-sized bed that occupied most of the tiny space. From there I just stared up at the rusted chandelier on the ceiling and tried to put everything that just happened to me into perspective. How did I allow myself to get so caught up? Why after all those times I disrespected Hi-C's marriage was that the only time I felt ashamed about it? How was he feeling about being locked up and how could I be working with the police to take him down? Maybe I had always been the selfish girl who only cared about what was in it for me. In fact, if it wasn't for my selfishness, Charlytte probably wouldn't be sleeping with random men for money. And I hadn't even talked to my mother, let alone my brothers. One thing for sure, I had become distant from the world, my family, and most importantly myself.

My brain had worked itself into a deep sleep and I found my body waking up about two hours later. I must admit, I did need the rest though. I even recall dreaming about my Aunt JoNell again. She was painting my nails and telling me girl stories, then she sent me into the woods and told me she had a gift there. I opened the big box that I spotted on the ground and there was a tiny baby inside. A beautiful baby too. When I rushed back to find JoNell she was nowhere in sight and then I found myself calling for her until I woke up. It was a strange dream nonetheless, but it wasn't the worst one I had. It could have meant that maybe I was progressing.

Feeling well-rested and fresh, I decided to dress myself up nicely and step out. I knew Detective Bailey said I should stay in and re-evaluate my life, but I didn't need to do that. My life was already figured out. I had everything I ever wanted, a good married man, money, and a job that made it possible for me to buy anything I wanted. That's what made me happy and nothing he could say to me would make me feel any different. My only problem was him coming in and interrupting my perfect world.

For my night out, I linked up with all my girls so I ended up meeting Shannon, Alicia, and Charlytte at a club called Frozen. It was the usual 'Grown and Sexy' night held on Fridays and we enjoyed the three dollar drinks and one dollar Jell-O shots that all ladies were entitled to have. All of us drove in separate cars and met up there, even Charlytte who had recently brought herself a Camaro with her trickin' money. She told me she got the car with her school refund check but I knew she was lying. I just went with the flow.

The girls and I kicked it until about one in the morning, before we all said our goodbyes. Shannon suggested the we continue our outing at my house, but of course I quickly curved that idea by telling them that I had a painter recently come by and that the fumes were so strong that even I couldn't stay there. That's one of the reasons I didn't trip on Charlytte for lying to me. Even I knew that sometimes that was just the way things had to be.

I made it home around two o'clock in the morning. The hotel was dead silent when I got back but many cars filled the parking lot. In fact, the only sign of life was the night auditor who was sitting with his feet propped up on the check-in counter watching some television. I quietly walked past him, careful not to interrupt his entertainment and stopped by the vending machine to grab a water and a pack of peanut M&Ms. The water I needed to lessen my chance of having a hangover the next morning and the candy was just a treat. I used my key card to enter my room, not knowing that when I stepped inside I would be in for an unexpected surprise.

"What in the entire fuck!?" I yelled after seeing all my belonging scattered all over the room. The covers were ripped from the mattress, the mattress was hanging off of the bed frame, and every drawer in the room was wide open. I immediately ran to the stash of money I kept under the dresser but it was gone. Nothing left but the envelope I kept it in. Three-thousand-four hundred-and-twenty-six dollars just vanished. It was strange because nobody knew where I was hiding my stash, not even Detective Bailey himself. Frantic, I grabbed my phone to make a call.

"Hello," Detective Bailey whispered. I could tell I had woke him.

"Hey, I know you're asleep but I need you to come here now."

"What's wrong, Keisha? Is everything okay?" he paused. "It's three in the morning."

"No, everything is not okay," I yelled softly. "Please just come over here now. Please."

"I'm on the way," he said before hanging up in my face.

I hung around outside the room until Bailey arrived, too afraid to go back inside alone. He made it to my spot in about thirty minutes, although he lived about forty-five minutes away. When I saw him approaching I rushed across the lobby to meet him.

"Thank you, thank you." I said gratefully, then grabbed his hand and led him to my room. "Please, come inside."

I allowed Detective Bailey into the apartment so that he could see it for himself. For a split second, he showed no emotion as he looked around at how trashed the place was. Then suddenly pulled out his gun and began checking the bathroom, under the bed, and behind the doors for any sign of an intruder.

"Well at least we know how they got in," he said once he got to the window and noticed that it was cracked open.

"You don't lock these things," he asked.

"I don't ever recall unlocking it. Ever. This is strange. Oh my god," I thought. "Somebody wants me dead."

I began to panic hysterically and Detective Bailey tried to calm me down. "I believe your overreacting. You do live in a cheap hotel. All types of people hang around here. You walk outta here every day with that expensive shit on and you don't think people are watching. I believe somebody from the area did it. I highly doubt that it's personal."

"But they touched none of that stuff," I pointed at my belongings. "I mean my money is gone but I have gold jewelry, purses, expensive clothes...all types of shit they could have made a fortune off of on the streets. This isn't about money. This is personal detective. I knew I shouldn't have testified today. Somebody from the OMC did this. They're blaming me for the reason the trial went sour."

"You're overreacting," Detective said.

I began to think deeper. "Oh my god! Tell me nobody followed me home and saw that I rode with you. Now they know I'mma snitch. Oh my God! I'm a dead girl walking."

"Keisha stop it. If someone wanted you dead, they would have waited until you came back here to do it. They're not gonna warn you or give you any reason to jump ship. I know that for a fact. I think this was random. One of these lowlifes around here. They studied you and knew you must have had money. Once they found it, they left. This gold bracelet was worth more than that money. That's how I know it was stupid amateurs. Trust me on this one."

"Well what about the cameras? Maybe the desk clerk can pull up some footage. I'm gonna go down and talk to them right now."

Detective Bailey stopped me in my tracks. "No! You don't need to bring all that attention to yourself. I am the law remember. Let me handle this."

"No disrespect, but every time I have listened to you, I have just ended up in deeper shit. I'm tired Detective," I said beginning to cry hard. "I'm just really tired of all this. That was all the money I had. And now I have not even one dollar to my name. This is not me. This is not Lakeisha Black."

Detective Bailey slowly walked over and hugged me. The warmth from his body soothed mine, for I had still been tipsy from Grown and Sexy.

"You are exactly who you are with or without money. When are you going to realize that? I told you to stay in and think about some of those very things. Why did you leave in the first place?"

"Maybe it was a good thing that I did. I probably would have been dead if I stayed here."

Without saying a word, Detective Bailey closed the window and locked it. Then he began pushing my bed back together and straightened what the intruders had messed up.

"I'll tell you what," he said. "It's already late and you look like you need some rest. I'm going to hang out around here and keep an eye out on you. I'll see to it that nobody bothers you. I promise. I'll be right downstairs."

Detective Bailey picked up a couple more items off the floor before heading towards the door. I wore the face of a sad puppy as my eyes reeked of terror watching him leave. As exhausted as I was, I didn't know how I was going to be able to sleep.

"Get some rest this time," he said after opening the door. "Or at least please try."

"Detective wait," I stopped him. "I'm afraid. Plus I'm physically and emotionally drained. I need some male energy around me right now. I know this may sound crazy but I just need to be held tonight. Please, can you just lay here with me? Just until I fall asleep. I'm begging you."

Standing outside the doorway, Detective Bailey took one look into my pleading eyes and another look down the hallway. I could tell he was uncomfortable about the situation. I was too, but my desperation caused me to overstep a line I knew I should not have crossed.

"Sure why not?" He surprised me and dragged his way to the edge of the bed. Then he sat down and began taking off his shoes, tie, and white-collared shirt. I didn't even bother to take off the short, strapless dress I wore for the club. Changing was the last thing on my mind.

After Bailey was finished getting as comfortable as he was going to get, I instructed him to turn off the lights and leave the one in the bathroom on. That's what I usually did. With the small amount of light shining in the room, I could see that he was careful not to get too relaxed. He still wore his black slacks and only revealed his chest through his sleeveless undershirt. I cuddled up on a pillow and rested my body on my side. Detective Bailey laid beside me on his back.

"Please Detective," I pleaded. "Just hold me. That's all I ask."

Uneasy, Detective Bailey rolled over and wrapped his arms around my waist. A feeling of relief came over my body. It was just something about a man, rather he was right for me or not, that gave me the sense of comfort and security I longed for as a child. It was a feeling that if only you were a bastard, you could described. I know I told Detective Bailey that all I needed was his energy, but I found myself becoming more sexually aroused by his presence.

Like a puppy looking for comfort from its mother, I waddled my butt up against his pelvis area until I had found his manhood. Strangely, he did not back away from me and, in fact, grabbed me tighter. It was in that moment that I wondered if he possibly felt something for me. Then I thought about how much of a failure I was to him and quickly rid myself of the idea. I just began to let my mind ponder on other things like my life, my future, and who was out to get me. In fact, the more I thought about it the worse I felt. I needed something to take my mind off it all and make me feel good.

"Detective," I whispered as a single tear trickled down my face. Then I grabbed his hand and placed it under my dress.

"Please, I need to feel loved right now. I need to feel something good, something that will make me take my mind off all this bad."

Detective Bailey rubbed my thigh gently and then squeezed it before breaking his grip from me. I knew for sure that I wasn't someone easy for him to resist.

"Keisha please, I am here with you, ain't I? What more do you want from me?"

I rolled myself over aggressively, sat on top of him, then slowly led my face to his."

"I want you to make love to me."

"Keisha, you don't mean that. You've been drinking. I can smell it on you."

"I know I've been drinking but that has nothing to do with what I'm feeling. C'mon, I haven't had sex in like four months. I need to rid this stress. I promise you, it will mean nothing in the morning."

Hearing those words, Detective Bailey aggressively flipped me around and was now on top of me. I gripped his left cheek with my right hand thinking he was about to take me, but he grabbed it and pinned my arms to the cheap mattress.

"Exactly. It won't mean a thing to you in the morning. So why do it? Huh Keisha. This is exactly what I'm talking about. You can't just go about life making decisions and then think that you can forget about it tomorrow. It doesn't work like that, at least not in my world. I'm a real person and I have real feelings. It will not just mean nothing to me in the morning."

"So that means you care about me?" Was all I could say.

"Huh? What Keisha? What are you talking about?"

"You can't just make this a sexual thing because you have feelings involved. That's what you're saying, right? That's why your so obsessed with me. Trying to take down Hi-C so you can have me to yourself. It all makes sense now."

"Keisha, when are you gonna stop thinking everything is about you. I must admit, you are physically one of the most beautiful women I have ever set eyes on and I understand what your accustomed to, but trust me when I say that there are some good men out here who can look past a gorgeous face to find beauty. And from what I see now, no disrespect, but there's nothing pretty about you. There is also definitely nothing sexy about you laying here begging me to have sex that will mean nothing to you by morning. I think it's best I sleep out in my car. I'll be watching your back from there. Don’t worry, I'm a man of my word."

Detective Bailey removed my hand from his cheeks and proceeded to rise, but I stopped him in his tracks.

"Wait no!" I begged of him. "You're right, I had a little too much to drink. Please. I'll moved over. Just don't go anywhere. I'm terrified."

Detective Bailey agreed to stay in my bed as long as I kept my distance. We both just laid on our backs about arm’s length apart. I looked up at the ceiling feeling so ashamed of everything I had done that had gotten me to that point. Everything even back to my childhood. That was my first time ever being turned down by a man, and although I wasn't happy about it, I honestly needed it.

"Thank you detective," I suddenly told him.

"Excuse me?" Detective Bailey asked.

We continued to stare at the ceiling. "I know you don't think so, but I listen to every word you tell me. And sometimes you’re right. So thank you, that's all I meant."

"I know you hear me Keisha. That's why I haven't given up on you," he said. "I just have one question..."

“What's that?"

"Why? Why are you so insecure? Like what made you this way."

"Detective Bailey, with all this confidence I have, there is no way I can be insecure."

"There is a big difference between being confident and being secure. In fact, some of the most confident women are the most insecure. Always having to keep themselves up. Wasting countless of dollars on hair, make-up, and clothing just to get the approval of other people. I mean, it's so weird, when I'm doing my detective work and I have used those computers and go on those media sites. Beautiful, gorgeous model-type, every hour uploading pictures of themselves just to be recognized. It's like they survive off the attention. The feedback is what feeds their ego. Those women really don't feel as confident as they pretend to be."

"I have no idea about those sites, but my girls said I would shut them shits down. When you're OMC you're not allowed on no internet. That's a major no-no. I'm kinda glad I'm not tho. Because if that shit hypnotizes me like it does my friends, I want no parts. I mean, hanging out ain't even the same no more. Everybody's just sitting round on their phones, not even talking to one another. Remember back when people used to really kick it?"

"Yeah, as a matter of fact I do," he replied. "But what can you say, times have changed. I guess that's just the way it is."

"You can say that again," I said. "But really, why do you think I'm insecure? Name one thing I have done to make you feel this way."

"Keisha, for starters just look at what you're doing right now. You're living in a rundown hotel just so you can have extra money to flex for people on the streets with. And you won't get caught out of the house if you don't look like a million bucks. You don't see anything wrong with that."

"You don't understand. You probably come from a good suburban family and that's what I hate about the law. Y'all don't know what it's like coming from nothing. To grow up in a trailer park or public housing, having to survive off syrup sandwiches and noodles. You probably don't even know how to spell struggle," I read him. "Well let me tell you something…people who never had nothing, desire to have everything. And if we have to deal, kill, or steal to get it then that's what we'll do. You don't have to like it, but you have to respect it."

"First off, don't assume that I had the perfect life. You don't know the half of my story. Second, I do understand. That's why I gave you another chance...And what about you settling for a married man? That doesn't count for anything on the insecurity chart either I see."

"You can't help who you love, Detective."

"You're right, but you can control your actions," he checked me. "Can I ask you a personal question?"

"Why?" I sassed him. "You seem to have all the answers."

Detective Bailey ignored me. "Was your father around?"

"Excuse me Detective?" I heard him clearly but I didn't want to go there.

"Your dad, or any father figure, did you have one around growing up?"

"Detective I don't want to talk about that."

"Why not? Did he hurt you? Touch you." Detective sat up. "Keisha, you can talk to me about anything."

"Wait…what...no way! My dad wasn't no fucking creep. He was a good man. Spoiled the fuck outta me. In fact, he was the one who instilled in me that I was beautiful. He'd tell me twenty times a day." I stopped and took a long deep, breath before building the strength to speak again. "But that's until they came and took him away."

"What? Who came and took him away?"

"You guys, you dirty pigs. The fucking law. That's the real reason why I hate cops. They took my daddy from me."

I suddenly began to cry. That situation involving my dad haunted me. I never wanted to talk to anyone about what happened with him but I knew I needed to. It was weighing heavy on my mind and heart and had been for a long time.

"I was about eight years old. That was a rough year for me. My favorite aunt died and not long after, the police stormed into our trailer and took him right in front of me and my older brother. My pregnant mama was there too, but she didn't even cry or try to stop them. She just sat there in a daze watching it all go down. But me, no way. I fought, bit, and kicked them off of him while they all laughed like it was cute or something. I mean seriously, how is anything funny when you are taking a little girl's father away from her? The only man I ever loved. It was one of the worst days of my life."

"Dozen cops?" he asked. "It must have been serious. What did he do?"

"Honestly, I'm not sure. My mama never told me. I'd try to ask her 'bout him, but she'd smack the taste out of my mouth every time I did. In fact, she was never the same after that day. It's like she turned in to a monster or somethin'."

"But your older now, can't you look it up for yourself? All criminal information is public information, ya know."

"Yeah I know, but I never knew his full name. Mama got rid of any trace of him. I mean, I know he's Mexican and his first name is Jose but that's about it. There are a million of them in the world.

"I see," detective said.

"You know what? You should go to him. I believe a lot of what's going on with you is the fact that you need answers. Get you some closure on the situation with your father. I've seen this work many times before. If you talk to him and find out what really happened maybe you can start putting your past behind you and move forward. What do you say?”

"I don't know, Detective. I don't think I'm ready to face that man. It's been twenty years since I saw him.”

"Trust me on this one," he assured me. "It will be good for you. Plus, I'm a detective. I can- I'm sorry- *I WILL* find your father for you. Then you can take it from there. In the meantime, get some rest and we will work everything else out in the morning."

CHAPTER 19: The Visitation

I had finally made the decision to do it. Wasn't easy but I knew it was necessary, and had I known the drive there was only three hours away I would have probably made it sooner.

I pulled up to Dooley State Prison at exactly ten-thirty. Visitation hours started at eleven but people were already lining up outside the main entrance to see their loved ones. I wasn't happy about waiting in a long line, especially outside of a prison, but in all of forty-five minutes I was identified, searched, and directed to go see my father.

Once I was led to the area he would be, I immediately began to scope out my surroundings. The facility looked like a school cafeteria, except with no tables and the room consisted only of strangers and chairs. I watched in amazement as everyone conversed with their loved ones and enjoyed each other's company. Fathers were laughing with their children, women were smiling with their men, and I even saw a few people crying. The emotional tension in the room was surely thick enough to slice with a knife.

I was directed by security to a spot in a rear corner. My father was already there. As I approached him, I realized how much different he looked from the man I remembered. The hair that used to sit on his head like a mushroom was now cut off, leaving him completely bald with a dark, thick mustache. Even his body was shaped different. The once chubby guy had become buff, toned, and was so covered with tattoos that seeing his skin was fairly impossible. I must admit, the old man looked good.

I hugged my father in just enough time for the guard to tell us to break loose, then we preceded to sit and catch up on old times.

"Oh myyee gawd," he smiled at me and spoke in his noticeably Hispanic accent. His English was still a bit broken.

"You are moore beauteeful than I pictoured you to be."

"Thanks," I blushed then reached for his biceps. "I see the prison life has its perks too."

"Si, I guess so." He smiled, then just looked at me without saying a word.

It was like he was astonished by something far more than my growth. I was uncomfortable with it but I knew the view of me sitting before him was a priceless one. I couldn't imagine going more than a decade without seeing a child of mine. He had every right to soak up the moment.

"You know I dreamed of 'dis moment," he said. "I prayed and prayed that just one of you would come through these doors one day. I guess the Most High does hear our prayers."

"Yeah I guess so," I agreed. "I would have come sooner, but I didn't know where you were or how to find you."

"I don't understand. Every letter I sent to you had my address on it," he informed me. "You didn't get any of them?"

"What letters?" I asked.

"The ones I sent to your mother's every week."

A blank look surfaced on my face.

"You mean to tell me you never got any of them?" he asked. "I must have sent hundreds. Your mom never read them to you?"

"No," I told him. "To be honest she never really mentioned anything about you since that night the police took you away."

"Oh," he said, before his entire mood shifted. "You remember that?"

"How could I forget?" I told him.

Daddy sunk his chin down deep into his sternum. I don't know if he felt shame, disbelief, or both. I, on the other hand, just wondered why Mama didn't give me those letters. My perception of many things in my life would have probably been a little different had I known daddy at least still cared enough to write me. Mama was definitely a selfish bitch and hearing this made it even more easy for me to hate her.

"Your mother...," he shook his head from left to right. "I should have figured. How is she doing by the way?"

I shrugged. "She's on the other side of the dirt so I guess she's okay."

Daddy sunk his head even lower. "Why doesn't this surprise me? I take it your relationship is not good."

“Far from good," I told him.

"Listen....your mother is not a bad woman. She's actually okay once you get to know her. She's just been through a lot of heartache in her life. Much of it has to do with me."

"But daddy, I always remember you being so nice to us. You'd tell me I was beautiful every second you got. You worked every day and came home every night. I just don't see how you could have been the problem."

"Often times we don't see things if they are not put directly in front of our faces. Keisha, I was far from a good man. I was a monster- selfish, sick and twisted. I hate to say it, but getting locked up was the best thing that could have happened to me. Wait a minute....," he paused. "You don't know why I am here?"

"No. Honestly mama never told me. In fact, she never really talked much about anything concerning you once you left. That's part of the reason why I am here. I'm having these crazy dreams about your van, dead babies, and dark forests. On top of all that, I'm dealing with so many issues of my own. I don't know, I think I'm just at a point in my life where I just need answers."

"Baby girl," he grabbed one of my hands with both of his. The guard came to interfere but the desperate look my father had in his eyes when he pleaded for her to allow him to enjoy his moment with his daughter caused her to relax a bit. "Believe me when I say I will never lie or hold back anything from you. Right now let's just enjoy the moment. Maybe you can come back and visit, then we can talk about that. But not right now. Please, I waited years for this moment."

I took a deep breath and then agreed to leave daddy alone. I could see that he sincerely just wanted to connect with me and I honestly wanted to enjoy him just the same. Besides, I had too many negative things going on in my world to add anything more.

"Okay. We can discuss it later," I agreed.

"Thank you baby girl," he said. "You know you always did listen to your daddy. What about Korey? How's my oldest doing?

And I can't forget about Keyshawn, you know I never even got the chance to meet him."

"Seeing the man Korey has become would make you very proud," I told him. "But that Keyshawn daddy, well that's another story. He's a little street kid. Way before his time."

"Just like his old man," daddy laughed. "But you tell that little joker that his daddy says he better clean up his act. That type of lifestyle is no good for him. He'll eventually end up dead or in jail like me. That's how it usually goes."

"I'll try but I doubt if he'll listen," I told him.

Daddy shook his head from left to right in sorrow. "I just wish I could have been there for you guys. I didn't realize until I got here, how important it is for a man to be in his household. It's us that keeps our families together. I know I failed you all, but there's nothing I can do about it now. I just pray that he'll end up alright."

"He'll be fine" I comforted Daddy. "And we all make mistakes so don't beat yourself up about it."

"Easier said than done," he said, before quickly changing the subject. "But what about you? How are you maintaining? That modeling life should be paying you a fortune, right."

"Never ever even considered pursuing a modeling career," I replied, truly flattered by my daddy's compliment. "Nowadays everybody and their mama wanna be a model, marry a famous rapper, or something' crazy like that. But not me daddy, my dreams are far bigger. That's why I'm in school now."

"School?" he scratched his head, forcing me to wonder if he knew I wasn't telling the truth. "And what are you taking up?"

"Business management," I said. "And I'm using the money I'm making from working at the bank to open a fashion boutique. I'm a great stylist daddy."

"Oh okay. I have a little entrepreneur on my hand. That's great. But please, stick with it. I don't want you working a nine to five, slaving for a company that makes millions while you struggle to make ends meet. Even those degrees can sometimes be bullshit. As long as you have a skill you can go far. Trust me, I worked all my life but I never once lived. I was miserable, taught to believe busting my ass for cheap pay was normal but I'm here to tell you that it's not. Listen, life ain't about waking up being told when to come in, when to go to lunch, when to go home, and when to come back. I want you to get to point in where nobody can order your steps nor your money but you. Get to the point where nobody has the power to hire or fire you because you will be your own boss. I want you to set your business up to where you can leave it to your children and they can leave it to theirs. That way your legacy will live on. You understand that."

"Yes daddy," I said. "I gotcha."

"I'm serious Keisha. Now I know I'm in prison, but I'm more free then some of those guys that walk past you every day. Freedom is a state of mind, so don't ever feel sorry for me. Feel sorry for those guys you see every day walking around with their pants to their ankles, killing each other over shoes and unowned territory, putting materialism before anything. Those are the ones who are locked up. Mental fucking slaves is what I call 'em. You stay away from those kind. And get you a man who's a leader. A man who has a plan. Not a drug dealer who kills his community by putting drugs into it, just so he can ride around in a fancy car and live in a fancy house. There is a difference between a man and a boy, and it has nothing to do with money, looks, or reputation. Remember my words to you honey."

The way my daddy spoke about dating drug dealers gave me chills. It seemed as if he knew of my life personally and was speaking directly to me and my situation. It was sort of weird. Had people been tipping him off about me? Maybe he had an ear in the streets.

I heard everything he said and I felt it, but of course, I couldn't show it.

"Dang, daddy," was all I managed to joke and say, "that was deep. Have you turned Christian up in here?"

"Christian?" he laughed aloud and then leaned in closer to me. He carried a really serious look in his eyes. "Let me ask you a question. If a man comes up in here right now, snatches me out of this chair, beats the hell of me until I'm blue, chops my dick off then puts a rope around my neck, hangs me from a noose, and then hands you a bible and tells you to believe in Christianity. Would you?"

"I dunno," I shrugged. "I don't think so."

"Good. So don't come in here talking about no Christians."

"So that means you don't believe in Jesus daddy?"

Daddy laughed again. "Jesus? Keisha Jesus is about as real as Santa Clause and the tooth fairy."

My daddy's words cut me like a sharp knife. To me, people who didn't believe in Jesus were devils. Judging by the uneasy look I suddenly gave him, Daddy caught my drift of me not feeling at all what he was saying.

"I know what you're thinking, babygirl. You don't have to be acceptant of my views but you have to respect when someone's beliefs are different from yours. People are more comfortable believing what they are told because searching for the truth is too much work. I was once like you. Sleep. Eventually you will see the light as I did and you'll know what feels right because your spirit will tell you."

"No daddy, it's nothing against you," I told him. "It's just that I have been taught one thing all my life so hearing your words...I don't know....just never heard anyone question religion like that before."

"Baby, religion is a business, a profitable organization. I am not a religious man, I am a spiritual man. When you learn the difference, you'll learn the key to life. I know I haven't given you much, so please even if you don't agree, just take these words with you."

Daddy then released my hands from the captivity of his. I was about to speak to lessen the awkwardness of the moment, but he cut me off.

"Although there is one thing I can say I'm proud to have given you?" he said.

"What? Life?" I responded.

"No. Something far greater," he said. "That thing they called melanin."

"Melanin?" I questioned.

"Yes. Melanin…carbon…it's a powerful thing. My problem was my addiction to it. I had to have it and it didn't matter where it came from," he said. "You know I wanted to name you that, but Joanne wasn't havin' it."

"Because she's smart," I said, thankful that mama didn't give in it to that foolishness. My daddy was really starting to make me believe that prison had made him a bit crazy.

"No, because like many of you, you don't know who you truly are."

"Daddy, I gotta be honest, your scaring me right now. I don't know what you are talking about. I don't even think *you* know what you are talking about. Can we just drop this and talk about other things? We have so much to catch up on and I have to be back on the road in a few."

My daddy paused and then stared at me for a second before shaking his head. He managed to still maintain a smile and then ignored my request.

"I know you don't know what I'm talking about and that saddens me. How could you not know the powers you possess? How the sun is the fuel for the earth, and how you- the original woman- is its best friend. That you were born from kings and queens and that your history didn't start four hundred years ago with no slavery. Hell, even us Mexicans know it. Why do you think that even in the presence of our own women, we lust shamelessly over you?"

"I don't know daddy," I began to get a little frustrated. "No disrespect, but I just thought it was because y'all were some horny freaks."

"No. It's far more deeper than that," he told me. "But as you wish, I'll drop it. Before I do though, I want to ask you one more question."

"Be my guest," I sighed. I really wasn't up to anymore crazy talk from daddy, but I would've agreed to anything if it resulted in him changing the subject.

"How many eyes do you have?" he asked.

"What kinda question is that?" I responded.

"A simple one, just answer it. How many?"

"Two, duh."

"No baby," Daddy said, as he just sat silently looking into my eyes in disbelief at an answer I just knew I had given correctly. Then he weirdly let it go and began to ask me questions about my personal life. I gladly began telling him about my plans to open a fashion boutique. Then for the next hour we shared a great conversation talking about any and everything that didn't involve powers, religion, and spirits.

After two hours passed, visitation was called to an end and the two of us shared one last hug before we went our separate ways. I smothered myself into my daddy's arms for as long as the guard would allow us. He dreaded having to see me leave and in the midst of everyone in the room, yelled out while walking away, "find the right answer to that question and the world is yours!"

All I could do was hold my head down from embarrassment and act as if I didn't hear him.

CHAPTER 20: Secret Meeting

After visiting my daddy, even as weird as it was, I felt a sense of relief. That may have been the only move Detective Bailey suggested I make that didn't steer me wrong. It was also good to know that my old man was cool as shit. Besides the fact he didn't believe in Jesus Christ and thought the sun was his best friend, he was a pretty decent man with a lot of wisdom. Although the important question, how he ended up in jail in the first place was never answered, I didn't worry. For I knew I would be paying him another visit for that.

A few days later, about eight in the morning, I was dead in the middle of my sleep when my phone rang. I scrambled around the bed for it and glanced at the screen.

Poncha? I thought. What could she want this early?

I answered and although I was surely tired, I added an exaggerated drag to my voice to let her know I wasn't too fond of her calling me at that hour.

"Hello," my voice crackled.

"*Wake up, waake up, waaake up it's the first of the moooooonth,*" Poncha sang my favorite bone thugs and harmony tune. "Get yo tired ass up bitch!"

"Girl, don't you know it's eight in the fuckin' morning?" I asked her.

"And don't you know I'm in town," she shot back.

Immediately, a burst of joy entered my body and forced me up out of my bed. My favorite girl was here. I missed her so much.

"No way heffa, why you ain't call me?"

"I thought you knew, you know the meeting is tomorrow."

"What meeting?" I asked.

"The OMC meeting girl, snap outta that sleepy shit."

Although I was indeed tired, I had no clue that the OMC was having another meeting. I didn't even get the notification in my phone. Our squad handled everything professionally and we used this app called LinkUp to stay connected and inform one another of all gatherings. Every member had an anonymous profile and we would use code words to set up important dates and times. That way we never had to speak of our business over the phone lines.

"I've been out of town for some time now and my phone wouldn't catch a signal for shit," I lied. "When did they send the memo?"

"Isis sent it about a week ago. She didn't put a subject code in it like he normally does so I really don't know what it's about. All I do know is that it's tomorrow at seven-thirty sharp, at the normal spot. She also requested we each bring at least one pool stick."

That fuckin' Isis. I thought to myself. She's trying to count me out. Now it all makes sense. I knew for sure Hi-C wasn't going to like it. In the drug game, business was kept business and personal was kept personal. As smart as Isis was, I'm surprised she didn't understand that.

"A pool stick? Girl what the fuck she got going on. It's cool though," I fronted. "I can always just call her and get the scoop. In the meantime, what's your plans for today?"

"I plan on treating myself to some good old Sunny Side Up then stop by your crib."

"Unfortunately that cannot happen." I shot her down quickly. "I'm over to my lil' boo thang's house and he is not letting me leave his side today. Maybe we can catch back up tomorrow. You know you're always welcome to my crib."

I knew I wasn't telling Poncha the truth, but I had to find a way to curb her. She would only be in town for a few days so I figured I could keep the lie going until then. Even though she too was affected by the shut down, I just couldn't tell her I had lost my place. She was a great money manager and was smart about her business. I knew she had a couple thousands saved up for her dry season and wasn't set back by much, if at all. Besides, her boyfriend in California was a military man and owned a successful construction company. She was good even before she started hustling.

"Okay, cool. Sell me out for some dick," she clowned. "But remember while you freakin', that I'm only in town for the weekin'."

I laughed at Poncha's crazy self and we both dismissed ourselves from the conversation. Even though it was early, I couldn't go back to sleep. All I could do was think about this secret meeting and what it was all about. I wondered why Isis didn't include me in it when she knew I was a major part of the OMC. She had never been in a position to call any shots pertaining to Hi-C's business, but she also respected everything he did, even if it was wrong and disrespectful. I just couldn't see her going against him by counting me out. Maybe they were all on to me, maybe they weren't. All I knew for sure was that the shit wasn't adding up.

I decided to make a call to Charlytte and get up with her. I missed her, but I really was hoping to pick her brain to see how much she knew about Cederick's little meeting. I could also find out exactly how she was making a living and see if she would open up to me about it. Maybe then I could school her on the do's and don'ts of the street life and how to move in that world.

Charlytte agreed to meet up with me and we went to get our nails done, did some outlet shopping, and then caught a bar called Long Branch. It was located on Ordale's eastside and it was a good place to go if you wanted to hear a mix of old and new school music, partake in some good eating, and hang around a more mature urban crowd.

I didn't have much money to spend, but I had just gotten my fifteen hundred in rent from the college girls, so I could play around a little bit. I also decided to listen to Detective Bailey's preaching about me splurging with all that money just to impress people who really did nothing for my life. Honestly I couldn't master the art of not worrying about what others thought of me, so I figured I'd just stay unseen.

We arrived to the bar a little after seven that evening. I knew the bartender very well so Charlytte didn't have to worry about getting

ID'ed. We both ordered Patron Margaritas and although we knew nothing about how to shoot pool, we decided to have a little fun on the table. Thankfully, someone had blessed the juke box with a few bucks so we were also able to enjoy the sounds of some classic hip hop jams while we played.

Charlytte and I shot a few games for fun and I allowed the alcohol to flow through her system before I decided to sit her down. I knew I would probably get her to open up to me more if she was a little tipsy. To top off the mood, the dimness of the lights called for a great, comfortable atmosphere.

"You sho you're not a pool player," I asked her after realizing she wasn't that bad for a beginner.

"I play the game a lot on my cell phone but that's about it. Pool is more of a mind game. I guess I'm just good at using my head." Charlytte said, as she bent over in her cream-colored dressed that closed up at the neck. It was so short that I was surprised her ass didn't fall out when she took the shot. It also didn't help that the lighting from above the table shined directly in her bosom, allowing me and whoever else watching a good view of her cleavage.

Peaches was right. Charlytte had definitely come up out of her shell and was much more confident than I once knew her to be. Although I must admit she had every right to be, she definitely had it going on.

"Ion know about that," I said. "You probably holding secrets from me. You had to have done this before."

"Never," she replied, then hit the white ball against the black one and made a clean shot for the win. I was tired of her beating me and she had finally grown weary of standing in her heels, so we decided to order one more drink. Then we took a seat at one of the open dining tables.

The hip hop jams had now turned into some smooth rhythm and blues cuts from the eighties after someone else gained control of the jukebox. It was the perfect mood for a good ole heart to heart girl talk, especially with the both of us now feeling a buzz.

"Isn't this spot dope?" I asked her, attempting to break the ice.

"Yeah, I love it," she said. "Just the right crowd and the drinks aren't cheesy."

"I know right," I agreed. "You get your money's worth here. That's why I fucks with this shit."

"I see," she held up her drink and we tapped our glasses for a toast. Charlytte took the shot and didn't even flinch.

"You hold yo' liquor pretty good for a sixteen-year-old," I told her. "How long you been drinking?"

"I just started like a year ago," she said.

"Hell I'd be drinking too if I had to still live with my mama."

"Yeah I know," she said. " I'm surprised I ain't end up on crack dealing with that lady."

We both laughed.

"So why did you leave anyway, did she beat you down with a bat too?" I asked her.

"Naw, but she did chase me out of there and threatened to kill me," Charlytte replied nonchalantly, seeming uninteresting to talk about it. I knew the feeling so I decided not to pressure her.

"It was just time," she continued. "You know yo' mama treated me like shit. Hell, if it wasn't for you, I don't where know I'd be right now."

"Yeah, I always did have your back," I replied. "You know, I was just thinking the other day, like even though shit was fucked up, and even though mama was crazy as hell, we still had some good times in that house."

Charlytte immediately shot me down. "Speak for yourself Keisha. All I remember was misery and suffering."

"Now c'mon Charlytte," I challenged her. "You can't think of even one good memory we had in that house."

"Wellll," she admitted, before brightening her mood a little. "I do remember the time she was gone and we took all the dish soap and spreaded it over the kitchen floor. That was the best slip-n-slide fun ever. Auntie Jo came home and the whole damn house was bubbling."

We both busted out laughing. It was actually my idea to do that one. I was supposed to be washing the dishes but I couldn't resist.

She continued cracking up and I enjoyed seeing her begin to smile. "Or what about the time we called ourselves rolling up school paper and burning it in the bathroom. Ackin' like we were smoking a damn cigarette. Auntie came home and got one whiff of the smell and was like 'WHO THE HELL SMOKING REEFA IN MY HOUSE!"

We both laughed again, so loud that some people even looked over in our direction to see what the commotion was about. We didn't pay them any mind though. "Like fa real, ma? REEFA? First of all, who says that? And second, we were too young to even know what weed was."

"I know, right?" Charlytte said as we both cracked up some more. "Boy was she pissed. She cut everybody's ass."

"But you gotta admit, that's one ass cuttin I believe we deserved," I simmered down. "Like the time Mama was dating that man who owned that seven-eleven, Mr. Otis. Remember the first time she took us to his store and I boosted Keyshawn up to steal a whole box of snickers off the shelf. Remember that?"

I continued on with my laughter, but for some strange reason Charlytte's began to fade. Then her eyes went low and shifted right. She seemed to mentally go astray from our conversation, before quickly bringing herself back.

"Yeah, I remember," she finally chuckled, then dragged her voice, seemingly to be uninterested in talking about it. "Then he had the nerve to blame it all on me."

"Oh snap, that's right," I recalled. "Keyshawn did say you did it. But hey, did you hear about what happened to him?"

"Who Keyshawn?" She asked.

"No, the old man Mr. Otis," I replied.

Charlytte suddenly seemed to get back excited. "No, what happened?"

"Well, I heard that some guys found him one morning unconscious in his office room naked and bleeding from his asshole. Apparently the niggas who robbed him had buttfucked him too. What kinda new niggas shit is that? These clowns these days be on some other shit man. That molly shit is the new-aged crack."

"Fa real. Damn, that's messed up," Charlytte responded, seemingly not sympathetic.

"To make the shit even worse," I continued, "they say the hood wiped his whole store out clean before they even called to get him some help. The next week he sold it and nobody has heard from him since. That's messed up, ain't it? He seemed to be a real good man."

"Who knows?" Charlytte replied. "Sometimes people ain't who they appear to be. Never know what he did to deserve that shit."

"Maybe," I shrugged. "All I know is that his store has been in that same spot for over thirty years. He couldn't have been that bad."

"Like I said, you never really know," she replied, before changing the subject. "I wonder what they did with the building though. Is it still even a store?"

"No. I drove by there recently," I told her. "I believe it's a laundromat now. If I had the money I would have bought the motherfucka. I've always dreamed of owning an elegant fashion boutique somewhere in the hood. What about you? What would you have done with it?"

"Probably nothing," she said. "I haven't discovered that thing that I'm good at yet. Maybe I should have just stayed in school after all."

"I'm glad you brought that up," I told her. "I was meaning to ask you about that. Why did you drop out in the first place?"

"I don't know," she sighed. "After I got expelled my seventh grade year for stabbing up that Samantha girl with a pencil, I haven't been back in the groove of it."

"Hold up. Wait a minute...what Samantha?" I asked.

"Samantha Hutchinson," she replied.

I placed my hand over my mouth and let a look of pure surprise show all over my face. I couldn't believe how small the city was.

"So you where the one who stabbed up Felice's sister? I can't believe this shit," I started to laugh. "Oh my God! That's crazy! I heard you sent her ass straight back to Philly too."

"I don't know where she went back to, but I do know she left town right after it went down. I was glad too. She was the fuckin' school bully but for some odd reason she only wanted to pick on me. And it was all because of a damn boy name Alex."

"Trust me Charlytte," I replied. "Samantha wasn't stressing you about no damn boy. I know that whole family very well and I used to babysit her. She always acted boyish, ever since she was little. I can bet one thousand dollars she's gonna grow up to be a lesbian, just watch."

Charlytte cracked a laughed. "Now that I think about it she did look a little manly."

"I know what I'm talking about Charlytte. Believe me, she wasn't worried about no damn Alex. Her issue with you was more personal than that. Felice must have told her we were related. That's her big sister and she hates me."

"Why though?" Charlytte asked. "Keisha, you cool as shit and you don't seem like you bother nobody."

"We were good friends before Shannon moved in to town. She started getting jealous and then tried to force me to choose between the two of them, but I wasn't having that. I sent her ass crying off the park in front of the whole damn neighborhood. We were kids then, but apparently she hasn't gotten over it yet."

"Damn, that' silly," Charlytte said. "Felice really needs to grow up."

"I know right. All I can say is just be careful. I know firsthand how them Hutchinson girls get down. They don't let shit go and they don't play fair either."

"Thanks, but I think that I can handle it. I kicked her ass before and I can do it again," she boasted. "And that's for any of them Hutchinson's that want it with me."

All tipsy-eyed, I looked across the table at Charlytte being super confident and shit. Although I knew she was no real match for them, I did admire her courage and don't-take-shit-from-nobody attitude. She was once so soft spoken and innocent that I thought she would grow up to be a little push over. But to my surprise,

Charlytte was a tough cookie and I knew it was the real world that made her that way.

We both went into blank stares, lost in our own little thoughts. Then I quickly came back to reality and tried to focus on my real goal of bringing her there. I had a mission with Charlytte and I definitely needed to stick to my plan.

"But forget all that," I said. "How have you been girl? I see you've been keeping up with yourself. You got taste like your cousin too. I like that."

"To be honest Keisha, I don't know the first thing about fashion. Cederick gets most of this shit for me."

"Cederick is a pretty sharp dresser himself," I gave him his props. "Speaking of him, what's the deal with you two? You guys don't seem to be as close as you used to be."

"We're okay," she said. "When I left your mama's house, I really didn't have anywhere to go and he showed me alotta love. I feel like I owe him the world for that, but at the same time, I still wanna make my own chips and learn how to stand on my own two."

"I hear that girl," I said. "Like I always say, we're Blacks and we don't depend on anyone for shit."

"Besides," she continued, "he just been acting different since, well you know, Hi-C got locked up."

"I figured that," I told her. "But I can't say I blame him. We all have been hit by this mess. I guess some people handle shit different than others."

"I guess I understand," she replied.

"All I know," I told her, "is that I'm ready for Hi-C to get out so we can start back making this real paper again."

"I feel you," she said. "That's pretty fucked up how they arrested him. Me and Cederick were together in Jacksonville when I first heard about it. All I will say is that it was one crazy night for me."

"I believe it was one crazy night for everybody," I agreed and immediately began to clean up our little area so that we could soon make our departure.

Although I was enjoying catching up with Charlytte, I realized from the little she told me that she didn't have the information I needed to know about the meeting. Sadly, after I came to that conclusion I wasn't as interested in talking to her anymore. With no sympathy at all, I made up a bogus reason to leave the bar and then dropped her off at the gas station that she requested me to. Although it was after midnight, she told me she was meeting up with an old man who was going to 'show her a car he was trying to sell her.'

I wasn't dumb by a long shot though. I knew when I saw that old broke down creep, who looked to be in his late sixties, smiling as Charlytte switched in her mini dress to his pick-up truck, I knew he was going to be showing her more than just a car.

CHAPTER 21: Stakeout

"I really can't believe they would do me like this," I said to myself as I sat slumped down in my lowkey little Camry. It was parked a couple blocks from Hi-C's house. I stayed far enough away not to be noticed, but close enough to get a good view of his front porch. Sure enough, at exactly 7:15 every member of the OMC began to arrive. Each of them carrying a pool stick and dressed in competitive attire. Even Poncha, who probably was expecting me to already be there, arrived pretty and ready for the meeting.

I watched enviously as Isis greeted the last member, before shutting the door and closing all the windows. As the anxiety of not knowing what was going on inside kicked in, I tried to remain calm but really it only made me more furious. It literally took all the discipline I had within me not to say fuck it and barge into the place. Yet, I decided it was best I played it cool and stuck with the plan of why I was even there in the first place.

In attempt to ease the stress, I found myself doodling on an old notepad that I retrieved from my glove compartment. About an hour had went by when I finally saw Isis swing open the door again to see everyone out. They were all in good spirits, laughing and mangling with to-go plates in most of their hands. This led me to believe that she had also cooked for them. She sometimes did this to support Hi-C and although I didn't care for her, even I appreciated the meals. I had to give it to her, the way she put together a Jamaican dish made me wonder why she became a lawyer and not a chef.

I watched carefully as all the members drove themselves out of the neighborhood and that was my cue to exit my car. I quickly, but cautiously, dashed across a couple streets and hoped to go unnoticed. Since Cederick was the second person in command he was always the last one to leave, so I knew it would be another couple minutes before he made his way to his vehicle.

As usual, he was parked on the side of Hi-C's house, a little further in the rear. Because of his position, he had to let the other members get spaces closer to the house. Dressed in an all-black body suit with ankle-length boots, I barricaded myself between two trees and waited for him.

"You mind tellin' me what the fuck is going on?" I said to Cederick as I crept up behind him after he finally made it to his car.

Cederick drew his gun quicker than I could inform him that it was just me and pointed it dead at my chest.

"Keisha, what the fuck?" he said, startled but relieved. "You know better than to run up on me like that. You trynna get yourself killed."

"Looks like I'm already dead, at least to the OMC," I fired back, "so what difference does it make?"

Cederick quickly attempted to unlock his car door with his keys, but not before he began to nervously look around. Hi-C's house being his main focus.

“You better get the fuck from around here now, before someone sees you,” he told me.

“No. And what do you mean *before someone sees me*? I'm a part of this circle too and I'm not leaving until you tell me what the fuck is going on."

"Keisha, you're really pushing it. Just leave now.”

“No!” I shouted. “I'm not going anywhere. Now tell me, why wasn't I invited to this meeting?”

After seeing that I was very serious about not budging, and hearing me get loud enough to possibly be heard by someone, Cederick gave in. He looked around once more, then snatched me up by the arm and walked me around his Monte Carlo. Then he opened the car door, threw me inside, and slammed the door. It was the first time I had ever had a guy open a car door for me and although it wasn't on the most romantic terms, I still appreciated the gesture.

“And they say chivalry is dead,” I said sarcastically after watching Cederick take his place in the driver seat of his car.

“You're gonna be dead if you don’t quit with your bullshit," he said.

My heart began to beat faster. I immediately thought that Cederick and the team possibly knew of my involvement with the feds.

“What bullshit?" I asked. "What are you talking about?”

“Calm down," he told me, before relaxing his own self with a hit of the freshly rolled blunt he pulled out of his ashtray. “Where did you park?”

“A couple blocks over on Quacco," I told him.

"I'm gonna take you there," he replied. "Just sit back and keep quiet."

As he wished, I said nothing the entire two minutes it took him to drive over to where my car was located. He was silent, looking as if he was in deep thought while he puffed on his blunt a few more times. He didn't even have the decency to offer me a hit. When we made it onto Quacco Road, he pulled up behind my car and put his in park.

"Look," he said, "I'm gonna tell you what the deal is, but you better not mention a word of this to anyone."

"I swear," I told him. "I just wanna know what's going on. That's all."

Cederick took another hit of his blunt before putting it back in the ashtray. Then he checked his banana-colored Polo shirt for any signs of ashes. Once he was pleased to know he hadn't damaged his fly gear, he turned his body towards me and began to spill the beans.

"Hi-C gave us the okay to start moving work again. He hooked me up with some of his people and trusts that I can handle the business. That's what the meeting was about."

"Okay, that's definitely good to hear," I said excitedly. "But that doesn't explain why I wasn't invited."

"Do I look like the guest keeper to you? I don't know anything about that. Isis was responsible for getting all the members there. And well, you are fucking her husband sooo…."

"Sooo what? You and I both know Hi-C don't mix personal feelings with his business. I'm positive he would want me back on my routes and if he finds out that Isis is out here interfering with that he's not gonna like it one bit."

"Relax," he told me. "Isis's only job was to get all the members together. I'm the one in charge of everything else from this point on."

“Oh thank Goodness,” I said. “So when do we start?”

“What do you mean, *we*?” he asked.

“We meaning you, me, the OMC," I said with a look of ‘duh’ on my face.

Cederick then shut off his car and let his seat all the way back. I watched him as he rested his head into his palms and relaxed as if he was on a beach or something. Then he closed his eyes and allowed a weird, devilish grin to appear on his face.

"I don’t know when *we* start," he replied while still smiling. "I guess that depends."

"Depends…?" I questioned. “On what?”

"Well...on you....I guess."

I got even more excited. "Okay cool. If that's the case, hell, I was ready yesterday. So what's up? When will you be ready to move?"

Cederick still remained calm and relaxed. "I dunno. As soon as *you* move?"

Then with one eye open, peeped down at his groin area. Only as a natural reflect, I also looked and to my surprise saw that his manhood stiffened. Ashamed and uncomfortable, I quickly turned away. Then suddenly realized where he was getting at.

"Cederick," I called out to him angrily, while trying to remain calm. I hoped that I was just overthinking the situation but I needed to be sure. "Are you asking me what I think you're asking me?"

"What do you think I'm asking you?" He said, still grinning.

"Look, I don't have time for these mind games," I said, beginning to get a little frustrated. "Are you talking about me fuckin' you or something? Because if you are you can kiss my ass on that one."

"Okay cool," he said, seemingly unbothered. "Well in that case, get out."

"Huh?" I mumbled.

"I brought you to your car, now get out."

"Boy you really have some nerve. Wait until I tell Hi-C about this."

Cederick busted out in a heavy laughter before rising from his position. Then he used his elbows to support his upper body so that he could look me in my face again.

"You think Hi-C really gives a fuck about you. Get real," he said. "You're just another one to him. Don't take it personal, but every chick from the OMC gotta do something for the boss in order to get down with the team. Sorta like an initiation. And well, I'm in charge now."

"Cedrick, I'm going to hope that whatever drink you had at the meeting got you trippin' like this. You are on some real bullshit. Besides, Poncha ain't sleep with him."

"Really?" he said. "And how do you know that?"

"Because she told me she never did and she wouldn't lie to me. That's my girl."

"And did you tell her you did?" he asked me.

"Well…no," I replied.

"So what makes you think she would tell you?" he chuckled to himself and then became serious. "Listen Keisha, the OMC is a business, not a friendship circle. Everybody gotta position to play. Trust me when I say that Hi-C don't work with no chick he hasn't touched. You better wake up and stop being so naive."

Cederick's words was a gut-puncher and really got me to thinking. If he were right, it would have definitely changed my thoughts about the OMC. Yet, I still couldn't bring myself to believe that

Hi-C's involvement with me was nothing more than a ritual. Everything he told me about his past, and running away with me, had to have been real. And I definitely couldn't believe that Poncha, as real as she had always been to me, would lie about something like that. I trusted them both and I just couldn't bring myself to accept that kind of reality.

"You're being ridiculous!" I shouted, trying to hide my hurt. "I can't believe you would even come at me like this."

"I'm not doing nothing but trying to put a bunch of money back in ya' damn pocket. When we want the finer things in life, we must be willing to do what we have to do in order to have them. Unfortunately, the greater the reward, the greater the sacrifice. That's just how it goes. I didn't make the rules. Bottom line, you need something from me, and I want something from you. So what are you gonna choose?"

"Wait until I tell Hi-C about this," was all I could say before I saw myself out of his ride.

Cederick shrugged his shoulder as if my departure meant nothing to him. He allowed his seat to rise, drawing him back up to the steering wheel. Then he cranked his car and fully blasted his music before positioning himself to take off.

"Hey Keisha," he quickly caught my attention after I slammed his door.

"What?" I gave him much attitude.

"Whenever you want your spot back," he threw a card and a condom into my hands, "you know what to do."

CHAPTER 22: Not so bad

It was just too much for me to take in at once. I was going broke. Hi-C was still in prison. Cederick was blackmailing me. And I was actually getting desperate enough to think about giving in to him. My tenants had also just told me that they were thinking about moving out. On top of all that, Mr. Zinc's wife had a stroke and he was too tied up taking care of her to be living out his freaky fantasies with me.

Wanting to be unbothered, I distanced myself from everyone and stayed shut up in the hotel room for weeks. I had a couple of missed calls from Shannon, Poncha, Alicia, and even Charlytte. But I ignored them all. Detective Bailey called me more than anyone else, every day to be exact. He was the only one I answered to, but ironically he was the one I wanted to hear from the least. I would always pick up his calls, but only to hit him with the same line, "not in the mood, try back tomorrow." Unfortunately, every day he would do just that. I don't even know why I entertained him. I guess I just wanted him to know how pissed I was with him. After all, I felt that my entire situation was all his fault.

It was a Sunday morning and my phone rang at exactly 11:30, same time it did every morning.

“You just don't quit," I said as I answered in the most aggravated voice I could possibly make.

"Quitting has never been my strong point. I wouldn't be where I am today if I was any good at it."

"And I wouldn't be where I am today had you decided to be a firefighter," I said sarcastically.

"How did you know I considered it?" he shot back.

"Look, I have told you for the thousandth time, I am not in the mood. I won't be today, tomorrow, or the day after that. So tell me, what exactly do you want now and make it quick?"

"I want you to throw on something nice and meet me downstairs. I've waited two weeks to speak to you. I'm sure I can wait another thirty minutes."

"You mean to tell me you're outside?" I asked.

"Looking at the front lobby as we speak," he replied.

"Detective, what the hell?" I said. "How many times have I told you not to pop up on me like that?"

"And how many times do I actually listen?"

Knowing I did not have much of a choice, I decided to just dress and head downstairs to take the mystery ride with him. I admit, I was growing weary of being trapped in the walls of that cooped up room. I decided to slip into something not too dressy, but not too casual either. A white fluffy blouse that draped across my shoulders and some skin-tight, light blue denim jeans was what I decided to cover my body with. I topped it off with some beautiful gold six-inch heels and gold accessories to match. Before leaving, I decided to bump a little curl in my hair to give my bob some definition. My hair was so naturally silky that even if I had not, it would have still fell beautifully down my face. I was dressed and ready to go in exactly thirty minutes. The detective was in fact waiting for me by the front entrance and as I usually did, I scoped out my surroundings before entering his vehicle.

"You happy now?" I said, pretending to not be thrilled by joining him. I watched him carefully as he backed out of the hotel and preceded to head toward the open road.

"I try to always be," he replied. "I have too much to be thankful for not to."

"You know you always have some clever shit to say," I replied. "Like your life is so peachy. Well good for you."

Detective Bailey let out a smirk and said nothing in his defense. In fact, we both sat quietly as we rode not one, but two, hours away from the city of Ordale. I pondered out of the window the whole time, listening to music in my headphones just thinking about my life and the direction it was going in. We were riding unusually further than I expected but I was too excited just to be out of the hotel to complain or even question it.

It wasn't until we arrived to a wooded area and turned into a lane away from the open road that I began to grow concern.

National Wildlife Center, I read on a huge wooden sign sitting at the entrance.

"Detective Bailey, where are we going? I know damn well you don't expect me to walk through these woods. And definitely not in these heels."

"Who said anything about walking?" he said as he rode fearlessly along the dirt road. The street of which we turned on to get there, could no longer be seen.

"Oh," I settled my nerves. "Then what are we doing?"

"It's a nature trail, but you can only drive through it," he said. "Besides, if you got out of the car the alligators would eat you alive."

"Alligators?" my nerves shot up again. "Detective Bailey are you trying to give me a heart attack?"

"No, I'm just trying to introduce you to something different. Life is more than high heels, the mall, and fancy night clubs, ya know? You have to be able to understand and appreciate this thing called the universe."

I ignored him and continued to look out of the window. As we rode deeper into the trail, the trees that we once looked up to had turned into swamps that we now looked down upon. The dirt road now seemed to sit high, while the water sat low on both sides of us. I couldn't believe people were actually allowed to ride on a trail that had no barriers. I mean really, if we veered a little too far left or right we would have been down in the swamp swimming with the creatures that occupied it.

"You mean to tell me that there are alligators down there?" I asked. "Where? I don't see nun?"

"Just keep looking," the detective said.

I removed the headphones from my ear and found myself getting more and more interested in my surroundings. Detective Bailey continued to ride about ten miles per hour as he searched his side and mine for any signs of gators. After only about five minutes I began to get frustrated, but shortly after my eyes rested on something peeping out of the water.

"Oh my god! There's one!" I shouted. "Right over there!"

Detective Bailey looked to where my fingers were pointing and put his car in park. I rolled my window down slightly but kept my hand on the lockpad in fear of my dangerous surroundings.

"See. There!" I shouted.

"Well I'll be…a big one too," Detective Bailey said after he spotted it, then suddenly reached in the back seat of his car and opened up a cooler. A horrible smell immediately reeked from it.

"What the fuck is that?" I pinched my nostrils then looked at a black bag that appeared to have some uncooked rotten meat in it.

"It's chicken," he said. "Or shall I say, *dinner.* Watch this."

I stared curiously as the detective opened the door to his car and stood out of it. He was sure to keep one foot inside as he began slinging meat into the waters of the swamp. He threw some far out and some close, but he made sure he never hit the same spot twice. He even dropped a few on the trail.

"Are you crazy. That sign clearly says to stay inside and to NOT feed them!"

The detective threw his body back into the car and had this look of excitement all over his face. Like he had just robbed a bank or something. I could sense that he got some sort of adrenaline rush by doing what he had just done. I was scared as shit but it kind of made me feel good to see him do something bad. Made him seem more human.

"You know what you just did was not only crazy, but against the law right?"

"So have me arrested," he mocked me. Sweat began to pour down his face and you could literally see his heart beating through his t-shirt.

"Well maybe I will," I said. "Under the grounds of a little thing called pay back. But seriously, you really just broke the law and that's exactly what I don't respect about people like you."

"People like me?" he chuckled.

"Yeah, you police ass muthafuckas. You wanna lock people up for stupid shit knowing very well you have skeletons in your own damn closet."

Detective Bailey was listening to me but at the same time he kept his eyes on the swamp. I watched too as I began to see more and more gators appear from the water to get a taste of the chicken flesh that had just been introduced to them.

"Well, I can't speak for anybody else," he forced his attention away from the water and then back to me. "But the difference between my crime and yours is that I ain't hurtin' nobody."

"...and who am I hurting?" I asked him.

"Your community," he replied.

"My community?" I got offended quickly. "Look, my community has been hurting since before I was born. Drug dealing, gangbangin', killing and everything else that has been going on in these streets didn't start with me, my click, nor my generation. I don't make none of the guns on the street and I damn sure ain't in no laboratory cookin' up no dope. I'm just using the resources that were already here before me to try and make a decent living out here. Regardless if it's me or not, somebody's gonna do it. Even you wouldn't have a job if it wasn't for people out here like us, so think about that before you judge. Besides, do you know how many local organizations- that your government won't even drop a dime to support- get funded by the OMC? Every winter we're putting smiles on these kids' faces with toys and giveaways. We're not just a bunch of crooks and dealers, we're actually trying to build our streets up."

"If you really want to build up your streets then stop dealing to those same kids fathers and mothers. One toy per year is nothing compared to living with a crackhead or a junkie every day. Material things aren't going to help these children. Always remember, family is the most important thing anybody can have."

"Okay Detective, gotcha." I said sarcastically. I really wasn't in the mood for the preaching, especially from someone who I just saw commit a crime himself. Didn't matter to me how small it was."

"I know you got me," he faced me with a clever grin and then winked. "Believe it or not, I got you too."

Detective Bailey turned his attention back to the marsh. The sweat was still dripping from his forehead and he had a very serious look on his face. He was so infatuated with the alligators that it almost worried me.

"Right on time," Detective Bailey said before I realized myself what he was anticipating.

"Oh my god, Detective!" I gasped. "Look at it."

One of the largest gators that I had ever saw in my life slowly crept its way on land, up towards the huge chunk of meat that Detective Bailey dropped on the trail. Literally just a few feet away from his car. I had never been so close to one and even though I knew we were safe inside, I still felt the need to grab the Detective's arm tightly to help me deal with the fear of what I was witnessing.

"He's the largest and bravest one out here. I call him Alpha."

"So you name them?" I asked.

"I name them. I learn them. I study them. I know them. I'd normally be standing out there watching him eat, but I won't frighten you any more than what I already have."

"Thank you for that. But I gotta say, you're even crazier than I thought you were. You don't ever get scared that one of these things might grab you one of these days? I hear an alligator's grip ain't no joke."

"Over two thousand pounds of force to be exact. Record breaking for any species," he informed me. "But I also know that an alligator's jaw muscles are very weak, which has always been a question for me. Like how can an animal bite down with that much force, but not have jaws strong enough to snap a flimsy rubber band from around its mouth. One night, I sat here for hours trying to figure it out until it suddenly dawned on me."

"And what did you come up with?" I asked, I was definitely curious to know.

"That life has a way of humbling every creature on this planet. There has to be a balance in anything that has power or else it can and will become a serious danger. See, I don't fear that animal because I understand it, especially enough to know its weakness. You understand that?"

"Yeah I guess," I shrugged. "I still think you're crazy as hell."

We watched Alpha carry his food back into the marsh. Then we continued to drive through the trail spotting more gators. Detective Bailey even showed me a few other animals and gave me the background on them as well. It was obvious that he was a huge fan of nature and I admit it was definitely something that intrigued me. I got to see another side of him that was more than a pesky investigator. I wasn't expecting that. I also wasn't expecting to go fishing with him for the remainder of the evening.

In fact, we went to a small river not far from the nature trail and sat along the pier. Judging by the two fishing rods, cooler full of sandwiches, and wine coolers, he had already knew what his plans were with me. It was the first time I had ever been fishing, but I enjoyed learning how to hook the bait, throw the rod, and be patient as I waited like a child for my first catch. We continued to talk more about life and the world, but decided to leave our lifestyles and separate viewpoints off of the table. By that water, we were just two people who enjoyed each other's company and it was perfect that way.

The sandwiches alone didn't do much for my appetite and the weak coolers just heightened my desire for an even bigger buzz, so I convinced Detective Bailey to hit up a small bar-n-grill to get some good food. Of course he wanted to shoot straight to Ordale, but there was nothing there for me to rush back to.

After a couple minutes of whining and bringing up the fact that I gut a fish for him, he rationalized and decided to let me have my way. We ended up at some hole-in-the-wall lounge called Quincy's that was urban but old school. The club wasn't the fanciest but the drinks were made how they were supposed to be and the guy in the kitchen made one of the best steaks I had tasted in my whole entire life. Detective Bailey first seemed a little uncomfortable being in that type of setting, but I managed to convince him to relax and have one drink with me. He stressed that he wasn't much of a drinker and after I saw how loose that one shot had him, I knew he was being honest about it.

The detective and I played a couple games of Keno together, hit the dance floor once to one of Michael Jackson tunes, and kicked it pretty hard until it was time to roll. I knew that he was in no condition to drive, especially being an officer of the law, so we both decided it was best that we just walked across the street and check in at the hotel that was conveniently there.

"You sure you don't want me to book another room?" he asked sluggishly, as he took a seat at the end of the queen-sized bed in our room and began taking off his socks.

"That's a waste of money. We'll be out of here in just a few hours," I said as I looked at my watch. It was approaching two-thirty. "Besides, it's not the first time we slept together... well you know what I mean."

"Yeah but it's the first time I've been drinking," he replied.

"I know. But I'm not worried about you trying anything." I assured him. "I know you're a good guy."

"Who said anything about me?" he questioned. "It's you that I'm worried about."

"Oh please Detective, I'm not attracted to pigs," I said, while ironically trying to stop myself from looking at the way his chest beautifully began to reveal itself as he unbuttoned his collared shirt. "They're one of the most disgusting animals on the planet. Living garbage disposals is what I call them."

"You're right about one thing," he said. "We do take out the trash."

Detective Bailey began to laugh but I didn't join him. I don't think he liked the fact that I called him a pig either, but I didn't care. I just called it how I saw it. Besides, even though we had a wonderful night together, I still hadn't forgotten how he ruined my life.

"I'm gonna ignore that, Porky." I teased. "Because you're just feeling good. Sometimes it's okay to leave the farm and lighten up, especially with a job like yours. Hell, I'd be relaxed every night if I had to make people's lives miserable every day."

"Look now," Detective Bailey laughed before trying to stand up. He struggled a bit but managed to get himself on his two feet. "We got along just fine today and I'd like to leave it that way."

"Agreed," I replied.

Detective Bailey headed to the bathroom that was centered at the back of the room. I could hear him freely take a piss before turning on the faucet to engage in a shower that only lasted about two minutes. After he was finished I followed suit. I was too drained and too tipsy to desire to bathe, but being around the marsh and fish all day left me no choice.

Unlike Detective Bailey, I took about twenty minutes getting a good wash in. Once I was finished, I threw on the same bra I had on before, but decided to free myself of my panties, jeans, and blouse so that I may get a good comfortable rest. I used a towel to cover me as I made my way to the bed, even though the absence of light that Detective Bailey orchestrated while I was in the shower, would have protected my bareness just fine. Detective Bailey was silently curled up on his side of the bed and I assumed he was sleeping, until I laid down and he slowly rolled over to face me.

"I thought you'd never make it out of there," he said in a weary voice. I could tell he was ready to crash at any moment.

"Unlike most men, I like to bathe thoroughly. Every part of me needs special attention."

"Is that right?" he asked.

"But had I known you were waiting for me, I surely would have been done quicker," I told him.

"I wasn't waiting on you. I just never sleep when there is motion going on around me. Been like that since I was a kid."

"I know. I'm kinda like that myself," I replied.

"Most people are."

There was a brief moment of silence in the bed while I just lay there thinking about the wonderful evening I had. I really enjoyed seeing that side of the detective.

"Detective Bailey, may I share something with you? "I asked, breaking the silence between us.

“Sure,” he replied.

"Now I don't mean to get mushy or nothin', because you know I'm a gangsta and all," I joked. "But I gotta admit that I really enjoyed being with you today. I honestly did think that you were this cocky dickhead cop, but you really are pretty cool and down to earth. You got some good dance moves too. I'm impressed."

"Well what can I say," he attempted to pop his collar but was only able to grab the soft handles of his tank. "I have always been smooth with my moves since back in the day. It's good to know that I still have it."

"Definitely gave me a run for my money," I said. "So I take it you don't get out much?"

"Not really," he said. "From sun up to sun down my life consists of work. I mean, even when I'm not working I'm still on the clock. It's like I've lost that 'fun' part of me."

"All work, no play huh," I said. "But you gotta have some type of balance."

"I know, what can I say tho. It's my life," he said. "Although I do appreciate those words. I know it took a lot for you to tell me that. And to be honest, I learned a few things about you too."

"Oh really," I said." "And what's that?"

"That you're not as simple-minded as I thought you were, no offense. That you were willing to explore and actually become interested in the world around you. That was cool."

"Well thanks," I was flattered. "See what happens when we put our differences aside."

There was silence again and immediately I drifted my weary mind back to the mini altercation we had when I first entered his vehicle. I thought hard about what he said about me being a source of the problem in my community and I wondered if he was right all along. Besides, thinking about how Cedrick tried to play me, I saw firsthand just how dirty the game could get and I wasn't quite sure I wanted to be a part of it anymore.

"Detective Bailey, can I tell you something else. I mean like completely off the record."

"Anything you want to. It'll just be between me and you."

"I have just been so down and distant lately because I can't wrap my head around how dirty the people in this game can be. I talked to Cederick the other day and he gave me word that Hi-C gave him the okay to pick up the business again."

Detective Bailey let out a deep sigh. "Not surprised, but isn't that what you wanted? I don't see what the issue is?"

"Well he has all the power now, I guess. And he's telling me I have to sleep with him in order to get my place back in the OMC."

"Man," he sighed even harder. "That is crazy, but does it really surprise you? Like really?"

"I mean, yes. Him and Hi-C are boys. He has to know how Hi-C feels about me, just like he knows how I feel about Hi-C. I don't know if it's a test of my loyalty or if Cederick is really that twisted in the head to think I would sleep with him. Either way, it's just a fucked up predicament to be in."

"Well, what can you say. You're in a dirty game with no rules. Anything goes."

This time I was the one who sighed deeply. As much as I didn't want to admit it or feel it, I knew that Detective Bailey had a point. I continued on. "It pains me to say this, but I've been thinking about what you said all day today and you might be right. Maybe I am hurting my community. I got a baby cousin out here trickin' and I've been too caught up chasing money to stop her. My best friend has kids and I couldn't even tell you there names. And I'm sitting here crying to you about how bad I feel about sleeping around on a married man."

The whiteness in my eyes became covered with tears. I placed one arm across the detective's chest, gripping him tightly for support, and unintentionally dampened his tank with my tears. Thankfully, he didn't seem to mind though. He just held me closely and surprisingly began to let out a few tears of his own.

"Keisha," he called to me in his now broken voice. "I need you to be strong. Don't beat yourself up for being human. We all have our own skeletons and baggage. Even me."

Detective Bailey threw my arms off of him and turned away so that I wouldn't see him cry. Yet still, the sobs he released were so intense that I couldn't help but notice. Surprised to see him weeping in that manner, I grabbed him and attempted to return the favor of comforting him.

"I know it's hard," I stroked his back gently with my soft hands, "but I told you you're gonna have to find balance between work and your personal life."

"It's not that," he sobbed mannishly. "It's much more deeper."

I was confused. Here I was thinking that Detective Bailey had all his ducks in order, but he was just an emotional wreck himself. I could only wonder how and why a man who appeared to be so perfect be in such turmoil.

"Keisha, can I share something with you? Off the record also?"

"Detective, I'm here for you. You can tell me anything."

The detective turned back around to face me. The room was dimmed but the nearby streetlight that shined through our window reflected from his watery eyes, putting a great spark into them.

"You are no more of a failure than me. I'm actually hurting the community more than you are."

"What? How is risking your life to take drugs and criminals off the streets hurting your community?" I interrupted.

"Because sometimes sitting back doing nothing while you're witnessing wrongdoing is worse than anything," he sighed. "I'm biracial, if you haven't already notice. And I have to come to my job every day and hide that side of me because I work for people who hate the look of blacks, the smell of blacks, and the ground they walk on. People who are on a mission to destroy and are not gonna stop until their agenda is fulfilled."

"Detective, I'm confused and scared here. What agenda? And who's not gonna stop?"

"The enemy. The power. You really think that folks are out here killing each other *every day*. I mean, yeah it definitely is bad, but the plot to oppress is even worse. What if I told you there was a reason so many black on black crimes go unsolved? What if I told you that every major city had a secret organization that was designed solely to aid in the plan to wipe out black men?"

I was still lost and the confused expression I wore on my face made it easy for Detective Bailey to grasp that.

"So it's like this," he began to explain, "if I find out Peter is beefing with Paul, I gun down Peter and now the streets automatically think Paul did it. I don't even have to go after Paul because the streets are gonna take care of that. Now I can arrest who shot Paul and throw him behind bars for life. His sons will grow up fatherless and more than likely end up in the system themselves. But most importantly, he can't produce any more seeds and populate the earth with more of his kind. Shit is so crazy, that sometimes killing the right person can lead to up to twenty deaths and hundreds of arrests. I've witnessed it happen far too many times."

"So lemme get this straight? A man- black man- can be chillin' in his house and a federal agent will run up in his house and shoot him dead. Now eastside beefin' with Westside."

"It's happen like that before," he nodded. "But it's never random. They only go after people that they know the streets will go to war over. People with a rep and a lot of love out there. It's a strategy to this thing, sort of like playing chest."

"So how do they know who to go after? Like where do they get their information from."

"That's the easy part. Snitchin' is at an all-time high, a base head will tell you anything just for a hit of crack, and you'd be surprise what you can learn from social media. But if all else, the All-Seeing-Eye."

"The all-seeing-eye." I said like a child, before sitting up from the bed. My right thigh was now laying across his chest.

"Yes. The eye in the sky. You never heard of it?"

"Nope."

"It watches over the world. That's all I can say."

"You mean like cameras?" I asked.

"Exactly like cameras?" he said.

"I don't believe that. The other stuff you just said was hard enough to believe, but this definitely is a stretch."

"Doesn't surprise me that you don't believe," he shook his head. "Because the thing about this world is that we only believe what's in front of us. What we think is impossible is really not. They send you flat screens, video games, and cell phones then make you think it's the latest. But who knows, may have been created hundred years before it got to you. You'd be surprised how advanced things have gotten and what you don't know."

"So you're telling me that there is a camera in the sky that is watching me right now? Can even hear everything I say, everything you're saying to me right now… and you're not afraid?"

"Yes it is. But it's not that simple. They're not sitting around watching people's every move. It's more for high-profile situations, only for the Big Fish. You wanna track down a terror, or a prison escapee, a mass shooter, that's when these people get involved. The manhunts are just distractions. I would only worry about being in those situations if I became important enough."

"But if that is true, isn't that illegal?" I asked. "Like recording people without them knowing."

"Illegal?" Detective Bailey laughed. "In this world there is no such thing as legal or illegal. Just a clever system of laws used to control people mentally and keep them in line."

"Well if they could do anything they wanted to, why not just tell people they are being watched. World would probably be more safer if people knew that anyway."

"Keisha, if you knew how much money is made off of crime, you wouldn't ask me that question? And that's why it will always be a secret," he said. "What type of world would it be if people knew their every move was being monitored? Who'd rob that bank if they knew they would be caught? Who'd murder if the evidence would trace back to them? No one. Trust me, the big guys aren't worried about finding out who killed Bam-Bam and Lil' Pookie. Let the locals deal with that. Like I told you before, it's only for power and the big fish."

"Would Hi-C be considered a big fish?"

Detective Bailey sat up along with me, clicked on the lamp beside of us, and then looked me dead in the eyes. He had his cap off and it was the first time I really paid attention to how curly his hair really was. Also his fawn skin tone let me know he definitely had some black in him. Kinda reminded me of Hi-C.

"I'm glad you asked," he said. "From a community stand point, eventually yes. Look, I may have gotten tipped off that the 'big boys' were gonna be getting involved with his case if my guys can't solve it. That's the last thing any of you would want. If they can't find the grounds to indict him, they will kill him and enjoy watching your streets turn into a blood bath. That's what they want. I don't want to see that happen to you or him and that's why I am so dedicated to this job. When I take these cases I'm trying to save lives, not destroy them. But I also have to live with knowing that I can't be superman to everyone. That's what hurts the most."

With both of my hands being swaddled into Detective Bailey's chest, all I could do was stare into his eyes. We both connected with each other's pain but had no more words to offer each other. Even in the midst of his sorrowful expression, I could still see his charm and judging by the way he looked at me I know I had the same effect on him. We were still buzzed from the alcohol and I could only hope that he didn't wake up regretting what he had just told me. I, on the other hand, was more thankful that he trusted me enough to tell me something like that.

"Thank you," I whispered to Detective Bailey before burying my face between his cheek and shoulder. Then I planted two wet kisses on his neck, while surprisingly he grabbed my hair passionately with one hand and my back with the other. Feeling like it was okay, I allowed my lips to kiss and lick all the way up to his face where I could see him enjoying it. Once I reached his lips, suddenly he placed one hand over mine.

"As much as I would love to go there with you, we both know this can't happen," he said disappointing me. "Let's just get some rest and be on our way back tomorrow."

Without saying a word, I nodded. Then I turned over and allowed my weary mind and body some much needed sleep.

CHAPTER 23: The Set Up

We made it back to Ordale around 11:00a.m the next morning. Would have got back sooner but we grabbed some breakfast and then stopped by one of the local flea markets. Neither of us mentioned a word about what we talked about the night before, although I could not stop thinking about everything Detective Bailey had shared with me. That conversation we had really got to me. So much that it made me think about wanting out of the drug game. And if he was right about the things he said, it was clear to see that I was playing a game I could not win. Yet still, I knew the only way to get out was to get back in and in order for me to do so, I had to beat the devil at his own game.

I made the decision to take Cederick up on his little proposal, or at least I would make him think so. Really I wasn't going to sleep with him. My plan was to drug him and just make him think we had sex. I knew a doctor that could get me some Xylolpol, a new drug that was made to knock you out for only a few hours. I dated him some time before but the relationship was short-lived. He was a sophisticated man with high expectations and I got tired of having to hold a fake persona just to keep up with him. I had him thinking that I was a dental assistant and the head of a local book club. I had to walk different, talk different, just move different every time I was around him and I grew weary of it. Besides, he wasn't breaking off none of his bread with me so it was nothing to cut him loose. He actually liked the person he thought I was and didn't accept my decision to leave him very well. All he could do was offer to be there for me if ever I may have needed him and only because of my current dilemma, I was glad for it.

After visiting the doctor and 'orally' convincing him to get me what I needed, he granted me my wish. I had no shame pleasing him in his office because although we were two different types of people, I was still physically very attracted to him. Besides, it wasn't the first time we had gotten down in his place of business.

After I had everything I needed to complete my mission, I made a call to Cederick to set up our little evening of fun. He agreed to meet me at the Quality Inn Hotel, which was located on the outer skirts of Ordale. I wouldn't see him for a couple hours because I had promised a girl named Quita that I would swing by the projects and watch her three kids while she went to work. Quita's real name was actually Shameka, but since I wasn't trying to know any more Shameka's, I made a joke one day calling her Quita and the name just stuck her.

It was actually Quita's cousin Vivica, who helped me obtain the lease to the apartment that Quita was living in, that I owed a favor to. After the college girls moved out of my townhouse, I wasn't able to afford rent or find another tenant willing to pay that much money, so I had to give the place up. Vivica was a case manager down at the Housing Authority of Ordale, who was also a client I used to steal for. We managed to use some bogus birth certificates and a host of other fake documents and she got me a three bedroom spot in the projects. Alongside my pride, I figured it would be much easier for me to rent out the place rather than live in it and before I could even think of who to ask, Vivica was telling me about her cousin. She happened to be moving into town and desperately needed a place to live. In the end, everyone got what they wanted. Quita got a spot and I got six hundred extra bucks a month, eight hundred if I stayed there and watched her kids for her at least three days a week.

I had gotten so distracted by setting up Cederick that I forgot I had promised Quita I would keep them. Not only that, but the

Camouflage Bash was going on that same night. It happened yearly at one of the hottest clubs in Ordale and it paid tribute to a rising local rapper who was gunned down in front of his recording studio. It was a tradition, in Army Boy's name, that everyone wear camouflage in order to get into the club at a cheaper price. It went down every year and I never missed one. I was upset that I couldn't make it but I knew that I had more important shit to do. That didn't stop me from telling Quita I needed her to make it back early so that I may get dressed and ready for it. She didn't make any promises, but she did say she would try.

Once I made it to Quita's, I did my usual tasks. I would cook for the kids, help them with their homework, and we'd all watch movies together. Quita came to Ordale to get away from the girl's abusive father, which also caused her to be very protective of them. She didn't even allow them to go outdside, especially when she was not home to watch out for them. I felt bad for them, but I was from Ordale and I knew firsthand that the kids in that neighborhood posed way more of a threat than their psychotic father.

In order to make the time go by, we normally just played games or watched a good movie. In fact, we were in the middle of *Corina Corina* when Charlytte rang my line. She figured I was going to the party and wanted to catch a ride with me. Even though she had just brought herself a Camaro, she didn't have any license or legit paperwork so she didn't want to drive. Because I couldn't go, I suggested that she catch a ride with Alicia, even though the two of them didn't get along. Charlytte caught a fit but once she realized I was standing my ground about not going, she decided to comply. They even paid me a visit and we smoked one before they headed to the club, which was only walking distance from the projects. In fact, Alicia kept her car parked in front of Quita's house and they all just footed it from there.

After getting my buzz on with the girls on Quita's back porch, I sent the kids to wash and go to bed. It was now ten o'clock and I had to start getting ready because I knew Quita would be coming home about a quarter past eleven like she always did. I began to run some bath water for Sabrea and Samyia, her youngest two, before being startled by someone else hitting my cell.

I told one of the girls, who was sitting on the toilet asking me a million questions, to grab my phone from out of my pocket and place it on my ear. Then I pinched it in place with my chin and shoulder bone.

"Hello," I answered.

"Hey Keisha, how's everything?"

"Who's this," I replied. Not catching the voice.

"It's me, Quita."

"Oh hey girl," I said. "I'm rinsing this tub out now. About to get the girls ready for bed. Sorry, I didn't even check my caller ID."

"It's okay," she understood. "How are they? Driving you crazy again today?"

"No girl," I replied. "You know those three never cause me no trouble. Brea is sitting here asking me a million questions though. You still haven't told her where babies come from?"

Quita laughed. "No, not yet. I haven't gathered myself up enough courage to have that type of conversation with a four-year-old."

I returned the laugh. "Well you need to go ahead and get it together because as good of a mother you are, if *you* can't do it then you know I can't either."

"I don't know about that," she disagreed. "You may be a little better at it than I am. But I'll talk to her though. Really soon, just trust me."

"It's okay, really it is. But what's up?" I asked her. "It's not like you to call me when you're not on break. Is everything okay?"

Quita let out a deep sigh. "Not really. My relief called out and my manager asked me if I could work a shift for her. She just left here from pulling sixteen hours and wants to get some rest before she comes back out."

"I don't know Quita, she may have to stop to Starbucks or something because I really have to go today. I know you're not from here but this party is a big deal."

"I know, I know. That Camouflage thing is tonight right? But please, I need you. You know I don't have anyone else."

"What about Vivica?" I said knowing that was a no-deal. I just had to test my luck.

"Now you know Vivica ain't leaving her man's side to come babysit no kids that ain't hers."

"I know, I know. But damn Queet, tonight is just not good. I'm sorry."

"Keisha please, I have no problem telling my boss I can't stay but I'm like this close to getting that morning position. I know if I help her out this time, she will definitely approve my request. Think about it. You won't have to do no more babysitting. And no more uncomfortable questions from a four-year-old. What do you say? Pleeeease, I need you."

The desperation in her voice activated the sympathetic side of me. I watched Quita struggle every day and I knew how much that morning shift meant to her and her kids. Besides, I was growing tired of being obligated to babysitting. As much as I needed that little bit of change, I was starting to feel like it wasn't worth it.

"What time will you make it back here Queet?" I asked, regretfully.

"A lil' after seven. And I'll pay you double."

"Okay. I'll do it." I told her. "And you don't have to double anything. Just give me my regular pay and have my crab stew ready for me next weekend."

"Even better, I'll have it as early as Sunday. Thank you so much Keisha. You're a lifesaver."

"I'll see you at seven," I told Quita and then hung straight up in her face.

I was pissed. Pissed beyond measurement. Quita was always on time to get back to the kids and the one time I really needed her to be home, she hits me with this crap. Seeing that my plans had changed, I called the hotel and cancelled my reservation. I spent about three minutes convincing the greedy foreigner not to charge me and I only hoped that Cederick would be as understanding as he was. After hanging up with them, I got enough guts to call him to reschedule our little appointment.

"Yooo," he answered confidently.

"Hey Ced, this Keisha."

"I know who this is. What's up? You ready for me?"

"Not quite," I said. "Something came up."

"What do you mean *something came up*?" his voice dimmed.

"You know the girl Quita, whose kids I'm over here keeping. Well she called and said that her relief got sick tonight and she wanted to know if I could watch them longer."

There was a brief silence before Cederick busted out into heavy laughter.

"That's the best lie you could come up with," he finally spoke. "I mean really, if you got scared and changed your mind then just say so."

"I didn't change anything, Cederick," I began to get upset. "You're talking to a girl who's over here babysitting fuckin' kids for a living. I need my spot back in the OMC and I'll do whatever it takes to get it. Even if that means fuckin' your pathetic ass. Trust me, I'm not bluffin'. Now what's your tomorrow looking like?"

"Tomorrow? Naw," he shot me down. "I want what I want today. Besides, I leave first thing in the morning and I won't be back to Ordale for another two weeks. This has to happen tonight or not at all."

Growing discouraged, my voice simmered as I tried to negotiate with Cederick. "Look Ced, you are really putting me in a bad situation. I already told her I would stay and keep them. I cannot just call her back and change the plans like that. What else do you want me to do?"

"Those little muthafuckas have to sleep, right?"

"Yea *the kids* have to sleep," I corrected him. "Why? What are you trying to say. These are babies. I'm not leaving them here alone."

"Who said anything about you leaving?" he asked. "When you go to sleep you just call me and I'll come there. I just need some pussy. I don't need no hotel for that."

I had never for a second considered bringing Cederick over to Quita's house. She didn't play that shit. Besides, all her bedrooms were occupied and I wouldn't risk having one of the girls spot us in the living room. The only other option was her bedroom and even I knew that was a bit on the shady side for me to do something like that."

"Cederick, you want me to fuck you in this girl's house. Are you crazy?"

"Look, I don't have time to do all this. I made my suggestion. You either call me when you sure the kids are good and sleep or don't call me at all. Choice is yours. Just text me the apartment number when you're ready. If I don't hear from you then I know what's up."

"But Ceder-" I called out before hearing my phone buzz to let me know the call had ended.

Cederick had really pushed his limit with this one. Even though I was plotting on fake sleeping with Hi-C's best friend, I still felt it was messy to bring him into Quita's home. Especially with her kids there. But what other choice did I have? I didn't have two weeks to wait on Cederick to get back in town to try to convince him again. Besides, it wasn't my fault that Quita had to work late. If I could sacrifice my plans for her, why couldn't she give up her bed for me? It took a minute for me to convince myself, but nonetheless I made my decision on what I was going to do.

Two hours had rolled by quickly and the kids were safely asleep in bed. It was now a little after twelve and before calling Cederick to come over, I hit up Quita to make sure she was still working and wouldn't happen to pop up early. After briefly talking with her and hearing her patient fussing in the background, she certainly was still working so I knew I had the green light. I hadn't felt that nervous since the time I snuck Kevin and Tre into my mama's house. Once I gave him the okay, within twenty minutes he was at the doorstep.

"You were so desperate to have me that you missed the RIP Bash," I said to Cederick who was standing on Quita's porch waiting for me to allow him inside.

"You know I don't do the club scenes like that," he fired back and then pushed his own way through the front door. He was looking rather sharp in his vanilla-cream Polo shirt and sandy, brown denim jeans. The gold watch he sported around his wrist glistened, complimenting his gold chain, while his Timberland boots brought it all together. I must admit Cederick was looking fly, but I expected nothing less of it. He was always well dressed- not quite the looker- but his swag made up for it.

"Whatever, just follow me." I said as I led him through the living room, passed the bathroom, and into the master bedroom.

Before closing us in, I peeped my head out of the door into the direction of both the kids' rooms to make sure they were sound asleep. Once I felt confident that they were, I shut the door. The sound of Bun B's 'Hold you Down' flowed from the small speaker Quita had on her nightstand and the single candle lit on her dresser made a dim impression on the entire room.

"Dang…is this chick from Africa?" Cederick said before sitting on the edge of the king-sized bed and placing his shoes neatly on the zebra-printed mat. He was making a mockery of

Quita's choice of style. She was into animal prints so her four walls were covered with lions, zebras, and leopard-theme pictures. The two dressers she had in her room were also filled with animal decors. I could tell wherever she came from she lived pretty decent because her entire house set-up was not too shady for it to be a project spot.

"Naw, she's just into that type of shit," I told him, while standing over the dresser getting ready to fill the two empty cups with alcohol. I could feel Cederick staring at my body and the slick grin he carried on his face let me know he felt certain that he would soon be having his way with me.

"Gotta admit Keisha," he said. "I didn't think you were gonna go through with this."

I took the Patron I had and the Xylolpol then put it behind the elephant that was staring at me. Then I slowly but seductively made my way back over to Cederick and positioned my body between his legs. Placing both of his hands in each of mine, I directed him to my butt cheeks. Cederick let out a moan as he cuffed them with no shame.

"I told you," I whispered softly to him. "I don't let nothing get in the way of me and my money. And I mean nothing. All I know is that a word of this better not get back to Hi-C. And who knows, if we can keep this between us and if it is as good as I hear it is, we just might be able to turn this into a regular thing."

Hearing those words, the now aroused Cederick lifted me from off the floor and laid his body down, causing me to fall on top of him. He then reached for his zipper and started to open his pants. I could feel his manhood began to rise and it confirmed to me that the rumors were true about him having a third leg. Feeling him stiffen between my legs got me excited and the hoe in me thought about just giving in and getting a taste of that monster, but I quickly rid myself of the idea. I had to stick to the plan.

"Wait a minute," I grabbed his hand from underneath me. "Not so fast. I'm still feeling a little awkward about this. I think I need to loosen up a bit. Why don't you have one drink with me? Quita doesn't get home until the morning so we have plenty of time."

Cederick wasn't pleased with my proposal, but he knew he had no choice but to abide. He let out a disappointing sigh and used his body weight to push us back to the position we started in. Once my feet hit the floor, I headed back over to the dresser to fix our drinks. Before doing so, I surprised Cederick by pulling my dress over my head and letting it hit the floor. Then I shot a peep at him and saw that he was mesmerized by the view he had of me in nothing but some laced panties.

I hated the thought of having the asshole see me in that manner but I needed him distracted while I laced his cup. The plan must have worked because he didn't even noticed me slip the Xylolpol into his drink. I also purposely wore no bra so that he could be so focused on my nipples that he didn't see the guilt I carried on my face as I looked him in the eye while handing him a spiked drink. After all, drugging men wasn't my profession.

"Here you go," I said to Cederick as I handed him his cup. "Patron on the rocks."

"Patron," he said. "Where's the Henny, I've been on brown tonight. I don't mix."

"One shot won't kill, I'm sure you've mixed before."

"Last time I mixed I woke up with the top half of my body in the tub and the bottom stretched out over the toilet seat. Don't ask me how because I still don't know."

"Crazy," I said as we both scooted our bodies up to the top of Quita's bed and let our backs meet with her headboard. "But like I said, it won't kill you."

Cederick gave in and agreed to take the shot. Then I gave a phony toast to seeing the OMC rise again under his leadership and watched him with a side eye as he down it. I swallowed mine and continued to make bullshit conversation with him while I waited for the meds to kick in. Sure enough about fifteen minutes later, Cederick's words began to slur and he started making complaints that he felt funny. I just kept convincing him that it was the mixing of those liquors that was most likely causing him to feel that way. Then once he started saying his head was spinning, I knew it was time for me to put my plan into action.

Clearly feeling slugged, Cederick laid his own body down flat across Quita's bed on his back and I used that opportunity to pull down his pants. There was a bit of a struggle trying to get them off without his cooperation, so I decided to just stop at the knees. Then I sat on top of him and watched his eyes go in and out of consciousness. Once I had him how I wanted him, I smeared red lipstick all over my lips and began to strategically plant kisses all over his body. I even grabbed my phone and began to take pictures just in case he tried to deny our little encounter. I decided to finish him off by laying on top of him and grinding my body erotically, while sucking the hell out of his neck to make sure I left marks. I also rang out soft moans in his ears.

"Ooooh Cederick, this feels so good." I whispered softly in his ears. Although he was nonresponsive, he showed movement and small signs of being aware. I just hoped that he would at least remember hearing the beautiful love sounds my voice sang out.

I continued for minutes just grinding on his manhood that didn't seem to at all be affected by the drugs. He was rock hard and clearly not dead.

"You're so good," I continued to chant for minutes on out.

By this time the drug had took full effect and he was finally a goner. Cederick was out and I mean cold. While looking devilishly in his face, I could only wonder why he was obsessed with having me, especially if him and Hi-C were boys. Could he have been doing Hi-C a favor by exposing me for the money hungry, disloyal chick I was? Or was he just jealous and wanted everything his friend had? It was in that moment when I started remembering all the times I'd catch him glaring over at Hi-C and I whenever we were together. The look of envy he displayed on his face anytime he saw us kiss or hug. His unexplainable concern for me dating a married man even though he tricked out young girls for a living. It suddenly dawned on me that Cederick could have possibly wanted me all along, and was using Hi-C's downfall to get to me. He was playing a dirty game but little did he know I could play it dirtier.

In fact, the more I thought of it, the more I became turned off and quickly tried to erase the thought of Cederick by mentally replacing him with someone else. I attempted to think of Hi-C, but strangely visions of Detective Bailey's face began to rule my mind. I tried to fight the feelings off, but it only managed to make me think of him more. As I rubbed my fingers through Cederick's low fade, I envisioned his hair being curly like Bailey's, and as I started kissing his lips I substituted them also. Not worried about the kids, I tried my best to make my fantasy seem real and began to moan louder and louder as I got deeper and deeper into my imagination. Then I sucked, kissed, and grinded on Cederick's lifeless body until I brought myself to a climax and was sure to let my juices fall onto his boxers. I could only hope that the residue and scent of me would further convince him that I had given him some. The moment was intense, so intense, that I found myself passed out alongside the fool.

CHAPTER 24: Caught Up

"Keisha! Keisha! Wake up right now!" A familiar voice, but not so familiar face, startled me right out of my sleep. I slowly opened my eyes and frantically jumped at the site of the very bruised person staring back at me. At first I thought it was Quita, but the scar on her face rid me of that conclusion.

"Shit Charlytte! Wha..what are you doing here?" I said as my memory started to slowly come back to me, reminding me of where I was and who I had lying next to me.

"Don't you mean…what the fuck happened to me?" she asked, tapping the blood on her nose with her index finger to show me that something terrible had just occurred.

"Yeah, I...I...I was getting there," I stuttered. "Wha..what happened?"

"Samantha and her girls jumped me in the bathroom at the club, that's what happened."

"Huh?...For real?" I said, still wondering how the hell she got inside the house. But once I saw small feet moving under the doorway, I knew it had to be one of the kids. Then I looked to Cederick, who thankfully was completely buried under the covers, and decided it was best that I gathered my clothes and lead Charlytte out of the room. There would have been no way to explain why I was butt-ass naked in bed with her boo.

"Yes! For real! Just now at The Bash! I ran all the way here!"

"Where's Shannon and Alicia?" I asked. "Wait...let's talk in the other room."

I quickly, but quietly, hopped out of the bed and ran to grab my bra and panties. I didn't panic too much because I knew that although it was well over the hours of effect, the meds should've still had Cederick in a deep sleep, but unfortunately I misjudged. The squeaking sounds from the loose mattress springs awoke him and he pulled the covers from over his head, revealing himself. Though the bruised eyes, bleeding nose, and clearly busted lip showed that she was physically hurting, it was nothing compared to the emotional pain she displayed across her face when she recognized who he was.

"How could you, Keish?" She asked, finally breaking the silence that covered the room.

I was so choked up that all I managed to say was the same line everybody said when they got caught up.

"It's not what it looks like sis, just trust me on this one."

"Trust you," she said. "How could I possibly trust you after this?"

"Because Charlytte, it's not personal. It's just business." I said still scrambling for my clothes. "You know how that goes."

"No. I don't know how that goes, Keisha," she replied.

Cederick just looked from my mouth to hers. He held a confused expression on his face as he rubbed his forehead. I didn't know if it was from the drugs, or the fact that he woke up to Charlytte and I arguing, but he surely needed answers as to what was taking place. All I could think about was not blowing my cover, so as much as it pained me to take it there, I had to continue to play my role.

"C'mon Charlytte, quit acting like you green to shit and stop trying to play Miss Goody-Goody all the damn time! I knew the minute you said you were with Cederick that you was either trickin' or about to be. Don't play stupid. You know how to fuck a nigga, get his money, and walk away without having any connections. That's all this is, so don't let it come between us."

Charlytte was shock by my betrayal and the fact that I seemed to have no remorse. "If it wasn't such a big deal, then why didn't you tell me."

"I was going too."

"I seriously doubt that Keisha," she replied. "Here I was all along thinking you changed, but really, you haven't changed since we were younger. Always thinking about yourself. You see Cederick taking over the operation and you're all over him, just like you did with Hi-C!"

Now it was Charlytte who hit the low blow, that seemingly let her true colors show. I didn't appreciate it one bit. Of course now it was personal. I just had to give her a piece of my mind.

"Oh, so you judging me now, bitch!" I yelled as I threw the baby blue Hollister t-shirt I wore earlier over my head. I couldn't find the night dress. "I'm not the one hoping and praying that one day the ghetto Cinderella is somehow going to make the broke down Prince fall in love with her. You damn right, I'mma eat off of these pussy ass niggas. They don't give a fuck about us. All they care about is money and that's all you should be worried about too. We're sisters and if you let this come between us, then you were never my family in the first place."

"Bitch, how-" Charlytte said, right before Cederick got offended and interrupted.

"Enough!" he shouted, still holding his head. "I can't take much more of this soap opera shit!"

Cederick then rose from out of the bed and let his big, hard dick dingle in our direction. Although I knew they were already fucking, Charlytte looked at it as if she never saw it a day in her life.

"It's real simple. Keisha, you a hoe, and Charlytte, you a trick. This whole fantasy about me and you being together, GET RID OF IT! I will never be with you. You fuck random niggas for money. You can turn a housewife into a hoe, but you can't turn a hoe back into a housewife. Once it's done, it's done. I don't care about either one of y'all slut bitches, so both of you need to just stop it."

I could tell Cederick's words really hurt Charlytte. Between my lie and his truth I knew the reality of the entire situation would have an effect on how she forever felt about the both of us. Probably mess with her trust in people for the rest of her life.

"Oh please Cederick, shut the fuck up!" she cursed him. "You try to act like you so real! Nigga you ain't shit! You fake and phony as a fuck. You just a wannabe pimp and Hi-C's yes man, you fuckin' powderhead junkie!"

Oh snap! I said in my head. It couldn't believe that Charlytte had the nerve to go there. She basically said all the things I wanted to say and I was glad someone finally had the guts to do so.

Cederick didn't like her words one bit. I don't know if it was what she said or the fact that she said it, but he charged at her like she was a white man and he was a bull.

"You dumb trick!" he ran with his right arm up in slap-a-hoe position. "I'mma fuck you up worse than ol' girl did!"

Not about to let him touch her, I jumped on Cederick's back to try to stop him from getting to Charlytte. We wobbled all over the bedroom and I held onto his back like I was the one riding the beast. Tussling all around the room, we created what appeared to be a stampede the way animals went flying everywhere. We even knocked a few pictures off the wall, allowing the contents on the dresser to also hit the ground.

"Xylolpol," Cederick shouted as he picked up the medicine container that came rolling over in his direction.

Shit! I thought.

"Bitch you drugged me!" he yelled, then with all his might reached his arm around himself and snatched me from his back, sending me flying down hard on the floor. I put up a protective shield as his fists painfully struck every part of my body. Cederick must have been a pro at beating chicks because although it was wide open, he made sure not to touch my face.

Charlytte's unhelpful ass took off running towards the front door. When she got to the exit she looked back and saw me begging and pleading for help, but instead of offering assistance she disappeared straight out the door. Cederick continued to take a few more swings until, Samantha, Quita's eleven-year-old and oldest, came running into the room with a phone in her hand.

"Miss Keisha! Miss Keisha! I called the police!" she cried. "They're coming to help you!"

Hearing those words, Cederick took his last swing before gathering his things. After his pants were fully on and his hat was rested tightly on his head, he began to tap his pockets for his keys. Then he remembered that he put them on Quita's coffee table in the living room and headed to retrieve them.

"Where the fuck are my keys?" he screamed, once he realized that they were nowhere to be found.

"I don't fuckin' know!" I yelled back.

"Bitch did you rob me too?" he yelled, then reached into his pocket and quickly began to rub his fingers through the money he kept in his wallet. I'm sure it was still all there.

"You broke ass nigga, what the fuck I'mma rob you for!"

Ignoring me, Cederick began to lift every pillow off Quita's suede blue couches. He looked under everything that allowed space and then went back into the bedroom to tear some more shit up. I knew damn well I hadn't taken them. Shit I wanted him out, especially knowing that Quita would be coming home soon. I just sat and thought hard about where his keys could have been and then it dawned on me.

"Quit fucking up this girl house!" I told him. "Charlytte took those fucking keys! I saw her! You betta leave before the police come because I'mma let them know you whipped my ass!"

"Fuckin' Charlytte, I'mma kill that bitch!" he shouted before running out the door. Before leaving, he turned to me in the doorway. "And you can forget about getting your spot back, you damn hoe. Once Hi-C gets word of me smashing you, you'll definitely be X-ed out."

His words cut me like a knife but I had to think of a fast comeback. "And once the hood get a hold of these pictures of me stuffing a pink dildo up ya ass, you definitely will be the talk of the town. Xylpolol is one helluva drug. I expect to be back on the road by the time you come back from Jacksonville."

The look on Cederick's face was priceless. He started to charge back at me, but the sirens that began to sound off from a distance caused him to flee. I immediately ran to comfort Samantha, who thankfully was the only child awoke at the time. I was glad she was there to defend me, but none of it would have happened if she didn't open the door for Charlytte in the first place. She knew her mama didn't play that.

"I'm so sorry you had to see all of that," I told her. "But you know it's all your fault."

Samantha's big bugged eyes got even wider when she heard those words. And although she was definitely cute with her huge puff ball and deep dimples, I still couldn't feel sorry for blaming her. I knew I was wrong for playing on her little mind but I had to save myself.

"My fault?" she said softly. "What did I do?"

"You opened the door for a stranger," I said. "What did your mama tell you about that?"

"She said don't open the door for anyone, especially if she isn't home."

"And if an adult is home?"

"Let them open it," she sighed.

"And did you do that?" I asked.

"No," Samantha began to sob which confirmed to me that my method was working. "But I did try to wake you up. I kept knocking on the door but you didn't answer. I thought it was mommy out there."

"Well it wasn't mommy," I told her. "Those were really bad people who tried to come in and rob us. The guy must have entered through the window. And when the police gets here that's exactly what you will tell them."

"But they're not coming," she informed me.

"Excuse me? Yes they are. I can hear them coming now."

"Well they must be going somewhere else because I didn't really call them," she held up a toy phone. "My daddy used to do this all the time. I know how to make bad people go away."

A breath of fresh air left my body and I grabbed Samantha tightly and hugged her. The last thing I wanted was for the pigs to get involved because anytime police got called in the projects all incidents had to be reported to the front office. With all the fraud going on surrounding my residency, Vivica neither I, could afford that type of attention.

"Oh good. Samantha you handled that so well. I'll tell you what," I said to her. "You don't mention a word of this to your mama and I won't tell her that you opened the door for strangers."

Samantha looked shocked that I didn't want her mama to find out what just occured. I could tell she knew something wasn't right. She was too smart for her own good, but she didn't want to get in trouble either.

"So we're not gonna tell her about this?" she asked for confirmation.

"No, let's not worry her. Your mom has been through enough as it is. Besides, I know those two. I'm going to the police station as soon as I leave here in the morning and they will be locked up in no time. You don't have to worry about them coming back. Besides, she might not trust that I'm good enough to watch you anymore and you may end up with the babysitter from hell."

I tickled Samantha and she laughed. I could tell she began to feel much better about the situation and I was proud of myself because I thought I handled it very well.

"Why don't you go back to bed and I'm going to get this house cleaned up," I told her.

"Ooooh, can I help? She asked eagerly. She was always so willing.

"No, not this time," I shot her down. "Get you some rest little girl."

Samantha sighed heavily and dragged her little head down all the way back to her room. Before she made it in, I stopped her.

"Wait," I walked over to the doorway. "Here is twenty dollars. You'll get that every time I see you as long as you don't mention a word of this to your mama. Or your sisters. Not anybody."

Samantha's frown turned into a bright smile as she took her twenty and skipped back into the room. Then I cleaned up the whole apartment and luckily the only thing I had to explain to Quita was how one of her elephants broke.

CHAPTER 25: DAMN DINO

"**I** fucked up really bad."

There was a brief silence on the phone before Detective Bailey decided to speak. He could only imagine what I had gotten myself into this time.

"What's wrong now Keisha?" he finally said, clearly forcing the words out of his mouth.

"Well...," I gathered my thoughts and even though I had practiced a thousand times how I would tell him, my words only seemed to fumble. "It's Cederick. I...I...decided to beat him at his own game and make him think that we had sex but…well…the plan backfired!"

A burst of tears began to shoot from my eyes as I thought about the events that took place the night before. How could I have let myself be so stupid?

"Wait a minute, calm down," he insisted. "I'm confused. First off, how can you trick someone into thinking you had sex with them?"

"Xylolpol," I told him.

"You tried to drug him?" he asked.

"I didn't try Detective."

"Keisha, what the hell!" he immediately got just as upset as I was. "How many times I gotta tell you to run your plans by me before you go out and take matters into your own hands? I could have told you that was a bad idea."

"But it wasn't a bad idea." I fired back, hating the fact that he doubted me so much. "It actually would have worked if Charlytte didn't come barging in all beat up and shit. She ruined my whole night."

"This is just too much," he said. "I'll get to this Charlytte thing later. But as far as Cederick, are you trying to tell me that he knows you drugged him?"

"I believe so."

"Dammit Keisha, he'll never let you close to the OMC now."

"That's what I'm afraid of." I said, although I was banking on Cederick thinking I had those embarrassing photos of him and that maybe I could blackmail my way back in. I decided not to mention that part to the detective. I had already put enough mess in his ears.

"You drugged him Keisha. That's definitely a done deal."

"I know, I know I fucked up." I tortured myself. "But the question now is what's next? Like how can I fix this?"

There was another brief moment of silence as both of us pondered on ideas. I could only hope his brain was working better than mine because the only thing I could come up with was nothing. Finally Detective Bailey spoke again.

"Welp. I guess we just have to go to Plan C. Keisha I have to go now. I have a situation I have to attend to. Let me get my thoughts together and I'll get back with you a little later."

"Okay. You promise?" I said, desperate for his, or anybody's, attention.

"I said I will call you back," Detective Bailey hung the phone up in my ear without giving me a chance to say goodbye.

With all my might, I immediately forced myself out of bed. It was about one o'clock in the evening and I had spent all morning having a pity party since thoughts of the night before conquered my mind. Every moment of it. Poor Charlytte, that hurtful look she displayed on her face when she saw Cederick in bed with me kept playing over and over in my mind. There was no way she would ever believe my side of the story, especially after all the mean things I had said to her. I wanted to just tell her the truth, but the hard part was getting her to even talk to me. I didn't really focus on the fight she had with Samantha because I knew those wombs would heal, but the pain I caused her, I wasn't so sure of.

As Detective Bailey said he would, he called me back and informed me that he would be picking me up within an hour. Without questioning him, I got myself together and prepared for our encounter. I wasn't in the mood to be cute or fancy so I decided just to throw on a grey jogging suit and then tossed a hoodie over my head.

When he arrived, I met him out front. At first I thought he was nowhere in sight, but then I realized he wasn't in his detective car. Instead he was driving a gold '98 Buick Regal with absolutely no tint on it. He also was unusually dressed very casual, wearing a fitted cap, a white t-shirt, and some denim jeans. It was the first time I had seen him in that manner. Uneasy about it, I took my place in this unfamiliar vehicle and tried to make myself as comfortable as I could possibly get.

"Is this your real car?" I asked him before flopping down in the passenger seat allowing the dust to pick up beneath me. "Damn. I didn't know a detective's salary was that bad. And why the hell you got me riding with you in a car that has no tint?"

Detective Bailey plucked the flap that laid across his chest as if it was a rubber band, reminding me to put my seat belt on. I obeyed and continued to wait for a much needed explanation.

"Although I am not a big fan of fancy cars, this one would not be my personal pick. My partner has my vehicle for the day. This car belongs to the department. We got some detective stuff to do later so I will be whipping this beautiful baby for the day.

"That's cool and all, but I really don't like that there's no tint in here."

"Don't worry about it," he told me. "Didn't I tell you you're always safe in my hands and that I would never put you in harm's way. This is my profession. Trust me. You're good."

After hearing those words, I relaxed a bit because by this time I had become comfortable and trusting in the detective's word. He had done a good job of keeping my ties with him under wraps this long so I had no reason to doubt him.

"If you say so," I calmed down, but I still let my seat way back just to be extra sure. "You haven't let me down yet."

"Exactly," he replied.

"And what's up with the cool clothes? You must be off the clock."

"I told you, I never have a day off. There's some private business involving another case that I have to attend to later today. Believe it or not, I'm working as we speak."

Although I was eager to know, I didn't dare ask him about what his other affair was. He clearly let me know it was a private matter, which was code word for *none of my damn business.*

"Word," I said. "I like this look on you though. You kinda look like someone I would date."

"Oh really," he chuckled. "Do I really look that worthless?"

"Oh please," I playfully jerked his arm but was very careful not to distract him while he was driving. "What does that supposed to mean?"

"It means exactly what I said. That you only date worthless guys. I probably gotta have my pants hanging down to my ankles before you would even consider giving me a shot."

"That is not true, Detective." I corrected him. "I have never been attracted to the ass-hanging-following-the-trend-ass-niggas like that. Neither the silly gold teeth. I mean, yes I love me a street dude, but it's more of the hustle that I get drawn to. Has nothing to do with a fake ass copy-cat image. Besides, he gotta have his own mind."

"Like Hi-C?" he asked.

"Yes, exactly like Hi-C."

Detective Bailey turned his eyes at the sound of his name, even though he was the one who brought him up. I could sense a little bit of jealousy coming from his end. I mean, I never felt that he wanted me in any kind of way, but I couldn't help but think that his obsession with taking down Hi-C was more personal than professional.

"Figures," he replied.

"I see you're being very judgmental," I told him. "And that's not cool at all."

The detective replied, "I just call it how I see it."

"Well if that's the case, I can say the same thing about you. You wouldn't give a girl like me the time of day either. I mean, I could be the most loyal, trustworthy woman on the planet but because of my lifestyle, you'd look right past me."

"You're absolutely right," he said. "The good Lord could break the sky right now, release a halo, and have it land straight on top of your head but because of your life, and I repeat *life*style, I wouldn't give you the time of day."

"So shallow," I said.

"You're wrong. Shallow is choosing not to date a woman because her nails are blue and her toes are pink. Now that's shallow. Smart is not dating a woman who has a possible future of spending the rest of her life in prison. I believe that's justifiable."

"But really, be honest Detective. I know I turn you on a little bit. I mean not physically, but the dangerous way I live. That bad girl, dare devil in me. The fact that I know the streets enough to profit from it and turn it into a business. That I'mma go-getter and a hustler, while these other chicks out here living off they mama, child support, and section 8."

"No. Nothing about what you just said is attractive," the detective shot me down with his words, although his eyes said something different.

"I'm attracted to a woman who doesn't value money and material bullshit. A woman who makes sacrifices and will struggle living with nothing but her dignity in order to remain true to herself and her values. A woman who would put her last dime into uplifting the community, rather than to profit and gain riches off of the destruction of it. That's sexy to me."

"Whatever," I said, allowing absolutely nothing he said to get to me. "You don't have to admit it, but I know you do."

The Detective and I said nothing to each other the entire ride to Ordale. I just stared out of the dirty window, watching the city as it appeared much different than I had ever saw it before. Spending so much time away from home made me suddenly have a deep appreciation for my city. The downtown squares I used to hate to drive through now looked like beautifully-patterned pathways that led to the heart of the river. The cheap discount department stores I used to think were low-class and too cheesy for my taste, now possessed those same tacky outfits I only wished I could afford. The whole vibe just felt different and I sat there like a little child soaking it all in. That's until I realized that we were getting too deep into the inner city, a place I didn't want to get caught dead with Detective Bailey. Immediately, the uncomfortable feeling I had when I first jumped in the car with him came rushing back to me.

"Detective, are you crazy?" I asked. "We're like a block away from Blackshear. You do know that?"

"I'm aware," he said calmly.

"Well are you trying to plan my funeral?" I shouted. "Take me back now. Or I promise I will hop out at the next light."

"You're not going anywhere," he said, still calm and unbothered.

"Try me," I said.

"Look, I understand your concern but you don't have to worry. I'm not going to put you in any danger. I'm headed to Thunderbolt Drive. I told you I'm in the middle of working on another case. I have to be in this area to check something out. Deep back on River Road is where I'm headed. We will be fine there."

I felt a little better hearing that we were heading to Thunderbolt. It was an upper-class small town near a marsh and River Road was a backstreet where outsiders would go to fuck in their cars, catch plays, and do other low-key shit like that.

There were only about four houses that occupied the street. I didn't worry too much because those homes were owned by retired old, rich folks. On my side, was a river with a single dock that stretched about fifty feet to the water. I'm assuming the people from the neighborhood would walk down it, fish, or simply catch the beautiful view of the sunset.

The detective was still very silent as he slowly cruised down the dead end street with a very concentrated look on his face. It was as if he was trying to locate the perfect place to rest his vehicle. After only a few seconds, he finally found a spot at the midway point of the street and fortunately the houses were so far apart that we weren't parked directly in front of any one of them. Once he was comfortable, he shut off the car's engine and turned down the old stereo system that was already at a low volume anyway.

I just sat quietly watching him from my peripheral view as he grabbed his phone. He was fumbling through it, typing, and had a look that was so focused I didn't want to interrupt. It was only after five long tormenting minutes of sitting in silence that I finally felt the need the speak.

"Detective, forgive me for what I said earlier about you being shallow and all. I don't know enough about you to make that call."

Without speaking, Detective Bailey glanced at his phone once more and gave it a few more seconds before acknowledging what I had just said to him. When he was completely done, he placed it down onto his lap, and shifted his body in the jammed up car as much as it would allow him to face me.

"Keisha, I'm not worried about your opinion. I know who I am and what I like. Besides, that's the last thing you need to be concerned with."

"And what do you mean by that, detective?"

"Keisha," he said, then released a great amount of air from his chest. I'm just gonna be straight up and tell you…You're gonna have to testify again?"

"What?...Are you serious?" I said. I wasn't too fancy of repeating the whole court thing again but a part of me wanted to have another face to face with Mrs. Lowisky. I didn't like the way she handled me and I knew if I ever had the chance to encounter her again I would surely be ready for her ass. Besides, I did miss my boo and was eager to see him, even if court was the only way."

"Okay, just act like I'm on Hi-C's side again. I think I can handle that."

"No," he took another deep breath before speaking again. "*Against* the OMC."

"What the fuck detective!" I jumped from my seat. "I hope that's not Plan C. You gotta be shittin' me right!"

"I'm not shitting you. Look, when I first took this case I promised the chief that I could take down the OMC and that I would do it in a timely manner. Well it's been quite a while now and I haven't gotten even a jaywalking charge on anyone involved. Now he's getting impatient and losing faith in my ability to deliver. If I don't start getting results, and getting them quickly, I will soon be taking a first class ticket of shame right back to Oklahoma."

"So you're gonna put a death sentence out on me in exchange for your freakin' pride. All because for once in your life you can't lose."

"It's not about winning or losing. It's about justice."

"Justice for who!" I yelled.

"Justice for my people!" he shouted back, clearly letting his anger get the best of him.

"Get real detective," I turned and looked him directly into his eyes. "You talk that 'we are the world' shit, but what do you really care about the people, huh? How many times have you pulled up to one of these homeless men and offered out a free meal? How many times have you used your position to voice your concern that there is no recreation out here for these same kids you're locking up. They takin' down the basketball courts and youth centers left and right, and I don't see you standing in the way of any of these bulldozers. This is all about you and your pride, believe it or not."

"Look Keisha, the last thing I'm trying to do is get you all upset again. I want us both to remain calm about this. I told you, I'm on your side and I won't put you in harm's way, but I need you to testify. That's the only way-"

"The only way what? That you won't lose," I interrupted him. "You and I both know that I just can't do that."

"Ok then, how much?" Detective Bailey asked.

"Huh?" I questioned.

"I said, how much? How much money would it take for you to do it," he asked. "You're about your paper, right?"

"Detective, I can't believe you're asking me this. I told you that's a death sentence. There's no price I would put on my own head."

"Look, I've talked it over with the department and everyone feels you're testimony, along with the other little evidence we have, would be enough to take down the organization. They are willing to pay you fifty-thousand dollars cash, move you far out of town, and change your identity in return. Just look at it as a cash reward for your services. I'm aware that it would be a major change for you, but the way I see it, it's better than spending the rest of your life in jail."

"Jail? Why would I be spending the rest of my life in jail. Thanks to you letting me go- and I'm not saying that I don't appreciate it- but you guys don't have a thing on me."

The detective turned his head towards the window. The guilt he displayed on his face let me know that he knew something I didn't.

"Detective," I repeated myself. "I'm asking you again…why would I be going to jail?"

"It's like I told you before…they are always watching, they know everything, and they pretty much have to power to do anything they want. Whatever happens to you if I have to go back to Oklahoma is on them and you, and not me. I won't be able to save you."

"Well then I'll go with you," I told him.

"And make me an accessory to crime. You know like I know that I can't be caught even touching you."

"Look, I know this is sudden. I know you'd be leaving everything behind and that's a lot to ask, but I need you to make a decision and I need you to make it right now. Keisha, I'm asking you to give me a straight up answer, are you gonna testify or not?" I looked Detective Bailey dead into his eyes. As wrong as it was for me to even be thinking about it at the moment, I had regretted even fantasizing about him the night before. Testify against the Ordale Mafia? There was a huge difference between being a traitor and just being plain stupid. No way I could put myself in that position.

"I'm one hundred and fifty percent certain that I'm not testifying against the OMC. I'm sorry."

Detective Bailey let out a deep sigh before grabbing his cellular phone and giving it the attention he had gave it before. I couldn't help but notice that his forehead began to leak sweat either.

"I figured you would say that," he said. "And now that I think about it, maybe I was wrong. I should have never even considered having you do something like that."

I felt relieved to know that the Detective understood my decision. It was surely comforting.

"So you're not mad with me?" I asked.

"No, why would I be?" he said before extending his arms to me for a hug. I proudly excepted his support and embraced him. I had gotten so worked up that I wanted to do nothing more than release some tears into his shirt, but I decided to just use all the strength I had not to let out any emotions."

"Everything's gonna be just-" Detective said before looking over my head towards the passenger side window. It looked as if his soul had been taking out of his body and his eyes widened at whatever he had laid them on. Curious to know what made the detective freeze up the way he did, I turned around to get a glimpse.

"Keisha, don't!" the detective shouted, then tried to push my head back down. But it was too late. I swung around and saw exactly who he saw."

"Dino?" I stuttered. "Oh shit! Dino!"

"What the fuck?" Dino's I'm-about-to-make-some-money-face turned into a stoned look when he spotted me, a member of his organization, staring back at him. "This ain't no damn play. This a set up!"

Before I could get another word out Detective Bailey screamed.

"POLICE! FREEZE! PUT THOSE MUTHAFUCKING HANDS UP NOW!

Out of instinct, Dino reached for his pistol and aimed it dead at Detective Bailey before firing off a couple shots. Detective Bailey in turn let off a few of his own before taking cover, using the driver's side of his vehicle as a shield. Dino followed suit and buried himself in the walls of the passenger side doors. They both took turns peeping over the border of the Buick passing shots to one another. All I could do was scream in fear of my own life while I watched them try to kill each other. The shootout lasted probably a short time but felt like forever to me.

"Keisha you're a dead bitch!" Dino yelled before he finally got up and pointed his pistol directly at the glass that stood as a barrier between the two of us. Everything moved in slow motion as I saw my life flash before my eyes and him pull the trigger in attempt to take me out.

Thankfully before he had the chance to, Detective Bailey fired off a clean shot that made Dino's whole right side lean. I don't know if he had been hit, but judging by the way his body jerked back I knew something had to have happened to him. Dino groaned heavily and then took off running towards one of the big houses on the street. I saw him hop the fence and head for the woods.

The detective immediately jumped from behind the car and ran toward me. "Keisha are you okay!" he panted before opening the door to check up on me. "Are you hit?"

Then he gripped my shoulders and frantically scanned my entire body with his eyes."

"No. I'm okay," I pulled myself together enough to answer him.

"Good," he replied. "I want you to stay here! I'll be right back!"

Detective took off running behind Dino before yelling out one more time for me not to move. Then I watched him disappear.

"Oh shit! Oh shit!" I said as I tried to gather what just happened and the position it had now put me in. Once I realized that Dino, one of Hi-C's most trusted members and stone-cold killer, had saw me hugging a damn detective my hands started shaking. So badly, that I could barely even unlock the door to make my escape.

"I gotta get the fuck outta here," I told myself.

Despite the detective's orders, I opened the door and ran like my life depended on it. I knew that if Detective Bailey didn't get to Dino before Dino got to him, or worse got away, I was a dead girl for sure. I had much confidence in Detective Bailey, but I also knew that Dino was known for successfully dodging police chases by any means necessary. He was a clever dude who knew every cut, corner, and back road in Ordale. On top of that, he was raised in Thunderbolt, just on the other side of River Road.

I continued running and even though my body wasn't conditioned to withstand the length and pace I was going, I didn't quit. My heart was racing. My blood was boiling. And my adrenaline was through the roof. I'm sure that was the only thing that kept me going.

Not too familiar with the Thunderbolt area, I cut a few lefts, a few rights and even jumped a fence. I didn't stop until I got to the back of a big lonely building of which I didn't know what rested on the other side. As I gave myself time to catch my breath, I grabbed my cell phone out of my pants pocket and called the only person I felt could help me.

"What's up chick," the sleepy voice answered.

"Hey Poncha, this Keisha," I told her as if she didn't already know. "Look, I need you and I need you like I never needed you before."

"Keisha what's wrong?" she asked. "What's going on?"

"Well first, I need you to trust me. Then I need you to not talk to or answer for anyone from the OMC until I get to you. Is there any way you can contact your cousin?"

"Keisha, you don't have to say another word. Just let me know how soon you're trying to get here?"

"Soon like yesterday," I told her.

"Gotcha girl," Poncha replied. "Say no more."

PART THREE

CHAPTER 26: Going back to Cali

I arrived at the LAX about three o'clock in the afternoon and the California weather was as wonderful as I imagined it would be. Poncha had a cab waiting for me and I was glad because I looked a hot, embarrassing mess. Especially compared to all the beautiful, star-studded people that crowded the airport. The folks there dressed, talked, walked, and just plain moved differently than what I was used to. It was crazy because I was so accustomed to being a big deal in the small city of Ordale, that it was the first time in my life I felt as if I was an invisible ant trapped in a giant new world.

The driver was exactly where Poncha said he would be and I gladly hopped in to take the hour and a half ride to her house with him. She lived in a small military town call Port Hueneme and although I had just took a stressful five hour flight, I still didn't mind the lengthy ride. It gave me a chance to see the unfamiliar city and soak in some of the many beautiful attractions that surely existed there. Cali was the longest distance I had ever been out of Ordale and I was nothing less than amazed by how much different it was from the East Coast. The fact that I could ride between an ocean and a tall mountain on the very edge of the country was something you couldn't pay me to believe was possible.

Poncha lived in a gated community near a private beach. When we arrived we had to call her so that she could buzz us in. As we cruised down the streets of her neighborhood, I gazed out the window and was truly impressed by all the beautiful houses that welcomed us. My jaw dropped even more when I saw the house that belonged to her. It wasn't very big, but it was surely two stories. I could tell whoever designed it was extremely creative and took their job very seriously.

After thanking the cab driver and letting him know that he didn't have to wait for me to be let inside, I took a slow stroll down the cemented pathway that led me to her front door. While doing so, I admired the pretty green grass and the two cars- a BMW and a Range Rover- that sat outside the garage. The type of chick Poncha was, I just knew her stuff was paid for, and if I was only half as smart as she was, I could have had just as much.

I made it up to the doorway and took a deep breath before reaching for the bell, but before I could get a chance to press it the door swung open.

"So some bad shit gotta happen just for you to come visit a chick?" Poncha happily greeted me.

A feeling of joy came over my body, for seeing my best friend gave me a sense of peace and comfort that I very much needed. Poncha was standing there shamelessly in nothing but a white t-shirt, looking at me with the brightest smile on her face. She was a true friend and it felt good to be with her in my time of need. Shameka was my girl too, but when it came to the lifestyle I lived, Poncha was the person I could relate to the most. I could talk to her about things that Shameka could never understand.

"Don't start," I blushed and then reached in for a much needed hug. Poncha embraced me wholeheartedly and I enjoyed every second of it.

"You know it's the truth," she said after releasing me. Then she reached over to grab my bags and once she realized I didn't have any, her big smile slowly started to fade.

"Come inside, girl. We definitely need to catch up."

I stepped into Poncha's home and was even more amazed by the inside than I was by the out. The smell that welcomed me was like fresh pumpkin pie and the carpet was so clean that I felt undeserving to step on it. Upon entering, I had a choice between taking a stairway that led to the second story or a hallway that took me through the downstairs portion of her house. I assumed the living room, den, and kitchen was there.

As I figured, we took the hallway and I followed Poncha enviously as she directed me to a kitchen that appeared to be bigger than my entire hotel room. The appliances in there, I could tell, was all top notch and her counters, along with her living room furniture, were all red. That was her favorite color.

Poncha's kitchen and living room was separated by a long bar stand. It was aligned with four tall stools that sat evenly on both sides of it and she directed me to sit in any one of them. I did as I was told and then watched her as she walked over to her cabinet and pulled two wine glasses out of it. Then she went over to another nearby cabinet, grabbed a fresh bottle of Patron, and began to pour us up a shot.

“Yesss, come through honey. Lord knows I need a strong one," I told her. "But do you mind if I get a little chaser with that? I'm kinda sittin’ on an empty stomach."

"Oh I'm so sorry Keisha, what was I thinking?" she tapped her own forehead. "I didn’t even offer you anything to eat. Are you hungry?"

After just hearing the word hungry, my stomach began to quietly speak a strange language. I hadn’t eaten a single thing all day. When I started to really feel it, I was about halfway through my flight, but the fact that I had not a single dollar in my pocket helped me make my decision on what I would have. Even after Poncha told me whatever I wanted was already taken care of, I still didn’t bother to indulge. I felt she had done enough just getting me on the plane, especially at such short notice. Her and her sister, who happened to be a direct assistant to the president of the airline, really didn’t see eye to eye so for her to ask that favor was enough for me.

"Just a little," I said, downplaying the severity of the situation.

"Well I can cook you up something really quick. If not, I have some leftovers in the ‘frige. But I forgot," she stopped herself. "All I have is vegetarian food."

"Ugh," I groaned at the sound of it. "I forgot you on that bullshit."

"It's not bullshit," Poncha corrected me. "But fortunately for you, I do take my house guests in consideration when I grocery shop. I have some chicken breasts in the freezer if that suits you better. I’m sure it won’t take long to thaw, but you'll have to cook that shit for yourself."

My stomach began to rumbled again. I sure as hell wasn’t strong enough to fix my own meal and I definitely couldn't wait for anything to thaw out. I needed food and I needed it fast.

"Just whip me up some of that shit you eat. I'll just have to deal with it."

"Sure thing," she said. "I have a burger I know you'll love. Won't even taste the difference."

"If you say so," I doubted.

I watched Poncha walked to the refrigerator and take some contents out. I always knew she was a vegan but I never discussed it or even cared until I was standing hungry in her kitchen. As I studied her silently, I couldn't help but wonder how a person who only ate boring meals like fruits and vegetable salads be so thick and have a booty so phat. Poncha's body was the shit and her skin was impeccable. She was thirty-six years old but she still got ask for ID whenever we went places because she was easily mistaken for a teenager. I mean, I looked damn good too, but for some reason people always thought I was older. Poncha, on the other hand, possessed a different type of beauty. Like she could have been a descendant of a real life goddess. It was obvious she took real good care of herself and I always admired that about her.

"Poncha, be honest," I said, forcing myself out of the trance of her beauty. "You don't ever get a craving for a big juicy ass hamburger. You know, with bacon and all kinda shit wrapped around it."

"I used to," she said, clearly unbothered by my attempt to tease her. "But that was during the beginning of my journey. Now that I'm more conscious 'bout it, I hate the thought of it."

"Conscious?" I asked. "What is there to be conscious about? Meat is here for us to eat, just like fruits and vegetables. Plants are living organisms too. I don't see you crying while you over there slicing up that spinach. And I don't see any vegans living to be two hundred years old either."

Poncha sighed and then placed a small pan on the stove. "It's nothing I can really explain to you. I mean I can, but I won't. You can't change the opinions of people who have been conditioned. If you can't think outside the box then I've learned from experience that it's pointless trying to get you to. My motto is to each his own. I just do what I feel is best for me. What I eat don't' make you shit, and vice versa."

"I feel you," I said, but deep down inside I really didn't. In fact, I pitied her for being so deprived of all the great dishes that were associated with meats. I just couldn't see myself living without some good ol' spaghetti packed with ground beef, fully loaded pizzas, and the way bacon smelled in the morning time, indescribable. I just had to have it in my life.

Poncha didn't waste any more time throwing her lifestyle choices on me. Instead she concentrated on fixing my meal and took only about fifteen minutes to complete it. When she was finished, she smiled at her creation and placed my plate in front of me. As I looked at it strangely, I saw that I was served some type of very brown hamburger bun smothering a patty that was not meat. Instead of the lettuce, mayonnaise, and pickles I was used to they were substituted for spinach, tomatoes, cucumbers, and avocado. The creamy spread she used, she explain, was some sort of vegan mixture with no dairy products inside. For my side, was sweet potato chips and dried apples. I didn't know what to make of it but I was so hungry that I wasted no time digging right in. Less than three minutes later, I had devoured my whole plate and was silently begging for another round.

"Damn Keisha," Poncha studied my plate after coming back

from taking a quick trip to the bathroom. “I never seen anybody eat that fast.”

"I’m sure it was only because I was starving, but that burger wasn't so bad."

"I knew you would like it," she said. "Got you another one coming right up if you want."

“Sure,” I shrugged as if it was no big deal. I couldn’t give Poncha the satisfaction of knowing that I could have eaten about five more of them. My loyalty to meat wouldn’t allow me. “It’s not angus beef, but it’s something I could get used to if it was the only thing left on the planet."

"Aaaw hush trick,” Poncha silenced me. “Just admit that you like it."

Poncha laughed then headed back to the stove. This time she fixed herself up a plate also. As I waited for her return, I finally took down the patron shot my body was now able to stand. Poncha whipped up our meals in no time, and with now two plates in her hand, she directed me to follow her into the living room.

"My husband would kill me if he knew I ate in here so try not to leave no evidence.” she told me. After sitting on the red leather loveseat, she slowly dragged her coffee table towards us so that we could place our trays on top of it.

"Those bar chairs do my back no justice and I’d be damn if I cook over a stove and can’t comfortably enjoy my meals.”

"Now you know whatever the husband says goes," I told her. "You better stop disrespecting that man."

"That muthafucka better stop disrespecting me," she said. “All these rules and shit. Sometimes I feel like I’m the one in the damn military."

Poncha went in a quick daze, probably thinking of her husband. I only personally met him once but the vibe I got from him was that he was a very good dude. He was a high-ranked member of the air force who used his money to invest in a construction company that was pretty successful in Cali. Unfortunately for Poncha, he was never home because of work.

"I miss him though," she finally said. "He'll be back in a month. Just for a few days tho."

"Damn only for a few days, must be hell spending all these nights alone in this nice ass house girl. I couldn't do it."

"At first I said I couldn't either, but love will make you do some things you thought you'd never do."

I dwelled for a minute on what Poncha had just said, then I busted into a heavy laughter. She just looked at me all crazy. She surely was confused.

"What's so funny heffa?"

"Girl please," I told her. "This is Poncha I'm talking to. I know damn well you got a six-inch, six-foot man somewhere ducked off round these Cali trenches. You know, for when the husband goes away."

"Maybe a six-inch dildo," she proudly admitted, "but no damn man."

"So you telling me you never crept around on your husband, not even once?"

"Not even once," she said with certainty.

"Ordale counts too now," I told her. "You don't have no secret boos back in Ordale either?"

"Keisha, have I ever told you I had anyone on the side? And I tell you everything. Just think about it."

"No you never told me, but I would understand if you didn't. All things ain't meant to be shared, even with your closest friends."

"Naw, I don't believe in that shit. If I have a best friend I should be able to tell that bitch everything and not have to worry about anything. That's how true friends get down. So you tellin' me you keep secrets from me?"

"I don't," I said, but really I didn't mean it. If Poncha knew the truth about me, I'm sure we wouldn't be best friends.

"And what about that doctor?" she reminded me of telling her about Michael. "Y'all still fucking around?"

"Hell no. I got tired of all that flexing' in shit. You were right, got old quick."

"I told you girl. I don't care how much money a man got, how fine he is, or how much he got it going on....if you can't be yourself around him then it's not gonna work."

"Oh believe me, I understand that now."

"And what about Mr. Zinc?" she laughed. "You still whipping on his old freaky ass."

"Well you know his wife got cancer now, so he's been stuck in the house taking care of her."

"Damn. That's fucked up," she said.

"I know. That stack a month I had coming in did some justice during this shut down."

"I was talking about her having cancer, Keisha."

"Oh, yeah right. That too."

Poncha shook her head. "Keisha, you know you are something else, I tell ya. You remind me of myself when I was your age. Cold and heartless"

"Well I'd rather be cold and heartless than used and abused. People tend to take advantage of you when you show them your emotions."

"Certain types of people," Poncha said.

"Well at least all the ones I've come across," I replied.

"Like I said," Poncha repeated. "You were so me back then."

For a second we both got quiet and devoured our food. I didn't know what Poncha was thinking, but I was wondering why she had started talking to me as if I was a child. *I reminded her of her when she was younger*? Poncha only had me by like seven years and she held the same occupation as I did. I mean yes, she had her shit together, owning her own house and all, but she had only been a homeowner for four years. Unlike her, I didn't have a sweet ass military husband who got me anything I wanted. I mean where was this I-eat-better-than-you-and-you-remind-me-of-when-I-was-young-and-dumb bitch coming from and what did she do with my best friend?

"So what took you so long?" Poncha suddenly asked, interrupting my thoughts.

"Excuse me?" I replied. I was already on defense and ready to give her a piece of my mind. "I'm not understanding?"

Poncha sighed deeply before directing all her attention to me. "Keisha, I already know why you're here?"

"What? Wait uh minute, why am I here?" I said.

I mean I knew why, I just hadn't told Poncha yet.

"Because you're wondering why you're not working for OMC anymore, right?"

Now I was completely lost. I didn't know what Poncha was talking about and obviously she knew nothing about Dino and the shootout. It was never a question about why I wasn't working for the OMC. It was because I hadn't gave Cederick's grimy ass any pussy yet.

"No, I'm not wondering," I said, thinking about how I had fucked up with Cederick the night before. "I already know why."

"Oh so you know about the meeting, that we voted you out? Who told you?"

"Wait ah damn minute!" I began to sit up, and even against my hunger, stopped eating. "What meeting and who voted me out?"

"Oh god Keisha, I'm sorry I thought that's why you were here. Well if that's not the reason then what is it?"

"No way," I told her. "I'm not talking until you start talking. I thought we were best friends. I guess being able to tell each other everything doesn't pertain to you."

"No, it's not like that. I was gonna tell you but only if you came to me first. They strictly forbid anyone from making any type of contact with you. I couldn't wait for the day you found your way to me."

The sincere look Poncha held in her eyes led me to believe she was telling the truth. I couldn't be upset with her anyway, because even I knew that there were codes and rules to the game.

"See, I didn't know until I got to Ordale, but the meeting- the one where we had to bring pool sticks- was all about you. Since you were the one in the house when it got raided, everyone felt it was best that you didn't come back to work once Hi-C gave the okay to start moving again. We just felt that you were hot and that the police would probably be watching your every move. To be fair, every member voted and it was unanimous that you be counted out."

"What do you mean unanimous? Poncha, you voted against me too?"

"Well yes," Poncha admitted, unapologetically.

"What the hell Poncha!" I cried. "And you're supposed to be my girl."

"I am your girl. That's why I voted against you. I'm smart Keisha, not stupid. If they were to trace anything that could shut the OMC down to us through you, how the hell would anybody make money? Trust me, as long as I was getting paid, so were you. I will always have your back."

"But how do you know it wasn't personal? What if it was because of Isis? What if she just doesn't like me? You know, I always got that snobbish vibe from her," I said, leaving out the fact that I had been sleeping with her husband for years.

"What? No. If anything Isis was the one who stuck up for you."

I sat up even more. "She what?"

“Yes. She was the one who suggested that we each took money out of our cuts and give to you. Ten percent was the agreement. And she saw to it that since Cederick was in charge, we give the money to him and he was to make sure you get paid. We're the OMC remember. We're more than a mafia, we’re a family.”

After hearing those words, a bit of relief, disbelief, and anger came over my body all at once. I was happy to know that the OMC members didn’t think I had anything to do with the Feds cracking down on us, but I was also furious when I recalled what Cederick had requested of me. He knew all along that I was voted out and still found a way to play me. I knew for sure now that him wanting to get in my pants was personal. Although I mentioned nothing to Poncha of this, I just knew that once I got back to Ordale, Cederick would definitely be hearing from me again.

“This is un-fuckin-believable,” I said to Poncha, who had no clue of what was really on my mind.

“I know. But it was for the best of the team," she said. “And what about you? Since all of this is new to you, what really brought you here?”

Instantly I thought back to the incident with Detective Bailey and Dino, and at that point, I really didn’t want to tell Poncha about it. Partly because I was overwhelmed with the information she had just laid on me but still I knew I had to say something. Besides, as sincere as she came off, Poncha could have already heard and was probably playing me too.

“You’re right Poncha, you guys made a good call, as much as it hurts me to admit it. As a matta fact, the feds have been on my ass since they raided Hi-C’s spot. One detective in particular. He’s been popping up on me often trynna get me to talk, but I always refuse. And well, this morning, I get a visit from him. He tells me that if I knew what was best for me, I'd ride with him so that we can talk. Then he tries to convince me that he had some type of dirt on my name and that it would be in my best bet to testify against Hi-C and the OMC."

"Oh my god Keisha...are you serious?" she said. "And what did you tell that bastard?"

"Girl I told his ass hell-to-the-naw. Next thing I know, I look up and there's Dino standing outside the window."

"What?" Poncha gasped. "Outside the car you were sitting in? With the damn detective? Wait? How?"

"I don't know girl. Looks like he thought he was about to catch a play or something. But once he saw that it was a detective in the car, they started shooting at each other and shit."

"Oh shit!" Poncha said in disbelief. "Are you fuckin' serious?"

"As serious as a fuckin' heart attack girl, I almost died today. It was the scariest shit I've ever been through."

"But do you think Dino recognized you, no offense, but you really don't look like yourself right now?"

"His last words before he ran off was, 'Keisha you're a dead bitch.' If that doesn't confirm it then I don't know what does."

Poncha placed her right hand over her mouth and just held it there without saying a word. I could tell by her sincere reaction that it was her first time hearing of this. I didn't know what she was thinking, but I hoped she believed the half-truth I had just told her.

“That’s why I asked you not to talk to anyone from the OMC,” I continued. “I didn’t want anyone putting a bad bug in your ear about me. I wanted to tell you my side of the story first.”

“Now Keisha, you know I trust you before I trust any of those other motherfuckers out the clique. You should know me better than that. Besides, how many times we talked about this. I told you what I would do if I ever got in a situation like that.”

“Yeah but I didn’t believe you, I thought you were just bluffing.”

“Just bluffing?” she gasped. “Girl, I would snitch on they ass in a heartbeat. Sing like a damn bird, hitting high notes in all.”

I laughed at Poncha who began to actually hit some notes to demonstrate. She didn’t sound bad either. I always told her that if the drug game didn’t work out then she should definitely pursue a career in singing. She was humble about it and always brushed me off.

“Girl that voice again,” my laughter faded into a chuckle. “But for real, I always said I would snitch too, but it’s different when you’re actually in the situation. I have to think about my life as well.”

“I feel you but I’d have to just take my chances. Them niggas would do the same thing to us. Like I asked you before, you think they would sit in jail for me or you? Hell no. We get locked up, their grind doesn’t stop. Long as I don’t bring you down, I would definitely get them. You do what you have to do, just don’t leave me in the blind so that I know how I need to move. And I told you if you ever needed me I would be here for you. Can’t nobody fuck with you out here in Cali. I got your back.”

“Thanks girl, I needed to hear that. You’re a true friend. But

I'm confused," I said to her. "Why do you seen so cool about all this? This is your lifestyle we are talking about? How could you not be against me coming between it?"

Poncha placed her plate of food, that she had only taken a few bites of, back on the coffee table. Then she turned her television's volume down and looked her almond-shaped brown eyes directly into mine. For some reason, a nervous feeling came over me.

"Because Keisha," she began to calmly speak. "Ever since we've been on pause I've had a chance to really think and evaluate my life. I've been so used to living this dream, that I never realized how fast it all can come to an end. I mean, I have a whole life ahead of me. I have a husband who loves me and I want to slow down and have children soon. I just started asking myself every day, is this really worth it? And the more I think and pray about it, the more I realize that it's not....And as far as the OMC going down, for some strange reason I feel that maybe if I get out before I'm forced out, the power of karma would have mercy towards me."

Poncha's words were a surprise to my soul. As much as she loved the game, I would have never thought she was starting to feel the same way I did. I knew there was a reason we cliqued so tight. Without saying another word, Poncha quietly rose from her seat and walked to the kitchen. When she returned she was holding something in her hand.

"Take a look at this," she said, handing me what I now recognized to be a small, wallet-sized picture.

It was a professional headshot of a teenage girl. You could tell it was an older photo because of the cheesy sky-blue background. Maybe it could have been a school picture. I didn't know. Just like I didn't know why Poncha was handing it to me.

“She’s beautiful,” I said as I faked being impressed. The woman was cute, but the extra fat on her face took away from her maximum beauty. I couldn’t see her whole body but judging by the plump cheeks and three rolls in her neck, I knew she had to have been more than two hundred pounds.

“Is that your mother?” I asked her.

“Look again,” Poncha replied.

“Your sister?”

“Harder."

I tuned out my surroundings to help me better focus on the image in front of me. I tried to figure it out but began to get frustrated because I was in no mood to play trivia with Poncha. I was just about to give in before looking at the mole the girl had under her right eye, which was exactly identical to the one Poncha had under hers.

“Oh my gosh Poncha, is this you?”

Poncha strangely did not hold her head in shame. Instead she looked at me with her chin high and smiled.

“Was me,” she replied. “Just eight years ago.”

“Poncha, you looked like this when you were my age. What? What happened to you?” I started rubbing her forehead. “Were you sick then? Are you sick now?”

“Sick?” she laughed. “Maybe I was sick….Sick of living. Sick of loving. Sick of myself. I never told you this but I was adopted. The family that took me in was from Nigeria but they moved to New York to open a midwife center. The man who raised me, well his name was Abilgal and he was one of the best black doctors to walk this Earth. His wife, Mrs. Abilgal, was an extraordinary woman too. She was an entrepreneur who made her own line of natural skincare products and distributed them wholesale to many of the local businesses in our area. Poppi, as I was told to call Mr. Abilgal, was a kind-hearted man and didn't believe people had to pay to be helped. So, when he saw my crackhead mama bangin' on the door of the center in labor after he was about the lock up, his heart wouldn't allow him to turn her away. With the help of his wife, they delivered me and before they could began to tell my mama where to go for assistance, she left me right there with not a thought behind it."

"So lemme guess," I went ahead and figured, "they legally adopted you?"

"Yeah exactly," Poncha said.

"Well, that was nice of them," I told her. "I'd take living with some rich folks over a crackhead any day."

Poncha then rolled her eyes and looked away. Then she laughed to herself as she clearly reflected on memories of growing up with her foster family.

"Girl, let's just say that they were some *very* cultural people. I mean, the word roots meant everything to them and that's why they never kept my truth away from me. They believed that in order to 'understand one's present, one must understand their past,' Poncha said in her best African accent. "Or at least that's what Mrs. Abilgal used to say. They never, and I mean never, steered from their customs and beliefs just because they moved over to this country and of course they raised me the same way. At first I was cool with it, but as I got older and started to be more exposed to the 'American way' I wanted to fit in with the people here."

Poncha's mood changed from a chipper to sadden one as she

reminisced on her past. "I remember being sixteen and telling my parents for the first time of my desire to go to a public school. They didn't want to send me, but being firsthand witnesses to my growing unhappiness, they agreed to grant me my wish. It was only under the grounds that it was private and all-girls school though. They also made me promise that I would stick to my roots and continue on with the customs of which they taught me."

Poncha rose from her sat and walked to the glass door of the patio that was right in her living room. I was paying attention to her but I was also watching the plate of food she seemed uninterested to touch anymore. My second serving was just minutes from being devoured, and I wanted to ask her if she wanted the rest of hers but then I decided that it just wasn't the right time.

"I remembered being so excited about my first day," she continued, "but when I got to school, all of that faded quickly. That's because I realized the world wasn't as nice as I thought it would be and high school students could be the most evil people on the planet. Keisha they teased me. They teased me because of how I dressed, how I didn't eat meat, what I ate, even because of my intellect. The popular girls would call me weirdo, an Albino-African, and animal lover. Sometimes I would come home to find notes taped to my back and one time someone snuck a piece of fried chicken in my lunchbox."

"Damn," I said, "that's cruel."

"I know... but I never told my parents about it because I didn't want them to say I told you so, or worst, embarrassed me further by coming to the school. Instead I just took the insults day in and day out until I met a girl who didn't seem to mind me being who I was. Her name was Virginia and she was one of the most popular and prettiest girls in the school. She would let me sit with her and her friends at lunch and they all treated me nice. About a month into our friendship, they invited me to a sleepover and although it was strictly against everything my parents stood for they allowed me to go. This would be the first time in my life that I had ever even been in the home of anybody's other than my own. Of course Mrs. Abilgal packed me with my own natural toothpaste, soap, and even sent me with food and a note to her parents that ordered me to eat only what I brought with me."

She laughed before continuing.

"But if mama knew that her letter never got to Virginia's mom, or that she worked overnight, she would have never let me go over. It was seven of us altogether. I had a great time with them and we got into all types of wild stuff night. Someone even suggested that we play make-up and beings that I was the one who'd make the most shocking transformation, I was their little project. Wanting to 'be down' with the crew, I allowed the girls to dress me in one of Virginia's older sister's mini dresses. Then they flat-ironed my naturally curly hair, laced me with big jewelry, and packed my face with tons of make-up. When they were finished, they revealed me to myself in the mirror and I admit I felt a confidence like I never had before.

Man those girls were so impressed by seeing another side of me that they made me the center of attention the whole night and because it was something I was never used to I was loving it. We ended our fun by playing a game of truth of or dare and I had watched as the other girls were challenged to called up their boy crushes, prank call 9-1-1, and even kiss each other. So, when I was asked take a picture bent over with my tongue out in this little dress, I didn't think that by Monday morning someone would tape it to the school bulletin board."

Poncha eyes began to swell but she held in her tears. I still felt the need to go over and hug her. But she stopped me.

"It's okay," she said. "I'm fine. It's just the look on my parents faces in that school's office when she saws those pictures. Not just with the dress, but with me eating a hamburger, me putting the cigarette to mouth, and all the other crazy things we did that night, would forever haunt me. I mean, I really thought they were my friends, how could I allow myself to be so stupid?"

Poncha banged on the glass of the patio door but still did not allow herself to cry. She did allow me to now come give her that hug I knew she needed from a true friend. Then I escorted her back to her seat.

"I ran away that same night and haven't saw my parent's since. I mean just like that I became a sixteen-year-old homeless girl but I somehow managed to hitchhike all the way until I made it to Philly. From there, I meet a dealer named Smoke who is good friends with Hi-C. He fell in love with me, showed me the ropes, and that's how I ended up where I am today."

"Wow, that's crazy Poncha," I said, completely blown away by her story. "But that still doesn't explain this." I held up the photo she had just showed me.

"Oh that, yeah how could I forget that," she said. "I got fat because I started to lose myself and I blamed everything I was going through on my parents shielding me. So as a way to rebelled against them, I began eating foods they warned me about and partaking in activities that I knew they would not approved of. It only took a year for me to gain all that weight and bigger I got the harder it got for me give it up. Depression, regret, shame, suicidal thoughts, they all took over me. Thankfully I got myself together and from there, I was able to go back the ways of which my parents taught me. I felt and looked better ever since."

"I see," I replied.

"You know why so many people are unhappy?" Poncha said, as if a thought had sudden popped into her little brain.

"No why?" I asked.

"Because so many of us are walking around in bodies that are not of our true images. See, the universe gives us everything we need to survive yet we had become dependent on man and man-made things to nourish us. You're eating double cheeseburgers every day and then you're looking in mirror wondering why you got a double chin, wondering why you aren't happy with your own reflection. Not to mention, the diseases that come with bad the nutrition. 'Everything starts with the food' as my folks used to teach me."

"Your folks seemed like they had a lot of knowledge," I said, yet still not convinced that eating meat was a bad thing. "Speaking of them, did you ever return home?"

"Yeah. I did," Poncha said then dropped her head. "But it was too late. When I finally got the nerve to go back to the house, the neighbors told me that when Mr. Abilgal passed, Mrs. Abilgal moved back to Nigeria. She also said Mrs. Abilgal sat on the front porch everyday waiting for me...You know what, deep down inside I knew my parents would have forgiven me for what I had done. They weren't like that. It was me who couldn't face them. And that's the hardest part of it all, knowing that when I did go, it was too late. You see, that's why I really don't care about this game, this money, none of it. I just don't want to wait until it's too late to do something. I'm ready to completely take back my life. I've started with my physical and now I'm working on the spiritual. I owe it to my folks."

Poncha words really made me think. I knew she told me that she was born to some pretty well-off people but she never mentioned that she was adopted or that she had run away at such a young age. Just looking at her, it would be impossible to imagine that those things she shared were true. It now explained why she was such a loner and only really trusted to hang out with me. I could only wonder though, what was it about me that made her trust me? I had to admit I wasn't the most loyal person, but nonetheless she saw me for what was in my heart. Hearing Poncha share her truth with me made me feel ashamed for all the lies I told her and made me want to open up about some of the things I was keeping from her in return.

"Poncha," I called out to my silent friend who sat emotionally in daze. "I appreciate you for sharing that part of your life with me. And since we're opening up to one another, can I share something with you?"

"Keisha, you know you're my girl," she said. "You can tell me anything."

"Well," I held my head down like a bashful little girl and began wiggling my toes. "It’s just...well it’s just that...I think I've falling with someone I probably shouldn't have."

"Who Hi-C?” she perked up and smile. “Girl, the way your eyes light up when he's comes around. Tell me something I don't know."

"No," I shook my head. “That’s not it.”

"So you're not talking about Hi-C?" she asked.

I nodded again.

"Then who?" she asked.

I sighed deeply before answering her. "The detective…I think I'm in love with Detective Bailey."

Poncha eyes were already red from her recent outcry, but what was once because sorrow was now because of anger. Immediately she leaped towards me and then ripped the thick cotton t-shirt I wore underneath my jogging suit with her bare arms like the female incredible hulk. She was obviously looking for a wire or something. Then she firmly grabbed a fist full of my jacket with each of her hands and pinned me up against the couch. I had never seen her so upset before.

"Bitch you better start talking and you better start talking fast," she replied.

CHAPTER 27: What Happens in Vegas

"**K**eisha have you lost your damn mind! I've been looking all over for you," Detective Bailey whispered through the phone after receiving an unexpected call from me. The commotion that suddenly faded in the background let me know that he had just removed himself from around a crowd of people. There was a brief silence and when the noise completely ceased, he spoke again.

"Where the hell are you?" he asked.

"I'm in Cali," I told him.

"California?"

"Yes."

"Keisha, what the hell are you doing all the way over there? You know what, nevermind," he said before even giving me a chance to answer. "If you're not kiddin', I'm assuming you're calling to tell me you're on your way back to Ordale."

"Negative," I told him.

"What do you mean, negative?" he asked, getting a little more aggressive but still managing to maintain his whisper. "You will be dead out here if you don't get your head together. You need to find your way back to me and you need to do it as quickly as possible. This is not a request."

"I don't take orders from anyone anymore, detective. I said I'm not going anywhere. I just don't trust anything right now."

"What are you talking about, *not trusting anything*?' he asked. "Is this directed towards me? Have I given you a reason?"

"Look, I have already spoken. The only way you're gonna talk to me is if you come to California. I'm not changing my mind on this one."

"You must be really losing your mind," he said.

I can tell he was very frustrated. Yet again, I had found another way to bring stress upon his life, but this time I didn't care.

"How do you expect me to just drop everything and come to California? Like really, how does that work?"

"Easy," I told him. "You just take your ass down to the airport and jump on the flight I have waiting for you. In fact, you better get to moving. It leaves in exactly three hours. When you land someone will be there to pick you up and bring you to me."

"Keisha," he sighed. "I just don't know what to say about you. You're the only one who can test my patience like this. Call me back when the joke is over."

"This is no joke," I told him while looking up at Poncha who had just set everything up with her cousin. She was bent over her fancy kitchen counter staring back at me as if I was about to reveal the night's winning Powerball numbers.

"I'm as serious as that look Dino had on his face when he was aiming his pistol directly between my eyes. I'm not going back to Ordale. I'd be a damn fool. You know you really put me in a fucked up situation and for once I'm calling the shots. Now I'm gonna say this one more time, if you wanna talk to me, catch this flight and I will see you soon."

"Keisha!" detective shouted out before hearing the sound of the disposable phone I was using click in his face. I immediately turned it off and stuffed it into the pocket of the sweat pants I had on.

"Do you think he will come?" Poncha wasted no time asking. She was desperate for the 4-1-1.

"If he wants this case bad enough, he will." I told her.

I got the call around 8:00pm. As I knew he would, Detective Bailey had landed in California and was hopping in the cab I had waiting for him and headed to me. I already knew he made it before he even confirmed it, thanks to Poncha, who was in her undercover gear waiting at the airport just to make sure that he had come alone.

"Elvis has landed and he seems to be by himself," Poncha, in her best spy voice, whispered through the phone.

"Perfect," I said then dropped the last artificial rose inside of the glass vase that rested in the center of the circular table we would be dining at. I took a step back and admired the gorgeous set-up before looking around to also soak in the matching surroundings. I couldn't believe I was thirty stories high on the rooftop of a beautiful five-star hotel. I also couldn't believe I went through all the trouble of hiring a personal chef, a personal waiter, and a decorator to dress the place up. Poncha paid for it and was the one who convinced me that all the extra stuff was necessary. She told me that her and her husband partook in the rooftop experience once a year and every time was life changing.

The top of the roof was filled with many round tables, but the single beam of light that glistened down on ours set it apart from the rest. Each of them were covered with a sheer, burgundy cloth and had fancy glass centerpieces resting on top. A trail of candles and rose petals were also planted carefully along the ground and created a pathway that led to the building's edge. I followed the path to see the great view of the cars and people on the ground below me. The commotion they caused seemed to be nonexistent in the heights, while the taller buildings that looked down on me aided as a shield away from the rest of the world. To top it off, the way the stars aligned around the almost-full moon made the night seem as if it arrived just for the occasion.

With the butterflies dancing around in my tummy freely, I waited anxiously for Detective Bailey to show up. The cab was directed to bring him straight to where I was so it wasn't long after I got word that he had landed, that our waiter was escorting him up the steps. Seeing them, I rushed back to the table, looked back towards the stars, and pretended to act as if I didn't know they were approaching.

"The lovely lady is right here," our host, who introduced himself as Joshua to me earlier, held out his arms and gave me a fancy introduction. Still pretending to be surprised, I jumped slightly at the sight of Detective Bailey who stood before me wearing his usual black suit and tie and greeted me with a phony smile. Joshua probably thought he was dressed for the occasion, but I knew by the untucked teal collar shirt, the stiffness of his dry hair, and the bags under his firey-red eyes that the last place he thought he would be meeting me was at an elegant dinner.

Detective Bailey took his seat and Joshua took a bow before dismissing himself to allow us some much needed privacy. He didn't bother to take our drink orders because there were already two glasses of wine on the table just waiting for our consumption. The clearly unhappy detective stared straight into my eyes and allowed his anger towards me to show all over his face. It was a bit uncomfortable to witness, so I decided to be the one to break the ice.

"Well hello," I said awkwardly. "So…uhmm…how was your flight?"

“Unexpected,” he said sarcastically. “But all that matters is that I made it safely.”

“That’s the spirit,” I said.

“I gotta admit,” Detective Bailey relaxed a bit and began to scope out his surroundings with his weary eyes. “This is very nice. I won’t dare ask how you could afford it.”

“Let’s just say it's not about what you know, but more about who you know.”

“I see,” he replied. “And is this your way of trying to smooth things over with me? Because if it is, it didn’t work.”

All I could do was smile at the detective’s weird way of thanking me. He was definitely playing tough but I knew he appreciated it. A getaway and an evening like this one was just what he needed to balance out his chaotic life.

“Well maybe you’ll find a way to forgive me," I told him. "Just like I’ve forgiven you.”

“And what do I need forgiveness for?” he asked. “Oh c’mon now, I know you’re not blaming me for what happened back there.”

“I told you detective, I didn’t want to ride with you in that car. I knew it was a bad idea and I don't see how you didn't know it either.”

“Look Keisha, it was never my intention to put you in any danger. It just happened that way.”

I began to get worked up thinking about Detective Bailey and Dino exchanging fire with each other. The loud shots that stung my eardrums, along with my screams, and the fear of feeling like I was going to die, was enough to mentally disturb the most sane person. It was a horrible experience and the last thing I wanted to do was to relive it.

“Look I don’t wanna get into all that. I’ve thought about it enough.” I told him. “But I’d at least like to know what happened to him? Did he get away?”

“No. We caught him,” the detective informed me, “but later that day. He got hit in the shoulder and thought that driving to a hospital an hour out would save him. We got the call as soon as he admitted himself.”

“Oh, so where is he now?” I asked.

“His injury was pretty bad so they kept him in the hospital for a few days, but after that he was expedited back to Ordale. Don’t worry, he shot at a cop. He won’t be getting out for a long time.”

“Good,” I replied. “That’s a relief.”

“I can imagine so. I have been trying to inform you about that,” Detective Bailey said. “Keisha, that was really selfish for you to just be calling me after two whole weeks. I was worried sick about you. I even went back to the hotel every day hoping you would return to your belongings, which by the way, I have in my possession.”

“Wait a minute, you have my stuff? Oh thank God.”

“Yes. Mrs. Burrows, you know the lady sitting at the bus stop with you when I picked you up for the trial?” he asked.

“Yeah I remember her,” I cornered my eyes. "Don't tell me she tried to steal them."

“Not even close. She owns that hotel and I know her very well. She made sure your stuff went unbothered and she seemed more concerned with your disappearance than I was.”

“What?" I sat at attention. "You’re telling me that lady’s not homeless?”

“No she’s not. And she wasn’t giving you her last dollar. She has *plenty* more where that came from. In fact, she owns three more hotels and over fifteen convenience stores. Sometimes things and people are not what they seem."

Learning this, I immediately felt ashamed for the way I treated her, for I had surely judged. Detective Bailey picked up on my sudden change of mood.

"Why the sad face?" he asked.

"I don't know, because of the way I treated her, I guess," I said to him. "I didn't know who she was."

"But would it have made a difference if you did?" he said.

Detective Bailey had a point and I didn't want to feel anymore wrong than I already did so I decided to just leave that one alone. "I'm sorry, detective. I didn't mean any harm with her, neither with you. It's just that for once in my life I'm doing what I feel is best for me. It's clear I have to look out for myself now."

"So then why not just hide in California. Why even reach out now?" he asked. "Trust me, I would have never guessed you were all the way out here."

"Because detective," I said, before grabbing my cup to take a swig of the expensive red wine. Then I attempted to tell him what was on my heart, but suddenly my mind wouldn't let me get a word out. All I could do was stare out into space with a look on my face as innocent as a newborn baby's. The detective locked eyes with me, just waiting for me to speak.

"Because what?" he finally asked, after realizing nothing would come out of my mouth. "Tell me something. I need to know. Why did you bring me here?"

At a moment that couldn't be better, thankfully, Joshua walked back through the entrance of the rooftop and saved me from answering Detective Bailey's question. He was carrying out what I soon made out to be a cart full of random foods. There I was thinking we had to place our orders, but Joshua informed us that the honeymoon special came with a small buffet where we could choose from what we wanted right at the comfort of our own table. The detective and I studied this fancy looking cart that consisted of three layers of food. Each layer had about ten small, rectangular hot pans that were individually filled with different types of food. I quickly assumed that the top row was the main entrée because it displayed all of the meats. Everything from fish, to steaks, to shrimp, even baked chicken was on that row. The second contain different styles of rice, mashed potatoes, and yams. And the bottom were the vegetables. Everything was perfect and appealing. To top it off, the aroma that rose from the blend of all the foods was soothing to my nostrils. This was definitely something I had never experienced and I couldn't wait to share my thoughts with Poncha.

"Oh my, I really wasn't expecting this," I told Joshua.

"Here at Bella's Rooftop 'decisions don't matter because we bring the menu to you on a platter," he said with pride. "And the best part about it is whatever you don't eat you get to take home. We also don't believe in aggravating our couples with silly questions like 'can I get you anything' so on that buzzer I gave you earlier, there are eight different options to choose from if you may so happen to need my attention."

Joshua grabbed his buzzer, which looked identical to the one he gave me, and demonstrated a few things. "This is a call device. If you want anything like water, just tap the button that has the picture of the raindrops. If you want more wine, just tap the champagne glass. For more of these delicious dishes, just hit the picture of that plate and spoon. And my favorite," he smiled, "if you don't want to be disturbed by my irritating voice, just hit the red X there. We also have a button on the side here that you can press and you can speak directly into it. Sort of works like a walky-talky. How cool is that?"

Joshua stood in front of us with the brightest smile on his face. Even though it was obvious that he recited those exact words every day, I could tell he took pride in servicing his guests. He was the type of guy who would probably be running the business in a couple years, maybe even opening a restaurant of his own.

"Definitely pretty cool," Detective Bailey surprised me by speaking up.

“I thought you’d be impressed," Joshua told him. "I’m going to be leaving you two love bugs alone now.”

“Thank you Joshua," I said. "You’ve been very kind.”

“My pleasure and remember,” he said before taking his buzzer out, pressing a button on the side and speaking directly into it, “Holla, if ya need me.”

The detective and I both laughed at Joshua’s keen since of humor before watching him leave us for good. Shortly after he exited, the lights dimmed even more and a sprinkler system that was prompted above our heads let out a crispy mist that gently graced our bodies. The music even seemed to get a tap bit louder, allowing Luther Vandross’s voice to bless our ears.

Without wasting any time, the detective and I led ourselves to the mini sink area that was also provided on the rooftop. Then we cleansed our hands before grabbing our plates and exploring our options of food. I ended up filling my tray with a grilled salmon, mashed potatoes, and asparagus while the detective tried the steak, grilled shrimp, crab rice, and steam broccoli. He must have been as hungry as I was because we both just sat in silence as we devoured the delicious meal. About ten minutes had passed before Detective Bailey decided to interrupt my grub.

“So you’re not gonna answer?” he spoke.

“Answer what?” I played ignorant. “What was the question? This food is so good that it must've effected my memory.”

“Very clever," he smiled. "But the question was, why did you bring me here? Why not just hide in California forever?”

Still no words exited my lips and I used the stuffing of my face as a silent excuse.

“Look Keisha, I don’t know what all this is about but I must know where your head is right now. Like what is your next move going to be? What are you thinking or planning? Please, just talk to me so that I can know how I need to maneuver on my end. With all that’s going on it would be in your best interest to face this.”

"And how exactly can I face it?" I finally managed to say.

"By stepping up and being brave," he replied. "You're gonna have to testify."

Immediately my body cringed just hearing the sound of that and doubts of us being able to have a good evening surely started to surface.

"I told you, I won't do it. Now please, let me just enjoy this outing without thinking about that. I don't want to regret bringing you here."

"Regret?" he chuckled, seemingly at the nerve of me. "There are a lot of things I regret about this whole situation but you don't hear me complaining. Testifying is your best option. Did you hear me when I just told you we didn't catch Dino until later that night? There is no telling who and what he told his crew about you. I hate to admit it but everyone probably already thinks you're a snitch anyway. Why not do it to save your life?"

"Because trying to save my life will only lead to me losing it. It's a catch twenty-two," I replied. "Now for the last time, I'm not testifying against the OMC. I mean that."

Detective Bailey shook his head in disappointment. "So this leads me to believe that you're planning on staying out here in Cali. If so, you gotta understand that you're putting me in a messed up position. I've always told you that I'm on your side, but at the same time I still have a job to do."

Knowing exactly what the detective was implying, my mood began to shift and my heart grew heavy again. There was no way he was leaving California without me, and if I refused to go, he most likely wouldn't keep my whereabouts a secret. It was clear that he wasn't going to give up until he got what he wanted out of me. At the end of the day, his very reason for playing it close to me was to get me to help him bring down my crew anyway.

I stared at my plate for some time just soaking in all my options until I made up my mind.

“Okay then,” I said to him. “How much?”

“Excuse me?” he questioned.

“I said, how much?”

“Keisha what are you talking about? How much what?”

Without answering him, I took a deep breath then I looked to the center of the floor. One of my favorite tunes from Eric Benet and Tamia came on at the perfect moment.

“You know what, let’s forget about that right now. Just come dance with me,” I said to him. “You know, like old times.”

Without giving him a chance to make the rejection that was surely about to come my way, I grabbed his arm and led him to the middle of the floor. Amazingly, the light that beamed down on our table followed us to the floor and continued to stalk our every step. Once I found the perfect spot under the stars, I put my arms around his neck and then placed his hands around my waistline. Detective Bailey was clearly uneasy about getting too close to me but that didn’t stop me from making my move on him. I led him into a slow dance as the music softly played through the speaker system and I appreciated the wonderful feeling of being in the presence of a real man again. Not to mention, the way the Detective embraced me tightly when he first felt my grip let me know that whether he admitted it or not, he yearned for me just as much as I did him.

We continued to slow drag around the floor for a couple songs, until I finally decided to follow up on our conversation.

“Detective Bailey can I share something with you?" I took a deep breath and then mustered up the courage to pour out my heart to him. “Like completely off the record again?"

“I told you before, anything you tell me stays between us," he said and then slid both his hands down my lower body until they rested on the arch of my back side. I moan silently at the sensation I felt from it. "Besides, I really need to know what's going on in that head of yours.”

"It's just that look, all my life I wanted to be somebody and I thought that being somebody came with price tags. You know, that having money was everything and that people could really buy happiness. Then I met you and you showed me another side of life. You showed me what living really meant and helped me to appreciate and see the world in a different light. Nobody's ever done that to me before, not even Hi-C."

Hearing those words, Detective Bailey pulled away from me.

"Keisha don't," he insisted, "Don't make this more complicated than it already is."

"Please, just let me say what's on my mind," I insisted then immediately grabbed his arms and pressed them firmly up against my body so that he could not escape my wrath. "I've always had to listen to you, now it's my turn to talk. You owe me this much."

Without saying another word, Detective Bailey eased his tension and once I felt certain that he would keep near me, I released the strong hold I had on him. Then we continued to sway our body's to the rhythm of the music, this time more passionately.

"When I met you, everything changed. Some ways for worst and some for the better. You were the first to ever reject me, but I get it, it was only because you respected me. You gave me the truth raw and uncut and made me see things about myself that I was blind to before. Really, you opened my mind so much to so many things and you don't know just how much I appreciate that."

"Keisha I hear you," he said, "but what does this have to do with anything? I've just been around a little longer than you and I don't want to see you spend the rest of your life dead or in jail. I hope you're not looking too much into this."

"Detective please, just let me finish," I begged him again. "Now I don't know the first thing about real love, so maybe you can help me with this....What does it mean when images of someone's face is the last thing you remember before you close your eyes at night and the first thing you see when you wake up in the morning? What does it mean when your heart beats a speed faster whenever you are around them while the bottom of your feet warms beneath you. When just the sound of their voice alone makes you feel secure and lifts the burdens of the world right from off your shoulders. Huh? Please, can you at least help me with that?"

Detective Bailey said nothing for a second and just stared at me standing there nervously before him. At that very moment there was nothing more I wanted than to know what he thought of everything I just said.

"Come here," he said finally, before surprisingly grabbing me by the hand. Then he led me to the edge of the rooftop while I trailed behind him like a little child did her parents. We made it to the metal rail that was about a foot thick, held onto it, and began staring down the thirty stories at the beautiful picture the ground painted for us.

"Everything looks so small from up here," he said, looking down upon the ongoing traffic and people. Then he looked up to the building that was twice as tall as ours was and pointed, "Yet no matter how big we are to that, we are just as small to this."

Detective Bailey took a minute to appreciate the view. Then he, at a moment that couldn't be any stranger, whispered something to himself.

"*You just can't lose*," he said.

"What?" I asked, hearing him clearly but was surely confused by his remark.

"I said," he repeated himself, "you just can't lose."

"What? That's not true," I told him. "I've been taking losses all my life."

"No, I'm not talking about you Keisha," he said before sighing heavily. "That was something you said to me a while ago, and as much as it pains me to admit it, you were right. Here I was thinking I was so clever, so experienced, so untouchable that I just couldn't lose. And it's that attitude that had you in a situation which could have costed you your life."

The detective grabbed my hands and turned my body towards his, pulling my attention away from the amazing night scenery. "Keisha truth is, when I saw Dino aim that gun at you, feelings emerged within me that I can't put into words. I thought I had lost you and I just couldn't live with myself knowing that I would have been the one to blame for it. Then when you ran off like that it made it all worse. I was worried sick, not once caring or even thinking about losing you as a witness, but losing you as a person. Don't you know I thought of all possibilities of why you disappeared? I did more than just go to that hotel. I searched the woods and the marshes, damn near every part of Thunderbolt thinking the worst had happened to you...I almost lost my mind wondering if you could have been lying face down dead somewhere. I don't know what I was thinking bringing you along with me on that mission, but trust me, I didn't mean to put you in harm's way. Dino was a part of another investigation and I had no idea he was even affiliated with the OMC until after we arrested him."

After hearing him bring up the Dino incident again, I yanked away from his arms and looked up towards the night sky in attempt to let him know I wasn't moved by anything he said concerning it. An apology or admission of guilt wouldn't take back the recent nightmares and flashbacks I had of that evening.

Detective Bailey sensed my anger but was unbothered. He aggressively pulled me back towards him, and with only the dimmed look in his eyes, dared me to do something about it. We were now so close that I could feel his breath tapping against the cheekbone of my averted face.

"Keisha please, don't be like this. Now you just sat here and asked me a few questions and it's only right that I return the favor,"

I tried to use the arms I had folded across my chest as a barrier between us, but our bodies were so compressed that my attempt was weak and meaningless. All I could do was stand there helplessly as Detective Bailey continued on. "I don't know much about love either so maybe you can help me too...What does it mean when you meet someone whose living purpose goes against everything you stand for, but yet you still can't help but fall for them? What does it mean when their beauty, even on their roughest day, has the power to make the strongest man weak? When someone can come into your life and challenge you in a way that no one has ever done before? What does it truly mean when the thought of losing them makes you question your own will to exist? Huh Keisha? Now you give me the answer to that."

The stars that I looked towards in attempt to shield out Detective Bailey's words, suddenly took turns winking at me. It seemed as if they were giving me the okay to relax, or at least that's what my mind made me believe. I turned to Detective Bailey and trapped myself in the captivity of his pupils and in that moment, my guards, worries, and fears were suddenly released in the heavy sigh I let out. Without saying anything more, we both silently marinated on our recently spoken words while at the same time admired each other's courage to express them. If the stars gave me the okay to relax, then I must have in turn gave gravity permission to allow him to let one soft kiss fall upon my lips because before I knew it, our tongues were dancing together to the rhythm of the music.

As our lips gracefully met, the detective passionately rubbed his arms all over my body while I gladly did the same to him. The feeling of his broad shoulders, squared thick jawline, and fully formed chest muscles all aroused me in a way that sent my body into an immediate state of ecstasy. After we released our faces from unity, I allowed my lips to trail down from the top of his shoulders, on over to his biceps, and then down his chest. I needed to let him know that I appreciated all the hard work he put into creating his perfect, masculine body. For it surely was a work of art.

As I knew he would, the detective held his head back and enjoyed the sensation my kisses gave him before picking me up, turning me around, and placing my bottom on the railing. The thick metal was first a little cold on my butt cheeks, but my rising body temperature quickly made me adjust to this dilemma. I was now sitting on the very edge of a building that was thirty-stories high with a great chance of falling to my death. In fact, the only thing that kept me safe me was his powerful grip, and although the wet kisses he returned to my neck turned me on, it was the risk that we were taking that excited me the most.

With my head back and legs wrapped tightly around Detective Bailey's waist, I moaned softly as he squeezed both of my thighs firmly and massaged my outer quads all the way up until he reached my panty line.

"Got damn," detective said when he felt the excessive amount of moisture that my laced underwear somehow managed to soak up. What they weren't able to hold came dripping down my inner thigh, some of it onto his attire.

After feeling this, he was certainly ready to explore me furthermore. With my body letting him know that I definitely was ready, he held me securely in his possession with one arm, and used his other to drag my panties down my thigh. With that same free arm, he unbuckled his own pants and then let them fall to his ankles. He didn't even care to remove them fully, just like I didn't mind that my panties were dangling from the tip of the six-inch pumps.

Unfortunately, our only form of protection was the gun he removed from his holster and placed on the side of us, but that didn't stop Detective Bailey from bravely entering me. Neither did it stop me from allowing it. Instantly his manhood, as it introduced itself to my inner walls, soothed me while I let out a cry that told him I definitely approved of the feeling. I freed myself of all insecurities as he began to plant long strokes in and out of my body and I periodically allowed my muscles to grip him just as tightly as he was holding on to me. It was even better that he enjoyed the view of the ground, as I looked to the stars and moon. I didn't know what was more beautiful, the scenery or the passionate love we were making.

"Feels so good," I said as I continued laying soft kisses on him, this time on his collarbone, as he began to go deeper and faster inside of me.

"I know," he replied, stroking me passionately at a steady pace. "And I'm about to make it even better."

Detective Bailey then picked me up and stood me up on the ground. Not even caring about his knees against the concrete, he bent down on them and before I could wonder what he was about to do, I felt his tongue flow in and out of my vessel as he clearly made me his dessert. Unable to fight the feeling, I began to rub my fingers through his hair and awkwardly the resemblance of Hi-C and our first encounter, caused my mind to ponder on him. Yet, I wasn't thinking about any betrayals or acts of disloyalty. If I was feeling guilty about anything, it was for enjoying Detective Bailey far more greater than I ever enjoyed him. When it came to love-making, Hi-C was an amateur compared to his adversary, who knew exactly how to please. In fact, our chemistry was far more greater than anyone I had ever been with, and I only hoped that afterwards, I wouldn't allow it to interfere with the situation we were in.

After I exploded all over his face, Detective Bailey rose up and stood confidently before me. I used the opportunity to try to tear apart his collar shirt, but he snatched my arms away and turned me over with another plan in mind. I don't know what got into him but he suddenly yanked me by hair and then bent my body over the rail in a very aggressive manner. Now fully turned on, I placed my spine in a perfect arch for him, looked back deeply in his eyes, and watched the facial expression he gave when he entered me from behind. I smiled victoriously as his eyes went to the back of his head, while mine went back to view of ground that I could now see again. Being face to face with the dangers of our acts still did nothing but only excite me more and more.

“This feels so fuckin’ good,” I moan, as I enjoyed it when he deeply massaged my back. Although being pressed against that metal made me slightly uncomfortable, the feeling I received from every stroked he offered me overpowered it.

"Well then, say my name," he demanded, while biting down on my earlobes as he began to stroke faster and faster. Then he gripped my hair again and then leaned over me. We both were now looking down from our high perspectives and equally became more aroused.

"Only if you fuck me harder," I challenged him.

"I said say my name," he repeated and then obeyed my request.

"Harder," I fought back, taking his pounding like a champ. I was surely playing tough but Detective Bailey knew he had me weak.

"Is this the best you ever had?" he asked.

"Harder," I groaned, challenging him even more.

"Huh, is this the best you ever had?" he repeated then rammed himself all the way inside of me and just he held it there.

"Oooh yesss! Oooh yesss!" I finally screamed out, unable to fight the feeling anymore.

Then like some sort of barbarian, Detective Bailey drilled me until he brought himself to a climax. I was already holding in my orgasm so it was nothing for me to explode right along with him. He took his final stroke and after he pulled out of me, I watched him as he sent his specimen flying freely over the balcony. The way it shot out I only hoped that no one was in the way of where it landed.

"Damn Keish," Detective Bailey panted deeply but still found a way to speak over the heavy breaths he was taking. His once stiff, dry hair was now soaked from the sweat that also poured down his face. "Shit was like a scene out of a movie. I thought I saw flashing lights and everything. I mean, it was even better than I imagined it would be."

"The feeling is mutual," I also panted, then wrapped my arms around him from behind and we both stared over the balcony.

"I just hope whoever's down there keeps a heads up," he joked.

Both very tired, we somehow managed let out a laugh at the thought of a blog of cum dropping on someone's forehand. Then he turned away from the rails and his mood immediately changed as he came to senses, obviously realizing what wrong he had just done. I could sense his arising feeling of uncertainty and immediately tried to comfort him.

"I know what you are thinking," I said as I turned my body and mounted myself in front of him. I tried to grace him with a hug but he pushed me away.

"How do you know what I'm thinking? I don't even know what I'm thinking," he frowned. "Hell, I don't even know what I'm doing."

"You know exactly what you're doing," I told him. "It's just hard for you to believe that you're doing it. It's a good thing though, you're starting to take chances and enjoy life. And hey, if you mess up, at least you know it's only because you're human."

"I'm not human, Keisha. I'm a detective."

"No you're a human being who just happened to take a chance on something and enjoyed it. That's all it was so try to not think too much into it."

"You sure about that?" he asked, seemingly beginning to feel better about the situation.

"I'm positive," I told him before planting one last kiss on his lips. Thankfully he accepted it. "And trust me, you don't have to worry about me letting a word of this get out because what happens in Cali, stays in Cali."

CHAPTER 28: Sweet Lick

Detective Bailey took a flight back to Ordale the next morning and made sure I went with him. We never mentioned a word about the night before, for we both knew that what happened on the other side of the country definitely needed to be left there. In fear of me running again, when we returned to Ordale he decided to put me in a place where he could keep a close eye on me. It was in a community called CAMP, which stood for Center Accommodating Mysterious Persons.

It was located inside of our military base and was secretly operated by the police department. Detective Bailey said that the community gave people, who like me were in hiding, a decent place to live and be comfortable. It consisted of about fifty houses that were very small and so close together that you could literally put your hand out of your window and stir your neighbor's pot of grits. The entire area was fenced all the way around and the only way out or in was through a highly-secured gate. Fortunately, everything we needed- grocery store, post office, gym, bank, even a movies- was provided there. The city did a great job of keeping the place lowkey too, because as long as I lived there even I didn't know it existed.

Although the one bedroom home was definitely more comfortable then that lousy hotel I was staying in, after an entire four months of being confined to a limited area and not being allowed to have any contact with the outside world, I began to feel miserable. In fact, the only excitement I got was sending and receiving mail from my father, which made looking forward to the next day a little easier.

I first wrote him one night out of pure boredom and then that turned into a daily exchange between us. We never got really personal in our letters though. I would just send him books and mere words of encouragement and he would send me articles relating to the true origin of African and Latino history, false religions, and even healthy eating. True enough, receiving those letters gave me much joy, wisdom, and a different insight on life but after a while that wasn't enough for me. I still wanted answers about why he was spending life in prison, so in a more personal letter, I finally found the courage to ask him.

Unfortunately, that was the last letter I sent out to him before he stopped writing. It was definitely heartbreaking but it was clear that he wasn't gonna give me the answers I was looking for. With no other choice, I had to finally just except it. That was until a few more months passed and on a rainy evening, my prayers had been answered.

I was having one of those days where I didn't even have the strength to fix me anything to eat. I would often get like that, down and depressed, just thinking about old memories of when life was life. The parties, the hustle, the money, I only wished I could have one day to relive it all again.

I took a slow stroll to the mail center, which was about a half a mile away. Even though there was a slight drizzle, I still didn't seem to care to shield myself from the drops that hit my oversized t-shirt and blue cotton tights.

It had been weeks since I checked my mailbox because after daddy stopped writing me, I felt I had no reason to. Because of this, I was greeted with lots of promotional mail and coupons. I grabbed the junk mail with one hand and used it as an umbrella to cover my head once the rain started to fall harder. I actually did not even see daddy's letter until I got back to the house and began throwing the mail away.

What the hell is this? I asked myself as I stood over the trashcan after noticing an envelope covered with his unique handwriting. The ink had smeared from the raindrops that landed upon it so the words were a bit smudged. The dark feeling I had before was now replaced by excitement as I rushed to the couch and opened the letter. It read:

My one and only babygirl,

I hope this letter finds you in the best of health and spirits. I apologize for taking so long to get back with you. I had to spend some time in the hole for damn near paralyzing one of these motherfuckers for disrespecting me. I did receive your letter and was in the process of writing you back when it all went down. I am happy to know that you are interested in learning more about me, and although I hate to relive my past, it pleases me to know that you seek the truth about your old man. For the more aware you are of your past, the more you have a great understanding of yourself in the present and hopefully that will lead to great things in your future. I will warn you that my truth is not a pretty one, but I pray you find comfort in just knowing the answers. I wrote you a link at the very bottom of this page. It will provide you with everything you need to know about why I am here. I hope to hear back from you after it is all out in the open, but even if I don't just know that I completely understand and I still love you the same. Take care my sweet baby girl.

One love,

Your old man

I sat there and read the letter what seemed to be a hundred times. Then finally worked up the courage to go over to the small desk space which held a computer that my room provided me with. After patiently waiting for the extremely slow PC to load, I began typing in the web address given by him. My fingers shook nervously and my body shivered as I wondered what would pop up on the screen. When it finally loaded, the link directed me to a clearly ancient newspaper article that was typed in such small print that I had to zoom in greatly in order to see it.

Along with squinting my eyeballs just to make it visible, when it got as clear as it was going to get, the first thing I noticed was the big headline congratulating Johnson High School's basketball team on winning the State Championship. But on the other side, in the righthand column, there was something a little less inspirational.

> *'DEAD WOMAN, SURVIVING BABY VERDICT REACHED'* was what it was titled. I continued reading.
>
> *Jose Pablo was found guilty on all charges that includes first degree murder, attempted murder, and child molestation. He was arrested April of last year for the brutal murder of the pregnant sixteen-year-old Jonell Black. Jonell was found by a man in a wooded area near Pinpoint with multiple stab wombs and later died at Memorial Hospital. Fortunately, her baby survived but was severely injured in the attack. During the trial, it was discovered that the motive behind the killing was to cover up allegations that Pablo had been molesting the victim. Jonell Black was living in the home of her sister, Joanne Black, who was married to Pablo during the time. She testified that Jonell had confessed to her that her husband had gotten the teenager pregnant. 'When I confronted my husband about the allegations he got really upset and denied them. Then he stormed out to find Jonell and two days later my sister was missing.' Joanne Black said, with a clearly heavy heart, while on the stand. She also testified that she discovered the murder weapon and bloody garments in a trash bag hidden in*

> *her home. DNA evidence that was tested from the garments found by Black did match that of the victim. The DNA test also confirmed that Jose Pablo was the father of the surviving baby, who is now in the custody of Joanne Black. Pablo pleaded guilty to avoid the death penalty. Sentencing is set for next week.*

I read the article only once. That was all I could stand, because the information was very difficult to digest. So difficult, that it even made me wonder if I was better off not knowing the truth. I could never in a million years accept that my father was responsible for my aunt's death. There was just no way. They were the two people who meant more in the world to me than anyone. On top of that, if he was the father of Jonell's baby then that meant Charlytte and I were real sisters. It was too much to take in at once.

Even though the evidence was literally in black and white, I still needed to get more answers. I sat in front of that computer for the next two hours just thinking, until an uneasy but necessary, idea popped into my head. I quickly grabbed my phone to call the only person I knew could help me out.

"How's it going?" Detective Bailey answered.

"Exactly how it was going yesterday and the day before," I sassed him.

"Cheer up sport," he said. "I told you if you get tired of staying in that cozy house then I will be glad to drive you down to the county jail. You will never get bored there. Now you won't have your own stove, cable access, computer, and a full-size bed to sleep comfortably on, but whatever amenities they have should suit you just fine."

"Detective Bailey, you know I don't want to go to no damn jail but can you blame me for being miserable. You promised me that after a few months I could start leaving, well a few months is here.

Besides, I really need to go visit my mom. There are some things, very important things, I need to speak with her about. Please."

"Keisha, we're still working on this case. Your name is still deadly around here. I don't want to take any chances letting you out of here and then something happens to you. I won't take that risk again."

"It's been months. I highly doubt the streets still think I set Dino up. And with Poncha vouching for me to the OMC, I'm sure my name is good."

"You'd be surprised. It only takes for a rumor to start for people to believe it. It doesn't have to be true but the fact that it is out there is more than enough to do some damage."

"To be honest Detective, I'm really starting not to care anymore what people think. Hell, the way I figure, if I lose my mind what difference does it make if I'm dead or alive anyway?"

"You're not gonna lose your mind, Keisha. "You'll be fine."

"Don't bet on it. I've already started to have full blown conversations with myself. Please detective, I'm serious. Besides, I already told you I would testify. How long does it take to set a damn court date?"

"It's not that simple Keisha, but I promise we are almost there. You're gonna have to hold on just a little while longer."

"Did I forget to mention I had a kickback last night with six of my imaginary friends? That reminds me, I still haven't washed the cups they were drinking out of yet."

"Keisha quit it," he said before taking a long deep breath. "Alright. For the sake of your sanity, I will talk it over with a few people down at the station. Stay by the phone and I will give you a ring back."

Detective Bailey called me about thirty minutes later and confirmed to me that I could leave. The deal was, I was only allowed to go to my mom's house and I had to be back before seven o' clock. I was cool with that. The CAMP also provided it's residence with vehicles we could rent to get around the large facility. It was for only people with children or handicaps but the Detective pulled some strings to allow me to have one. Mostly all of the cars were repossessions, and ones that wouldn't even sell at an auction, so none of my options were fancy. I ended up getting a 98' Toyota Camry because it was the only one with tinted windows. It ran poorly and was nothing like the Impala I had Detective Bailey take from the hotel and put in a safe lowkey place for me, but it would do me just fine for the occasion.

Without wasting any time, I grabbed my purse and keys then headed out of the miserable place. The security guard who sat at the booth was already informed that I would be leaving, but I still had to sign out on a logbook. I gladly took the thirty minute trip back to the area of which I grew up and was happy to see that the neighborhood hadn't change much. When I pulled up to my mama's house, I saw her car parked in her driveway so I figured she was home and a tingly feeling immediately came over my body as I didn't know what would become of this unannounced pop-up. I only hoped no one got hurt and that I could simply get some insight about our family's past.

After exhaling deeply, I stepped on the porch and nervously took a couple swings at the door. Then I witnessed someone take a peep through the blinds and watched the door as it flew open, revealing the person on the other side.

"Well look what the money brought here today," Keyshawn smiled, showing off his mouth full of gold teeth as he extended his right arm to dap me. I was more of a hugger, but I followed suit.

"Boy stop it," I said as I sized my little brother up. He wasn't the pest I was used to seeing running around in his ninja turtle drawers fighting imaginary criminals anymore. From the looks of it, he was now the damn criminal.

"And look at you, all buff and stuff. You're still short tho. Just like those little ass locs in your head." I joked.

"Yeah but ain't shit little about me, don't let it fool ya," Keyshawn bragged, probably on his manhood. "And where that fine ass Shannon at? Tell her I think, no I know, I'm ready for her now."

Keyshawn rubbed his lower abdominal area that consisted of his forming abs. He was always pretty cut as a kid but now he was fully defined. Hearing him bring up Shannon's name quickly took me down memory lane. I immediately thought back on the good ole times that I certainly missed.

"What's goin' on with ya sis?" he said, bringing me back to reality. Then he opened the door wider to allow me to enter. "Nevermind. Come on in. We're in the back."

I obeyed, followed him into the house, and embraced the smell that was old, but familiar, to me. In fact, everything was set up exactly the way it was the last time I had visited. The two velvet couches with the patches of cotton sticking out of them both sat in their same positions and the fifty-inch old timey television that filled up the entire living room was still holding on for its dear life. Mama hadn't changed a thing, but due to her lack of empathy, it still didn't surprise me one bit.

When we made it to Keyshawn's room he quickly closed the door behind me. I got a sexy surprise when I saw Teon, the neighborhood cutie, sitting on his bed. He had a very focused look on his face and seemed to be in the middle of something.

When he saw me come through the door, he swung his neatly-layered, medium length dreads in my direction and looked as if he saw a ghost. I was his crush growing up and although I thought he was cute too, because of his young age, I could never give him the time of day.

"We good. This just sis," Keyshawn said as he chained three locks behind me and secured a deadbolt that I didn't recall being there before. Then he snatched back the sheet from off the bed and revealed the huge amount of dollar bills that covered it. Teon had already had about ten small stacks counted in rubber bands. I assumed he was working on the rest of it.

“Keisha, the one and only, the top female hustler, and the finest girl in Ordale?” Teon said, letting me know that his feelings for me had not changed.

“Stop it,” I blushed. “It’s not even like that.”

Keyshawn turned his body from the desk he was sitting in to join us in conversation. I could see he was stuffing marijuana, that he was pulling out of a gallon-sized zip lock bag, into tiny little jewelry bags.

“Big sis, you gotta know you a fuckin’ legend in the city,” he said. “You know how much love I get off ya name alone. We just respect the hustle. That's all.”

Keyshawn’s statement made me think that either he wasn’t fazed by what he heard about me setting up a crew member or that no one was really talking about it. He didn’t even seem uncomfortable at the fact that I was there with him while he was running his little drug business. Even I was smart enough to know that whether it involved family or not, you never trusted a snitch.

“Yeah, the grind sure as hell ain’t easy tho.” I replied, trying to dead the situation.

“But you doing it sis,” he said. “I’ve always looked up to you even though you don’t come around. Shit, if I was making good money I wouldn’t come around this bitch either, so I don’t knock you for that. You big sis and always gon' be big sis. Hell I got more respect for you than I do for Korey's country ass."

"Korey?" I asked, remembering that I even had an older brother. I hadn't spoken with him in years. "Speaking of him, how is he? Have you talked to him lately?"

"Yeah, him and his nosey ass wife bring the kids over here sometimes. But I don't fuck with that clown nor his bitch or his bitchmade babies. Always preachin' to me about my life and always trynna turn me on to these bullshit ass jobs. Naw, I'm good bra."

"Well you know how Korey is. Always wanna live righteous and shit. Like he too good."

"Exactly sis," Keyshawn agreed. "That seven hundred a week you seeing at that bullshit ass UPS job ain't gon' help you see a million. Ain't no way I'm working for these crackers, slaving check to check, while they sitting up doing nothing livin' it up in mansions and shit. Fuck a job, I'mma be a future boss."

"I feel you on that," I told him.

"I'm for real," he continued. "He's just like Charlytte's dumb ass, out here tricking for chump change. I don't know where they come from sis, but they just not built like us."

Keyshawn had the right idea of success but I could tell he was a bit ruthless and ignorant. I did admire his drive though. It was very consistent with mine. Watching him sitting there putting weed on a scale reminded me of the day I first knew he would be a little go-getter. He comes running up in Mama's house after school one day with a face full of tears. When I asked him what was wrong, he told me that someone from his class teased him for wearing girls' clothes. Mama was pregnant with Keyshawn when she took Charlytte in, so it was very hard for her to provide for two babies at the same time. Whatever clothes she had for Charlytte would be passed down to Keyshawn and even though she tried to keep the attire universal, sometimes you could tell. He was so angry that although she did nothing wrong, he wanted to beat Charlytte's ass too. He just felt that she was the reason he couldn't have anything of his own. I tried to help him understand Mama's position and tell him it wasn't Charlytte's fault, but he wasn't hearing it. Last thing he said before he left my room was, "Fuck Mama and Charlytte, I'mma make my own money from now on. Just watch me." He was only five years old.

"I fuckin' feel you on that. Nobody built like us true Blacks," I said, drawing myself back into the conversation. "What about ma? I see her car out there. Is she here?"

"Naw she doing that cleaning house, or should I say house-nigga, shit for that doctor five days a week now. Lewis done got sick of her crazy ass so you know he slowly faded out of the picture. I try to help her but she tries to take advantage too much. I done peeped game and fell back myself. She needs to get out there and get it on her own anyway."

"Oh damn. I'm mad I missed her," I said, truly a bit disappointed. I really wanted to talk with her and I didn't know when the next time Detective Bailey would let me out the CAMP again.

"What about you tho, sis? Besides making money and living it up with the OMC, how have you been?"

"I can't lie, shit's kinda crazy right now," I replied. "But I'm still here so I'm good."

"Yeah we heard about that," he told me. "That's fucked up how they ran down on Hi-C. And I heard they don't have shit on him but still won't let him go."

"Ya heard right. They don't have shit on him," I said. "But you know how the folks can play it. Man shit got everybody's pockets fucked up around here."

Teon butted in, as he swiped the fives he was counting sharply from one hand to the next. "Everybody but ours."

Keyshawn quickly through a bag of weed at Teon and hit him in the forehead, punishing him for the statement he had just made. It didn't bother me one bit though. I was glad someone was winning off of our lost.

"Yeah sis, don't mean to shit on ya downfall," Keyshawn couldn't help but admit too, "but small time niggas like us really done picked up since y'all slowed down. Money good right now so just let me know if you need some work. Ya know lil' bra got you."

"I'm aiight," I lied. "But thanks."

As much as it sounded and looked good seeing all the money they were getting, I couldn't let Keyshawn know how desperate I had gotten. He respected me too much for that. Besides, all I knew was drive and drop off. The measurements and mathematical science that came with selling was very unfamiliar to me.

"Ya sure?" he insisted. "It's a lot of money to be made."

"I'm good on money," I lied again. "I'm just using this little time to slow down and enjoy life. The OMC will be back shortly, trust me. No one can stop us."

"You right. Them pigs can't stop shit," he agreed.

"All I can tell ya is to be careful because just like it can all go good, in a matter of time, it can all go bad."

I adjusted my purse and since Mama wasn't there and got ready for my departure. "I think I'm going to head out now. Don't tell Joanne I came by. I want it to be a surprise."

"I'm no snitch sis," Keyshawn said, and although it was probably innocent, I couldn't help but to wonder if it meant something more.

Keyshawn walked me to the door and I convinced him that with everything he had going on in the house, it would be best to go ahead and lock up behind me. Truthfully, I was more concerned with him seeing me ride off in a car that was older than him. He agreed and I made my way down the street, feeling that my trip there was a complete waste of time. I still desperately wanted to find out what really happened to my Auntie Jonell. I also had to know whether or not daddy was the person to blame. To make matters worse, there was no telling when Detective Bailey would allow me to leave CAMP again. All I knew was that I had a little more time left to be back before another idea had popped up in my mind. There was this one place that probably held some clues about my past and although it was surely out of my jurisdiction, I could not pass up the opportunity to go.

CHAPTER 29- Trailer Park Cash

I pulled up to a secluded area a little ways down from the trailer park and although the open, treeless land allowed no room for secrecy, I still did not want to be noticed snooping around the place. Besides, I had completely stepped outside of the boundaries Detective Bailey had set for me and if he found out I disobeyed him he was sure not to trust me again. Hoping no one heard my loud engine, I turned off the car and made my way up to my old neighborhood. Then I walked swiftly through flimsy clothes lines, abused but clearly used toys, and newly added mobile homes, until I found the one that was most familiar to me.

"So weird being back here," I whispered to myself as I stood in front of the trailer that I spent a big part of my childhood in. I couldn't help but stare in its presence while soaking up the past

memories that instantly came to mind. It had been decades since we lived there but the absence of soul the place possessed, along with the huge tree stomp that grew underneath, gave me the feeling that no one had occupied it since we did. I had no intentions of going inside until I made it around back and saw a broken window that would grant me the privilege. Allowing temptation to take control of me, I took a deep breath then stuck my hand through the hole and felt around until I found what I was looking for.

"Got it!" I said once I felt the lock pop and the door ease open. Then I looked over my shoulders to make sure no one saw me entering. Thankfully, besides the few kids who were running around playing hide-and-seek, no one worth worrying about was paying me any attention. With no time to procrastinate, I made my entrance and then quickly closed the door behind me. The first and only thing in the empty place that I noticed was the Cabbage Patch doll I knew I must've left behind the day we moved. It was lying face down in the center of the floor, but the lip stick I spread all over her face somehow managed to still be intact. I picked up Maria, as I used to call her, and with the tip of my two fingers, allowed her to dangle freely in front of me. Although the dust went flying from her filthy body, I could only smile as more memories of my childhood came full surface. Then I slowly eased her down, placed her back where I found her, and headed off to explore other parts of the house.

Besides the missing cheap furniture and decors, everything had looked exactly the same. In fact, the only thing in there that really changed was me and how much I had outgrown the place. The windows and door frames that once stood taller than me now made me look like a giant. I even spotted the wall my father used to measure our heights on. I remembered he would carve it with his butcher knife and Mama would always fuss at him about possibly causing her to not get her rental deposit back.

My room was the last one I went to, and unlike the others, it gave me an unpleasant and eerie feeling in my gut. It was because the thought of Auntie Jonell and the memories we had there made me hesitant to enter. That's where she would be whenever she would visit and never left it unless she was headed to the bathroom or out the front door. We had so many good times, from girl talks to salon treatments to simply playing dress-up, that I just couldn't go inside without being saddened about her death. Yet still, that was the main reason I wanted to revisit the house. I hoped to channel some type of spirit or receive even the slightest indication of what may have happened to her.

I had remembered seeing once on television a documentary of a lady who talked about her experience when she visited the slave dungeons in Africa. She said when she was alone inside she began to hear the voices of her ancestors speak to her. She heard their cries first and then they comforted her by letting her know that everything would be okay. I only wondered if Jonell would do the same thing with me once she felt my presence in that room. I mean it wasn't a slave dungeon, but living with Mama, it may have been pretty close.

After building up the courage, I eased into my room slowly and carried myself to the middle of the floor then stopped there. Keeping very still, my body shivered as my ears, my heart, and my mind opened to the idea that Jonell would somehow feel my presence and come to me spiritually. Maybe she would speak in that pleasant, sweet voice and let me know exactly what happened to her. Maybe she would reveal to me the sounds of her cries, her screams, or her laughter. If nothing else, at least let me know she was okay.

"Jonell! Auntie!" I shouted softly then waited patiently for some type of response. "Are you there? Please talk to me! Tell me what happened to you! Please!"

I opened my ears but heard nothing, except for the voices of the children roaming outside. Then I began to quickly grow discouraged.

“Please, send me a sign or something!” I yelled again. “I need you right now!”

Still nothing and after realizing how ridiculous I was being, my eyes suddenly began to feel heavy. Unable to hold back my emotions, I let out a heartfelt cry while my knees locked up and my body weakened. That caused me to sink to the ground and from there all I could do was curl up in a fetal position as I soaked the floor with my tears. It didn’t even matter that it was unclean and unsafe. I didn’t care about that. All I cared about was knowing the truth and it looked as if I was never going to get it.

After spending some time weeping on the floor, I finally pulled myself together and made my exit out of the room. When I reached the bedroom door, I took one last look at it because I knew it would be the last time I saw the place. Then I preceded to leave the same way I came, but was startled by the approaching presence of unfamiliar male voices and the obvious sound of back door reopening.

"Oh shit! The police!" I whispered to myself before my quick reflexes led me to dash in the small hallway closet that held the air conditioning unit. I used to hide there all the time when I didn't want to be aggravated by Mama. Safely trapped inside, I quickly placed my hands against my nose to stop myself from sneezing because of all the dust I rallied up when entering. Not to mention, the smell of mildew and decaying flesh, probably from a recently deceased rodent made it even harder to withstand. Luckily the closet did provide a vent to aid in my breathing. But most importantly, it allowed me a fairly decent view of the four men, who I soon made out to be Hispanics, clearly not cops, that entered the house and took their places in the living room. Judging by how they all went and stood in a particular spot, I knew they had been there before.

The strange guys positioned themselves across from each other. On one side were two younger amigos who appeared to be in their late twenties. One was tall with long hair and a thick mustache, while the other was short, bald, and carried a black suitcase in his muscular arms. The two men standing across from them were the total opposite, for they were much older and either they had been friends for a long time or were identical twins because they looked just a like. One of them also carried a suitcase.

"Es todo lo que hay," the older man said, kicking off their conversation.

"Abrirlo," one younger bald replied.

"Si."

Suddenly the tall young man grabbed the suitcase from his partner and then kneeled down to open it. I mutely gasped at the sight of all the cocaine I was able to see packed inside. The older cat studied it with only his eyes and then made a gesture with his finger.

"Bien, bien." He said before now opening his own suit case to show the younger guys what he brought to the table. Their backs were turned to me so I couldn't get a view of what they were carrying, but I had a pretty good idea. This was a drug trade and I was witnessing it. Realizing this, I tried more than ever now to keep a calm composure and hold it together. Although the dust and particles that floated around me still made that very hard to achieve.

"Todos cien mil," the older man said while the younger two's eyes also examined what was in the box that stood before them. Then I watched carefully as they switched packages.

"Placer hacer negocious con usted," I heard one of them say

before they all shook each other's hand.

"Asimismo mi amigo," said another.

The tall one peeped the outside view before giving the okay for them to all make their way out of the door. When it closed, I saw an arm reach through the hole of the window and I watched it as it locked the door from the inside. Then I waited until I heard no more steps before quickly making my way out of the closet. Once I was free, I let out a much deserved sneeze and added some exaggerated coughs in hopes of releasing as many germs as I could from my body. I quickly ran to the windows, hid behind the flimsy blinds, and began looking out of them. From there I could see the two older guys hop in separate cars and follow each other towards the open road, while the other two dudes carried their package inside of the trailer that sat directly behind ours. Before entering the house, the short bald man kissed all of the kids then handed each of them some dollar bills. While they were distracted by the money they had just received, I used that opportunity to make my exit then ran all the way back to my car where I wasted no time speeding off.

A rush of adrenaline flowed through my body while I drove away to safety and as I traveled, I eased my nerves by finding humor in how close I was to almost getting caught. I even pondered on what would have happened if I did, then quickly erased the thoughts that came to my mind. Nonetheless, I was impressed with my hiding and spy skills but was more enthralled that the little Arsley Parks community, as poor as it was and looked, had some major work shit going on in it. I wasn't the best at speaking Spanish but I did still remember much of what my daddy taught me so one hundred and fifty thousand dollars wasn't hard to hear in the midst of their foreign communication. Seeing that large sum of drugs also made me wonder if my daddy had some involvement in the dope game. Hopefully that could have been the real reason he was put away, not for harming Aunt Jonell. I could have accepted that more. To give it even more thought, maybe me being there, at the right place and the right time, was the sign that Jonell was trying to send me. Maybe she was providing me with a ticket to get myself out of the messy situation I was in. Why else would the timing be so perfect?

With less than an hour to make it to CAMP, I used that little bit of extra time to make one more much needed stop and in less than thirty minutes I was pulling back up to Mama's house. This time I parked in the driveway with no shame and rushed to the door. Wasting no time, I began hysterically banging on it and as I expected Keyshawn reappeared in the doorway. Unfortunately, he wasn't as happy as he was to see me as the first time and that was probably because it seemed I had awaken him from a good sleep. The rubbing of his eyes, confused look on his face, and trail of drool that drained from his bottom lip gave me that impression.

"Why you back here?" he asked, clearly upset by my disturbance. "You left something?"

"No," I replied.

"Well didn't I tell you Mama don't come back 'til later?"

"Yeah, I know that."

"Then what's up?" Keyshawn said, before looking at the beat up '98 Camry I had in the driveway. "Tell the troof, you need money don't cha sis?"

"You know what, as a matter of fact I do," I admitted. "And I know just the way to get it. You down?"

CHAPTER 30: Pinky Promise

I was able to make Detective Bailey believe that I met up with my mother and that we had a nice conversation at her house. I told him that she even invited me back to spend the day with her, have lunch, and catch up on lost time. Of course, he didn't want me to leave the camp again, but he couldn't resist the begging and fake sobs I let ring out over the phone when I tried to convince him how much it mattered to me. I promised this time to be back by two o'clock, for I figured the real business I had to attend to would be taken care of by then.

As Keyshawn ordered, I arrived back at Mama's house at exactly eight in the morning. She was gone for work and just seconds after I pulled up in the driveway, a lowkey black Kia with Teon behind the wheel was sliding in behind me. It was a bit of a downgrade from the T-top Monte Carlo he was known for, but I was glad he had the sense enough to know not to bring his own vehicle.

Keyshawn wasn't in the house but was sitting in the car with Teon. Shamefully, I got out of my car and headed towards the two of them. My little brother signaled for me to hop in with them so I led myself to the back passenger seat where the smell of marijuana greeted me before they did. Although it was soothing to my nostrils, I declined the offer Teon made me to partake. I hadn't smoked in a while and even though I needed to release some built up pressure, I decided not to get back caught up in the habit.

"What's up, you guys?" I said to them as I immediately laid eyes on a big duffle bag full of strange items. It was slightly open so I was able to see the two big guns and a face mask that reign on top.

"You already know sis," Keyshawn told me. "We geeked up and ready to roll."

"And remember," I told him. "It's the trailer directly behind the one we used to live in. I don't know how much you remember about it, but I'm sure it'll come to you once you see it. Their house is the one with the small trampol-"

"Trampoline and those raggedy ass tricycles sitting on the porch," he cut me off.

"Yeah, exactly." I told him. "But wait, how did you know that?"

"Where you think we coming from sis? We've been there since you told us about it. It's a little short notice for the amount of bread you talking about so I needed to scope it out. Just get a feel of the place."

"Damn," I said to Keyshawn. "You on ya shit, lil' bra. I'm impressed."

"That little nigga might be young, but he is way before his time Keisha," Teon finally spoke.

And you might be young but you sholl is fine, I said to myself as I took my focus off the mission and put it on the angle I had of Teon's face. His smooth, chocolate skin and narrowly structured jawbone in relation to the dreadlocks- that had went from little beads on his head to now full grown strands- made for the perfect combination. He was always too young for me but Shannon and I would playfully joke about who would put it on him first when he got older.

"I told you I ain't built like these flaw ass niggas sis." Keyshawn bragged. "Speaking of flaw ass niggas, what's up with Ski? It's 8:05 and he ain't here yet."

"Just be patient," Teon said. "He'll be here."

"Listen, I don't see why we had to bring a third man along anyway. I told you I don't roll with all types of dudes. The less niggas involved the better."

"Man chill, I told you Ski is good," Teon told him. "My cousin been solid as long as I can remember. And plus he's sharp on his feet. You ain't see it was about four a them Mexicans coming in and out of that house. Trust me, we need a third man. Plus, I told him it was ten bands in the house and he only wants three. That's still a hundred and forty seven to split between the three of us."

"If you say so man," Keyshawn surrendered his thoughts. "But

I still say we should have went alone."

I listened quietly as they both let their voices be heard. I wasn't too particular about having another guy in the mix as well but I trusted a more mature opinion. As I quickly noticed, Keyshawn could be cocky and hotheaded at times, so much that if he wasn't careful it could be his downfall.

It was about 8:15 before this mysterious Ski dude came walking down the street and that was my cue it was time to exit the car. Keyshawn gave me the keys to Mama's house and told me they would be back soon. I hugged my brother tightly, told him I loved him, and repeatedly warned them to be careful. Then I watched the little car they drove off in all the way up until it turned off the street.

"God please let me be successful," I prayed selfishly after they disappeared, as if I was the one who was about to run up in a trailer full of Mexicans and rob them for a suitcase full of cash. But hey, in my opinion, I was the one who turned them on to the gig. Now they wouldn't have to be bundling up ones and fives and if they were as smart as I thought they were they would flip the fifty thousand and soon be young bosses of their own. Me, on the other hand, had a different plan. I was gonna take my money and disappear. I figured that would be enough to go far away, find a low-key town to live in, and build a new life. I was gonna have to leave Ordale when I testified anyway so why not go and still keep my dignity. I was gonna miss my family and my city, but maybe I would find a husband to create a new family of my own. As far as Detective Bailey, I'm sure he would have felt betrayed and ashamed, but if he cared about me the way he said he did, he wouldn't come looking for me.

After entering the house and heading straight to the room where I used to sleep. I laid across my bed, which to my surprise, was exactly how I left it. The anticipation of what was going to happen and whether or not they would pull off the mission, sent my mind into heavy pondering until I eventually drove myself to sleep.

A loud bang and heavy stomps awoke me before Keyshawn even had a chance to barge into my room. I open my eyes while laying across the bed still trying to get a grip on my whereabouts.

"WAKE THE UP FUCK SIS!" my brother shouted as he grabbed me with his two hands and shook me by my shoulders. He was too excited to even realize I was conscious and staring straight back at him.

"Shit sis, wake up!" he continued shouting. "Wake the fuck up right now!"

"I'm up! I'm up dammit" I said as I jerked away from his unnecessarily strong grip. "What the hell is wrong with you? Is everything okay?"

Keyshawn was frantic and he was pacing so hard that my tired eyes could barely keep up with his movements. Understanding what was coming from his mouth was even more difficult.

"I…I…mean… yeah and no," he panted. "Shit Keisha! Shit was crazy man!"

Keyshawn then exited my room, ran towards his, and I had sense enough to follow behind him. When I got inside, Teon was kneeled over the bed in a praying position. He was panicking too and also crying. I would have been concerned about him, but once I laid eyes on the suitcase that he was hovering over- the suitcase that was identical to the one I saw the Mexicans with- my feelings were replaced with pure victory.

"I don't think it was worth it! It wasn't worth it man!" Teon kept repeating like some sort of mad man. He was clearly flipping the fuck out. "Shit wasn't fucking worth it! Aaaaw fuck."

"Nigga you better pull it together!" Keyshawn angrily ran over to Teon and kneeled into his ear. "Shit over for cuz. I told him not to get out the damn car."

"But how you know that? Huh, how you know that?" He shot back as he rose from the bed and headed for the door. "Fuck this, I'm going back man. I'm going back for my cousin."

Confused as hell, I stepped out of the doorway to allow him to pass. But Keyshawn, being quick on his toes, beat him to the door and used his back as a shield to block the exit. The two good friends now stood face to face as rivals. They were close enough to smell each other's sweat.

"Are you fucking crazy?" Keyshawn looked up to his much taller and older friend. You wanna get yourself killed too. You're not going back. I told you, it's over for cuz. He dead."

Hearing that, I placed my hand over my mouth and unable to stand being in the blind any longer, began to voice my concerns.

"What? Whose dead? What happened to Ski?" I asked.

Even though I didn't know him personally, I had literally just saw him. The slim dude with the long head and face was one you could never forget. Besides, I just wanted to make us some money. I didn't want anyone to get hurt in the process.

"He got himself killed. That's what happened," Keyshawn said, seemingly unbothered. "I told him...stay in the fuckin' car. All he was supposed to do was drive. Soon as we busted out of that bitch, he hops his ass out of the car shooting and shit. He wasn't in place and almost got us all killed."

"He was just trynna to cover us," Teon defended his cousin. "Those motherfucking came out shooting too. What else was he supposed to do?"

"Back up and shoot out the window, if anything. We had those fools. You see how quick I hopped in the driver's seat, peeled off, and saved our asses. I told you, I live for this type of shit."

"Yeah, you peeled off and left cuz screaming for us to help him. I can still hear that man's voice in my head. That was fucked up. We blood."

"Look, Ski was already hit, in the chest at that and by the time I got in the car they had already grabbed him. What the fuck was I supposed to do? Just get us all killed. Shit's fucked up but that's life. We all knew when we left it was a possibility we wouldn't be coming back. That's just how the game goes. Charge it man."

"But what if he ain't dead? What if they got him up in the basement or some shit, just torturing the man? What if he ratted us out to them? Or the police? And what am I going tell his mama man? This shit just ain't right. It just ain't right."

"First of all, trailer parks don't have basements. And I told you, he got shot. He probably died before they even had the chance to kill him. And you worried about the law? Man type of niggas like that don't get the police involved. They gonna make him disappear. Worst case, he'll just forever remain a missing person. But don't worry," Keyshawn opened the suitcase and revealed the many stacks of crispy cash to the both of us, "we gonna make sure his family straight. And we ain't never gone forget the sacrifice he made for this shit."

Even Teon's cat-eyes widened and quickly became less concerned with his cousin and more for the cash that Keyshawn began to start distributing amongst the three of us. It took us almost two hours to count and sort it but we got it done. It probably would have been done sooner but we got caught up in conversation, as we all shared our plans of what we would do with our portions. Of course I made up some bullshit about opening up a fashion boutique, while Teon discussed buying fancy cars and jewelry. Keyshawn, on the other hand, shocked the hell out of me when he began to talk about his plans to invest in stock and real estate. I was very impressed at how business-minded my little brother was and it made me realize that he was more than just some gang bangin' street nigga. Little man was a future force to be recognize with, if only he could put his energy on more positive things. I sat there clinging on to his every word while I soaked in as much of his presence as I could. With my plans to take the money and leave Ordale now officially confirmed, I knew it was a great possibility of that moment being my last time ever seeing him. Any of my family and friends for that matter.

Once we were ready to break from each other, Keyshawn led us into the backyard. There he poured out some of the Hennessy he kept under his bed onto the ground and buried a fully rolled blunt for Ski. Then we took a moment of silence to pay our respects. Clearly still torn up about his cousin, Teon's silent moment turned into a weeping one. I immediately rushed over to comfort him while Keyshawn just kneeled down in the ground and continued to pat down the hole he had just created with dirt.

"What I'mma tell his mama bro? My aunt crazy 'bout her son man," through his tears, Teon managed to ask again.

"You ain't gone tell her shit," Keyshawn replied as he slowly rose from the ground and looked to the both of us with eyes that had no soul in them. "In fact, none of us gonna speak a word to anybody about this for as long as we live. Got that shit?"

"Got it," we both said in unison.

CHAPTER 31: Man down

Everything you need to know is here," Detective Bailey said as he placed a white envelope into the palm of my hand. I sat slumped on the couch with my heart-theme robe covering my body, as I pointed the remote at the television and tried to find something worth watching. Even though I knew I wasn't much of a T.V. person, I had to seem interested.

"Thank you," I smiled and took the paper from his grip then stared at it. "Gotta admit, I didn't think you would find her. I'm very impressed."

"Well, it wasn't easy," he informed me. "If Charlytte's mission was to stay low. She definitely did a good job of that. Geesh."

"Well, where is she?" I asked. "Looks like she's out in Hinesville. Has an apartment with her boyfriend and two year old son."

"Boyfriend? Son?" I said in disbelief. "Detective, are you sure you have the right girl?"

"I'm positive," he said. "But if you're not certain you have the number."

I looked down at the paper again before stuffing it into my bra, then I pondered on the information Detective Bailey had just shared with me. Charlytte was a prostitute. There was just no way she could have had a boyfriend and a baby, plus she was just a kid herself. I knew a lot could change in almost two years, but that seemed to be a bit of a stretch. Yet still, if it were true, my attempt to try to clear my name and say farewell wouldn't be as important to her as I thought.

"Thank you, Detective Bailey. You've been a great help. You just don't know how much this means to me. Setting things right with Charlytte will surely take away some of the stress I have built up from just sitting here day in and day out."

"I know," he said. "You're doing the right thing. As long as you don't say anything to incriminate the case. But I trust you know how to handle it."

I nodded in the detective's direction and he continued to encourage me.

"She'll definitely understand," he said. "You don't have to thank me. If anything, I should be thanking you. I know this isn't easy, but it will all be over soon. Next week Monday is the date of court. They finally set one."

"Oh thank God!" I hugged the detective. Then I used the opportunity to slowly run my fingers down his back. He caught my drift of me trying to seduce him and quickly pushed himself away. Then he headed towards the door.

"Now we both know that can't happen again," he told me.

"Detective Bailey, I'm lonely here. Please."

"No."

"I guess it's because were not in Cali," I told him.

"No, it's because it shouldn't have happened in the first place," he said. "Keisha please, don't make this any harder than it already is. I have to go now."

Detective Bailey let himself out without giving me the chance to. I didn't even bother to watch him leave and proudly let the door close behind him.

"You're not the only one who has to go," I whispered as I smirked devilishlyy after the door slammed shut.

The time had come for me to make my move. Now with everything I needed, I rushed to the closet where all my belongings were packed and began transporting them to the living room couch. From there I did a quick run through to make sure I had everything. I was packed and ready to flee from Ordale and I was confident that I would be successful.

My plans were to head as far west as I could possibly go. Detective Bailey wouldn't be calling me until the next morning so that would allow me at least a twenty-four hour head start. All I wanted to do was get to Arkansas or one of those low states, then I would ditch the car and pay a taxi to get me further. I really didn't have a plan other than to just stay out of sight until I could somehow swindle my way across the border. I knew this wouldn't be easy, but the hardest part was missing my family and friends.

Just the thought of it all sent my mind traveling into another place. I took a pause from packing and began to let my little brain ponder on the people I loved. Although I hated my mom, I couldn't help but think about the times we shared growing up together. Those nights she would come home drunk and make us laugh while she wobbled around the house dancing and singing. The times she would curse out the entire neighborhood if she got a simple word that someone was picking on us. Even the time she tried to murder me and Tre had started to seem kinda funny. She wasn't all bad and I appreciated her now more than I ever did before. Shannon-my ace, my sister, my best friend that not even the love I had for Poncha could compare to. I hated that we had become so distant over the years and only wished that I could have took some time out of my busy life to see her and her children grow. I also thought about Korey, my older brother. Even though I felt I barely knew him, I would miss him dearly. I really couldn't be mad at him for wanting to do the right thing and take care of his family. He wasn't trying to be better than anyone, he was just trying to be better for himself. Quita's girls, the OMC, hell even my rival Felice Hutchinson would be missed. And Hi-C, the true love of my life, just the thought of not being able to ever talk to him again made my gut cringe. I only wished we could have spoken at least one more time. I needed to know how he felt about me and what was going on through his head the months he spent in jail. What did bring me peace about it, was the fact that I would have rather lived without him than live with myself knowing that I had betrayed him. All of them and everything about the city of Ordale, I would keep near and dear to my heart as I traveled on my new journey.

But there was one person whose voice I just had to hear one last time and it was Charlytte's. I felt I owed it to my Aunt Jonell to at least try to make amends with her. She was the driving and motivating force for me growing up. Those times I wanted to give up or run far away, I'd look into her innocent eyes as they possessed the power to calm me. She was my everything and even though I took advantage of her many times, I still knew how much she meant to me.

With Charlytte heavy on my mind, it was now or never to make the call. I grabbed the phone and stared at it, but was quickly distracted by a news reporter and a familiar scene that flashed across the television screen.

"Shit! That looks like my old neighborhood," I said as I turned the volume up on the monitor and stood directly in front of it.

"Donna Summers reporting live from the 100th block of Price and Reynolds Street, following an incident that left one man dead and another in critical condition. Witnesses say that around 12:00p.m. yesterday, a car riding eastbound slowly strolled down this street and stopped directly in front of this house. Immediately the people occupying the vehicle opened fire on the two men sitting on the porch. The police have identified the victims as twenty-three year old Teon Albright and sixteen-year-old Keyshawn Black. Both Albright and Black were transported to Memorial Medical Center. Black died from his injuries and Albright is in serious, but stable, condition. The OPD is currently investigating the motive behind this attack, but says that they do not believe it was a random killing. WSOT also spoke with the Chief of Police who discussed with us his plans to try and control the gun violence that has been becoming more and more of a problem for the city of Ordale. Here's what he had to say....

The television flashed to another scene while my mind flashed into another dimension. As much as I wanted to grab the remote and hit rewind to make sure what I saw was real, I knew it would do me no good. The evidence was all in plain sight- Teon's front porch, his car in the driveway, and the fact that just two days before we had robbed some Mexicans- all let me know that what I was seeing was definitely real and true.

"Nooooo. Please god," I cried out as I placed my hand over my mouth and let out a gut-wrenching cry. A heavy weight suddenly fell upon my chest and caused my entire body to hit the floor. From there, I just lay crying my heart out and what made it all the more worst was that I knew deep down it was all my fault.

If I had any doubts of calling Charlytte before, there was no room for them now. I was certain she hadn't heard of Keyshawn's death and as much as I hated to be the bearer of bad news, I knew it would be best that I be the one to tell her. After I had made a few phone calls to confirm the situation and gather as much information as I could, I finally worked up the nerve to reach out to her.

"Hello," Charlytte answered cautiously.

My jaws locked and for a second I couldn't say anything.

"Hel-lo," she repeated. This time a little louder.

"Hi, is this Charlytte?" my voice finally cracked open.

"Yes, this is she. Who is this?"

"Charlytte, this is Keisha," I told her.

"Keisha who?" she asked, as an unpleasant tone in her voice abruptly surfaced.

"Your big sis," I mumbled.

Charlytte let out a deep sigh and immediately let me know that she wasn't happy to hear from me. "Look, I don't know how you got my number, but I honestly don't want to hear no sob stories about how sorry you are! My life is perfectly fine and I'm over that. Goodbye."

"Wait!" I began to cry harder. The tears flew uncontrollably from my eyes. I didn't know if I was more upset about Keyshawn being dead or Charlytte's love for me. “I’m not calling to apologize. Something bad has just happened."

"Keisha, what’s wrong?" She said, suddenly putting her negative attitude on pause to show genuine concern for me. It was refreshing."What happened?"

"It’s about Keyshawn!" I started to cry even louder.

"What about Keyshawn?!" she asked. "Keisha, calm down. What happened to Keyshawn?"

"He’s…he’s...he’s dead!"

I heard a loud thump, as if her phone fell to the floor, followed by a horrible scream. Charlytte clearly allowed her love for him to pour out of her soul and I just waited patiently as she released her emotions. Hearing her cries, made me feel a thousand times worse about it.

"Charlytte, you there?" I finally asked, after I could take no more of listening to her sobs.

"Yeah, I’m here. Just trynna get my thoughts together.” She answered. “You okay?"

"Yeah, I’m just in a state of shock right now." I replied. "I still can’t believe it."

"Me neither," she cried. "Do you know what happened?"

"Not really," I lied. "You know I barely watch the news, but something told me to watch it today. A story came on about a drive–by shooting turnin’ fatal. As usual, I thought it was some ole stupid motherfuckers out the hood, until the news anchorman said the two victims were twenty-three year old Teon Albright and sixteen-year old Keyshawn Black. I was hoping and praying that it could have somehow been another kid who goes by that name, but after they showed a clip of Teon's orange chevy, I already knew."

"Is Teon dead too?" she asked. I knew she remembered him from the neighborhood. He would always beg her to tell me how much he liked me, then give her candy as a bribe.

"No. They say he in the hospital with minor injuries. I think he got hit twice in the arm or something. The police are questioning him down at the hospital and from what I hear, he ain't talking. His cousin Sharice say they got him handcuffed to the bed and all. Apparently they had guns in the car and you know he a felon so he going straight to jail, probably five to ten."

"Damn," was all she could say. "What about Auntie? Does she know?"

"She's out of town with Evelyn. I'm not telling her until she comes back. I don't want to ruin her vacation. Keyshawn wouldn't have wanted that. She don't have a cell phone so hopefully the word won't get to her, but Korey is on his way down here as we speak. The whole neighborhood is meeting up at mommy's house tonight. You should come."

"To be honest Keisha, I can't go back there," she told me. "I'm just not ready for that. It's too many memories. The last time I saw Keyshawn we weren't at....Nevermind that story. I'mma just have to pass on that. I'm in no condition to drive anyway."

"Okay, but if you change your mind, we'll be there."

"Okay thanks sis." Charlytte said, then called out to me before hanging up. "Hey Keish, can I ask you a personal question?"

"What's up?"

"I know I may just be being a little paranoid, but honestly, do you think that this has anything to do with Cederick retaliating for that little debt I created?"

She was referring to the night she stormed out of Quita's house. I heard that after she stole his Monte she flushed a lot of his work down the toilet in revenge. Then she parked the car at the mall and left it there. After the car was reported for just sitting for a long period of time, the police ran the tag and found that it belonged to Cederick. Because he had a warrant for his arrest, they tipped him off about where his car was located and then arrested him when he finally came to retrieve it.

"I heard about that," I told her. "You a fool for that one, but naw, I'm positive Cederick didn't have anything to do with this."

"How can you be so certain?"

"Because he's in jail, and has been for the past year."

"Oh," she said, clearly relieved.

"It's not your fault Charlytte," I comforted her. "Keyshawn made mistakes and he paid for them with his life. We'll talk more in person."

"Okay sis," she replied. "Stay strong."

"I'll try."

CHAPTER 32- THE FUNERAL

African Baptist was already one of the largest churches in Ordale, so to see it packed to full capacity was a shock for me. People literally had to stand up against the walls to enjoy the service. I didn't realize that my brother was so popular and that so many people had love for him, but the turnout of the city most definitely made it known.

With my share of the invasion money and Keyshawn's cut that I found tucked deeply in the closet of his room, I felt it was only right that I paid for the funeral. It cut me short about eight grand, but I still had more than enough to make that departure I had plan on making once everything was over.

The funeral was two hours long but it probably would ended sooner if it wasn't for the big scene that took place in front of the entire congregation. Mama and Charlytte got into a verbal argument and the shit was crazy, like something straight out of a movie. During the middle of the service, when we were allowed to view his body, the two of them somehow managed to exchange words and it was on and poppin' from there. It got even more chaotic when my uncles got involved and reminded Mama of something terrible that occurred in her past. From there she had a very intense emotional breakdown, were she finally shared the details of her past and confirmed that the things I had recently learned about my daddy were in fact true.

She told everyone how she felt she was the blame for Keyshawn's death, saying that she knew all along of his drug activity and didn't try to teach him better. She admitted to holding a hateful grudge against Charlytte and her reason was because she felt as if her mother was the one who broke up her happy home. I couldn't believe Mama actually blamed Aunt Jonell for my daddy molesting and killing her, but I was glad she finally realized that she was wrong for it.

With her hands held high, my mother begged for mercy and forgiveness and it was a very joyous moment to witness. Then entire family hugged, cried, and made up while the congregation rejoiced at the miracle that had occurred right in front of their very eyes. Pastor Williams ended the service by speaking a powerful eulogy and all we met up at the cemetery where we peacefully laid my little brother to rest.

While everyone headed to the repast, which was held at Mama's house, I stayed behind at the burial site. The cream-colored pumps that went beautifully with my gold dress showed no mercy on my toes and my heels, but I still planned on standing there with Keyshawn for as long as I could. I figured he would hear me better when I asked him not to be angry with me. And just maybe he could talk to God and ask not to punish me for the death I brought upon his life. Besides, it would be my last time visiting him since I already had my belongings and the money packed in the trunk of the car and was ready to move soon as I left Mama's.

Once everyone was out of sight, I said a few words softly to

Keyshawn and must have been deep my conversation because I hadn't noticed the company that had come to join me.

"Wha... what's going on here Detective Bailey?" I stuttered when I turned around to see him and the three other police officers that accompanied him. The way they all circled around me, I knew they had not come to pay any respects. The detective just held his head to the ground like a little boy who had just asked his crush for a dance. As hard as he tried, he could not look me in my eyes. That let me know that something was surely wrong.

"I'm sorry but this is out of my control," he finally replied, then flicked his index finger at the officers and watched as they closed in on me. The only one who was a female patted me down, while the other two grabbed my arms and placed me in handcuffs. I was surely confused.

"Detective, what the fuck is going on?" I asked, with no energy to resist or put up a fight. "Why are they arresting me?"

My heart immediately changed its pace, as I wondered what I could have done so wrong and I could only pray that no one found out about my involvement in my brother's death. With my car being gassed up and ready to hit the road, that was the last thing I needed stopping me.

"Relax," he replied. “You didn’t do anything.”

"Then what the fuck is going on?" Learning of my innocence, I now began to resist and get a little more aggressive. "What the fuck are they doing!"

"Looks like she's about to have another anxiety attack," he lied to the other officers. "Let me have a word with her alone. She's comfortable with me."

Without questioning or even saying a word, the team followed orders and headed back to each of their own vehicles. Even though they were many feet away from hearing us, Detective Bailey still watched them all the way up until they closed their car doors before whispering to me.

"Listen, you're not being arrested because you did anything wrong," he told me. "It's just that soon as the chief found out Keyshawn was your brother and that he was murdered at the very place I let you out to go to, he feels it's best that we hold you in jail- well protective custody- until your court date arrives."

"What? Wait, no! The OMC had nothing to do with that. My brother's been heavy in the streets since he was knee high. No telling what type of beef he had or with who! This can't be happening. Please nooo, right now is not the time. I just buried my brother."

"The chief doesn't care about that, Keisha. He actually didn't even want you to be here today. It was me who talked him in to allowing you to at least make the funeral."

"And should I be thanking you for that?" I said sarcastically.

"Keisha, I tried. But this is what they wanted, not me, and there is nothing I can do about it. Look on the bright side though, court is only four days away."

"Four days seems like four years behind bars and I have to be on lockdown at that, all alone. Please Detective Bailey, did you not hear me when I told you I just buried my baby brother? I wouldn't be any good mentally come time to testify if this happens."

I admit, I was trying to play that whole psychology game again but unfortunately Detective Bailey wasn't buying it. Funny the other attempts were exaggerations, but this time I really was concerned for my well-being. Twenty-four hour lockdowns and being shielded away from the free world, would only lead me to think. And that was not what I wanted to do, especially when the truth still ate at my conscious. I mean, I could alleviate some of the pain by listening to some good music and drinking the shooters I had stashed for the ride. But jail, that certainly was the last place I needed to be.

Tears began to fill my eyes because I knew deep down I was going down to the county and there was nothing I could do about it. And worst, if he discovered those luggage bags and over $90,000 cash money I had in the trunk, he was surely going to know that I had plan on ditching him.

"You'll be fine," he tried to comfort me. "Like I told you before, this is really outta of my control. In fact, I was taken off of the case today. Chief said I'm becoming too emotionally tied and more concerned for you personally than professionally. He also thinks that this murder could be a retaliation against you. Now he's back in the spotlight about gun violence and he's not happy about it."

The detective bit the bottom of his lip to help ease his anger before continuing. "Crazy, all the work I put into this case and this is how that motherfucker thanks me. I'm staying for the trial but after it's over I'm taking the first flight back to Oklahoma and never stepping foot in Ordale again."

Without giving me a chance to respond, Detective Bailey took the keys to the CAMP house and the keys to the CAMP car right out of my hands then headed off across the field. Immediately after, the three officers exited their vehicles and headed towards me.

"You just can't lose, can you?" I said, throwing my voice at Detective Bailey as he walked away.

"You just take care of yourself," was all he could say before I watched him ride off with my car, my money, and my very last hope to create a new life.

CHAPTER 32: Traitor in the Court

Nothing. That's exactly what I felt as I stared emotionlessly at the back walls of courtroom B. Although the place was filled with people, including Hi-C who sat in the short distance, it seemed to feel as if my presence was the only one that existed. I had no feelings of fear, no anxiety, no nervousness, not even a single goose bump- all the things that I should have been feeling knowing that I was about to go against everything and everyone I stood for. Not even my appearance mattered. I usually wouldn't be caught dead looking anything less than perfect, especially in the eye of the public, but the stale white t-shirt and dingy black slacks I unapologetically wore revealed a side of me that not even I knew existed.

Sitting behind her desk, Mrs. Lowisky's eyes pierced mine after she watched me take the stand. Even she could feel that I wasn't the same girl she challenged before, and although she wasn't impressed with my exterior, she was proud to see that I had at least showed up. For she knew I was the key to her winning her big case.

In fact, Mrs. Lowisky looked very calm and at ease. Her dark hair that was before pull back into a tight ponytail, now dangled freely down her shoulders, appearing just as relaxed as she did. My hair, on the other hand, was a hot mess. I managed to pull it all back into the smallest ponytail I had ever saw in my life, leaving the pieces that didn't make the cut dangling irresponsibly down my cheeks.

After I took the oath of truth, Mrs. Lowisky asked the judge for permission to approach the bench. Then she rose from her desk, straightened her knee-length black skirt, and made her way to me. Although I longed for the day I could face her again, the grudge I had against her had slowly faded along with all the other fucks I no longer cared to give.

"State your name for the record," she said.

"Lakeisha Monique Black," I mumbled barely.

"And may you tell the court your age?"

"Thirty-two."

"Mrs. Black, I'm going to need you speak a little louder so that all the people in the courtroom may be able to hear you."

"I said I'm thirty-two," I repeated, but this time a little louder.

"Hmmm...," she scratched her chin and then continued on questioning me. "And where do you live?"

“Do you mean currently?”

“Yes currently.”

“I was released from the Ordale County jail yesterday because of a prior situation unrelated to this case," Detective Bailey prompted me to say. "And now I'm at a location I cannot disclose for safety reasons."

"A situation unrelated to this case? Just yesterday?" she asked. "Mrs. Black, I just have to ask, have you been offered any exchanges or reduced sentencing for your testimony here today?"

"No. I have not made any deals with anyone for this testimony."

"Thank you. I guess I’ll just have to take your word for it. And before you were in the jail, where did you reside?"

“Bates Inn Hotel.”

“A hotel huh. And before then?”

"Riverside Complex," I told her.

“Hmmmm. The Riverside Complex is one of the nicest communities in Ordale, while Bates is one of the cheapest. Quite a bit of a stretch if I had to say so. What brought about this change?”

“My financial situation.”

“Your financial situation?" she repeated. "But those townhouses, they are fairly expensive, might you agree?"

“It depends on what one would consider expensive,” I replied.

“Starting price is about fifteen hundred dollars per month, does that sound about right to you?”

“I could have paid about that much.”

“But the average monthly rent in the city of Ordale is about eight hundred and fifty dollars, would you agree with this statement also?”

“I guess that sounds about right too. I don't keep up with the statistics.”

Mrs. Lowisky began to walk back to her desk and proceeded to grab a piece of paper, then she quickly returned back to the stand.

“So you must have worked for a pretty high paying company in order to afford that type of rent, right?’

“No, I didn’t work for any company.”

“Well what type of degree do you have? I’m sure a Master’s to say the least.”

“I don’t have a degree either.”

“You own a business or something?”

“No.”

“Inherit any money from your family?"

"No."

"Win the lottery?”

“Nope,” I said nonchalantly.

By now I knew that Mrs. Lowisky was trying desperately to get under my skin. Truthfully it was only her presence and the fact that I had to be there that aggravated me. For all I wanted to do was get it all over with so that I could get on about my life.

“So then tell me,” she dramatically dragged her index finger back and forth across her temple, “how is it that you can afford to pay over fifteen-hundred dollars in rent every month?”

“Because I hustle,” I said blatantly.

Small chatter began to emerge from the courtroom. The judge was about to call for order but it simmered just as quickly as it started.

“You hustle?" she mimicked me.

“Yes.”

"Mrs. Black, I’m a law student. I never mastered the art of street talk. Can you explain to me and the people of the court what exactly does that mean?”

“It means I make my money off the streets, by drug trafficking.”

More gasped sounded.

“So you’re saying that you trafficked drugs and get paid cash money for doing so?”

“Yes,” I told her.

“Mrs. Black, who pays you?”

“The organization I work for.”

“And which organization is that?”

“The OMC, Ordale Mafia Circle.”

The chatter that started earlier began to make its way back to the room again. I glanced over to Hi-C, who looking pretty dazzling even in his white jumpsuit, now had the courage to give me contact. His eyes deeply penetrated mines and he seemed to begin to let a little emotion show. It still wasn't obvious exactly what he was thinking, but the guys from his crew who watched in the back made gestures that surely let me know I certainly crossed the line.

"The Ordale Mafia Circle, is that right?" she smiled victoriously. "So by the name of it, I take it this mafia is local, based right here in Ordale."

"Yes."

"So how did you carry these drugs for the Ordale Mafia Circle?"

"In the trunk of my car," I told her.

"And what type of drugs did you carry?"

"I don't know."

"You don't know?" she asked. "Well do you know, on average, the quantity of drugs that you would transport?"

"I don't know that either. Look, I never touched or saw anything. I drove whatever was in my trunk to whatever destination I was told to and then I collected my chips. It wasn't in my job description to keep up with the numbers."

"I understand, Mrs. Black," she dropped it. "Well, do you at least know who ordered these runs?"

I paused almost an entire minute and allowed the look of fear to come across my face. Then I sighed deeply before answering.

"Yes."

"You do?" she asked, pretending to act surprised. "And is that person here in the courtroom today?"

“Yes,” I sighed again.

“Can you identify him, I'm sorry *or her*, by not only telling the court who it is, but pointing in their direction if you see them here today?"

“Yes,” I drew a single finger up and placed it towards where Hi-C was sitting. “His name is Herbert Isaac Cooper.”

The voices that were before cheap and low had now began to roar from the back of the courtroom. The outpour caused me to unblock my mind and put my focus on the people who had become rallied up. I could now make out a few members of the OMC sitting in the back along with a host of others from the community who were there because they simply supported the mafia.

“You lying bitch!” I heard one woman yell, while the other voices shouting all types of damning phrases made its way across the room into my ears. One of the guys, who was unable to stand the sight of me any longer, silently put up a trigger finger before sliding quietly out of the courtroom.

Hi-C's head now sunk down to the floor and he clearly couldn’t bear to look at me anymore either. Strangely, still I showed no emotions and neither was I bothered. The judge quickly called for order and even had some people thrown out of the courtroom. Mrs. Lowisky, now with all she needed, continued on.

“I would like to note that the witness has identified Mr. Herbert Isaac Cooper, better known as Hi-C, as the leader of the victorious, but vicious, drug operation called the Ordale Mafia Circle. I have no further questions your honor.”

"Would the defense like to cross examine?" the judge asked after the court was finally in order. As I knew he would, Hi-C's lawyer, who was the head of the firm Isis worked for rose from his seat. He was stalky and bald, and put me in the mind frame of Danny DeVito. In the middle of a serious trial, I still managed to find some humor in that.

Mr. Patillo, who had been a lawyer for over thirty years, also asked the judge for permission to approach me before proceeding with his questioning. Hi-C still kept his head down, now completely uninterested in the case anymore. I couldn't help but think that he thought he was finished.

"How are you doing today, Mrs. Black?" Mr. Patillo said.

"I'm as good as I'm gonna get," I replied.

"Those are some pretty serious accusations you just made against my client," he said. "That type of thing can have someone put in jail for a long time."

"I'm aware," I said.

"You said you worked for the Ordale Mafia Circle, under my client's orders, trafficking drugs. Is this correct?"

"Yes. That's what I said."

"And how long did you work, allegedly, for Mr. Herbert Cooper?"

"About eight years," I answered.

"Yet you stated you are unable to tell the people anything about how much drugs, or even what type, you carried in the trunk of your car? Is this true."

"Correct."

"Eight years and you're not able to give one figure?"

“Like I said before, I just did the driving.”

“So you could have been transporting a bomb, or chocolate candy, in your trunk and you're telling me you wouldn’t have even known it?”

“I guess you can say that,” I replied.

“And you did it all for the money?” he asked.

“Yes. I just wanted to live a better life than the one I had growing up.”

“I see,” he said. “Miss Black, are you familiar with a woman by the name of Mrs. Isis Cooper?”

“Yes, we went over this before. That is his wife.”

The rumors of Hi-C and I had already spread through the city so it was no surprise to anyone, not even the judge about our affair. All I could do was look for Isis in the crowd, only to find that she was nowhere to be found.

“Yes, she is Mr. Cooper’s wife. She also works at my firm. We usually take on cases together but she told me that she wanted no parts of this one. Not because her husband was involved but because, well, she couldn’t face you. Is there any particular reason why?”

“Objection! That’s hearsay.” Mrs. Lowisky said, rising from her seat.

“Objection sustained,” the judge said. “Mr. Patillo you know the rules. Please leave hearsay out of the courtroom.”

“I apologize your honor, allow me to rephrase my question. I can assure you that it is relevant.”

“Get to your point and do it quickly,” judge ordered.

“Miss Black, if I was to tell you that Isis Cooper, the wife of Mr. Herbert Cooper, told me that she couldn’t face you in court, would you believe this to be true?”

“Yes, honestly I would.”

“And why would you believe this?”

“Because I was sleeping with her husband.” I said unbothered.

“So clearly you had a romantic relationship with my client, Mr. Herbert Cooper, is that correct?”

“That is correct.”

“And how long did this relationship go on?"

“Eight years.”

“Judging by your previous testimony, that means this affair was going on the entire time you worked for him. Is this accurate?”

“Yes.”

“I see,” he began to pace back and forth. “Eight years is a very long time. Can you say that you were very much in love with him?”

“Yes.”

“Do you still feel the same way about him?”

“Yes, I’m still in love with him.”

“But you are willing to testify against someone that you are deeply in love with. How is that so?”

“I’m not testifying against him, I’m just telling the truth. It’s a difference.”

“Well since you are in such a truth-telling mood," he said sarcastically, "is it true that you asked Hi-C to leave his wife to be with you?”

“I never asked him to leave her,” I replied, “but I wanted him too.”

“And did he ever give you any impression that he would?"

“Yes, he hinted on it once. The last time I talked to Hi-C, before he went to jail, he told me that he wanted to leave her and run off to be with me?"

“And did you believe him?”

“Yes, I did.”

“And to your knowledge, do you know if the two of them are still together? Or if he has went through any processes of divorcing her while he was incarcerated?”

“No I don't know, but I don’t believe that he did.”

“But even in the middle of all his down time, he still has not inquired about or attempted to take the steps of leaving his wife, who happens to be a lawyer that specializes in divorces. I’m sure that made you angry,” he said.

“Not so much of ang-”

“So angry,” his mellow voice began to harden, “that you would get revenge by any means necessary. Even by lying to a jury to have him put away for a very long time! Would you agree?”

"Objection!” Mrs. Lowisky called out again.

“No further questions,” Mr. Patillo, said before walking smoothly back off to take his place next to Hi-C.

After the brief outpour of excitement simmered, the judge ordered for the jury to disregard Mr. Patillo's last remarks. Then he ordered for both parties to approach the bench. With no more use for me on either side, the court decided to take a break before their last witness, Detective Bailey, took the stand. I had the option of leaving the courthouse, but I just had to stay and witness that.

After everyone was dismissed, I spent the intermission in the restroom. I decided to fix my hair, apply make-up, and undress my old clothing to reveal the much nicer outfit I had on underneath. Court was back in session after an hour and I took my place in the far back of the room, but was sure to sit next to the jury. There were two sheriffs who sat alongside me, as they figured it would be best with so many people now wanting to kill me. It took some time but I eventually ignored all of the dirty looks I was given by them.

Mr. Benson, a middle-aged German with a deep accent and dark brown hair, met Bailey at the stand and began to examine him. He was always present at every trial but he normally took a back seat while Mrs. Lowisky did all the talking. Somehow I believe it was part of a tactic, allowing two powerful men to face each other. Still, Bailey looked unbothered as he sat handsomely on the stand. He was sharply dressed in his usual gray suit and tie, but instead of having his badge on his hip like he normally did, it dangled around his neck for all to see. His hair also looking exceptionally nice, extra curly and trimmed with enough grease in it to fry a bucket of chicken.

"Can you state your name for the record?" Benson started off.

"My name is Owen Bailey," the detective said confidently.

"And may you tell the people what your business of being here today is."

"Certainly, I am a Drugs and Narcotics Agent and the lead detective in the investigation against Herbert Isaac Cooper and the Ordale Mafia Circle."

"Detective, I took a minute to view your resume when I first learned of you and I must say that I am quite impressed with your track record. You served in the army at age eighteen, joined the police force at twenty-one, and you were named Detective by twenty-seven."

"Yes. That is correct," Detective Bailey smiled, clearly appreciating the recognition.

"And if I may ask, how old you are now?" Benson inquired.

"I'm thirty-nine," he said, still smiling.

"So you have been a detective for over a decade?"

"That is also correct," Bailey said.

"Yet you seem to have successfully solved more cases than many of those who have worked twice as long as you have. Again very impressed."

"Thank you."

"I also see that most of your work was done in the state of Oklahoma, which is where you were located before you took this case. Is your impeccable record what landed you the assignment here in Ordale?"

"Yes, something like that," he boasted. "But to be more accurate, I inquired about moving to Ordale a short time ago. I always enjoyed the southern hospitality here and the historical feel that the city keeps alive. I visited Ordale last year and spoke with the chief about transferring my position from Oklahoma. From there, he took one look at my resume and made me an immediate offer to take on one particular case that I just could not refuse."

"And what case was this?"

"Ultimately the case against drugs and the rising number of criminal activity related to it here in the city of Ordale. But more specifically, the department had gained reason to believe that a man named Herbert Cooper was running an organization that brings in and distributes a high amount of illegal drugs into the community. My job was to turn these suspicions into factual evidence so that we may clean up the streets and make them a little more safe for our residence."

"I see. And what made you think you could take on this case especially with no, or little, knowledge of the city of Ordale. You must have taken down drug operations before?"

"Yeah, quite a few," he said. "But I will say I was insecure about this one."

"A fine man like yourself, why would you have any doubts? What would have been your biggest challenge."

"Well first off, as you stated, the city was unfamiliar to me." Detective Bailey answered. "But mainly because going after the head of any organization is never easy."

"And why do you say so?"

"Because like many businesses, the person on top usually never does any of the dirty work. They have people they pay to do it for them, while they keep their own hands clean. Nonetheless they are the ones calling all the shots and making everything possible. Without the head, there is no body."

"Make sense to me," Mr. Benson said. "So what, in your professional experience have you found is the best way to take down the head?"

"With the body," he answered.

"With the body?" Benson caressed his chin. "Can you explain exactly what that means?"

"It means that, from my experience, somebody from the organization, usually a trusted member or someone who actually is getting their hands dirty, has to give up information."

"And do you have that in this case?"

"Yes. A member of the OMC, James Williams also known as Squirrel, was caught attempting to sell thirteen kilos of cocaine to an undercover agent, which estimated to over $300,000 in street value. When he was arrested he informed us, and the jury here today, as we clearly all heard, that he was working for Mr. Herbert Cooper. Lakeisha Black who also testified today, was also caught transporting an undisclosed amount of cocaine in the trunk of her car. She also testified that Mr. Cooper was the head of the organization. That's confiscated drugs and two confessions, which should lead to one solid conviction."

"You mentioned Mr. James Williams, better known as Squirrel. We learned today that he pled guilty to the drug charges he faced and received a lesser sentence for his testimony today. But what about Lakeisha Black, did she serve any time for the drugs you found in her trunk?"

"No. LaKeisha Black was never even arrested under the grounds that she worked as an informant to help us obtain factual information against Mr. Cooper. She was the closest person to him, besides his wife."

"I see. And did she cooperate with you?"

"Yes, she did her part."

"So even during this drug bust, where she was also arrested, she was working for the police?"

"Yes. She knew all about the drug bust prior to it happening."

Hearing those words, Hi-C exhaled heavily then dropped his head into his sternum and I did not have to see his face to know it displayed hurt. I could only think back to that day he poured his heart out to me about his family's past. It must've brought him much sorrow knowing that the person he trusted the most and gave a chance to when no one would, could betray him the way I did. Many of the people in the courtroom also looked to me and shook their heads in disbelief, while the officers who protected me had sense enough to draw closer. Still I kept and nonchalant demeanor and waited to see how it all played out.

"Understood. I believe I'll stop here," Mr. Benson said. "I do just have one more question though. After the take downs of these operations, what in your experience has been the outcome, as far as a community standpoint?"

"Wc usually notice a decrease in drug related arrests, but most importantly, an amazing drop in the number of violent crimes we have in the city."

"I see. Thank you detective, I have no further questions."

Mr. Benson rested while Detective Bailey held a calm composure because he knew he had handled the situation well. Between Squirrel's testimony, mine, and the way he charmed the jury, everyone had a good idea of which direction the case would go in. Mr. Patillo, who had also gave up hope, tried to hide his discouragement with a fake smile and phony display of optimism. With the detective being the last witness and the last hope, he decided to go ahead and cross-examine him.

"Hello, how are you detective?" he said, as he rose again and dragged himself to the stand. He wasn't the type that liked to lose so I knew the predicament he was in was a very heartbreaking one.

Before Detective Bailey could answer, suddenly the double doors of the courtroom pushed open and revealed Isis as she strutted hard in her royal blue shirt that displayed her beautiful chocolate thighs. The matching jacket, that went extremely well with her pearl accessories, looked as if her entire outfit came straight out of the closet of a queen. Clearly the aisle was her runway, and she was nothing less than a supermodel as she held and captivated the attention of everyone in the room. We all watched in amazement all the way until she met her legal partner at the stand.

"I'll be taking over from here," she looked to the judge. Even he was astonished by her beauty.

"What can I say," he sighed. "If you think this is good idea....Unfortunately there's no law against you defending your husband."

"Thank you, your honor," she said, before turning to give Detective Bailey her full attention. She was holding a manila folder in her hand that she hugged tightly.

"Hello Detective Bailey, I'm Isis Cooper and I'm one of the lawyers representing Mr. Herbert Cooper."

The detective nodded and showed a clear sign that he wasn't interested in her nor her position. He dealt with big time crooks for a living and this petite woman who stood before him posed no threat, no matter how intimidatingly gorgeous and headstrong she was.

Ignoring his slightly disrespectful gesture, she turned to the jury. "I have been a lawyer for over thirteen years and this was the hardest case that I ever had to sit through. The lies, the betrayal, the humiliation, is a feeling that you would only have to experience in order to understand. I thought about jumping ship, assigning it to another firm, even divorce, but then I realized something....I realized that when I took my vows, I made a promise to love through sickness and through health, through thick and through thin, through right," she turned to Hi-C and took a deep breath. "And through wrong."

A heartfelt silence was heard around the courtroom before it was interrupted by the sound of dry and widely spaced out claps.

"That was beautiful and moving, Mrs. Cooper." Detective Bailey smacked his hands together for the last time. "But may I remind you that this is a court of law and not marriage counseling."

Knowing the situation could have got out of hand fairly easy, the judge quickly intervened.

"Detective you know the rules, try to only answer when you are being asked a question and Mrs. Cooper, you're hanging a very thick rope around your neck already here, let's just get on with the case."

"I'm sorry, your honor." She said.

"Don't be sorry, be a lawyer." he replied.

Isis pulled herself together and continued. "Detective Bailey, I was sitting outside the courtroom there and couldn't help but over here

Mr. Benson talk about your credentials. I reviewed them myself and I'm also quite impressed by it."

"Thank you," Detective Bailey began to straighten his collar. He was definitely feeling himself.

"You've been a detective just as long as I have been a lawyer," she said. "So it's safe to say we're both professional, highly experienced, and we know our rolls very well?"

"I can only speak for myself," he said. "But yes, I can agree with that."

"I'm going to cut right to the chase," she said. "During this indictment you asked my client to provide documentation and financial proof on how he was able to afford a million dollar home and four cars totaling about one hundred and fifty thousand dollars in value. Is that correct?"

"Yes, we did ask for these documents."

"And what did you find?" she asked.

Detective Bailey paused before speaking. It was clear he did not want to answer her. "We found that his assets were accounted for?"

"And how?" she asked.

"Apparently he had inherited a large sum of money from an insurance policy after his parents died."

"So the amount exceeded the cost of the house?" she asked.

"Yes."

"And the cars too?"

"Yes."

"And how long after he received this insurance money did he purchase this home?"

"The house was paid off about a year after."

"So is it safe to say that he used the money he inherited from his parents to do this?"

"Yes, I guess you can say that."

"Detective Bailey, did you also tap into phone lines any time during the investigating of this case?"

"Yeah."

"And do you have my client on any of your recordings attempting to buy or sell drugs?"

"Not Mr. Cooper himself, but alleged members of the OMC, yes."

"Alleged," she repeated purposely. "And this bust, did you find any drugs in the home of my client?"

"No."

"Did you find any in his personal possession?"

"No," detective sighed again and clearly began to appear frustrated. "But as I stated before, these guys are smart and they never get their hands dirty."

"So is it safe to say that your strongest piece of evidence against my client is the testimony of two witnesses who are merely pointing the fingers at him?"

"Yes, but they are solid," he said.

"Solid huh," she said. "Mr. James Williams, also known as Squirrel, are you aware of any prior charges he had before you arrested him for selling to an undercover?"

"Yes," I could now see the balls of sweat he accumulated appear on his forehead even from where I was sitting. "He had a warrant for his arrest for a separate drug charge. But it was only minor."

"I agree it was a minor charge. But if convicted it would have been his third, so he was facing up to what? Anywhere between four to fifteen years I believe. Probably why he didn't turned himself in. Is this correct?"

"Yeah, that's one way to look at it." he said.

"Detective Bailey, now I don't mean to change the subject, but how common, from your expertise, is it for a witness to lie in order to avoid or get a reduced sentence."

"Objection!" Mrs. Lowisky shouted again.

"Overruled," the judge shut her down.

"I believe I'm perfectly within my limits but let me reword this anyway," she glared at Mrs. Lowisky. "Detective Bailey, have you ever witness where a person has blatantly lied on someone or something in order to get themselves out of trouble?"

"Yes. But not in any of the cases I have worked?"

"Understood," she said. "And what about Lakeisha Black? Are you aware if she has any prior legal situations?"

"Mrs. Black has not even a speeding ticket," he smiled.

"So after you pulled her over and found these drugs in her trunk, did you arrest her?"

"No."

“Funny you say that because I noticed that drugs you confiscated from Mr. James Williams was admitted into evidence, but not the drugs you found in Lakeisha Black's trunk. Can you explain why this is so?"

"We allowed Miss Black to make the drop in exchange that she worked with investigators to help expose the organization."

"So you, an officer of the law, allowed Lakeisha Black to leave your sight with a trunk fill of cocaine, meaning all of that went back on the streets. Would that make you a drug dealer too? Or an accomplice?"

The detective began to swarm around in his chair. He was clearly becoming upset with Isis and his once calm composure had surely started to fade.

"As an officer of the law, sometimes you have to make uneasy decisions, like sacrificing the little fish in order to get to the Big fish. As detectives we have to trust our judgments and sometimes that comes with taking great risks."

"I understand," she said, but her face said the opposite. "And whose idea was it to let her go on with this load?"

"It was mine," he lied. "Like I said, she had not even a speeding ticket. I needed something solid to hold over her head in return for her cooperation. It was my plan all along."

"Clever. So you allow her to smuggle drugs into the city of Jacksonville, she does it successfully, and then what? She begins to start giving you insight on the Hi-C and the Ordale Mafia Circle."

"Yes, basically."

"Detective Bailey, I don't mean to get off track or personal but I must admit, I've always noticed that Miss Black is a very attractive woman. Would you agree?"

Isis began to steer her eyes in my direction, which prompted others to do so also. I had made a full transformation as I sat elegantly in the back, wearing an all-black romper that hugged my body not too tightly but not too loosely either. My diamonds earring glistened with the permission of the lights from the ceiling and my hair that was before pulled back messily was now comb down and tamed. Some people didn't even recognize me.

"Yes. She's very beautiful. But so are many other women I have worked with, even you." he said.

Isis ignored his weak attempt to flatter her and continued to drill him.

"Did this make it difficult for you to work with her?"

"Not at all," he said. "I'm a man of integrity. Very strong-willed. I wouldn't be where I am today if I was anything less."

You sure?" she asked. "So you never thought about her, shall I say, sexually." Sudden gasps came over the courtroom. Even I was surprised by her boldness.

"I believe you're getting personal again," Detective Bailey said to her. "You might want to let your partner take it from here."

"I'm afraid I may have to agree," the judge butted in.

“Your honor, I know what I'm doing," she informed him and without saying a word, he turned and looked away.

"Detective I don't mean to throw you off but those are very nice loafers you're wearing," she said, referring to the shoes he sported on his feet. "Are they real gators?' she asked.

"No they're fake. I appreciate a gator too much to wear his skin."

"I'm not a big fan of wearing animals myself. I just noticed the shoes because my father used to own a pair just like them. When I was a kid he used to stand me on top of them and slow dance with me around the house," she said. "Detective Bailey, when's the last time you had a real good slow dance?"

"Excuse me?" he questioned.

"You know, a real good slow dance," she said. "Remember, you're a man of integrity and you're under oath."

Detective Bailey blew a heavy amount of air out through his mouth and nose. "Probably about six months ago."

"And where were you?" she asked.

"I was having dinner at a restaurant."

"I have been trying to find a place where I can eat dinner and slow dance, but I've had nothing but trouble. Is this restaurant located here in Ordale?"

"No," he answered hesitantly, clearly knowing where she was now headed. The balls of sweat that began to appear on his forehead earlier now began to trickle down his face.

"Well where is it?" she asked.

"It's in California."

"California?" she questioned. "I hate to get personal again, detective. A nice looking man like yourself, I would hope I'm not stepping on any toes when I ask this, but who did you share this dance with?"

Detective Bailey's chest now sunk to his stomach. Although he tried his best to hide it, the look of discomfort he showed on his face was present and obvious. I just sat there calm with my eyes glued to the show that was certainly playing in front of dozens of us. We are all so curious to know where Isis was going.

"Lakeisha Black," he sighed.

"You mean the witness who testified here today?" she asked.

"Yes," he replied.

"So you were slow dancing with Lakiesha Black at a dinner in California, yet you deny her beauty interfering with your ability to work with her professionally."

"Correct. I was being professional," he said. "In fact, I'm glad that you mentioned this. I'm so dedicated to my position that the only reason I was even in Cali was because that's where she went in attempt to flee from testifying. I didn't know I was going to dinner until the cab she had waiting for me took me there. As far as the slow dance, sometimes you have to get in people's head psychologically in order to get the results you want. You're a lawyer, you should know this. Again, I was just doing my job."

"Yes, I see. And you're right, psychologically you do have to sometimes get into people's head so I can understand that. But what about sexually...have you ever went as far being sexual with a witness to get a confession?"

"What? No!" he blurted. "I don't know where you think you're going with this, but I can assure you I never had sex with Lakeisha

Black, or anyone for that matter, to persuade a case. I told you I'm a man of integrity."

"I believe you," she said. "So this only leads me to believe that you had sex with her because there was love involved."

I collection of gasps sounded again.

"What! No!" he shouted.

"Well, then how do you explain this!"

Isis immediately threw down the folder she held tightly in her hand into Detective Bailey's lap. When he opened it, it revealed a stack of pictures of the two of us getting down and nasty on The Rooftop in California. The one where he had me bent over the balcony while he thrusted himself deep inside of me reigned on top. We choose that one because it was the most dramatic. The clear angle of Detective Bailey and I, while I smiled up into the camera that Poncha had pointed on us from her hotel room, was one that not even a blind man could deny.

"Objection!" Mrs. Lowisky shouted before struggling in her heels to make it up the judge. "Those documents have not been admitted into evidence!"

Without a single care, Isis then held up two more photos in each of her hands and then dragged her body back and forth across the jury box. The mostly white jury, that ranged from men and women who were in their twenties to their sixties, look appalled as they got a clear view of the explicit images that tainted their unprepared eyes. Some of their bland asses looked as if they could have used the entertainment.

As I imagined it would, the courtroom quickly turned into a full circus as a mix of feelings of surprise, confusion, joy, and even hurt surfaced. Even the judge could not immediately call for order because he was so busy trying to get a glimpse of new evidence that had been introduced in the room.

"Your honor!" Mrs. Lowisky yelled to him as she quickly reminded him of his obligations. Only then did he began banging his gavel against the sound block in an effortless attempt to calm everyone down.

"Mrs. Cooper!" he yelled to Isis. "Are you out of your mind! You cannot show these photos!"

"But I can," Poncha said as she stood up from the back of the room and began to pass around the rest of pictures she had taken to the people near her. She got them developed in extra-large sizes so even the ones who weren't trying to look could not ignore."

"So you, a man of integrity, a professional, a lead detective with a high level of expertise who knows his roll very well, thinks it wise to fall in love with the key witness in the case against the man you are trying to put in prison for life. This case is too messy for any jury to have to decide on." Isis shouted through hell and chaos that surrounded her then began to make her smooth exit. "Judge I would like to call for the immediate dismissal of the State's case against Mr. Herbert Isaac Cooper under the grounds of a little thing called, shall I say, *tampering with the evidence*."

"Mrs. Cooper you get back here!" the judge ordered, but his words were meaningless when the doors shut behind her.

The feeling of sweet victory came over me and it was soothing to my soul. I knew I had saved my family, my man, and most importantly my life. In fact, hadn't smiled that hard since I saw the money that Keyshawn got from the Mexicans at the trailer park. The people who were rooting for Hi-C cheered on while a host of officers made their way through the courthouse doors to gain order. Hi-C just sat still and emotionless, even he did not know what had just happened, while the very excited Poncha, rushed to me and jumped for joy.

"I told you it would work!" she yelled. "Didn't I tell you!"

I wanted to celebrate with her, but her words only became background noises as I locked eyes on the clearly embarrassed detective who rushed off the stand and tried to make his way through the crowd of people who began to attack his character. The commotion I witnessed also became nonexistent as I carefully watched him take this walk of shame, and only with the help of those same fellow officers he had arrest me, attempted to make it out the door. Unfortunately, we had to cross paths in order to exit and the closer he got to me, the more my heart began to beat faster. When he finally made it within arms reached, I literally thought it would jump straight out of my chest.

"So it didn't mean anything to you huh," he managed to whisper to me once he got close enough for me to read his lips. "None of it?"

While the detective glared down at me with a look that could have killed, I just sat still with a clever grin on my face.

"I guess you really can lose," I told him. "You just take care of yourself, detective."

CHAPTER 33: Runaway

"I couldn't rest without knowing," I said to Hi-C who stood in the doorway of his home unexpecting me to be knocking at one in the morning. It was two days after he had been released from jail, with all charges against him dropped. Gladly, this was also the third weekend of the month so I knew Isis would be out of town.
Hi-C was standing in the doorway wearing nothing but a black robe, clearly enjoying the benefits of his freedom. Without saying a word, he went back into the house and signaled for me to follow. It had been a long time since I had seen the place, but I still got the same bubbly feeling every time I stepped in. The house's entire vibe, and even the aroma, was still the same. The sweet, pure smell of ginger hit my nostrils instantly and gave me a high that my body had been withdrawn from.

"I've been waiting for you," he finally said, then he made his way in the bedroom. I followed and watched as he rested his body right in the middle of his bed. Not wanting to get too comfortable, I decided to remain standing.

"Waiting for me?" I questioned.

"Yes. I gotta thank you for what you did for me. Took some real courage and loyalty. I will forever be indebted to you."

"You don't owe me anything. I did what I had to do. I may be a lot of bad things, but a snitch is not one of them."

"I never thought for a second you were," he said before placing three taps on his chest, signaling for me to come and lay down on top of him. Despite my plan not to get too close, I obeyed and crawled what seemed to be miles across his extra-large bed, then smothered myself inside his chest like a spoiled newborn. As much as I wanted to resist, it felt good to be back in his arms.

"Are you sure about that?" I asked, planting two soft kisses on his chest.

"I'm positive," he said.

"So you didn't think for one second that I switched sides? Even when I had my fingers pointed at you."

"You know what, honestly never," he said before running his hands down my denim tights and squeezing my ass firmly. Judging by the way he instantly rocked up, I knew he wanted what he had been missing from me while he had been incarcerated. Unfortunately for him, all I could think about was Isis and how she helped me and I was pretty sure she had already broken her husband off a piece of ass when he got home. Besides, as much as I wanted pull his robe back and give him the best sex of his life, I also wanted to start making better choices.

"Look, I don't plan to stay long," I said, pulling away from his grip. "I'm actually headed out now. I just wanted to see you before I leave."

"Before you leave?" he lifted his body over mine and stared directly in my eyes. "I don't understand."

"I'm ditching Ordale for good," I told him. "And honestly I don't know if I will ever see you again. I have a car outside right now with nothing in it but a full tank of gas and a suitcase loaded with cash. I'm getting on the road, going to wherever the universe guides me, and I'm never looking back."

Hi-C just continued to stare down at me in silence. The expression on his face let me know that he didn't care for my words one bit. After finally digesting what I had just laid upon him, he gently lifted me from his chest and took a slow stroll towards his window. I watched him carefully as he pressed a button on his wall that automatically pulled both of his suede, black curtains into opposite directions. He then took his place in front of the window and centered his focus on the night scenery that revealed itself on the other side. I stayed on the bed with my ears fully opened, eager to know how he felt about my departure.

"Leaving huh?" he finally came to say while he continued to gaze out of the window. Although there was a great view of his neighbor's solar night lights and the moon as it reflected perfectly off of two live oak trees, his eyes gravitated more towards the ground.

"Yes, I broke my promise with the police and I know they're going to be on my ass. Besides, there's some people here in Ordale that still probably want me dead. It's just too risky to stay. There's nothing left here for me anyway."

"I'm disappointed in you, Keisha. Very disappointed," he said as his words cut me deep. The last thing I wanted was to leave him on bad terms.

Seeing how hurt he appeared forced me to jump from the bed and rush over to comfort him. When in reach, I wrapped my arms tightly around his waist and then I looked out the window in the same direction as he did. I wanted to appreciate just what he saw but I realized that there was something far greater capturing his attention.

"So what am I going to do with this?" He said as he pointed down at his driveway, to the old school Chevrolet classic that stared back at us.

"Oh my god, it's beautiful!" I said, soaking up the view. The car stood out effortlessly amongst all the others that surrounded it and the way the streetlights reflected off its wide body allowed me to really see every detail. The wet, baby-blue paint went well with the cream colored leather interior and the fact that it was a convertible made it a hundred times better. It was always a fantasy of mine to cruise down the highway in an old school with my hair blowing in the wind and that was the perfect ride for it. It was truly one of a kind.

"The mayor didn't want to sell it," he said. "But once I offered up my house, he changed his mind. I sacrificed a lot to make this getaway just as I imagined it. So yes I'm disappointed. Disappointed that you would leave without me."

A smile big enough to squeeze two suns in my cheekbones appeared across my face. Although I had long time rid the idea of Hi-C and I going anywhere together, let alone being in the presence of each other again, it brought me great joy knowing that a dream of mine was about to come true. I immediately began to picture all of the things that we would do on our adventure and the places we would go.

"But what about Isis?" My concern suddenly overpowered my excitement. For once, I symptomized with her and felt very guilty about involving myself with her husband again.

"What about her?" he said.

"She's your wife. How could you just leave her like this?"

"Isis knows what's up. This distance gave us plenty of time to discuss our relationship. Come to find out," he snickered to himself, "we express ourselves better over pen and pad. She has a clear understanding of where our marriage stands and she also knows where my heart is. Isis has always been loyal to me no matter what. Why do you think she helped blow the case? Listen," he grabbed both my hands, "Isis will always be dear to me and I love her very much, but we both just want to see each other happy, even if means we are not together. Besides, she confessed to me that she's in love with someone else and that he was man enough to plant the seed that I wouldn't inside of her while I was away."

"Oh wow," I said, completely blown away by what Hi-C had just laid on me. "So you mean she knows that we're leaving together? And she's okay with it?"

"Yes. She's happy and okay. So don't you worry about that."

Hi-C's words sounded like a sweet symphony playing in my ears. It brought me great pleasure knowing that we were really going through with running away together, but the fact that I could go guilt-free made for a much better departure.

Unable to hold back any longer, I aggressively spun him around and threw his back up against the window. It didn't matter that the lights on his chandelier was shining over the entire bedroom, allowing whoever was able to see us a good view. Hi-C gripped my hair tightly and moaned as I opened his robe and kissed his bare chest. Then I allowed my tongue to roll in a circular motion down his stomach until I made it to his pelvis. Without wasting any time taking them off, I pulled his manhood through the slit of his boxers and began to slowly stroke him with my mouth. He closed his eyes, placed his head back against the window, and enjoyed the wonderful feeling I blessed him with. After only three minutes, he was filling my mouth with his juices and I made sure not to let any of it go to waste.

"Why don't you wash up and let's get out of here," I told Hi-C as I rose from my knees and kissed him passionately in the mouth. He didn't even mind tasting himself.

"Okay baby, give me ten minutes," he agreed and then pulled himself together.

Hi-C left the bedroom and made his way a couple feet down the hall to the shower. I led myself back to the bed, where I just lay with a huge, irreversible smile attached to my face. I hadn't felt that happy in a long time and I was definitely going to enjoy it. It amazed me how, even though I had a bunch of cash in the car, all I wanted was Hi-C. In fact, the only reason the money mattered to me was because I knew it would cost for us to travel. I didn't care about hitting the malls nor the clubs, but was more anxious to see the mountains, the valleys, and the rivers as we were sure to pass them by. I was also thankful that Detective Bailey showed me how to appreciate nature and I was sure to carry his advice with me every step of the way.

I watched the fancy wall clock constantly and counted down the minutes until his return, but my smile faded as the ten turned into twenty and twenty turned into thirty. Hi-C hadn't made his way back to the bedroom and he normally didn't take long to dress. Besides, he wasn't carrying anything but his body, so I could only wonder what was the hold up.

It was only after a whole hour had passed that I figured it was best I went to check on him. I rushed down the hallway and called for him, but no answer. As I got closer to the bathroom, I could hear the shower running so I knew he was still inside. I tried not to get upset because I knew that was the last shower he would have in his home and with a bathroom as beautiful as his, I couldn't blame him for wanting to savior the final moments in it.

The door was open slightly, so without knocking I eased my way inside. Instantly, thoughts of taking my clothes off and hopping in with him ruled my mind. He deserved some great sex to accompany that great head.

"Bae, it's me. Are you almost- " I said, before receiving yet another surprise. This one was not as pleasant as the first.

"What the fuck? Baby are you okay!" I dropped to the floor and landed where Hi-C was laying, unresponsively. He had a huge knot on the back of his head with a little bit of blood seeping from it that I knew wasn't there before. While trying to remain calm, I hung over his body and tried to shake him a few times, but still no movement. Then I began to check his wrist for a pulse, and although thankfully did I feel one, what I did not feel was the approaching presence of the person who crept up silently behind me. At least not until their legs were on my back and the tip of a hard object was firmly pressed against the back of my head. Before I could fully turn around to get a glimpse of this mysterious presence, the pain from a blow that I too received sent my conscious mind into a state of darkness that I could only pray I would wake up from.

CHAPTER 34: FAMILY TIES

"Rise and shine, sleepy head," a male voice manifested its way into my discombobulated mind. As my blurry vision slowly cleared, the bright crescent moon and gloomy night sky began to reveal itself. "Glad you could join us. We thought you'd never wake up."

"What? Wait. What's going on?" I struggled to mumble, then attempted to relieve the pain I immediately felt on the right side of my head by rubbing it, only to find out that my hands were confined to my side. As I gradually brought myself to consciousness, I soon realized that they were tied down by a thick rope that tightly coiled around my body from my shoulders on down to my feet. My heart began to pound rapidly at the very notice of it and I surely started to panic, but was slightly relieved when I rolled my weary head around and spotted Hi-C sitting next to me. Unfortunately, he was in the same predicament I was in and was staring at me as if he was more worried for my well-being than his own. We were both propped up in what I soon recognized to be the Buick Classic he had just purchased from the mayor. I was in the passenger side, he was in the driver's, and the convertible top was let back.

"We've just been waiting for you, that's all. That Xylolpol works better than I thought," the voice said again, now seemingly more familiar. A cloud of cigarette smoke blew in my face and when it cleared, it revealed the person I could only assume was responsible for us being in that dilemma.

"Detective Bailey?" I gasped with what little breath I could.

The man before me, who was clearly the detective I learned to know so well, stood with his back up against the passenger door. He was calmly looking down at me as he continued to puff the cigarette smoke directly in my face. Strangely, he was dressed in an all-black, thick long-sleeved Dickie jumpsuit even though it was over eighty degrees out. His hair was also unusually untamed, and his eyes were weary and baggy, as if he hadn't had a minute of sleep since the last time I saw him in court. In fact, that was the worst I had seen him look in all of my entire time knowing him. On top of that, the clear smell of alcohol coming from his sweaty pores let me know that he had been doing something he told me he normally didn't do, drinking. I was surely in a state of disbelief and couldn't figure out what to make of any of it.

"Nope wrong," he said quickly. "Although that name was starting to grow on me."

"But I don't understand," I slurred. "Where…where am I?"

"You don't remember?" he extended his arms and waved them across the air, introducing the scenery. Even in my weakness, I managed to slowly lift my head and rotate it before finally recognizing the familiar place.

"The National Wildlife Refugee?" I asked.

"You guessed it," he replied.

"But why? What am I doing here? And why are we tied up?" I began to cry as the reality of the situation began to sink in. "Please. Why are you doing this to us?"

"Why?" Detective Bailey busted out into a quick, but heavy laughter. "Because of a little thing called *revenge,* that's why."

"Revenge?" I tried to sit up, but then realized that the rope was not only tied around my body but also to the seat of the car, allowing not even the slightest bit of room for movement. It was an uncomfortable and rather painful situation to be in, but still I tried with everything in me to remain calm.

"Look, I'm sorry for what happened at court," I pleaded. "It wasn't personal. It's…it's... just that I had to do what I had to do in order to save myself. If you care for me like you said you do, then you have to understand. Believe me when I tell you that the feelings I have for you are still the same. Please."

The laughter that Detective Bailey had earlier simmered down from made its way back to surface again. He clearly wasn't trying to hear anything I said and he quickly let that fact be known.

"Keisha, don't bother trying to run game on me. Besides, you think this is really about you? Or that fuckin' court thing? In fact, I should be thanking you for that. I mean really, that was the highlight of my career. If I'm going to go down for anything, getting caught fuckin' a beautiful woman would be at the top of my list. You saw those photos. Those shots made me look like King Kong," he chuckled, then lifted his body from the car and knelt down on the side of me. Placing his lips against my cheeks, he slowly dragged his tongue up my face. "This is way deeper than how far I was inside of you. This is a family matter."

Disgusted, I turned my face away, allowing just enough room for the ball of spit that flew out of my mouth to shoot towards him. Luckily, he was successfully able to dodge the matter that was headed his way. Then without a second thought, he slammed one hard backslap across my face to show me that he wasn't too fond of my disrespectful gesture. My head bobbled from the impact and I could instantly feel my lips began to bleed and swell.

"Watch yourself," he said before being interrupted by the sound of Hi-C's voice as he began to yell and toss around in his seat like a mad man. Seeing this, the unbothered Detective Bailey danced his way around the car towards him.

"You crooked pig!" Hi-C shouted fearlessly as he looked to Detective Bailey once he had made it to the driver's side. "Let us go now. Or at least let her go."

"Calm down," the detective replied with a smile still on his face. "Don't worry. *I'm* not going to kill the bitch."

"Well untie her and then face me like a fuckin' man," he said.

"Although I'm certain that even if you had a fair chance against me, I could still take you," he bragged, "I'm afraid I can't do that."

"Then just tell me," Hi-C pleaded, "what's going on here? What are you doing to us?"

Detective Bailey spoke not another word then reached into his pants pocket, pulled out a knife, and flicked it open. I watched as he aimed it at Hi-C and slowly guided it towards his face. In great fear, I squinted my eyes tighter and tighter the closer he got to his throat but was still sure to keep them open just enough to vaguely see what he was about to do to him. Even though Hi-C looked unafraid as the sharp object came only centimeters away from his skin, it was certainly a big relief to both of us when the detective suddenly turned it away from him and then put it towards his own face. Hi-C and I looked with both confusion and curiosity as he started dragging the knife towards one of his eyes and allowed the tip of the blade to merely touch his eyeballs. Then he precisely slid the weapon over just enough for the brown-colored contact lens to depart from his cornea. He did the other eye just the same, and once he was finished creeping us out, he suddenly grabbed Hi-C around the neck with one arm and smashed their heads together. Then he turned to me so that I may get a good view of them both side by side.

"A good ole' family matter. You still don't understand?" he said as he just stood there giving me time to figure out what he was implying. As I carefully scanned both of their faces, I was still completely clueless. It wasn't until I focused in on their eyes that an eerie feeling came over me. There was something very similar about them. They both had that same weird hazel-blue color.

"Still don't get it?" he asked again before insolently throwing Hi-C's head away from his grip. Using only his legs, and obvious plyometrics training skills, he then jumped on top of the hood of the car and mounted himself before us like he actually was King-Kong.

"Maybe this will help," he said before he put his arms to his chest and began to rip the thick jumpsuit apart with all his strength. I didn't understand why he could not just zip it down like a normal person, but I guess his way called for a more dramatic effect.

Detective Bailey now stood before us with a chest that was bare and a set of lungs that throbbed heavily back and forth within it. A big portion of his stomach was blackened, charred, and just looked completely different from the rest of his body. Unless he had an usually strange birthmark, something had clearly happened to him in the past.

With a clear view from the passenger's side, I watched the detective and Hi-C. The moment was very intense as they both looked long and hard into each other's eyes, while I just waited patiently to see what would happen next.

"Simon?" Hi-C broke out into words first. "Is that really you? But this can't be. I..I..I… thought you were-"

"Thought I was what?" he said. "Lemme guess…dead."

"Well…yes," Hi-C replied. "I thought you were dead. Better yet, I just knew you were dead. I went to your funeral."

"Lemme guess again," Detective Bailey replied, "it was a closed casket?"

"Yes…but…huh…wait a minute. How is this possible?" Hi-C said in total disbelief. "I must be dreaming. Yeah that's exactly what this is, a dream. Because there's just no way you could be alive."

"How could you say that? I mean, how could you not know? How could you not feel it?" Detective Bailey's body slowly sank down until his bottom was resting on the hood of the car. Then he folded his legs Indian-style in front of us and sat like he was about to read a children's book or something. His eyes were a extremely red and the way he was tossing that sharp knife back and forth from each of his hands, I was glad that the glass windshield could be a barrier between us.

He continued speaking as his eyes began to tear up. "You were my big brother. I always had your back. But clearly, you didn't always have mine."

"Huh? What do you mean, Simon?" Hi-C looked Detective Bailey into his eyes, this time more passionately. "And you were my little brother. You and Mama were all I had and I loved you both with all my heart. I don't understand any of this. I swear I thought you were dead. Mrs. Brockington said-"

"Mrs. Brockington said what?" Detective Bailey intercepted, chuckled, and then shook his head. "You mean the same Mrs. Brockington that I caught walking off the backyard with a gas can that night the shed caught fire."

Hi-C's eyes widened hearing those words, but still the detective did not give him a chance to marinate on them before he continued.

"Herbert, I looked up to you," he said. "I loved following my big brother's footsteps. Every move you'd make, was a move I'd make. Think about it. That night you were in the woods and you heard that noise, who do you think it was? Who do you think went behind you and picked up those cigarette buds every time you snuck out? And all so that you wouldn't get caught… It was me. I always went out behind you. In fact, I watched you that night jumping around kicking invisible shit in the woods. Hell, even from the distance I helped you fight off some of those bad guys. Little did I know the bad guys were really out there and they weren't imaginary."

Detective Bailey paused, clearly visualizing the terrible moment in his past, then took a minute to pull himself together. Tears began to flow even harder down his face and he used his palms to aggressively wipe them away. I could see that he was mentally torn by the spaced-out look he possessed. Also by the way he could barely get his words out.

"That's when the worst happened," he continued. "I saw a huge cloud of smoke that was too big to be coming from your cigarette and I quickly noticed it was near the shed. I didn't want to disappoint you by letting you know I was there, so I just ran back alone to check on Mama. But by the time I made it to her, the smoke had turned into full blown flames."

Hearing his brother's words, Hi-C closed his eyes tightly and he began to sweat drastically.

"It was a painful thing to witness, big brother," the detective said. "Mama was just screaming and crying for help. She was trying her best to get out of there but couldn't because for some odd reason, the door was tied shut with a thick piece of rope. And me, well I just stood there crying too, at the same time trying to pull it open. Only problem was that my little hands weren't strong enough to do it alone. That's when I started calling for your help, but you were nowhere to be found."

"Please stop it! Shut the fuck up right now!" Hi-C now suddenly began to scream out and shake his entire body, attempting to break free from the shackles and the unwelcoming words that troubled his ears. Detective Bailey knew he was tearing his brother down, but he still didn't hold back the truth.

"I was able to get it open just wide enough for her to get her arms threw it and I held on to her tightly not even caring that the heat from the door was burning my chest badly. Herbert, I listened to Mama until she screamed no more and then I blacked out. Next thing I know I was waking up in a burn center."

"I said I can't take this!" Hi-C continued to shout, now with more meaning, "Please stop now! I'm begging you!"

"I couldn't take hearing it either!" the detective began to get a little aggressive himself. "But I have had to over and over and over every single night of my entire life! The sounds of her screams are something I just can't shake. They torment me. They haunt me. They consume me. Just picture it, having to look your own mother straight into her eyes while you just watch her die."

"Please," Hi-C's cries slowly festered into regretful sobs. He calmed down greatly, but his emotions were clearly still in an uproar. It was evident that every word laid upon him took a bigger and bigger piece of his life and the detective showed no signs of making anything easier for his brother.

"And what's worst," he continued, "waking up in the hospital bed to Mrs. Brockington and her ol' dirty ass sheriff daddy standing over my aching body fussing about why we weren't all dead. I had to hear him curse her and question her about how she made the mistake of not knowing the two of us weren't in the shed before she set it on fire. Then I had to listen to their plans on trying to fix it by having her adopt us. How they would get some of his friends down at the news station make her a huge headline for having a heart big enough to take in her deceased nanny's *black* kids. How that would be good for business and future elections."

Detective Bailey took some more time to reflect. This time much longer than the first couple of ones. I just sat there with my eyes glued to his lips while I hung on to every word that came out of his mouth.

"But unfortunately," he finally said, "Mrs. Brockington said she only had the heart to, as she put it, *'do one'* and the oldest would be the better choice. '*He'd be leaving the house faster and as soon as he turns eighteen I'm gonna send that nigger straight to the army,*' is what she said. As far as me, they decided they would give me a new identity, tell everyone I had died alongside Mama, and send me to an orphanage hundreds of miles away. Mr. Dave was in the room too."

"What? Daddy knew about this? All of it? Even the fire?" Hi-C quickly asked. He now appeared to be more acceptant and interested.

"Well they only talked about the fire when he wasn't in the room, but he did know about me being sent away. He tried to talk them out of it, got all upset and even broke down awfully when they told him about shipping me off. That's when I learned that he was my real daddy. He didn't want it to happen but apparently they had some type of dirt on him, so he was forced to just go with it. Why do you think he killed himself? I mean yeah, it hurt him deeply to know Mama was gone, but he could have lived without her. Now knowing he had a five-year-old son somewhere out there that he abandoned too....that was just too much pressure on him."

"Whoa," Hi-C said in total disbelief. "This can't be real."

"It's real," he sighed. "As real as those abusive foster families I somehow always managed to end up in. Real as these scars and bruises I received growing up…real as those grown men who used to touch me inappropriately."

Suddenly Detective Bailey rose back up on the hood and allowed his jumpsuit to fall completely off him. He now stood before us with no shame in only his boxers. Wounds, lashes, and all types of legions covered his entire body. It was clear that he had been through a great deal of hardship in his life and even though he proved himself to be the ultimate deceiver, I couldn't help but feel that everything he said was the truth.

"No…no…no!" Hi-C screams began to resurface as he thrusted his head from side to side. "I told you I can't take any more of this! Please stop it! You cannot blame me for that! Believe me, I didn't know!"

"Bullshit!" Detective Bailey slammed both his fist down on the glass, almost shattering it. "You weren't there to help mama and you didn't come for me neither. Don't deny it. Just admit it. You failed us."

Detective Bailey jumped up from the car and met Hi-C again. He grabbed his brother by the face with one hand clinching his chin, forcing them to lock eyes. "I remember I couldn't wait to turn seventeen and get out of that group home. In fact, the first thing I did when I left was take the little bit of money they sent me on my way with and buy a bus ticket straight to Ordale to find you. Here I was thinking shit had been just as bad for you growing up, only to sneak through that back gate of the Bluff and find you throwing the dopest party I had ever saw in my life. I mean, that smile you had on your face while that pretty little trick was throwing her ass on you in that bikini devastated me. You didn't seem to have one care in the world. Even worse, you had everything that should have been shared with me- the house, the cars, the money, and all I got was the shitty end of the stick. Then to dig deeper and find out you were dealing drugs... As many times Mama talked against that shit, and as hard as she worked and the sacrifices she made to protect us from that lifestyle, you shit on her grave by being a dealer?"

Detective Bailey suddenly threw the pocket knife directly at Hi-C and the sound that let off when its' steel handle met with his face caused even me to feel the pain. He landed a clean shot on his brother's nose and when I saw it began to leak blood, I could only hope it wasn't broken.

"All the respect I thought I had for you was instantly lost and it was in that moment that I put it in my mind to stop at nothing to take you down."

"So then what!" Hi-C shouted, becoming angry from just being suckered while having to deal with the reality that there was nothing he could do about it. "You became an officer, then a detective? Just to take me down?"

"Exactly," he said. "Now you're starting to get it."

"Yeah I get it now," Hi-C shook his head, slowly making sense of everything that had just been presented to him. It wasn't an easy truth to except but he knew he had to. "I just have one question though?" he asked.

"Be my guest?" the detective replied.

"Who helped you?"

"What?" Detective Bailey looked bewildered. "What do you mean?"

"C'mon Simon. There is no way you did this alone. Dragging two unconscious bodies, this entire set up, getting two cars out here," he looked out towards a wooded area at a vehicle I hadn't noticed before ducked off behind a tree. "You had help. Just tell me, who was it?"

"Damn, you're good," he surrendered and then threw his hands towards the woods and called for someone. "Baby, come on out and join us! They're on to us!"

Instantly a body appeared from out of the car, but the dark night sky protected their identity. It wasn't until the person made their way out from the trees and drew closer into our company that we both recognized who it was. Hi-C's heart seemingly fell right out of his chest as he watched his wife walk up to his brother, wrap her arms around him, and then lay one passionate tongue kiss on his lips.

"What!" I cried, now being the one to get upset. "You backstabbing bitch!"

Isis just smiled as she looked to us while they both stood in front of the car. Even in the swampy and mudded area, she wore her usual business attire. Funny she chose to rock all red for this occasion. Hi-C just sat quietly, mentally trying to process everything. I could only imagine how he was able to deal with what all that was being thrown his way.

"I just wanna know how long?" he finally spoke. "How long has this been going on?"

"Seven years," Isis boasted, clearly with no regret. "We've been planning this for seven years."

"But why? I don't understand. I gave you the world. There was nothing I wouldn't do for you."

"And there was nothing I wouldn't do for you either," she said as she walked over to the car, opened the door, then took a seat on her helpless husband's lap. Even though it was out of Hi-C's control and he couldn't touch her, I still didn't like that she was all over him.

"I remember the first time we met. I had just come over to this country. A hopeless little foreign girl… innocent, gullible, naïve, and had to learn the hard way about the insensitive, unapologetic ways of these heartless American men. I met you and instantly fell in love because you were different. You treated me like nothing less than a queen, the way they treated our women back home, and the feelings grew even stronger once you made me your wife. Baby, you had me head over heels and I would do anything for you, even carry your drugs back and forth across the country."

"So that's what this is about? Me putting you out there on the strip. That's why you did this?" he said. "You still think I didn't love you because of that?"

"No that's not why. There's so much more to it," she said. "You remember that last run I went on. The one where I came back a day late and told you I wanted out because I got arrested on my way back for a nickel bag. Well I wasn't caught with any weed. I was caught riding down I-95 with a trunk of cocaine by a handsome young detective, with your eyes, that handcuffed me, drove me all the way down to Oklahoma, and placed me in a small room where he gave me a choice between my loyalty and my freedom. Of course at first I was willing to ride for you, but once he showed me photos of you and all of the women you had been fucking around on me with every time I'd leave to go on those runs, I no longer knew what loyalty was. It was heartbreaking. In only the few months of him following you there was over a dozen of them. Some who I even considered to be my friends. Where I come from, that's not love. Love doesn't deceive. It doesn't disrespect you. It doesn't *slap you in the face*. Or make you second to any of these bitches out here."

Isis planted one last kiss on Hi-C's cheeks before rising from his lap and exiting the vehicle. She took her place next to Detective Bailey, before turning to me. "Didn't I tell you I would get my fifteen years back from this man one way or the other?"

I quickly deterred my attention away from them both and gazed upon the trees, not wanting her to see the stupid, defeated look I carried on my face. I hated that I had allowed her to get over on me and wished that my hands were free so that I could have laid upon her the ass whooping I felt that she deserved. Hi-C, on the other hand, seemed to have no more fight in him. He just held his head low, incapable of enduring any more pain, and surrendered to his brother.

"If this is your way of getting revenge out on me then you won," he sighed. "You took my freedom. You took my wife. And you've taken my spirit. All I have left is my flesh, so if you want that you can take it too. Just go ahead, kill me now."

"Say no more," Detective Bailey replied then snapped his fingers at Isis and pointed towards the wooded area where the car she came out of rested.

"I'm on it babe," she said, before strutting back to where she came from. We all watched as she began to drag what appeared to be a white cooler back towards us and it must have been extremely heavy because she was struggling with two arms to carry it. Detective Bailey just looked at her tussle with it, without offering her any assistance.

"You know what?" he said as he turned his attention away from Isis and placed it back on Hi-C. "I thought about just killing you but then I realized, that would be too easy."

"Don't make this any harder than it has to be," Hi-C said. "Just tell me?...What exactly do you want from me?"

"To see you suffer," he replied. "That's what I want...I want you to know what it feels like to hear the Mama you love screaming in pain as you watch her die. And I want you to know what it feels like to have your brother watch and do nothing to help as it happens."

Detective Bailey then walked towards me and pulled out a comb from one of his boots. My heart began to beat very swiftly as he grabbed my face with one strong arm and began to roughly rake my hair back into a ponytail with the other. The tears came when he rubberbanded it as tightly as he could and with no remorse yanked out a piece in the front to attempt to create a bang. The pain was worse than the slapped I received from him early and it hurt me even more when I saw a chunk of my hair leaving with the comb.

"Mama used to wear her hair just like this. Remember how beautiful she was," he tossed my head towards Hi-C. "We both know why this one is so special to you."

"You sick bastard!" Hi-C yelled to his brother. "Untie me right now and face me like a man!"

Detective Bailey chuckled again before watching Isis finally return with the cooler. She was breathing heavily and her nose was turned up in disgust.

"Damn baby, how long did you have these things sitting out?" she panted.

"A whole week," he replied then slapped her on her ass, congratulating her for a job well done.

He took the cooler from Isis, pulled it next to me, and then opened it. Immediately a terrible and rather familiar smell reeked from it, almost causing me to skip a breath. Judging by the way Hi-C began to cough, it clearly had the same effect on him too.

"A whole week in the scorching sun," he said as he pulled a raw chicken leg quarter from out of it with his bare hands. He began to smear it all over my face and then dropped it in my lap. I gagged instantly and tried with all my might not to vomit on myself. After putting some gloves on over her French manicured nails, Isis took over tossing the meat on me while Detective Bailey grabbed his knife and finished his business with Hi-C.

"Here's exactly what I'm gonna do," he said as he began to cut the rope from around his brother's seat. "First, I'm going to roll this beauty- along with the girl- down into to swamp and after we listen to her scream while we watch these gators eat her pretty ass alive, then I'll deal with you. You know, I thought about just setting you up for the murder and making you spend the rest of your pathetic life in prison where you belong. But then I realized that if I kill you that would make me the only living son of Dave Brockington, your next of kin, and the next in line to inherit the millions."

"Are you crazy?" Hi-C replied. "If I die everything goes to my wife."

"What wife?" Detective Bailey said before aiming his pistol at Isis and firing one clean shot in her chest. The next piece of chicken flesh she was about the throw on me flew out of her hands as her body drew back. We all watched as her eyes widened in disbelief before she dropped and fell straight on top of the cooler. As messed up as it was to admit, the way she landed over it, I was just happy no more chicken would be thrown on me. On the other hand, Hi-C's devastation was not hard to notice. Even though she had betrayed him, he still seemed to sympathize with her.

"I wasn't ready for kids anyway," Detective Bailey said remorselessly before he turned back to Hi-C like he just didn't shoot someone. "As I was saying, I'm going to kill her, then you, and finally get to live the life that is owed to me. You know, see how it feels to live in your shoes."

"You could never live in his shoes," I finally took the courage to speak up. After seeing what he did to Isis I knew we were both goners anyway. "You're not even a quarter of the man Hi-C is."

"Oh really," Detective Bailey stopped cutting on the rope and made his way back to my direction. Then he squatted down next to me so that he may look me straight into the eyes. "That's not what you said on the Rooftop. I'm the best you ever had, remember? Which can only mean one thing…that I'm better than him."

"I knew it," I looked to him with even more disgust in my eyes. "I just knew that your beef with Hi-C was personal. This had nothing to do with you saving no communities and getting no drugs off the streets. You've been playing me all along."

"You're absolutely right," he smiled. "You got played. Everything from the hotel robbery to the-"

"Wait a minute," I interrupted. "That was you?"

"Of course," he chuckled. "I needed to make you dependent upon me. You want to control someone, strip them to nothing."

"And Dino?" I asked.

"You were all over the place Keisha. I had to put fear in

you so that you could be in my sight at all times. How else was I gonna convince you to stay at the CAMP?"

"What about the bust? That was a set-up too?"

"Most definitely the bust."

"But why?" I sighed regretfully. "I don't understand."

"I knew about the security box long before you told me, thanks to Isis. And since she couldn't successfully get into it, I figure I'd had a better chance with you. See, from the first moment I saw you, I knew exactly why Hi-C kept you around and I knew it would only be a matter of time before he shared with you his family's past. Keisha, I never cared about any financial documents. Don't you get it? They destroyed my entire identity. I just needed solid evidence that could better prove I am his brother and those family photos in that security box were perfect. Trust me, they're gonna come in great handy once you two are out of the picture."

"You will never get away with this," I told him. "Never in a million years. The police will figure this out."

"The police? Don't you know the Brockington bloodline is all through the justice system? How do you think I obtained that warrant? Or got the job down here so quickly?" he laughed. "My granddaddy was the sheriff, my uncle is a judge, and they both were in on sending me away. They thought they would never see me again and man you should have seen their faces when I caught up with them years later. I have enough dirt on them to turn the whole department upside down, so they know what's best for them. And trust me, they'll do anything I ask. As a matter of fact, I'll be lead detective over this triple homicide."

"Well none of you can hide from the All-seeing eye," I told him. "It sees everything, remember?"

Detective Bailey laughed in my face again. "And you believed all that conspiracy bullshit. That was just another one of my fear tactics. I'm glad to see it worked."

The detective stopped and looked out to the woods then snickered again, before turning back to me. "You gotta understand, the whole arrest, TMSD, this entire investigation was just fun and games for me. I just wanted to show the spoiled brat here what it was like to have access to nothing and be isolated from the world. I never thought the case would make it to trial, but I too learn how flawed the legal system could be. Once I realized it was taking longer and longer to release him and that they were really trying to put him away by any means, I spent this entire time trying to get him out, not keep him in… Can you believe I almost thought I lost this thing? I almost thought they were going to convict him and that I wouldn't be able to carry out my plans. It wasn't until you came to Isis with those pictures of us making love in California that gave me hope again. Without you none of this would be possible. Thanks for saving us Keisha, I will forever be grateful for you."

I sunk my head ashamed of my own stupidity, but the detective quickly grabbed me by my measly ponytail and rose from his squatted position. Then he forcefully turned my face to his and attempted to hypnotize me with his erotic eyes. They were so much like Hi-C's. I tried to look away but for some strange reason I remained trapped within them.

"Now here's what I'm gonna do… I'm gonna remove your little boyfriend from this car and then put this baby in neutral and push it down into this swamp. And as you die, here's what I want you to do…I want you to look directly into his eyes and scream from the strongest part of your gut. Make him feel it. You love puttin' on a show right? You love being the center of attention? Well this is your stage tonight. And if it makes you feel any better, you'll probably drown before the gators even get to you."

"You really are a piece of shit!" I shouted before I made my second attempt to fire off a ball of spit at him. This time I didn't miss. One clean shot of blood and slime landed directly between his eyes and the rage that appeared in them sent a chill down my spine.

"You dumb bitch," the detective said as he raised both his arms up with his pocket knife sitting in the realms of his tight grip. With his weapon positioned to land down directly on the top of my head, I squeeze my eyes tightly together and tried to prepare myself for the pain, and possible death, that I was about to face. Detective Bailey let out a heavy groan and fixed himself to strike, but his attack was interrupted by something that none of us saw coming.

Pow. A single shot suddenly rang out and caused the detective to stand at attention. The still look that quickly came across his face let me know without a doubt that he had been hit. I turned my head in the direction of where the shots rang out and saw the very weak Isis with her arm stretched out, a pistol in it, and the back of her jacket lifted up. I guess that second gun finally did come in handy. Isis then took what appeared to be her last breath before returning motionlessly to her slouched position.

"Aaaw shit...goddammit!" Detective Bailey moaned in obvious pain then weirdly laughed again. This time even he knew nothing was really funny. "Out of all fuckin' places, you hit me in my spine! You fuckin' bitch."

Most likely only out of shock, was he able to take a few steps towards the front of the car before he dropped to the ground. Hi-C screamed out for his brother and now that he was cut from the seat he was able to move around a bit more. Unfortunately, his hands and feet were bonded so his movement was still limited.

"Brother, if you can get the knife to me, I can at least help you!" Hi-C yelled. "Please, let me make it right this time!"

"Fuck you!" the detective said ungratefully. "Besides, I can't fuckin' move if I wanted to, I think the bitch paralyzed me!"

The detective just laid there squealing for minutes while we both watched with no help to offer. It wasn't long before the sound of his agony was interrupted by the sound of motion coming from the swamp. We all got silent and as our hearts pounded in fear of the unknown, while the biggest beast in the water made its way to surface.

"Alpha is that you?" Detective Bailey called once he located the distinct features that identified his dear reptilian friend who was coming to formally meet his acquaintance. "Yes, that is you. Come to daddy."

The anticipation of what was to come was torture as Alpha moved slow as a snail and stopped every couple of steps, just staring at the body lying before him. It was as if even he had a hard time believing that what he was witnessing was real. Not long after, more gators started to appear and head towards the direction of the smell of chicken flesh and blood. Even though I was covered in it I didn't panic because I knew I was safe inside the vehicle.

"It's me, remember? I'm the one who feeds you," the detective said with a confident uncertainty. He wanted to believe so badly that the creature would not see him as a meal, yet he was an alligator expert and couldn't deny the reality that he didn't stand a chance.

"I know you won't bite the hand that feeds you," he continued to plead and once Alpha made it within a couple feet, he finally started to panic.

"Please big brother," he began to cry for Hi-C's help. "Do something!"

"I can't!" Hi-C yelled out. "I'm tied up remember. Please just try to toss me the knife."

"I told you I can't move, you idiot!" he yelled back, somehow still finding room to insult. "Please help me. I don't wanna die like this!"

As the tears whelmed up in his eyes, Hi-C pleaded for his brother to remain calm while struggling to free himself so that he may rescue him. I just wondered how he could have pity towards him or anyone who tried to kill him. I guess family really did mean more to him than anything when it came to matters of life and death. I, on the other hand, still felt no remorse. I just wasn't mentally strong enough to witness anybody die like that.

With Detective Bailey in front of me about to be alligator's dinner, Isis lying dead to the right of me bleeding from her chest, and Hi-C to the left of me screaming his heart out, it all became a bit overwhelming. With no other direction to turn, I had no choice but to look up to the sky for strength to cope with it all. Magically, the way the stars were aligned sent my mind in a trance, where one of the most memorable moments of my childhood came to surface. Suddenly, the night sky transformed into day and the grown men screams turned into giggles that got louder and louder as I got deeper and deeper into my daydream.

"Huh Keisha!" a pleasant voice said unto me. "Huh Keisha? What did I tell you about saying mean things about your mama?"

Aunt Jonell tickled me until I almost urinated on myself. When she stopped, we both laughed but it was short-lived because Mama somehow always managed to put a cease to our happiness.

"What's that kee-keeing I hear in there? Fuck is so damn funny?" she yelled as the steps she laid down on the wooded hallway got louder and louder. As the noise grew heavier, so did our hearts. "Nothin' funny about what you just came here and told me. You better be packing your shit to leave. You got one more minute left!"

Understandably, the smile Aunt Jonell had just recently possessed slowly faded at the sound of her sister's voice. She quickly kissed me on the cheek, rose from the floor, and grabbed her little bag before heading for the door. Then she slowly reached for the handle, but suddenly paused before turning it.

"You know what?" she looked in my direction. "Get up. Come with me."

Auntie Jonell took my hand and snatched me from the floor without even my permission. Seconds before Mama made it to the door we pushed it open, rushed past her, and unintentionally knocked her big body to the ground. Then we ran full speed straight out the back exit.

"Just keep running," Jonell told me as we dodged through mobile homes and headed straight for the woods. "Run until I tell you to stop."

Mama flew out the back door behind us with a huge pot in her hand. Although she cared little for me, she began screaming for Jonell to bring her child back. She followed us a good distance but even though she was a brave woman, she didn't play around with those woods. Besides, she was no match for the unlimited energy of children.

"Bring yo' ass back her now! I'm gonna kill you!" was the

last thing we heard from her before she gave up on chasing us. "Jonell, you're a dead bitch!"

Ignoring her, Jonell, her unborn baby, and I dashed through the woods what seemed like miles and once we had completely felt safe our fears transformed into excitement. Thrilled by what had just occurred, we began to laugh even harder than we did at the house. For some strange reason, although we were playing a dangerous game, we still couldn't help but find humor in our rebellious actions.

Aunt Jonell and I entertained ourselves by mocking Joanne all the way up until we got to a small bypass that oversaw a river. I continued to follow as she led me past docks, boats, and fishermen until we rested on a big rock that gave us a clear view of the large body of water flowing in front of us. We were only kids but we somehow managed to appreciate the beautiful scenery.

"I think we're safe now," I panted, allowing my breath to catch up with me. "I know we lost her."

"You're always safe with me, Keisha," Auntie Jonell replied.

"But that's the problem," I looked to her troubled. "You're not always with me. Why don't you ever stay long?"

Auntie Jonell hesitated then placed her hand on top of my tiny one. In great need of security, I moved in closer to her and rested my head on her shoulders.

"I'm afraid I can't answer that. It's a very complicated story... But listen Keisha, when I'm not with you is when I'm with you the most. Always remember that, okay."

"Okay," I nodded, but honestly was too young to understand her meaning.

"Now I gotta take you back soon, and it may be a while before you ever see me again but remember what I told you. As a matter of fact, I want you to repeat those words. Say them right now...when I'm not with you is when I'm with you the most."

I closed my eyes tightly and tried to memorize what she told me, then attempted my very best to repeat it. "When I not with you, is when I with the most of you," I mumbled.

"That's good enough," she smiled, then removed her hand and continued to stare out at the water.

I looked too, and couldn't help but become saddened once I thought about having to return home. As usual, Auntie Jonell sensed my change of mood and became concerned.

"What's wrong?" she asked. "What did I tell you about holding your head down like that?"

"Auntie, please. I don't wanna go back," I said to her. "Why can't we just keep running?"

"Because," she said, "you can't just run from reality. You'll never solve anything like that. You gotta be tough enough to stand and face your problems. In the end it always makes you stronger. Always remember that too."

Still confused, I simply nodded again. Auntie Jonell knew too that I understood nothing of the words of which she spoke. She just wrapped her arms around my shoulders and laid her head on me as well.

"But forget about all that. Let's just enjoy the view right now. It's too beautiful not to," she said. "Do you know that the water has magical powers?"

"It does?" my eyes lit up.

"Yes, it's a healer. Anytime you're faced with a problem, you just take it to the water and I promise all your worries will go away. Don't believe me, try it now."

I obeyed Aunt Jonell and we gave all our troubles to the waters. Then we stayed and watched it until the sun rose, or at least until I returned home to face my own reality.

When I snapped out of my daze, I realized that I must have been out of it for a while because the sun was beginning to creep through the night sky. Hi-C was slouched over the steering wheel, and the deep breathing coming from his nostrils let me know that he certainly was alive. He must have just cried himself into a deep sleep.

I looked around at my surroundings in fear of seeing the worst, but strangely saw no bodies or no gators. Unfortunately, two heavy trails of blood visibly flowed down into the swamp and gave me a pretty good idea about where Isis and Detective Bailey were located. Even in the midst of the horrible chaos, I suddenly felt a sense of peace all over me. I wasn't afraid anymore. Neither was I worried and it was because I knew I was protected. I knew that the sign that I had been once looking for had revealed itself to me.

"Thank you, Auntie." I whispered, as I looked back up to the sky and smiled. "Thank you."

THE OUTCOME

I could bet that after she had her morning coffee, the Ranger who worked at the Refugee did not expect to arrive at her job and stumble across a horrific crime scene. We weren't found until Monday morning, which meant that Hi-C and I were tied up for over a day. It didn't bother me because I knew I could have been discovered in an even worst predicament.

In fact, the whole time I waited for savior I was totally at ease. I never complained. I never got scared. I never even got hungry. Hi-C and I just sat speechlessly not speaking a single word to one another, both caught up in our own web of quandaries. I don't know what his mind had been pondering on, but I was beginning to re-evaluate the entire world and my purpose of living in it.

There must have been a hundred police that flooded the nature trail and even though my head was bruised, my lips were badly busted, and my body was in excruciating pain, the real hurt came from the two of us being treated like the villains instead of the victims. Once the OPD got word that the two members involved in the gruesome mess were Herbert Isaac Cooper and Lakeisha Black, and that a respected, fellow detective and well-known lawyer was killed, the media had a field day destroying our reps. The judge and sheriff, who were also a part of the family scandal, took advantage of Bailey's death by using his silence as a way to cover up their dirt, and making us out to be the bad guys in the process.

Even worse, the investigators found a huge amount of cash in the trunk of the Classic Buick. 8.5 million dollars to be exact. Hi-C had wiped out his entire bank account, I matched my ninety thousand, and we planned on taking the money cross country to start a new life together. None of it could be touched by the Feds because it was all accounted for, but when the police found a little bag of marijuana in the car that we were going to use to smoke on the road, the dirty scums hollered 'attempt to distribute.' That gave them grounds to arrest us and confiscate every penny. Of course, only three million was reported, but as I always say, you know how the folks can play it.

Unfortunately, in a little less than six months, Hi-C and I were convicted and sentenced to prison. Although the State aimed for the maximum, they had to settled for the ten years Hi-C received, while I had to serve seven, plus an additional five for fraud. Apparently, Mrs. Lowisky did her homework on me and dug up the fact that I had a government assistant housing apartment illegally in my name. She offered me one year jailtime along with probation, but since I did not give up Quita or Vivica's involvement, she hit me with the max. This meant that I would be locked up two years longer than Hi-C and the only thing that made that easier to accept was that I would get to see if he would hold me down like I did him. Being in my forties when released, I'm certain that I would have no time to waste on anyone who did not have my best interest at heart.

Actually, one of the good things about being in prison was that it gave me the opportunity to filter out the real people from the fake. To see who really had my back and who was just riding a wave and within a few months of me being incarcerated, I had learned just who those people were. It turned out I had a good judgement of friends because my top three girls definitely held me down. Since inmate to inmate communication was not allowed, Shannon kept it G by making sure I kept in contact with my father and Hi-C. She did this by playing middle man with our lettering. Poncha stayed down by making sure I was financially straight, putting more money on my books than I would ask even for. And Charlytte would regularly visit me, keeping me updated on the family. Even Mama surprised me by sending pictures from time to time. They all in their own way made life easier to cope with and I appreciate them for it.

Another thing that made time easier for me was the memories I could look back on, especially on those extremely lonely nights. I spent all my life in the free world putting material things first, but what was so ironic was that when I was locked up not once did I think about missing out on the next Chanel bag or pair of Red Bottoms. When I smiled the most, I was thinking about those times I danced the night away with my girls at the club. It was the laughter Qutia's daughter's and I shared when we played Monopoly. Or the way Charlytte would squint and I would fuss as I cornrowed her hair when we were kids. All the things in life that didn't cost me a thing.

I remember this one night- cold and lonelier than the others- I began to do my usual reminiscing. This time, I thought back to the day when Shannon and Charlytte visited my townhouse for the first time. We were sitting out on the balcony kicking it and I remember pitying her for having that measly gas station job. I remember trying to convince her to get down with the OMC and I could hear her voice clearly in my head as she gladly turned down my offer. She told me, without a doubt, that she would sacrifice having only a little than do anything that would put her at risk of losing her children. But me, I wasn't trying to hear that. In fact, I was so persistent that even on the way taking her home, I was still trying to convince her to quit that store. Then once I got completely frustrated by her stubbornness, I just had to ask her 'how could you be so content with being so broke?' She froze as we pulled up to her spot and before getting out of my car, looked me dead into my eyes and said to me, '*That money shit don't impress me, you can build a house with it, but you can't build character. Trust me, it's the people putting a hundred dollars' worth of gas in their big trucks who are rudely throwing the money down on the counter at me, while the people who scrape up change make sure they respectfully place it in my hands. Eventually you'll have a lot of free time, and when you do, you make sure you dwell on that."*

I didn't understand then, but the free time that she predicted I'd have surely came and allowed me to understand now. Shannon was right all along. Even though I was the one with the money and all the fancy things, she honestly had so much more than me. She had four beautiful children that she could call her family, while for my selfish reasons, didn't have any kids nor a strong tied with any of my folks. She had a loyal man, who even though she struggled to make ends meet with, loved and cared for her. While the one I flourished with was married and the rest didn't seem to stick around any longer than a week. But most importantly, Shannon had a sense of peace and a clear understanding of the true meaning of life. Realizing this partly made me sad, but I did find joy in knowing that I wasn't living in the blind anymore. I was beginning to get smart enough not to allow the pressures of a broken society continue to make a fool out of me.

In fact, my father would always tell me that the first steps in solving a problem was recognizing it. It puzzled me how a man as wicked as he was could turn out to be so spiritual and enlightened, but if he could turn his life around despite his dark past, then I know I could have. As hard as it was to accept what he had done to my Aunt, I had to admire him because he was the one who played a major role in my spiritual development. It was his letters, his teachings, his book referrals, that helped me understand my present, my past, and ultimately my purpose. It was his guidance that allowed me to discover that third eye I never knew even existed and none of it would have happened had I not decided to make a couple wrong turns in my life.

Those wrong turns also allowed me to bring joy to more women's lives. I started a styling business right out of my cell and would do the girls' hair, make-up, and even spiced up our jail jumpsuits with creative designs. I gave birth to Kool Keisha's Klothing again and with limited resources, I made broken women feel good about themselves. When I first got to prison, I told myself that I would keep a low profile, do my time and go home, but I guess that spark I always had inside of me wouldn't allow me to hide my shine. I was always a go-getter by blood and a hustler by nature, and even if it was for only for measly headphones and cheap snacks, I put passion in my work and took pride in my rewards. Yep, prison was just a pitstop for me. A chance to take a break and fix some things in my life so that I may dash back into the world fully equipped to win the race called life. Believe me, Lakiesha Black is gonna come in first place again, now which road I take to get there and what being in first place actually means for me this time around, who knows? I guess we'll just have to let time answer that…

THE END....

WORD TO THE READERS

Thanks for taking the time out of your lives to read the novel. I hope that you enjoyed it. Lots of hard work and dedication goes in to creating these stories and the greatest reward I can receive from it is hearing your feedback. Please feel free to leave a review regarding your experience with my book(s). I have many different avenues- whether it be amazon, social media, or email- that you may do so. I also have a P.O. Box address for those who desire to write me. I do respond!!! Thanks in advance for your cooperation and support!

If you would like to reach out by mail, you may do so at:

Jessica Germaine

P.O. Box 24356

Savannah, Georgia 31403

Other Outlets:

www.facebook.com/jessicagermaine2
IG: jessica_germaine
darkblackthenovl@gmail.com

L.O.R.E.T.T.A

I would like to dedicate this page to my mother, Loretta, my hero and my lifeline. You are strong, beautiful, and one of a kind. I know that I have not been the best daughter or made some of the wisest decisions in my life, but you have always been there for me through my right and my wrongs. You have a heart bigger than the ocean itself and it may seem sometimes to us as if you're smaller than a grain of sand, just know that we all love and care about you. As I get closer to understanding my purpose in life, I am feeling better, thinking clearer, and having a greater appreciation of the many things I took for granted in the past. I thank you for the values you instilled in me, to be straight-forward and less concerned with material things, but most importantly, to be there for the ones you love. I'm aware that I have no idea the amount of weight you carry on your back, the sacrifices you have made and continue to make to see everyone happy, nor how strong you truly have to be, but I do recognize it. As our days get shorter and shorter, I realize it's a blessing to still have you around and I'm thankful for each moment. In this journey of pursuing my dreams, my ultimate goal is not to see a million dollars or million sales, but to see that million dollar smile when you see me reach the peak of my success. I love you.

-Jessica

SHOUTS OUT TO:

My daughter Alourie Hancock….you mean to world to me. I'm not perfect but the sacrifices I make are all for you. Keep a positive attitude and you can be anything you want to be in life! Always remember that.

My KNUCKLEHEAD brothers, Lorenzo & Quentin. I love y'all genuinely!

Jennifer 'Jenny" Wallace, for just being a call away for babysitting. I thank you so much.

My Stepfather, Theodore, Love you! Thanks for your ongoing support.

Carl Ski----- just wanted you to see your name in print big cuz…skys the limit! You're here for a reason.

To my very smart and charismatic nieces and nephews- Lariah, Qamyra, Qaelyn, Qayla, Kennedy, Baby Q, and Camell ...Family always stuck together. Remember that too! I love watching you all grow!

SPECIAL SHOUT OUTS FOR YOUR EXTRAORDINARY SUPPORT:

The entire Unity in the Community organization, Sharon and Craigs Butts. Whitney Necole Smith, Quinton Todd, Kamilah Bazemore, Christina Drummond, LaDrann and Linda Godwin, Julian Moore, Stevie Habersham, Sam and Tiffany Tolbert, Ontreal Bowers, Robert Jordan, Nia Singeton, Mary Nevins, Summer Bess, Tall Angie, Robert Jordan, fellow author Aisha Patrice, Dr. Joseph Washington, Antwon Bryant, Mrs. Tilly, Eric & Raz (and Tre), Lionel, Jazz, and Chris Brown, Taj Pace (Cover Design) Ray (Chevron) Jacorius David

You all have had a special impact on me and inspired me in some type of way, whether it be big or small. There are so many more people to thank but just know that you are all recognized and appreciated more than you will ever know! Peace and Love. Until next time!!!!!

Special Thanks to James Smalls…

From set up to break down you've been there for me. You believe in my success and have been supportive since the day we met. I, along with my family, are glad to know you and call you a friend. Let's grow together with this thang and continue to have fun making them think we 'go together.'

Check out a sneak peek from "IZZA BELLA"

"I'm telling you the truth ma, it did happen! Why won't you believe me!" Sarah rushed down the hallway to her bedroom as a flood of tears whelmed up around her eyeballs.

"No it didn't. You're lying through your fucking teeth," said her mother who sat on the old, worn down leather couch that was holding up by only three legs. "Take your fucking clothes off and I'll be there in a second to whip yo' womanish little ass."

Sarah was unbothered by her mother's threat and instead of undressing for her punishment, she ironically began to put some more clothes on so that she could make her escape out of the window. She knew her mom would be out like light once she drugged herself up with the heroin she was just getting ready to inject into her bloodstream and by the time she'd wake up she'd forget that they ever had a falling out.

You would think that after ten years of Sarah accusing every man that came into their home of being perverts her mother would believe her, but that wasn't the case with Mrs. Heather. Only thing that didn't come before her and whoever she was dating that month was the shit she stayed high off of.

Sarah slipped into a white blouse and a very short denim skirt. Then she carefully climbed out the window, trying not to let her skin get burned by the metal lining that was forced to embrace all of the sun's heat. It was record breaking summer weather but that didn't detour her from taking her a much needed walk to the park that was located just a couple blocks over. As Sarah got closer to her destination she was happy to see some of her friends sitting at their usual spot by the merry-go-round.

"There goes the baddest white bitch I know," Monique said to Sarah as she saw her best friend approaching. Sitting with her was Ash, Lexus, and Charcoal.

"What's up milk chocolate," Monique continued to innocently throw racial shots at her friend. Normally Sarah would laugh or have a fancy comeback, but this time she was in no mood. She just lazily threw her hands up to acknowledge them and then flopped down on the bench.

"I guess somebody's having a bad day," Monique said, before sliding her massive body weight over to allow room.

"I'm fine," Sarah groaned. "Fine as I'm gon' be."

"Ya Mama tripping again?" Monique replied, taking a wild, but obvious, guess.

"You already know," Sarah told her.

"What's the matter with her ass now?" Lexus butted in as usual. She was the smallest, but the nosiest, one in the group. Lex knew all the gossip about everyone in the project buildings of which they all resided. She was the go-to person when you wanted to know what, when, where, and with who. Sarah was already two steps ahead of Lexus though and knew not to put her in too much of her personal business. Besides, she wouldn't dare tell them about the men in their forties who tried to touch her. It was just too humiliating.

"Not nothing major," she lied. "Just about me washing the damn dishes."

"Man, it's always something with that lady, " Monique jumped back in. "Don't worry about it though girl, you'll be eighteen in two years and you can ditch her pathetic ass."

"I know that's right," Sarah begin to cheer up before clapping her palm against her best friend's.

"Speaking of pathetic," Monique continued, "girl why Destiny came strolling pass here not too long ago? She had a couple other girls with her too. Looks like she was trying to start some shit."

Sarah rolled her eyes and then in her soft and squeaky voice responded confidently. From hanging around the hood people all her life she had quickly picked up on the street lingo.
"I'm not worried 'bout that girl. If I kicked her ass before, I can sure as hell do it again. And that's for anybody she tries to bring with her too."

"Now I know you done proved you ain't to be messed with around here, but Sarah you can't beat everybody. I saw those girls Destiny had with her and they were big. Soon as folks round here find out you finally got yo ass whooped, they're gonna go right back to fuckin with you like they did before. Remember, you're the only white chick that lives here and you always been an easy target. I would choose my battles wisely if I were you," said Charc, the only boy of the group. His real name was Cole but because of how extremely dark his skin was people would tease him and call him Charcoal. Eventually Charc just became a name that the hood shortened and gave to him.

Charc normally stayed out of the girl's drama but somehow felt obligated to kick some much needed game to Sarah. She had become quite cocky since she proved that just because she was petite and white, she could still hold her own. After all, Sarah had to fight men from off her and her mother all her life and didn't realize how much that conditioned her for the real world. That's until one day the toughest chick round the block learned a good lesson about picking on her. Ever since then people started to respect Sarah and the ones who didn't, well they just knew not to fuck with her.

"But enough about Destiny and her ugly ass weave," Charc continued. "I got something that'll take your mind off all that bullshit."

Everyone's eyes focused in on Charc, who reached into his pocket and grabbed a small sack of marijuana. It was actually some shake his older brother- a nickel and dime dealer- gave to him. He normally gifted it to his baby brother to bride him into keeping his mouth shut about him selling drugs out their mama's house when she was at work.

"That's my nigg," Monique applauded Charc for always coming through with the smoky things. They had all recently started getting high once they found out that it helped them escape from the problems that they each definitely had. Sarah especially, she needed a hit more than any of them at the table.

"We going to ya mom's house again?" Charc asked Sarah. "I ain't trusting doing this shit out here, remember how the folks ran up on us last time."

"Yeah, we can go but let's just wait a while to give her a minute to fall asleep. She was just about to take a nap before I left," Sarah replied.

She never told her friends her mom did heroin, even though they probably already knew. You could take one look at her anorexic body and stale, lifeless face and know that Miss Heather was on something serious.

With their plans set, Sarah, Charc, Ash, Lex, and Monique headed to the convenient store that sat right outside the projects. It was connected to a liquor store and a Chinese restaurant. Charc bought two packs of Swishers and some snacks to munch on after their session. He was only sixteen but he stood 6'2 and looked much older than his age. Because of this, he barely got checked for ID. Once the crew left the GRAB-N-GO, Charc tried his luck at the liquor store but the employee wasn't gonna let him buy alcohol just off the strength of his height.

When they arrived to Sarah's house she made them wait outside so that she could check her mom's condition and do what quick little cleaning to the filthy apartment that she could. As she expected, Miss Heather was knocked out cold on the couch with her mouth wide open. Sarah took a big blanket and covered as much of her face and body as she could with it, for she knew her friends would have to pass her when entering the house. Once she was finished getting the place in whatever order she could, she quickly ran out to let her crew in and led them to the back screened-in patio. When inside, they all took their places in one of the four white plastic chairs that was decorated in the small, enclosed space. Everyone except for Monique, who sat on the cooler because she was too big to fit in any of the chairs. There was nothing else on that patio but a flimsy stand holding up a small tv that was so old looked like Adam and Eve could have owned it. Sarah was ashamed of her mom's furniture because even though her friend's parents were struggling just as bad as she was, they at least had nice things in their places.

Lexus took it upon herself to turn on the television. She already knew there was no cable at Sarah's house, so without complaining or questioning, she flipped through the six channels until she found the one most entertaining.

"Ain't nobody wanna look at no damn Jeopardy?" Monique yelled to Lex.

"Well, that's the only thing on so hush," Lex fired back. Monique was twice her size but she wasn't afraid of her.

"Alright ni, we all know Fox is the only the thing to watch when you ain't got no damn cable. Don't act all bougie cuz y'all mamas stealing y'all shit," Sarah joked.

Everyone laughed except Charc, who was busy concentrating on how to roll his blunt. He was still new to the process and needed no distractions.

"I told ya to let my cousin come over here and hook y'all up. He only charge fifty," Monique told them.

"You know my mama ain't got fifty dollar and her sorry ass boyfriend ain't gonna pay it either."

"Well why don't you pay it? The way yo' mama sleep you'll be the only one watching it anyway," Monique said.

"And where I'mma come up with fifty damn dollars?" Sarah asked.

"Shoot, you can get a damn job. We all sixteen now. Brea, that live next door to me, just started working at Kentucky. She said they paying like seven-fiddy an hour and it's in walking distance. I think I'm going there to talk to the manager tomorrow morning."

Sarah had never thought about working. Just waking up in that dysfunctional household was already a job in itself. She wasn't too fancy of it being at a fast food restaurants either, but the more she thought about it, the more she figured it couldn't hurt to make a few extra bucks. Although her mom would more than likely take her for every dime she had and used her living in her apartment as an excuse for it.

"I don't need to work right now," she sighed. "It's best I focus on just trying to stay in school."

"That's what my mom said too," Lex butted in. "I asked her 'bout it before and she straight up told me hell-to-da-no. Apparently, I'm too young to be needing to pay for anything. Besides, my daddy give me whatever I want anyway."

Lex was right. Her dad was different from all the other dads they knew in the area because he came around regularly. Lex's mom was fairly decent too. She worked at hospital and you could tell the hood was just a stepping stone her for. She was one of the very few parents that actually cared about her kids. She even used her mother's address to have Lex attend a school that was thirty minutes away so she didn't have go to the crappy one in their district.

"We all know you a spoiled lil' brat. You don't have to rub in it," Monique jealously said as she swiped Lexus brand new Jordan shoes with her fingertip. Then she continued.

"When I get older I'm gonna live just like yo mama…I mean not in no projects, but I'mma have me a good job and I'mma spoil my kids just like yo' folks do you."

"Girl, I feel ya but with great things comes great responsibility. Hell I wish I had it as easy as y'all," Lex told her friends. "Besides, why we even talking like this?"

"Like what?" Monique asked.

"Bout kids and our future and shit," Lex replied. "I mean, we got plenty time to think about that later."

"Girl please, I think about it every day. We'll all be grown sooner than you think and I'm just trying to get my shit together now. I wanna own me a hair salon and that ain't easy," Monique said. "C'mon now, y'all ain't never thought about what y'all wanna do when y'all grow up?"

"Well I do see myself being a teacher," Lex admitted. "Or a nurse like my mom."

Ashley finally broke from her silent. She was always the most antisocial one of the group. Sometimes they didn't even know why she even bothered to come around. "Well I wanna be a veterinarian," she replied.

Everyone look to Charc. He was the next person in line to give an answer.

"I don't know what y'all looking at me for?" he said. "Man, I just wanna be alive."

"Alive is not a job," Monique said truly appalled. Everyone else was surprised as well.

"For a black boy in America it is," he answered. "Niggas round here don't make it to see twenty-five."

"Whatever boy," Monique rolled her neck.

"Just drop it," he told them. It's a guy thing. Y'all wouldn't understand."

"Let's just let him have his opinion," Sarah quickly defended him. "Maybe we really don't understand."

Charc glanced over at Sarah and cracked a smile that he tried so hard not to show. He admired her for sticking up for him the way she did.

"Well, what about you missy?" Monique turned her attention to Sarah. What do you want to do when you grow up? With a name like Sarah Isabella Perkins and that 'privileged' skin color you so blessed with, you shouldn't have a problem finding work anywhere."

“For one, stop thinking us white people got it easy, cuz I'll be the first to tell you that it's not all like that. Second, I've thought about it before....but I don't wanna tell y’all."

"Why not?" they all now looked more eager than ever to know.

"Because it's almost impossible," she told them.

"Girl my mama said nothing’s impossible," Lex said. "Just tell us."

Sarah let out a long deep sigh before surrendering, "Okay, only if you promise not to laugh."

"We promise," Monique was the first to comply.

"Okay well, I always dream of being a Hollywood ....well…uhm....actress."

Everyone looked at each other quietly, and despite their promise to their friend, they all laughed. Even Charc, who didn't have the courage to stick up for Sarah like she just did for him. She felt slightly betrayed by that so she attacked him first, before having to at laugh her own self.

"Welp, it's better than just wanting to alive dumbass," she sucker punched Charc in the arms and they all continued to crack up. Sarah did dream of being a famous actress. Marilyn Monroe was her idol, and despite her 'free' lifestyle, she wished to have the same charisma, beauty, and impact on the big screen as she did.

"Sarah please, the closest you'll probably get to acting is shaking yo lil phat vanilla ass in a rap video," Charc shot back at her. "You know you're pretty thick for a white girl."

Although she in fact wasn't built like the ordinary white chick, Sarah had never heard her male best friend talk about her body in that manner. It was only the guys in the neighborhood who reminded her of how shapely she was. Even the older cats lusted over her and would probably have tried something if she had given them the opportunity.

"Well Monique, I have yo mama to thank for all this ass," Sarah rubbed her hips. "Eating all that mac and cheese, greens, and pound cake for five years at your house would do that to you, ya know. I'd be aneroxic for sure depending on my mama to cook a damn meal."

They all laughed again, then took turns passing around the blunt Charc tried his best to roll. The higher they got, the less conversing they began to do, until eventually all their talking ceased to exist. They pretended to be glued to the television but really each of them were thinking about their own little problems. About an hour had passed before Lex was the first to realize it was time to go. It made sense since she was the only one with a curfew and parents who cared what time she got in.

"I don't know about the rest of you but I'm headed home now." She took some Visine of out her Mk purse, laid a couple drops in her eye, and then passed the bottle around for the rest of the group to follow suit. After they were done, they all jumped up behind Lex and Sarah walked them to the door. Fortunately, her mom was still sleep and unaware that anyone had ever been in her apartment.

Feeling very buzzed, Sarah said her farewells to her friends and closed the door once they were all out of her sight. Then she headed back to the patio to rid all evidence of having any herbs and company. She began by straightening the chairs and sweeping the ashes off of the ground, before being frightened by something approaching from the outside.

"What the fuck Cole!" Sarah's heart almost jumped of out her chest after hearing two soft taps on the screen door. She knew without a doubt it was Charc's eyes staring at her.

"Scary ass," he chuckled a bit. "Put that damn broom down and meet me at the front door."

"Why? You left something?" Sarah hesitated and then asked, before considering to act on his demand. She hadn't recall seeing anything unusual as she was cleaning.

"No. Just meet me at the front," he told her again.

Obediently, Sarah crept back to the front of the house and opened up for Charc. He stood in the doorway with a smirk on his face holding a small bottle of wine that he had stolen from the liquor store just a few hours earlier.

"What?" Charc shrugged. "He should have just sold it to me."

Sarah smiled then shook her head at her naughty friend.

"Boy, one of these day that man is gonna catch yo ass," she said as they headed to the back patio again.

"Maybe," Charc replied, not denying it.

"But why you wait 'til everybody leave to pop that open. You know when one got it, we all got it. " Sarah said. Loyalty meant everything to her.

"I know, I know. But I was only able to get this small bottle. It wasn't enough to share with everybody. Shit, you the one who always letting us come through. Smoking and dranking out ya place, so why not let you get first dibs tonight. Besides, Monique get too damn loud when she drink. Be blowing my high and shit."

Charc did have a point. Monique got ridiculous when she got even the slightest bit slithered. Even Sarah knew how irritating she could be but she just couldn't agree with him.

"Well you know she is the life of the group," Sarah said. "Monique's just naturally a loud person. That's what makes her so fun to be around."

"Yeah but damn, you know it ain't lyin."

They both laughed before Sarah headed to the kitchen to grab two glasses and then poured up the wine in them when she returned. She was much more a liquor drinker but when you had to steal alcohol in order to consume it you couldn't really be picky. Silence came upon the two of them as they both attempted to enjoyed the bitter taste of the extra dry wine that truly dissatisfied their taste buds. Still, they were smart enough to know that the whole purpose of them drinking was to feel the effects.

By now the sun had completely gone away and darkness took over the sky. The backyard patio's view showed nothing but two dumpsters and all the trash that flooded the ground, but the way the stars were glowing beautifully, the night sky made up for it.
It was awkward for Sarah to be around Charc at that hour, especially when the others weren't around. In fact, it was her first time ever being alone with any boy she actually trusted and she quickly realized how much that thrilled her.

"Do you know what amazes me about the sky?" Sarah broke the silence with a ditsy question.

"No…what?" he replied.

"Just that… no matter where you live, from the raggediest projects to the damn nicest surburbs, we all look up to see the same view of it. Like really, somebody over at The Mansions is sitting on their upstairs balcony seeing this shit the exact same way we see it."

"Yeah, true. But when they take they eyes of it at least they don't have to dash to the ground after hearing a damn gunshot. So what's your point? I hope you not trying to make any comparisons, or come with that universal equality shit, because I'm not buying it. Life ain't fair, never will be, and that's just the way it is."

As the words exited his lips, Charc formed the face of a cold-blooded killer. Still, he could hold a beautiful conversation. Sarah had always noticed and loved that about him. What she hated on the other hand, was how he always so negative.

"Why do you believe that Cole? And why are you always so negative about everything?" she asked.

"When you witness yo' oldest brother get shot right in front of your eyes, it's hard to be positive Sarah."

"I mean, I know being eight-years-old and seeing him die like that must have really did something to you, but c'mon, you can't hold on to the pain forever."

"Like I said, when it happens to you then we can talk about it," he replied.

"I didn't have to happen to me, Cole. You not the only one going to through shit or have had bad things happen in your life. I just know that sometimes you have to let that shit go."

"And this coming from the pretty little white girl with the drug addict mama who lets her do whatever the hell she wanna do. No rules, no pressure, no nothing. Life must be really hard coming in and going out as you please. Having your friends over kicking it every day getting high and shit. Yeah, sound like a pretty rough life to me."

Sarah was offended by Charc's lack of understanding of her situation but the only thing she could concentrate on was the fact that he had just called her pretty. It was the second time that night that he had complimented her and she was surely taking notice of it.

"Look, you don't know the first thing about my life. I wake every day with some new shit to deal with. Going to sleep with a chair underneath my doorknob and one eye open because I know one day David's perverted ass is going 'make my sexy ass feel like a woman' like he always threatens to. Did you know that just this morning he had the nerve to bust into the bathroom while I'm showering, pull the curtain back, and ask me if I wanted any breakfast? Then tells my mom that I attacked him because he was simply trying to feed me. And on top of all that, guess who she believes?"

The tears almost started to whelm up in the her eyes but she was mentality strong enough to restrain them. "Listen, you don't know where I have come from before I even got here. This project shit is like a mansion compared to those dirty trailers, filthy cars, and bus stops we used to sleep at. Man, every day I have to fight a man off of me and then y'all think I'm flattered when these guys around here tell me how fine I am 'for a white girl.' Well, I'm not. That's the most degrading thing I've ever heard. And worse, I got these black chicks constantly trying to tell me how I'm trying to act, talk, and look like them when in reality I'm just being myself. Really, I've lived here since I was ten years...this is all I know so what am I supposed to do? It's really no winning or fitting in this world for me. I end up being too hood for the white folks and not hood enough for blacks. To be honest, if it wasn't for you, Monique, Lex and Ash understanding me, I probably wouldn't have anybody to call a friend."

Those tears Sarah tried to hold back finally came out. Charc rushed over to her and allowed her to cry in his arms. He hated that she was so emotional but he enjoyed them being close. In fact, he liked her a whole lot more than what he pretended to and had ever since the first day he introduced himself to her as Charcoal. She was only ten but she was disappointed with how mean people could be to him and promised that she never would never call him that. As the years pasted she only referred to him as Cole and every time she said his real name it reminded him of the day she made him feel confident. Only now the older he got, the more he desired to hear her say his name under a different, much more mature, circumstance.

Charc continued to console Sarah the best way he could and informed her over and over that everything would be okay. Feeling a little frisky from the weed and wine, he confidently took his long arms and rubbed them slowly along her backside. Sarah's whimpers slowly turned into soft moans as she realized that Charc was slowly trying to make a move on her. Conditioned to always be on the defense, Sarah suddenly drew back.

"Relax, don't think too much," Charc sensed her uncertainties. "Just go with the flow. I am not one of those guys who tried to hurt you. Believe me, I've always wanted you, but I've always respected you too. And…well… It's just that…I don't wanna respect you right now and I don't mean that in a bad way."

Charc grabbed Sarah's face and because he was so tall, had to kneel way down to kiss her. To her own surprise, she met him halfway on her tippy toes and they began to devour each other like there was no tomorrow. While still kissing and rubbing, Charc led Sarah to his usual seat and placed her on top of his lap. Now facing him, she watched as he slid his manhood over his jean shorts and her eyes widen when she realized just why the black man was truly a powerful work of art.

Once he knew he had Sarah, Charc then reached his hand under her skirt and slid her panties over a bit to allow himself entrance and for the next seven minutes he guided her up and down his lap until he let off pieces of him deep inside of her. No concern for her mother in the other room, no care to wear protection, and no idea that she would be telling him a couple months later that she could possibly be carrying his child…

22597045R00293

Made in the USA
Columbia, SC
31 July 2018